TEFLON

A Lincoln Lee Novel

B
BLACK PEARL BOOKS PUBLISHING
www.BlackPearlBooks.com

TEFLON

A Lincoln Lee Novel

Published By:

BLACK PEARL BOOKS INC.
3653-F FLAKES MILL ROAD – PMB 306
ATLANTA, GA 30034
404-735-3553

Copyright 2005 © Lincoln Lee

All Black Pearl Books titles, imprints and distributed lines are available at special quantity discounts for bulk purchases for sales promotion, premiums, fund raising, educational or institutional use.

Special book excerpts or customized printings can also be created to fit specific needs. For details, write to Black Pearl Books: Attention Senior Publisher, 3653-F Flakes Mill Road, PMB-306, Atlanta, Georgia 30034 or visit website: www. BlackPearlBooks. com

FOR DISTRIBUTOR INFO & BULK ORDERING

Contact: **Black Pearl Books, Inc.**
3653-F Flakes Mill Road
PMB 306
Atlanta, Georgia 30034
404-735-3553

Discount Book-Club Orders via website:
www. BlackPearlBooks. com

ISBN: 0-9766007-8-1 LCCN: 2005936490

Publication Date: December 2005

ACKNOWLEDGEMENTS

First off, I would like to thank Jesus Christ my Lord and Savior, for constantly having patience with me. Don't give up on me yet; because you know my heart, it's my mind that has taken in so much madness. Thank you for this gift and plenty others that I'm starting to realize that I have.

I would like to say thanks to Felicia Hurst and the rest of the Black Pearl Books family.

To my mother, sorry for the pain I've caused you. But as long as I'm free and not in the grave, the people will hear the truth without the tie-ness of any tongue.

To my father, I feel like I failed you due to the evil I kept amongst me. We'll talk again old man. Hopefully I will have made a total transition.

Grand-mom, Grand-dad what's happening, and to the rest of my family, I mean whole family, because there's a lot of ya'll, what's the deal. I will name no names of any of my kin, because I was taught to keep the most precious thangs tucked away. And to my relatives, who passed, see you on the other side hopefully.

To some of the real people I ran across in the street, and trust me there was very few. Babyface, Ghost, and Wiz. There may be a few more I forgot.

Shot out to some of the writers that gave me advice, Dwayne S. Joseph, Brenda L. Thomas, JD Mason, Sammie Ward, Carla Dean and Kalisha Buccannon. And there's a few others I might have forgotten, get to you on the next go around.

To my cats locked down, never lose hope.

To the poor, for I am not just an author, but also a spokesman for ya'll.

And last but not least, a special shout out to my buddy Kilo.

As for the readers, whether you're in jail, prison, home, or a bookstore, sit tight as I borrow your attention and take you into a glimpse of the Illinois underworld, trust me, it's like a movie.

TEFLON

A Lincoln Lee Novel

B
BLACK PEARL BOOKS PUBLISHING
www.BlackPearlBooks.com

PROLOGUE

SUMMER OF 1999

Lightening flashed across the sky so vigorously, at times, you would think it was daylight in Kankakee, Illinois – just 35-minutes south of Chicago. As the rain heavily hit the pavement it portrayed the sound of a running heard of cattle. The thunder was so loud and deep that it made twenty-eight year old Shawndra Coleman jump at times, pulling the cover half way over her face and clutching the phone in her right hand thinking, "*Two hours have passed and this fool still ain't called, why do I put up with this mess, why do I waste my time? I know what he does in the streets and I deserve better.*"

Shawndra glanced at the clock on her bedside table and thought, *Damn it's after 12 o'clock, and I'm up waiting on a phone call that I know I'm not gonna receive* ....Ring...Ring...Ring...

Shawndra checked the caller I.D. before answering, and noticed that the call was private. Her first thought was not to answer, but she remembered that Cleofis sometimes called from private numbers. After a few more rings she quickly picked up the cordless phone.

"Hello".

"What took you so long to answer the damn phone?", said the demanding voice on the other end of the line.

"I told you about calling my house private -- you know I don't answer private calls."

"I'm calling from somebody else's phone..."

"Who, Natalie's phone, I'm sick and tired of your shit Cleofis. When you gonna step up and be a man. I'm tired of you threatening me, talking that abortion shit because I'm keeping my baby."

"You sure about that", said Cleofis, "Or are you just talking out your ass? But forget all that, I was just calling to check up on you sweetie."

"You ain't just calling to check on me, you calling about that damn money, and I told you Cleofis, I spent it on baby clothes."

"Look Shawndra I know you ain't that stupid, you only three months, just get that abortion before it's too late you hear me? And, I want my money, before you make me do something that I don't wanna do." His voice went into a rage then back into a calmer tone.

"What you gonna do huh, kill me too, like you did them boys in that house?", Shawndra snapped back.

"I don't know what you talking about and you need to watch your big mouth on this phone. I told you about your mouth, don't ever let me hear you talk like that over a phone again." "You don't tell me what to do. When your ass was locked up, who was there for you huh, me? Then when you get out, you dog me like I don't mean anything to you. Was that bitch Natalie coming down there to see you every week? Huh? No! Was she putting money on your books every week? Hell NO! And when you got out, I'm the one who put you on your feet! And this is how you treat me after everything I done for you? I'm tired of being disrespected and I'm tired of fooling with you, when there are men out there that will treat me better."

"I ain't gonna stop you from talking to nobody, but that money belong to me and the guys. Now, I gave you a couple of days to cool off, do you need a couple more?" Cleofis said sternly.

"What I need is for you to stop calling me until you get yo' shit together." Shawndra threw the phone against the wall disconnecting Cleofis instantly. Click…

"Shawndra…Shawndra….you still there?"

As she buried her face into the palms of her hands, tears of hurt and frustration slowly seeped through the creases between her fingers. Slowly wiping the tears from her eyes, she got out of bed and worriedly walked to her seven year old daughter's bedroom to see if she had awaken her. She peaked into the bedroom and saw a small figure in pink Barbie doll pajamas stretched out across the bed, still sound asleep. Shawndra walked back to her bedroom and pulled out a shoebox from under her bed, containing all the letters she had received from Cleofis while he was incarcerated. She dumped the letters onto her silk bedspread. Shawndra started ripping a couple of letters into small pieces, and then suddenly realized how much the letters meant to her. She began to laugh softly, remembering when she first fell in love with Cleofis.

Lying across the bed, she listened to the pattering of the rain against the window, it gave her a soothing feeling as she thought about how things used to be. And the good times she and Cleofis had shared together. As she began to fall asleep the rain pattering against the window was the last thing she heard, before a loud noise that made her jump, someone was at the door. BOOM BOOM BOOM…. BOOM BOOM BOOM… The knock was loud and heavy. She frantically got up out of her bed still half asleep, she approached the front door and looked through the peep hole.

"Who is it?", she asked.

"Open up the door it's us, Teflon stranded", responded the nervous voice from the other side of the door.

"What?" Shawndra yelled through the door before recognizing the familiar voice.

"Teflon stranded!"

Shawndra opened the door, it was raining heavily now she realized, as James (Jackpot) Love and James (JW) Wells stepped into her apartment, drenched from head to toe due to the heavy rain.

"Did you say Cleofis was stranded?"

"Yeah", Jackpot replied, "We need a ride to go get him."

"Where is he", she asked worriedly.

"Not far away from here, the car broke down on him and we need you to take us to go and get him", said Jackpot.

"But my daughter is in the room sleep…

"It ain't far, it won't even take ten minutes."

After throwing some water on her face to wake herself up fully, Shawndra quickly grabbed her coat, purse, and car keys. Still in her pajamas she locked the door behind her, hoping that her daughter would not wake while she was gone. The thunder had stopped but the rain was still coming down, as the three of them entered her vehicle.

"I don't know why ya'll call that fool Teflon, his momma named him Cleofis Jackson. Don't nobody call him Teflon but ya'll and these lames that's scared of him in the streets."

"Just make a left up here at this stop sign", JW uttered.

This would be the first time JW said anything since they had come in contact with Shawndra. Shawndra didn't trust JW, and wouldn't have opened her apartment door if it wasn't for Jackpot.

"What? Ya'll ain't talking mess like ya'll usually do when I see ya'll?", Shawndra asked, expecting them to start talking shit at any given second.

But the car was silent except for the static from the radio and the tune from the windshield wipers.

As JW sat on the passenger side everything seemed to be going as planned. His cold wet clothes gave him the shakes along with his intentions. And the cold steel rubbing up against his bare skin was a reminder of an undecided decision. His heart was beginning to beat like a drum. You don't need to do this, there is still time to turn around, he reflected.

Turning left on a very dark road Shawndra noticed a parked car a few yards ahead. JW now having second thoughts was now in the process of changing his mind.

Good it wasn't that far now I can get back home to my daughter. Shawndra reflected, while JW nervously retrieved a black object from the side of his waist that appeared to be a gun.

The seriousness of the situation hadn't fully set in on Shawndra when he pointed the gun at her, demanding her to pull over. His hand vibrated the automatic and when he realized the power he possessed it ruled out the nervous feeling that rattled his body.

Pulling over to the side of the road, Shawndra couldn't help but to come to the terms of this being set up and Cleofis was no where in sight. "What's going on James", Shawndra asked Jackpot in the backseat with a rising fear in her tone. "Shut up", JW replied, not giving Jackpot a chancc to answer. "Stop movin' bitch!" The harsher his words flowed, the more his confidence to kill began to take over. "I know you ain't gonna let him do this James", Shawndra started through sobs. "What about my daughter?"

Jackpot was speechless wanting to respond once again, but his fear caged his tongue.

"STOP MOVING!", JW interrupted her pleading after thinking about the price of getting caught. His eyes had quickly glanced at the get-a-way car which brought him to his decision.

As the barrel of the automatic rose to Shawndra's face and the twitching in JW's hand stopped, she knew it was over.

"Jaaaaaaaaaaaames!" She yelled in an earsplitting scream, just before a bullet ripped through her skull and shattered the window as it exited out the other side. Seconds later another bullet tore into her forehead, scattering brain fragments, putting an end to the nerves that jerked her body.

CHAPTER 1

ENDING OF '96

THE GIFT AND THE CURSE

The closing of the county bars was all very real to Cleofis Jackson, having been to prison already at age seventeen. He quickly adapted to the county jail rules. April secretly ratted him out to collect on a thousand dollar reward. Sergeant Fox couldn't wait to pull the van over that chauffeured him in the back under tinted windows. The top floor of the county jail is where he was stationed, where they kept some of Kankakee's worse criminals. Cleofis was in the north east cell block where there were ten cells, five on one side, and the same on the other. You had to walk in a circle to view all ten cells. Cleofis was housed in the fourth cell with a cellmate named Bootleg that he woke up to every morning. The fifth cell was the last cell before turning the corner to go to the other side, which had cells six, seven, eight, nine, and ten.

More than anything he stayed on the phone in the day room trying to get his fifty thousand dollar bond lowered by his lawyer Mark Galante. The normal bond for a person being charged with attempted murder was twenty-five thousand. But because Detective Diamond and other law enforcement spoke with the State Attorney, they went for the highest bond possible.

A lot of inmates thought Cleofis still had money, and figured if he didn't bond himself out, then Bruno, his ballin' ass cousin, would come to the rescue. But they were sadly mistaken, and Cleofis drowned himself in shame, not able to bond out for what some felt was nothing to him. Very few expected his stay in the county jail to be long and in a strange way, considering how much money he once possessed, Cleofis felt some way some how he would bond out before coming to the actual terms of exile.

Ninety-seven rolled around, and it was kind of chilly waking up in the morning "BREAKFAST", the trustees yelled, "Naw I'm straight", Cleofis replied. Splashing some water on his sleepy face, he recognized his cellmate was still asleep. Looking in the tainted small mirror the inmate noticed a change, "Shit this filthy ass county breaking my face out." His face looked nasty, and it was spreading rapidly! Taking off his white tank top he searched his upper body to make sure it was just on his face. "What's wrong with you?", asked his cellmate. "Man this damn county breaking my face out." He responded, jumping on the top bed of the bolted in the wall bunk. "I need me a request slip." He bent between his swinging legs and said.

Bootleg looked up at him from the bottom bunk with his eyes half way opened. "It ain't like they gonna do shit, you gonna have to see the nurse."

Bootleg was fighting a secret indictment. He was a chocolate complexioned, cocky fella with braids. He enjoyed being housed next to the widely spoke about Cleofis Jackson. "Man if I find a way to break out this bitch, they'll have to kill me to get me back", Cleofis said, tired of the living conditions. "Well if you find a way out let me know 'cause I'm coming with cha", replied Bootleg.

Bo Pete was out in the world running his big mouth, smoking crack and telling the triple murder story that involved Cleofis, to anybody who would listen. "I was there, CJ killed all three of them boys, and da nigga woulda killed me if I wouldn't of jumped out of the window", Bo Pete continued, "I'm telling you, that boy is a cold blooded killa, with silencers and all. That's why nobody heard anything…I'm for real. The nigga had silencers, no bullshit!"

The story started in a crack house and in no time it was all over the city. Disco couldn't control his tongue, neither. "I'm telling you Cliff, CJ is a killer. The nigga killed Toby, Muddy, and them niggas in that townhouse."

"I thought Marvin killed Muddy", Cliff said naively. "Naw stupid, I just told you, I don't know how he got outta it, but CJ smothered dude and set his body on fire. Toasted the nigga, motherfucka looked like a skeleton", Disco exaggerated a little.

"I know Cleofis Jackson killed my boy", the mother of the little white boy Toby cried. "Everybody knows it! Why isn't he being charged with my son's murder?" Detective Diamond tried to calm the lady. "We have no proof, ma'am, but were working on it, just give us some time."

Every actual murder Cleofis did, that was uncertain to people, eventually became certain to them. Bo Pete spoke about him as if he was some myth. Hustlers spoke about him as if he was Robert Di Nero off the movie *'Heat'*. Gangsters talked about him like he was one of them. Women pictured him as a gangstafied Tupac figure or something. The newspapers described him as notorious, after Marvin yelled, "Cleofis Jackson did this shit, not me", in court, while he was on the stand. Citizens thought of him as a monster, and vengeful family members of the victims prayed for his death or life imprisonment. His absence gained him street credibility beyond his childhood dreams. "If CJ was out, this…., if CJ was out, that…", was some of the things his followers would say to eager listeners. Plenty of niggaz talked shit though, but the majority who talked shit feared him in physical form. His presence was felt, even though his body was locked inside a cell.

In Chicago, he would be just another gun-slinger, but in Kankakee to get away with that many murders without being charged was genius, especially considering the fact that murder was hard to get away with in the small city.

Majority of all the murders from the early nineties was brought to justice by a right hand man who caught a case and chose to rat on his homic, or simply from killers having big mouths. It was a few silent killers that dwelled in the night, but for the most part the late nineties was full of big mouths, bragging about murders they didn't do or see. Once you was suspected or charged with a murder the gossipers would implicate you in other murders. The stories about Cleofis was so added and subtracted, by the time it would reach a different set of people, it was a totally different story than the first. Kankakee was full of gossiping, miserable people that would lie about a cup of coffee just to hold conversation.

"Mail", she yelled, handing out mail to the first cell. Cleofis jumped anxiously off the top bunk, squeezing the steel bars impatiently, I better have some mail, he said to himself before seeing her. "Jackson", she yelled when approaching his cell. And there she was, Natalie Knowles, and for a second, Cleofis' heart skipped a beat. The encounter was brief, but it was breath-taking. *Damn she bad!*, He said to himself after making the eye contact.

Natalie reached out to hand him his mail, "Quite a bit of mail you got there Mr. Jackson."

Delighted by her comment and appearance, Cleofis replied, "Thank you, and how do you do today? You look a little tired to be new, 'cause I haven't seen you before."

Natalie checked on cell five and remembered that Cleofis' money order receipt was in her shirt pocket. "Here you are Mr. Jackson, I almost forgot", she said, handing him his receipt. "I never worked this floor before that's why you never seen me before."

"Well you need to work it more often", Bootleg yelled as Natalie walked off and over to cells six, through ten to finish handing out the mail.

Natalie was 5'4" with caramel skin, honey brown eyes, full luscious lips, and plenty of cleavage. She didn't have big hips, but she did have a very large bottom that stuck out as if it was swollen. No garments could hide it! Besides the small gap between her top front teeth, she had crazy sex appeal. She had long black hair that reached the middle of her back, even when she wore it in a ponytail. Her ears almost looked like elf ears, how pointy they were at the top, but Natalie was still a very attractive woman with a round baby face.

Her thin textured hair she'd been growing since birth was a fairly decent strain, which she usually kept professionally done.

"That bitch raw ain't she?", Bootleg replied, star-struck. "She decent", Cleofis merely expressed, not wanting his cellmate to know he was head over heels, and didn't even know her name yet. "Who wrote you?", Bootleg asked, trying to be nosey. Cleofis sat on a stool, built into the wall along with a desk, "None of ya business, chump", he replied jokingly, "Jus' moms and a couple of folks."

Looking at the fifty dollar money order receipt, Cleofis smiled thankfully. "*Gabe always lookin' out for me, man that's my nigga*", he said proudly to himself, opening a letter from Shawndra Coleman.

Hey little Bro,

This is your big sis Shawndra. I was just thinking about you, I've been trying to come see you but this job has had me working crazy hours. My little girl still asks about you, saying "Where Cleo at momma?", I tell her you're at school. It's amazing how she still remembers you. I hope they lower your bond soon, so that you can get out, 'cause I miss your little bad ass. Call me as soon as you can. Take care of yourself and I'll keep you in my prayers.

From your big sis Shawndra

Cleofis set his mothers letter to the side, for an unknown letter caught his attention. It had no name, no address, and no city state or zip code. *Who could it be?*, he thought. Opening the small folded letter, he was instantly curious because it was an anonymous sender. But he didn't recognize the hand writing, so his first thought was it was an old fling or female he probably was involved with in the past, so he started to read.

How are you doing Cleofis Jackson?

I don't think you know me, but I know you. You're the one that killed my little brother. I've dedicated my life to tracking you down, and I hope so bad they set you free. No need to know my name now. Just pray you never meet me, 'cause I will never grow to accept your presence on this earth. You a dead motherfucker, and you don't even know it yet.

Bootleg could see the displeasure in Cleofis' face. "You straight 'Moe'?", he asked concerned as Cleofis balled the letter up into a compressed paper wad, and threw it in the toilet aggressively. "Who was that?" Bootleg asked.

Cleofis jumped distraughtly on the top bunk, laid on his bed and replied, "Nobody."

When the inmates on his cell block went to the day room, Cleofis stayed in his cell in deep thought about what victim's brother that letter came from. Staring at the graffiti covered ceiling, it dawned on him. "CHOPPER! Travis' older brother, I bet that's who it is", he spoke out loud to himself while he tried to picture the man's face.

"Jackson you have a visit", a white guard yelled. He was so into thought, he didn't hear the big key they used to open the northeast door. "I bet you that's Kim", was his thoughts as the cell door rolled back. "Let's go Jackson", the white guard yelled again.

The visit was in a first floor room, with thick glass in between the visitor and inmate. Communication was by phone, sight and sign language, if hearing impaired.

Kim was already sitting waiting when Cleofis arrived, as a streak of joy came to his face, when seeing the woman he loved. Wanting so bad to know why Kim hadn't written him, Cleofis took a seat in the hard chair and grabbed the phone that strongly resembled a pay phone.

"I hope you got a good explanation young lady", he said sarcastically, "You haven't written me and you haven't been to see me in a while. What some nigga got ya time or something?" Cleofis was becoming frustrated with her complete silence, and her lack to look him directly in the eyes. "What the fuck is wrong with you?" he yelled.

Kim stood erect and Cleofis knew what it was before she could get it out, "I'm pregnant can't you tell?"

He sat with a confused look on his face before asking, "By who?"

Kim glanced totally in a different direction, "Gillmen", she spoke in a low nervous tone. "I'm sorry CJ….. I still love you no matter what."

His heart felt like it was ripped out of his chest, the phone slid slowly through his fingers, as a force field of sickness rattled his body making him feel very weak. Gathering strength, his mouth could barely muster the words, “Get outta here”, he began in a hollow whisper, “I betta not ever see yo’ face again, you filthy disgusting bitch. I hate you!” The last words came out hoarse for the thought of betrayal took his breath away. *‘Out of all the niggaz in the world, she had to sleep with my enemy,’* he thought hurtfully banging the phone on the thick glass, as Kim walked out of the visiting room in tears. Cleofis sat their for a minute visualizing Gillmen on top of Kim and how happy he must have felt impregnating the young woman that he loved.

The guards physically escorted him from the visiting room, trying not to have a conflict with the infuriated young man. Cleofis went to his cell and threw a tantrum, throwing all of his cosmetics all over the place.

Bootleg was in the day room with the other inmates, wondering why Cleofis didn’t come out of his cell.

“Ay ‘Moe’ you coming out today?”

Cleofis corrected his sobbing voice into a stern reply, “Leave me the fuck alone!” he yelled in response.

The broken heart brought many sleepless nights and many refused meals. The thought of Kim made him sick to his stomach, and resulted in him losing weight.

Finally, after weeks of staying in his cell twenty four hours a day, by choice the sick villain was recuperating. He grinned and laughed like an old hoodlum when receiving news of Bruno’s widely discussed murder. Cleofis knew that Chicagoans got word back to the powerful figure that they tore off in Maywood, because of the dice game incident, along with Bruno not bonding him out and for sleeping with Kim. Cleofis vowed to disclose Bruno’s role in the tremendous come up. The hit men practically turned Bruno’s five hundred Benz around with choppers, leaving Bruno’s body riddled with heavy artillery. You could barely identify him because pieces of his face were missing. Kankakee’s king pin was dead, and the funeral brought in tons of women from many different states and dealers, who wanted a last look at the street legend.

Inmates thought the news would send Cleofis back into depression. They all were naïve to the fact Cleofis was the cause of thc murder, and that he could barely control his smile around them. After reading an influential book on John Gotti, the villain decided to call himself Teflon, The Untouchable. And the name stuck to him in no time, the whole cell block referred to him as Teflon, But Cleofis was still a number one fan of Al Capone. He mentally noted that he was going to call his crew the Capone gang, when touching down.

Cleofis was now fully understanding his power to control, and became a master at manipulation. He used to do it unconsciously, but now he was fully aware of what people expected out of him -- leadership, money and to feel protected. And he wanted something in exchange, the assistance to murder anyone who stood in the way of him getting money.

The mafia bosses he read about all had a similar past to his own, and Cleofis came to the conclusion that, that's what he was, a boss.

"What's up lil bro? I tried to call you earlier, but nobody answered the phone."

"Who the hell is, Teflon", Gabe asked in a joking tone, "I started not to accept the call, till I recognized your voice."

"That's what niggaz call me now, but when you write me, don't use that name 'cause them people try to read every square inch of my mail. And I don't want them having that alias before I get out. But anyways lil bro I was calling to tell you thanks for the cheese. It was right on time and them bitch ass niggaz out there gonna make me fuck them up if they don't start matching what you bring down here."

Gabe listened carefully, to his friend that some people was starting to forget about, "Man I don't mean to cut you off, but I seen this fine bitch the other day with that thick bitch you used to creep with, Makcela."

"Oh, and thanks for reminding me, the fine bitch you talking about is Kiara, and she told Makeela she wanted to holla at you."

"Stop lying nigga", replied Gabe not believing his friend, "You serious, straight up."

"Would I lie to you? I talked to Makeela last night, and she said the bitch asked about you."

"Man that bitch, bad she look like a fuckin' model."

"I know lil bro", Cleofis spoke through a slight giggle, "And I think she a virgin, so don't mess this up, 'cause I tried to get her but she wouldn't go, and she went back and told Makeela like that's my woman or something."

Gabe broke off into a humorous laugh, "How do I get up with the chick? Where she stay?"

"Don't worry I'll have that all hooked up by tomorrow, thanks to you big bro Teflon, 'The Untouchable'."

Gabe and Shawndra started coming to visit him together and Gabe was getting close to Kiara in a way Cleofis could only dream about. Kiara most definitely looked like a model, it's like she just hoped out of a magazine or TV. She was a tall beautiful light skinned girl with Chinese eyes and long hair. Gabe was appreciative for Cleofis putting in a very good word with Kiara, and when visiting him with Shawndra, Cleofis could see his friend was full of joy and happiness.

"I heard about that guy Bruno, somebody said that was your cousin", Natalie said, observing Cleofis as he was reading a book in the library."

"Yeah, that was my cousin", he replied with a straight face, "Did you know him or something?" he lowered the book from his squinting eyes.

"I've seen him around, when I was younger, but I didn't know he was this big time drug dealer that everybody's talking about."

Cleofis stood up, and walked to the bars that locked him in the library, "Tell me something. Why are you working here? You seem too intelligent for this job." Natalie gave a bashful look, "'Cause the extra money really helps, and work takes my mind off of other things."

"Is that right, Ms. Knowles?"

"That's right, and how come you don't ever smile? To be so young, I never seen you laugh since I've been working this floor."

Cleofis put up the best happy smile he could produce showing all thirty two teeth. But his smile could not hide his heavy heart, and Natalie could tell he was stressed.

"See I knew you could smile", she continued, "I came up here to see if you were ready to go back to your cell block?"

"Do I have a choice?"

"I'll let you stay out a little bit longer."

"I appreciate it pretty lady", the eye contact between the two sent chills down his spine, and Cleofis went off the Scarface theory, "The eyes never lie, chico." Cleofis almost forgot about Natalie in his time of heartache, but now was open to a mutual encounter of flirting with the eyes.

"Look at her", he said to himself in a low tone, "She know she wants a thug in her life." She looked just a little too long, and that's all Cleofis needed to build off of.

Time plus pleasure has granted me this golden opportunity to correspond with a lovely lady such as yourself, I couldn't help it I had to write you regardless of a response or not. The flirting going on between us is obvious, and a nigga want to know, how can he get the time of day? I know you probably get a lot of attention from guys but I'm definitely a unique one. I didn't see a ring on your finger, so I would assume you don't belong to a man. I'm about to shake it out of here soon, and it would be nice to have your friendship out in the world.

Cleofis was waiting on a response from this letter he wrote Natalie, but never got it. He didn't let it bother him though because his trial was coming up, and he was trying so hard to get in touch with Gillmen over the phone. "You got his number?"

"Yeah I got it", Shawndra answered.

"Well, click over and call him on three way."

Gillmen's cell phone rang until the last ring finally he answered.

"What it is man?"

"This Cleofis homie, my trial is about to start and I was wondering what you was going to say."

"What'chu mean, what I'm gonna say? You shot me, you bitch ass nigga. I'll be in court before the scheduled time." Gillmen hung up the phone after the statement.

"Hang the phone up Shawndra, that nigga hung up on me." Shawndra clicked Gillmen's line off. "Damn he wild, I thought he was a street nigga, how he just gonna come to court on you like that?"

"'Cause they stool pigeons, what'choo expect, but fuck it. I'mma still take it to trial, 'cause everybody else say it wasn't me, and that rat ass nigga know he was coming to kill me."

It took an all white jury no time to find Cleofis Jackson guilty of attempt murder. Gillmen came to court, and gave a partially false statement of what happened. Cleofis went to his cell and contemplated all night on hanging himself. And the double digits the judge was going to give him were hard to swallow. More sleepless nights came, but this time not from Kim's heartache. He didn't feel like Teflon the untouchable anymore, and the verdict seemed to take the fight out of him.

Until a wise old inmate took a look at his case, and enlightened him to a lot of errors. The old man gave Cleofis life again, when he felt like it was over. He immediately went to work, reading anything in the law library that had something to do with his case and situation. Cleofis started showing the old man more errors that were made. The old man advised him to set a meeting with Mark Galante as soon as possible. Mark was stunned by the intelligence of the young man for recognizing things that he didn't. He presented the errors to the judge on the sentencing date.

The judge agreed to postpone the sentencing and to look over the questionable evidence for a new trial.

1998 came as a shock to many inmates when Cleofis was granted a new trial. Feeling very good about himself, he strutted around the catwalk like a humble sophisticated lawyer wearing prescription glasses that fellow inmates joked about. The glasses made him look intelligent in a Muslim perspective, reading the Kuran occasionally. Cleofis face was begging for a grooming, due to unkemptness from depression. But with his new mindset he kept himself shaved and had a low hair cut. The favorable clean cut look also made him look wiser, and more in control of his destiny. Cleofis prayed for forgiveness' of his sins, and truly believed God had forgiven him. The second chance at freedom, he felt was Gods way at giving him a shot at a second chance in life. He promised he'd be better if receiving a second chance. He felt cleansed and carried a slight attitude adjustment.

'Dang', Cleofis said to himself quietly, *'If I would have known that, I wouldn't have ever gotten back serious with Kim, I would have stayed right where the hell I was'*.

Cleofis reflected on the situation after reading a letter Shawndra wrote to him, revealing her desire for him when she harbored him. He was kind of surprised, especially since he thought of her as a sister. This made him want to be free more, and the letter he wrote her back let her know it was a mutual desire.

Shawndra's visits became more frequent, along with her letters and commissary money. They grew closer through correspondence. Shawndra grew emotionally attached to the twenty year old inmate. Cleofis wrote Natalie again, but came up empty on a response. "No, this *heffa* just ain't gonna ignore me like that." Cleofis expressed sarcastically in silence.

Cleofis asked Natalie if he could go to the library. She had said, "Someone's already in there."

He hoped he could get the chance to holla at her in private some more. Whenever Natalie worked the top floor, she made excuses for his request to the library.

Cleofis thought he was reading between the lines, even though Natalie remained in a philandering manner towards him.

'She wanna flirt with a nigga, but that's it. It's cool, it ain't like she hospitable. She could be an asshole like some of the other guards. But she does tend to most of my requests. Maybe she thinks, I'm doomed or something, I don't know, fuck it, I ain't fenna let her bother me though', Cleofis thought while resting his back against the wall and sitting curiously on the top bunk.

He glanced at Bootleg, doing pushups, as the cell next to him opened, and a guard brought in a new inmate.

"Did they just bring somebody in?", he asked Bootleg.

"Think ssssoo", Bootleg replied, pushing up on his last push up.

Cleofis jumped down softly off the top bunk, and approached the bars, "Who is that in cell three… is you deaf of somethin'… who dat be in cell three?" He again asked, more curiously.

CHAPTER 2

Cut Throat

"This me", A voice said shamefully. A split second of silence occurred, then Cleofis responded jokingly, "Get the fuck outta here – this my little brother", he replied to his cellmate, Bootleg. "What the hell you in here for? You supposed to be out in the world helping me." He continued, easing his ear to a small opening between the wall and the steel bars. "Man little homey I can't believe it's you."

"Yeah me neither, they picked me up on a secret indictment, some pussy muthafucka set me up."

"You ain't tell them people nothing did you?"

"Come on man. Don't ask me no stupid shit like that."

"I'm just asking nigga, but I'm fenna go and lay back down, we'll holla when they let us back out in the day room."

Gabe held the steel bars, barely in his hands, not yet fully aware of the seriousness of the situation. He sat on the steel chair with a steel desk top, and replayed everything that happened with him being set up, in his mind.

"How could I have been so stupid?", he thought to himself. Gabe's cellmate was a young Italian fellow who wrote his girlfriend everyday of the week, and loved to draw pictures of people.

"Can you move some of this shit, so I can have some room for mines?" Gabe asked sternly.

The Italian finished the sentence on a letter he was writing, "Okay okay, no need to be rude." The Italian then moved some of his belongings saying, "Make your self at home."

"Chow time", a guard yelled from a distance. "Now you fenna get to see this bullshit they feed us", Cleofis began honestly. "So what you think about this hell-hole so far?"

Gabe could see the trustees coming to hand-out supper. "It ain't so bad, I don't see what ya'll tripping about."

Cleofis blew through his lips, "Okay little nigga, wait till you be in this boy a little longer."

The trustees slid two trays through the chuckholes for him and his cellmate, "What the hell is this?", Gabe replied seriously. "Food muthafucka", Cleofis spoke in an 'I-told-you-so' voice.

The tray was laced with cold green beans, a cold chicken sandwich, and a foam cup that contained a terrible tasting gulp of red Kool-aid.

"The people at the homeless shelter eat better than this. How you supposed to eat this cold shit?" Cleofis took a hungry bite out of the sandwich, "You'll eat it when you get hungry and commissary low playa." The Italian chuckled at Gabe's displeased comments. "Bambino you want some Mickey Dee's", he chuckled louder, "Betta bond out of here 'cause this as good as it gets."

"Would you tell em?", Cleofis yelled obnoxiously from the cell next door, agreeing with Gabe's cellmate. "Pass me yo' tray if you don't want it", Gabe stuck his tray through the chuckhole as far as he could, then swung it to the right. "Good lookin out", said Cleofis.

The orange two piece jump suit was tight on Gabe's fairly tall figure. The brown criss-cross laced sandals were worn out. The mat he slept on was very thin with a thin sheet and a thin wool cover that only covered the lower part of the body from the shoulders down. They were also provided with state soap, toothpaste, tooth brush, and other state accessories that seemed to be a glitch, compared to the ones out in the real world. A person usually lost a massive amount of weight in the Kankakee County Jail, you also gargled with the same water you pissed and shitted in. They fed you just enough to keep you alive.

Gabe took a seat on one of the stainless steel picnic tables in the day room, waiting on Cleofis to come in from out of his cell. "Aye lil homie, come back here", Cleofis yelled out to Gabe. Cleofis was choosing to stay in his cell so he could go over some things in his case. "What's up lil' bro?" he spoke casually. As Gabe came into the cell it began to shut. "Long time no see", Gabe was glad that the guards put him in a cell next to Cleofis. He now felt amongst family and a little more secure. Cleofis looked so different to him, maybe it was because of the massive gossip behind his name, or the glasses he used for reading. "Pop a squat", Cleofis voiced, sliding on a long sleeve long john shirt that curved to his muscular physique.

Gabe disclosed everything about his case in hopes of Cleofis telling him some good news, "Man, Gabe you might have to do some joint time, but don't trip it won't be that much. This yo' first offense, they gotta be lenient on you." Cleofis took his glasses off and blinked, "I bet you trippin' off of seeing me in these glasses." Gabe sat there coming to terms of possible penitentiary time. "Yeah you look like a four eyed frog", he unconsciously replied after swallowing the bad news. "There you go with the jokes. I been in dis muthafucka almost two years and it seems like ten. I'm ready to get the hell out this muthafucka."

"So what happened in that townhouse?", Gabe cut him off, "Damn lil homey you sure is nosy." Cleofis rubbed his nose with his thumb and index finger. He then started showing a demonstration of what happened in the town house, using body language and folding his index finger pointing it like a pistol. Gabe could actually picture the scene he was re-enacting using no words but shot gun sounds with his mouth. *It was like it was all too natural for Cleofis*, Gabe thought. Then Cleofis started speaking about other things people accused him of, like the little white boy Toby. He responded with, "I didn't try to kill em, he was just in the way, and got hit. I heard his moms went to the police station saying Cleofis Jackson killed my son, crying and shit. But she shouldn't let her son be out playin' late at night", Cleofis explained with no remorse. He took a sip from his foam cup and continued, "And that dumpster shit, I don't know why the hell they keep saying I did that, when I woke up, the whole neighborhood was at the scene wondering who Muddy was." He tapped Gabe's leg, "So see homie, I'm not so bad after all."

A little time went by and Gabe worried that the guards might say something about him being in another cell, but Cleofis reassured him by explaining the pull he had on the cell block from his reputation. Cleofis broke out the photo album from under his bed and they spent the day reminiscing.

Days passed and Gabe was really becoming annoyed with being incarcerated, he also disliked many guards, especially one in particular, the one all the guys called stuck up. "Stuck up Bitch", He yelled loudly right before Natalie closed the entrance door to the cell block. "Gabe!", Cleofis yelled angrily, "Don't do that, don't disrespect the female guards, 'cause they the only ones who tend to our needs." He really only meant don't disrespect Natalie. Cleofis continued, "Them asshole men guards don't even see to it that they get your requests downstairs, we need the women homeboy, for a lot of…"

"The bitch don't see to it they get my request", Gabe interrupted the sugar coated advice. "Fuck her, that bitch walk around here like she on a high horse or something." Cleofis shook off the statement. "Keep being hard-headed, you here?" Grabbing a dry off towel, deodorant, and petroleum jelly for a shower. While waiting for the cell doors to pop open, he shook his head in disappointment to Gabe thoughts. Gabe wiped off of the stainless steel toilet connect to a stainless steel sink, after a much needed piss. He threw the tissue in the toilet and flushed the loud sounding thing.

The sound of the cell doors opening was good music to his ears. Gabe walked out of the cell with a smile on his face, "What's up 'Moe'? What's up 'Moe'?" was all you heard from inmates speaking to Cleofis who trailed behind him. Gabe had not yet copped to the fact that his friend was a blackstone. Calling Cleofis 'Moe', sounded unreal to him, and that was something he chose not to do. Even hearing other people call him Moe sounded funny to him.

Cleofis sat down next to Gabe in the day room and Gabe glanced at him, then smiled still full of jokes about Cleoifs flipping to another organization. "Quit smiling so much", Cleofis started directly. "Killas don't smile -- when you smile a lot people don't take you serious." Gabe didn't want to hear any of the villain's theories. He got up and moved closer to the TV, which showed sexy female actress Pamela Anderson on Baywatch. The inmates enjoyed flicks like this and you would hear seldom say I'm fenna go back to my tip. Meaning they were going to their cell to masturbate. Gabe just couldn't see what kind of pleasure they got out of beating their meat. *How could they even reach a climax?*, he thought. Cleofis assured him that if his stay was long enough the feeling would eventually creep up on him.

"Damn you acting like you about to go out on a date or something."

"I gotta keep my hygiene up", Cleofis replied arrogantly, "The fresher you are, the better you feel about yourself. So of course, I'm a over do it, 'cause I'm confident in my abilities."

Gabe raised his eyebrows, as his friend put some petroleum jelly on his arms, "Aw I see you trying to impress these female guards, huh?" Cleofis cut him off before he could get anymore out, "Nigga", came out loudly, "I ain't trying to impress nobody, but myself silly lil nigga."

Gabe glanced at the stainless steel shower walls, "Let me use some of that deodorant when I get out the shower."

"You ain't even gotta ask that", Cleofis began, "What's mine is yours and you paid for most of it anyway."

The shower was a sanctuary, for Cleofis and he took as much time as he possibly could in it. He used the shower to drift off into the past and into the future mentally. Thinking about changing his life and settling down with a good woman. Shawndra crossed his mind. He frequently asked himself, if she was the type of woman to settle down with.

The sound of Gabe's cell phone kept ringing in his head. He was so used to it going off every five minutes. He'd reach for his side only to discover it was just his mind still stuck in its hustling state.

"You getting down son?", the old man who helped Cleofis replied, "Do you wanna play chess youngsta?"

"Yeah, I'll play", Gabe exclaimed, turning inward to the round table. "Go on and beat his ass real quick, maybe he'll learn somethin'", Cleofis said. Gabe sat the chess pieces up, blinking tightly at the old man's horrible breath. The smell of it turned his stomach upside down.

"Mate", the old man spoke after a few moves. "You must ain't played in a while huh?" Gabe shook his head no.

"You got him with the old one, two, and three." Cleofis smiled as he started, "I didn't think that he would fall for the okey doke."

Felling discouraged to play again, Gabe managed to get up enough guts to take another shot at it. What Cleofis did to others didn't work on Gabe. By the time Cleofis got done joking about somebody, their confidence would be torn down and would have to be rebuilt. So Gabe came out viciously exchanging major pieces, this made the old man bothered, and if it wasn't for lack of experience he would have beat the old man.

"Good game fella, I like the way you attacked me, most players fall back and let me attack them while they defend their house, but you wasn't intimidated by my skill." The old man expressed, pulling the gray hairs out of his beard.

"Don't tell that little nigga that, 'cause it'll go straight to his big head", said Cleofis, putting in his two cents. "Quit throwing salt in a nigga game Cyclops."

The old man laughed at Gabe's sharp and also hilarious comeback. The coldness of the semi smooth concrete floor felt like breath under Gabe's feet. Not yet adjusted to the temperature, he sniffed frequently and his sinuses were bothering him.

Later that night Gabe laid slightly asleep in his cell when he was fully awaken to the marijuana aroma that quivered passed his congested nose. No matter how bad his sinuses bothered him, he knew that smell from anywhere. "Yo homeboy, Gabe yelled as he stood to his feet, are you sleep?" A couple of coughs was let out, "Shhhhhh keep it down... you wanna hit this or what?"

"Naw I'm cool", Gabe was tempted due to his now becoming stressed incarceration. But he didn't want to risk the chance of getting caught. And on the other hand it just wasn't his cup of tea. Gabe was still astonished by a smell he thought he would never smell behind bars. "Well lay yo' ass down and go to sleep den, motherfucka…….. Nigga need to hit this green, it a probably take his mind off that girl."

"My mind ain't on that girl", Gabe's voice grew in the silent cell block, "At least I wasn't chasin' that rotten bitch Kim."

Cleofis laughed gently, "That's why I got love for you, 'cause you never let nobody get the best of you." You could hear a strong pull from him inhaling the weed as he stepped closer to the wall that separated them. "Man I ain't even gone lie to you, I was hurt when she got pregnant on me, but I now realize it was a blessin' in disguise. I didn't really want that rat like that, I just loved her as a child and that was a part of the hold she had on me. Sheeiiit, I don't even think about her no more. But Kiara she a good girl, she fine, and you the only one that's done had her. You better keep that."

"I know, I know, trust me, she ain't going no where." Cleofis hand reached out for him to move closer to the wall. "I'm tryin' to plug with that guard you don't like."

A sudden pause occurred, "See she diggin' a playa right, so just be cool, 'cause once I'm in da car it will be a smooth ride for you too."

"Homeboy" Gabe began, changing the subject, "What was that with Bruno, a hit or something?", a sharp smirk came across Cleofis' face. "You could say that… but that was my doing, I sent that." He whispered. "That nigga stepped on my toes too much, you feel me?"

"I thought ya'll was cool."

"Looks can be deceiving… the nigga was a cut throat just like me, I'mma cut throat too"

Gabe, only interested in hearing more about the street legend carried on paying no attention to what was just said at the end of Cleofis statement. "They say that nigga was a millionaire."

"He was, cuz did have millions ain't no denying that, I wonder where all of is at now. I know he had lots of real state and shit, if anybody got a nice cut of that change it was Shanice, his main bitch."

Gabe was just getting fully adjusted when relatives came to bond him out. In a way he didn't want to leave his friend that he grew so close to in jail.

"I'm outta here, Cleofis."

"I know nigga, I'm just putting the finishes touches on what I told you last night." Referring to a third letter he was writing to Natalie. "Just stand on that business I told you about." Meaning, try to kill Bo Pete, and Gillmen if he could.

Though they argued like they were enemies, they had a lot of love for each other, above their disagreements. And the cruel and unjust treatment they suffered in Kankakee County Jail was unbelievable.

CHAPTER 3

Natalie's Perception

It was a special day for Natalie Knowles, being that it was her 30th Birthday. She was kind of feeling old, 1998 was turning out to be a good year for her. She was working two jobs, buying the house she lived in, had a new vehicle, and was very independent. She dreaded having to go into work on her birthday, although she loved her second job as a Kankakee County Correctional Officer, she hated the pay. Natalie's first job paid very well, so well she didn't have to work the second job. But being a correctional officer had its advantages for her. She loved gossip, she liked attention, she made friends with police officers, and most of all she had a fetish for street guys. Natalie was very flirtatious with a chosen few of the inmates at the jail. But one out of the chosen few she really looked forward to seeing.

Entering her restroom, she turned her shower on. She looked into the mirror at her puffy face from a short nap. She deeply yawned saying to herself, '*Do I really wanna go to work today? Maybe I should just call off. But then again I'm really looking forward to seeing Cleofis. And I know my co-workers are going to spoil me rotten.'*

Natalie reached into a small drawer pulling out a black silk scarf. She tied it neatly around her fresh new hairdo. She pulled back the shower curtain after undressing, and tested the water with her hand to make sure it was the right temperature. Natalie realized the water wasn't hot enough. She turned the nozzle a little more, and glided back in front of the mirror. Confidently gazing at her reflection she heard a knock at the bathroom door. She immediately knew it was her ten year old daughter Dasia by softness of the knock. "It's me mommy", was the response form the other side of the door, "Auntie's on the phone for you."

Natalie halfway cracked the door, grabbing the phone out of her small hands. She excitedly put the phone up to her ear saying, "Why are you just now calling me? You should have been calling to wish me a happy birthday at twelve o clock a.m., on the dot."

"Girl who said I was calling you, to wish you a happy birthday", her sister said jokingly. "Nat you know I'm just playing. Happy birthday girl, so what are you going to be doing for the big THREE - O?"

"I have to work today, but when I get off I'm gonna party till I pass out."

"Don't party too hard -- you know what happened on your last birthday. I can't believe you thirty girl, you getting up there with us old folks."

"I can't believe it neither, it seems like just yesterday I was a teenager. My age might be getting up there with you old folks, but my looks definitely not."

"Girl, please. I know I'm fine. These young men try to holla at me everyday at work. Anyways I was thinking about coming down there to Kankakee, but my husband has really been tripping lately. I don't know what I'm gonna do with that man."

"What's the problem you ain't giving it up enough, because if that's the case you should be trying to give him all he can handle."

"I just be too tired for all of that, and he thinks it's because I'm cheating on him. He's been accusing me about that a lot lately."

Looking into her bathroom closet for a face towel, Natalie jokingly said, "Well are you cheating on him?"

"Yeah I did recently, but I doubt if I do it again. The thought of it makes me very paranoid around the house. I would hate for that to surface, 'cause if he found out, he would probably kill me girl."

"Girl, I can't believe you creeping, it's been a long time since you did something like that. Tell me how it was, was it at least worth it?"

"Every minute of it, and he was such a gentleman. He took his time and made me feel very comfortable. My body needed every bit of it. It's been a long time since it's been that good. Enough about me, tell me more about this guy you been fantasizing about at work"

"His name is Cleofis, he's alright looking, but he got a body out of this world. We flirt with each other everyday at work, but I think things starting to get kind of serious. Girl if he wasn't locked up, I would have been put it on him."

"Girl, you mean to tell me you been talking about an inmate all this time. I thought you were talking about one of your co-workers. You always go for the rough ones. I hope you being careful, you wouldn't want to lose your job."

"Girl I'm always careful, and no one sees us when we talk seriously to each other. There are a couple places in the facility that don't have cameras. That's where we do the most of our conversating. He's a cool young man and he does not have a big mouth, he stays to himself."

"Did you just say young man? So, not only are you getting involved with a inmate, you a cradle robber too." Her sister said before letting out a very loud laugh.

As the bathroom began to fill with steam from the very hot shower, Natalie offensively replied, "So you a comedian now, and for your information he's about twenty years old, and anything over the age eighteen is legal."

"Well why don't you tell me why he's in there, Ms. Smarty pants?"

"Well, it's really none of your business, but if you must know he's in for an attempted murder, and please don't blow this out of proportion. I just like him a little, and you know I can't stand lames."

"It's always the dangerous ones that get your attention, huh?"

"Girl please, I don't have time for the lecture, let me get in this shower before all the hot water runs out."

Aware that she was running low on time, Natalie showered very quickly, drying every inch of her body. She started to get dressed putting her work shoes on, as she took the black scarf from around her hair she walked into her bedroom to throw on some of her best perfume. While spraying more on than usual, she began to look forward to having a spoiled day at work.

Exiting her front door with her daughter following behind her, she pointed her key chain towards her vehicle to unarm the system. Natalie turned the radio up before she pulled off, and started singing the R & B song that blasted from her radio. Moving her body back and forth while driving, her daughter laughed at the sight of her mother moving to the music. While pulling up at the baby sitters she glanced at the radio clock. She realized she was running later than she thought. The babysitter walked towards the vehicle ready to tell Natalie some juicy gossip, but she sped off like a mad woman yelling, "Girl, I'm running late." She didn't have time for their routine gossiping session. Approaching the Kankakee County Jail, she could see the police bringing in a young African American male. She shook her head slowly thinking, "There goes another brother, which will fall victim to the system, man he looks so young."

Entering the facility, she could hear one of her co-workers whisper, "There she is."

Natalie smiled as her co-workers started to wish her a happy birthday. A few greeted her with cards asking her what she wanted for lunch today. "Whatever you guys wanna treat me to." She responded. Her boss telling her that she wouldn't have to do any work today, that made her very relieved. As the afternoon turned into night, she sat in her bosses chair doing mostly nothing, until she was asked to pass out the commissary sheets. This would give her a chance to see Cleofis at least once before she left. Anxious to do the job she took the elevator to the top floor. While passing out the sheets, she could see that the inmates had been waiting to place their orders for a while.

Almost done with passing out the sheets, she saved Cleofis' cell block for last. Walking through the cell block she noticed his firm arms sticking out from between the spaces of the bars, before she reached his cell. Looking at the five foot four, brown skin, muscular young man with a very large wide nose. She could see that he was holding an envelope in his hand. Cleofis gave her a smile and a wink. "Could you mail this off for me Natalie?" He asked softly.

"Sure can Mr. Jackson, is there any other mail that you want mailed off?"

"No, this is all I have tonight. Do you think they're going to be late with our commissary like they was last time?"

"They shouldn't be, it should only take the regular two days, this time."

"Do they have you working over-time tonight?" He asked to carry on more conversation.

"No, I'm about to leave in a little bit."

Passing the last inmate on the cell block a commissary sheet, Natalie turned around and started walking back through the cell block getting one last glimpse at Cleofis. To Natalie, he stood out amongst the other inmates. He was most definitely an Alfa-male in her eyes. She walked back past him. He presented a smile of a misunderstood man who was nothing like the things people said about him. She had to take a deep breath after the short encounter, trying to rid her mind of the lustful thoughts while waiting for the elevator to come up. While stepping in the elevator she thought to herself, "He always got his shirt off trying to show me his body." Very pleased with what she saw, she just couldn't shake him out of her mind. She not only lusted over him but she wanted to get to know him.

She pushed the envelope that he handed her deeper into her pocket as she stepped out of the elevator. She knew that the letter wasn't to anyone on the outside, and she couldn't wait to get off of work to read it. This was his third letter to Natalie, she wanted to write back the other two times, but was scared of losing her job.

As she got off of work, a co-worker of hers asked for a ride home. Her name was Tracy, a female she associated with occasionally at work. Natalie said yes, and then asked, "Where do you live at?"

"Around the corner from the police station."

Already knowing what Cleofis was locked up for, Natalie asked her co-worker anyway, just to find out more about the young man that other co-workers said was a suspect in many deaths. "What is that Cleofis Jackson guy locked up for?"

"I heard he's in there for attempted murder, they said he killed a few people, but I guess they don't have enough to charge him."

"He don't even seem like that type of person, he's always nice and clean and respectable to the officers. It makes you kind of wonder if he's innocent."

"I doubt that very seriously, but when I was working the top floor he was very nice to me too. They say he's kind of smart, they found him guilty of attempted murder, but he went through his papers very carefully, and found a bunch of errors. The judge had to grant him a new trial."

"Yeah, I noticed that he reads a lot of law books out of the library. His bond seems extremely high compared to the other attempted-murder inmates."

"They said he's a high profile criminal, that's probably why. They say he made a lot of money when he was on the streets, and became a number one target for law enforcement in Kankakee County."

"He must have been terrible on the streets. I'm surprised I've never heard of him before. He just don't seem like that type to me, and the glasses he wears makes him look like a Muslim or something."

"I try not to even look at the inmates, 'cause sometimes they get the wrong impression if you look too much. The dude you talking about though, the Chief is always careful about who he is around."

"Yeah, I can see why, if he's killed a lot of people. Which street you want me to turn on?"

"Turn on this one right here. I stay in the second house to the left. What you doing for your birthday tonight? I know you not going to go home and go to sleep?"

Natalie yawned very deeply, and said, "Shit as tired as I am, I might just go to sleep and call it a night. Girl let me quit playing, I'm getting my party on tonight, and probably gonna take somebody man home."

Natalie's co-worker laughed as she got out of the vehicle, closing the passenger side door she quickly said, "Have fun girl", as Natalie pulled off.

Already arranged for her daughter to stay at the babysitters longer than usual, Natalie rushed to get home. Almost busting down her door to get in, she had to use the bathroom so bad she barely made it. After using the restroom she took her work clothes off, leaving only her bra and panties on. She bent down to pick her work clothes up. Getting the letter Cleofis wrote her, out of her pocket. She walked to her bedroom, and threw the clothes on her bed. Checking her answering machine she could see that she had quite a few messages. She pressed play on the machine, and started looking in her closet for what she was going to wear for the night. Grabbing one of her outfits out of the closet, she threw them on the bed along side of her work clothes saying to herself, "I'm gonna shut shit down when I step in the club tonight." With her hands on her hips, she looked at her outfit for a few more seconds. Then said, "What did I do with that letter, that boy wrote me?"

While her answering machine continued to play, she looked for the letter saying to herself, "I Just had it in my hand." Lifting her outfit off the bed she found the letter. She quickly opened it and started to read.

Greetings

This is Cleofis better known as Teflon the untouchable. This is my third letter and you ain't wrote me back yet. I understand that you would be taking a risk, but I thought we made some kind of connection when we were in the library talking? I just couldn't stop thinking about you since then, and that's not jail talk. I had a dream about you last night. I dreamed me and you were together on the outside. You had got to know me and saw me for who I truly was a warm hearted loving person. You was in love with me and you always wanted me with you. You never got tired of me. I was the man in your life, I was so happy I felt no pain, no regret, no fear of taking it to the next level. I'm pretty sure you've been hurt before and you're not into trusting men. If you would give me the chance, I could show you that I'm very trustworthy, even after betrayal, I've received from people on the outside, since I've been in here. I know that you like me and know that I have a new trial, hopefully soon. I could show you how much I like you. This is my last letter to you, if you respond we could get to know each other a little better. If you don't then I won't write again.

P.S. happy Birthday, If I was out I would shower you with a dozen roses.

Natalie plopped down on her bed paying no attention to the family and friends messages that continued to play on her answering machine. She started thinking to herself, *"Should I write this man back, he seemed so certain that I like him, if he only wasn't locked up. Me and him could most definitely be involved with each other. He's a hustler too, shit! I'll put this thing on him and he'll want to give me all his money. I wonder if he working with something big or is he little down there. 'Cause he sure look like he can handle a woman. Yeah, I think I'm going to write him back."*

She stood up off the bed after making her decision, and started to get dressed. Natalie wasn't really attracted to hard working men. She had been around hustlers the majority of her life. Watching her brothers sell drugs, as a young teenage girl, she saw the money, cars, clothes, and women of their choice. She loved the way they talked, the way they acted, and also their style. The ones that demanded a lot of respect, along with power, were the men that Natalie was attracted to the most. Natalie had a very big family, lots of cousins, aunties, uncles, brothers, and sisters. Her father had also made some children besides the ones he had with her mother. But because she hadn't seen her father since a young girl, she could never find out who they were. She was still very curious about her fathers' children.

Two months later... Natalie and Cleofis was corresponding every chance they got. Every time she would work the top floor, she would take him to the library. At the library they would talk the whole time Cleofis was allowed out. Majority of the time it be no more then two hours. The letters that they wrote each other had started to become sexual. By the intensity of the letters it would be a matter of time, before Natalie would risk her freedom for her own lustful desire.

Bringing restaurant food for Cleofis was a risk she was already taking. She would laugh while watching Cleofis eat quickly, Natalie wasn't the only one who did this. Some of her co-workers had their favorites too, and they would all cover for each other. They would gossip amongst each other about which they felt was the sexiest inmate.

Always careful that nobody heard them, Natalie and her co-workers would only talk about this in private.

Natalie and her co-workers had a very tight circle, which only consisted of people that were like her. Half way through her shift, she and Cleofis entered the library. Usually when an inmate is in the library the officer would close the cell door until their time was up, but Natalie always left the door open with Cleofis. And for the past month she would stand in the cell door way when they held their conversations. Only one inmate was allowed in the library at a time, and because of that, there wasn't a camera that faced directly in front of the library. This gave them the opportunity to correspond with each other without anybody knowing.

The library was small and usually referred to as the law library by the top floor inmates. It was one of the only places on the top floor that didn't have a camera directly on it.

As Cleofis took a seat on the desk, that was built in the wall. He grabbed a book off of the shelf. "Woman, I've been thinking about you all day, what took you so long to come and get me so that we can talk", he said.

"The Chief been tripping today, he didn't even let us leave out to go to lunch. That's why I couldn't bring you food, 'cause he been hounding us since we got here. He's still here and he was supposed to been left a couple of hours ago. I think he woke up on the wrong side of the bed today, or he probably going through some shit with his wife. I don't know it is all I know is I am tired and I'm ready to go."

You only been herc for about three or four hours, and you tired already. Shit the presence of me should have made you energetic!"

Natalie laughed slightly, while standing in the cell doorway. "You always got something to say to make me laugh, where you get your joy from considering the fact you're in the situation you're in?" she asked.

"My joy comes from God, him knowing the things that I've been through, and still he allows me a second chance at life. When they found me guilty, I felt like killing myself. I really felt like going in my cell and hanging myself. Something told me don't give up the fight because I knew it was self defense. I was just protecting myself, that man came to do me harm so I had no choice. I knew it was a lot of errors in my case, so I started to read these law books. The more I read the more I started to realize my whole case was bogus, but I'm not surprised I got convicted in a way. The State made me look like a monster to an all white jury.

"If it was self defense, why you didn't tell them that, instead of just saying you weren't there?"

"Because I knew they wouldn't understand. I never seen him grab for his gun, I didn't give him a chance to grab for his gun. He had already told so many people that he was going to kill me, so when I ran into him I didn't give him a chance. What was I supposed to do, wait until he pulled his gun out and shot me? My lawyer told me the jury would never buy that story, that's about the only good advice he gave me because I could have represented myself. That's how bad of a job he did, but what could I expect out of a public defender."

"Yeah, I know what you mean. Them public defenders don't help nobody. You talk so old to be so young, you seem to smart to be in here. All you do is read law books, how come you never thought about being a lawyer?"

"I don't know I guess I was running the streets too much. To busy chasing a dollar, I was young with a nice amount of money, and I didn't know what to do with it. Now that I've been in here for a while, I've learned a lot about investing, and I read every book I can get my hands on. And by people turning their backs on me since I've been in here, it's taught me not to trust anyone. Only person that sent me some money besides my mother was my little homey Gabe. Everybody else disowned me except for a couple other people, who write me every now and then. Everybody gonna be surprised when this judge cut me loose in this new trial."

"You sound so confident like you just know they gonna set you free. But I hope they do 'cause I would like to see you in the free world."

Cleofis then stood up and took a couple steps towards Natalie and said, "You can see me now. Plus I don't think I can control myself any longer." With his right hand holding a book, he put his left hand on Natalie's waist and stepped forward to kiss her. Their lips met with a very passionate french-kiss, which Cleofis finally got up enough guts to try. He moved in closer and the book dropped out of his hand. He then gripped her bottom very tightly. You could hear the smacking sound form the moist kiss between the two. Kissing her neck very gently, he relaxed her body from an early irritated day at work. Stimulated by the touch of his hands and lips, Natalie exhaled with a slight moan. With her back against the library wall, she felt like she was momentarily paralyzed. Cleofis moved his hands from her bottom up to her chest, and began to loosen a button from her uniform.

Mesmerized by his muscular build, she said to herself, "I can't believe I'm letting him unbutton my shirt. Am I dreaming? Is this real?" She could then hear her walkie-talkie say, "Ms. Knowles do you copy?" She then pushed Cleofis onto the library seat and said, "What did you say?" Then the voice came in again saying, "The Chief wants you down stairs now."

Frantic from the disturbance she quickly buttoned her shirt, and then she closed the cell door to the library and told Cleofis she would return shortly."

Returning to the first floor had her kind of nervous, at first she thought it might have been another camera some where hidden that she didn't know about. But the Chief just wanted to tell her that she would be in charge tomorrow, when she came in. She sighed in relief and waited a while until she got on the elevator to return upstairs. When she got off the elevator, she could see Cleofis looking inside of a book, through the jail bars. He looked up at Natalie very calm, but still excited from the incident. He was expecting them to continue with their act, until she said, "I'm about to take you back to your cell block, we can talk again tomorrow."

"Is the Chief trippin again or something? 'Cause man girl you got me feeling real good right now."

"You had me feeling good too, but we gonna have to put things on a hold for now. I just don't know what I'm gonna do with you. Boy I don't want to get in trouble."

"I ain't gonna get you in trouble, we'll be cool as long as we keep playing it smart. It ain't no camera directly on the library, so they ain't gonna know shit, stop being so paranoid."

Natalie opened the bars to the library, "I have to be careful, and this is my job. Not to mention that this is my freedom we talking about. You won't get in trouble, so of course you not going to be paranoid", she replied while walking Cleofis back to the entrance door. She then continued, "Just have some patience, don't rush things, because you know our situation. If it's meant to happen then it will."

"You're right, but those letters you been writing me lately got a nigga hormone jumping like crazy. It's just so many things I want to do to you, and if we be careful, we won't have to wait until I'm free."

"Just play it smooth, like I told you and anything could be possible with your sexy self, she tapped him on the butt softly. How come you didn't wear your glasses, they make you look very sophisticated and attractive?"

"I didn't know you like when I wear 'em, shit I'm gonna wear them all the time now. The fellas in here say I look like a nerd when I have them on. But I really don't care about what they say."

"And you shouldn't."

Opening the entrance door to the cell block, Natalie could feel Cleofis touch her bottom quickly, as he walked in before her. She then opened his cell and watched him as he walked in. The cell closed when Natalie pushed a switch that was by the entrance door to the cell block. The inmates in the day room yelled her name as she walked past to check on them asking for everything that they could think of -- medicine, toilet paper, request slips, but most of all they wanted their pencils sharpened. So she walked through collecting pencils as the inmates stuck them out through the bars. She could smell the foul odor from some of the guys that hadn't showered in days, as she collected the pencils.

Natalie loudly said, "Damn, who over here smelling like that?" She could hear some of the inmates mumbling "Not me" as she exited the cell block entrance. She then said, "Well it's somebody, and they ought to be ashamed of they self."

Natalie was exhausted when she made it in the house with her daughter. They routinely took off their shoes when they made it through the door. She unbuckled her belt and unbuttoned her work pants, making herself more comfortable. She turned her cell phone on because she always cut it off while she was at work. She could see that she had messages, but she didn't feel like listening to any of them, so she sat her phone on the counter. She opened her refrigerator, and looked for some leftover food to heat up. After moving a couple of items around she found what she was looking for, she threw it in the microwave.

The house phone started to ring, she yelled to her daughter, "Don't answer that phone, 'cause I don't feel like talking to nobody tonight." The phone continued to ring as she took her plate out of the microwave. Most of her friends basically knew what time she got off work, so they all would call the minute she stepped through her door. Nothing made her feel much better, as she sat down in her lazy boy chair, and kicked her feet up. Grabbing her remote control she turned on her big screen TV and started to flick through the channels. Discovering that it was nothing on interesting, she ate a couple of more bites out of plate. She then took the plate into the kitchen and headed for bed. Natalie undressed out of her work clothes, and removed her bra leaving nothing on but her panties. Her bedroom was very roomy with a walk in closet. She had grabbed her silk pajama set out of. Putting her top on she could hear the phone continue to ring from numerous calls. Agitated by the noise, she cut the ringer off, laid down in her bed and buried herself under the covers. With her body tired, but her mind still at work, she tossed and turned. She just couldn't shake Cleofis off of her mind. She started to fantasize about him.

Turning over on her back, she started to touch herself. Thinking about the incident that took place in the library at work, she started to imagine Cleofis in the bed with her. The thought of him made her body yearn to be satisfied. After tending to her body's needs, she fell into a deep sleep.

The next day was a normal day for Natalie. She was just finishing up at her first job, and getting into her car when George called her cell phone.

George was one of Natalie's best friends, that she loved to gossip with, and was now out in the open with being a homosexual. George cut men's hair and did women's hair for a living. "Girl, you act like you can't answer your house or cell phone, I been trying to call you since last night."

"Boy I was so tired last night, I cut off the ringer on the house phone, and left my cell phone on the kitchen table. I just cut my cell phone back on, you know I usually don't cut it off when I'm at my first job, but everybody calls so much it be hard to get stuff done."

"Girl, that's all them men you got, you need to give me some, 'cause this one I had the other night was coming up short."

"Uh-huh, who was he? Boy, forget I even asked you that 'cause I really don't want to hear about you and another man."

"Okay then, Miss Thang. What about you, what man been in your bed lately since you don't want to hear about who been in mines."

"Ain't nobody been in there lately, but last night I sure could have used a man who knew what he was doing. I had to hook myself up last night, but it is somebody that I'm thinking about putting it on. I'm not going to tell you who this time."

"You better tell me who you talking about, because I might be able to tell you something about them. You don't want to be in the bed with somebody I done had, do you?"

"I know you ain't had him, or none of your friends that you be with had him. This person I'm almost for sure that he doesn't go that route."

"If you talking about a thug, they like men too, I don't care how tough some of these men may act, 'cause it be the tough ones that like men the most.

"I ain't gonna argue with you about that 'cause you out of all people would know. But, anyways -- Are you doin' my hair this weekend?"

"Girl, you know I got you. Just make sure you on time and call me as soon as you make it in the house this time."

"A'ight, holla at you later, you big old playa you."

Natalie was dressed for her second job and had left out of the house. Her mind was fully made up about Cleofis. He had won her over, and she knew that she could get away with it. She would say to herself, "I am really going to do this", as she stepped into work.

Being in charge for the day made her able to work any floor in the facility that she wanted to. She chose the top floor, and told her co-workers that she trusted to watch her back. Her co-workers knew nothing about her intentions. They thought she would be feeding Cleofis restaurant food as she did on occasions. Her mind was on something totally different from what they thought. Opening the door to the section that Cleofis was in, on the top floor. Natalie could see that he was in the day room with the other inmates. He had just got out of the shower and was sitting on a table putting lotion on.

Cleofis put his tee shirt on as Natalie walked around both sides of the cell block, checking on inmates. His colorful county pants that was given to all the other inmates, were very big on him. Considering his small height, the County wasn't concerned with what size fit who. Natalie recognized Cleofis cleaning his glasses, when she came from around the other side of the cell block. Cleaning his glasses gently with his shirt Cleofis yelled, "Hey can you take me to the law library today?"

"Yeah, you ready to go now? Let's go."

Natalie opened the gate to the day room, and waited until it was closed, before opening the gate which let Cleofis into the area where she was at. She controlled every door by the press of a button except for the entrance door to the section that she used a key to come through. This made sure an officer only dealt with only one inmate at a time. The entrance door closed and Natalie locked it while Cleofis stood to the side of her. He walked behind her until they reached the library cell. Natalie then opened the cell Cleofis went in and took a seat. Natalie stood in the cell door way for a couple of minutes, having second thoughts, but her hormones along with her infatuations couldn't take it anymore.

She started to unbutton her work shirt, taking a couple of steps forward towards Cleofis. Cleofis took off his glasses and remained seated as she came closer. With her bosoms in his face, she started taking off his shirt. She rubbed his muscular chest a little before his hands went from her stomach, up her bra. He pulled her bra forward and up letting her breast pop from out of the bottom. Holding her shirt up with one hand and unfastening her belt with the other, Cleofis kissed and dealt with her chest very softly.

Sliding his hand down to her front, once he got her pants open, she aroused him in a way he hadn't felt in a long time. He could tell she was ready pulling down her pants to her ankles. He could see that her panties didn't stop her front from bulging out of the sides. Natalie stood there making soft moans as Cleofis kissed her stomach. Moving down to her waist, she took a deep breath as he slid her panties down to her ankles. Her front was shaved and freshly groomed as she kept it most of the time.

Natalie bit her lip and closed her eyes while Cleofis kissed her all over the bottom half of her body. Still seated while Natalie stood, Cleofis turned her around, she extended her arms out so that they would touch the wall. Her work shirt and under shirt raised up, showing her whole back side, while she stood there tilted, in a frisking position. Cleofis kissed her bottom, while doing this he rubbed his hand up and down the crease of it. He was becoming through with the fourplay, so he stood up as she looked back at his pants, and seen that he was excited for the occasion. He slid his baggy pants down to his ankles, grabbed Natalie's waist from the back and entered her body.

He went back and fourth, looking at himself as he went in and out her body. Her walkie-talkie still hanging on to her belt, hit against the floor repeatedly. Natalie tried her best to keep her voice down, but she was filled with sensation that caused her to yell. As she yelled Cleofis could feel the warmness in the liquid that traveled out of her body on to his man hood. Natalie started to shiver, her legs got weak, and for the moment she could no longer move along with Cleofis. She would yell a little more until Cleofis uttered, "Shhhhhhhhhh you don't want nobody to hear you do you?" After she reached her climax, Cleofis braced himself as he pulled back for the last time mumbling, "Damn girl."

Grabbing her waist very tightly, his knees started to buckle as he released his lust into her body. Momentarily drained of energy he fell back on to the library seat. With her legs shaking from the sexual healing, Natalie could barley get her clothes on. With her back against the wall she let her body slide down, until her butt touched the floor. She said to herself, "I need to sit down for a minute, I could barely even stand up and I know I don't want to fall 'cause that would just make his day."

Cleofis sat there motionless with a smile on his face, as he watched Natalie sit on the floor, with her legs still shaken. "I can't even get up and walk, my legs might give out."

"Hmmm, I told you about me, you thought I was playing didn't you? I tried to last a little longer but that thang just felt too good for me. Give me about five minutes and I'll be ready to go for some mo."

"Is you crazy? I'm through for today. And anyways, we can't be doing this all the time. Pull your pants up and you better not tell nobody!"

"I can't believe you would even talk to me like that, you should already know I'm not one of them niggaz who like to run they mouth, I don't even get down like that."

"I know you don't run your mouth like that, but you might tell that young boy that you said you could trust."

"I don't trust nobody, and my little homey Gabe already bonded out so I don't got nobody else that I could talk to, and if he was in here I still wouldn't tell him about you."

Natalie took Cleofis back to his section on the top floor after going down stairs, and returning from the bathroom. She finished her shift and turned on her cell phone as she backed out of the parking lot. Her cell phone wasn't on for one second before George called.

"Damn! You don't even give me a chance to cut my phone on do you?"

"Girl, what's wrong with you, you had a hard day at work or something?"

"I'm alright, I'm just a little tense, but I do got something to tell you, this nigga put it on me today, I had to sit down, I couldn't even walk."

"Put it on you where? You mean to tell me you skipped work for some meat. Tell me all about it girl, I wanna know detail, and who was he?"

"Well you know we got a lunch break, and I'm definitely not going to tell you who he is, but shit, he sure knew how to work it. even though it wasn't that big."

"I bet you it's one of your co-workers and you ain't got to tell me who. If it wasn't big then I don't want to hear about it anyway."

"Yeah right, you know you want to know, 'cause this dude got a hell of a body. And his sex appeal is through the roof. I just wish we had more time to do our thang. He kissed me from head to toe, and the position he had me in wasn't one of my favorites, but some how I was very satisfied."

"Oooh wee, I know what position that was girl", George yelled. "You a freak!"

Natalie laughed loudly, driving in traffic, and said, "I'm gonna just stop by your house after I pick up Dasia, and I'll tell you more about it."

Natalie didn't want George to know she had sex with an inmate, so she changed the truth a little bit still keeping George in mystery of who she was talking about.

Natalie and Cleofis would have one more sexual encounter before he was released, due to his attempted-murder case being overturned. But he would still be going to court for a gun and stolen vehicle case.

Natalie went by Cleofis' place of residence on her day off, it was hard for her to believe that he was free. She pulled into the driveway honked the horn and Cleofis opened the screen door to step out. Wearing some blue jogging pants with no shirt on Cleofis walked to the driver side door.

"I know it's hard to believe ain't it? I'm free as a bird", he said, glancing up at the clear baby blue sky.

"You better go put your shirt back on 'cause I know you probably already got a lot of girls chasing you." Natalie replied, watching Cleofis inhale the fresh air.

"A lot of them have stopped by but I wasn't really trying to hear that bullshit they was talking about. I'm just being cool, I'm not thinking about any woman right now. All I'm thinking about is spending some time with my family." It was a moment of silence between the two, while they both stared at each other.

"So this is your mother's house, 'cause I didn't know whose house it was."

"Yeah, this mom's spot, I'm gonna introduce you to her when she gets back in."

Natalie could see a familiar face sticking out of the screen door, "Who is that, he look kind of familiar, where do I know him from, is that your brother?" She asked curiously.

"That's Gabe. You don't remember he used to be in the cell next to mine? You can say he's my brother, 'cause he did a lot for me, we've known each other since we were kids."

"You ain't nothing but about twenty years old -- you still a kid. When you get my age then you can talk about when you was a kid", Natalie said jokingly.

"Damn, you got a smart mouth, for an old lady. Baby girl I'm far from a kid and you should know that by the way I demonstrate." Cleofis said jokingly.

"Boy I was just playing with you, trust me I know you all man baby, all I want to know is when do you want me to come and get you?"

"Write down your number and I'll call you and let you know. It a probably be soon though, I just need to spend some more time with my family."

"Well don't let it be long 'cause I doubt I if I can wait any longer."

CHAPTER 4

Guns and Roses

"Ain't that, that correctional officer from the County?", asked Gabe. "Yeah that's her", Cleofis stood in the doorway watching Natalie ride off. "Wasn't you fucking her in the County or something?" A grin flashed in his face, "Mmm hmm, but keep that to yo' self."

Cleofis turned the Jay-Z 'Hard Knock Life' CD up on the stereo in the living room. Moving his head strongly to the beat, Gabe chuckled loud at the energetic villain. "I'm bout to take over this city like Al Capone, you with me?" The tall figure nodded in agreement at his long time pal. "Did I tell you my ma said some niggaz was lying in the grass waiting fo' me?" Looking out the blinds he continued, "I guess when they seen it was her they got up and left. She said the niggaz was in all black too." The blinds shingled as

Cleofis released his hand that kept them opened. “That girl won’t let me chill fo’ twenty four hours.”

“Who”, Gabe asked anxiously.

“Shawndra, she pulling up right now, so I’m probably fenna dip with her.” Gabe walked to the door, Cleofis had just opened, “But who you think that was, that was waiting in your grass?”

“I got an idea… I’ll let you know when the time is right.”

Gabe stepped out into the cold and headed for his car.

“Hey, Gabriel”, Shawndra spoke after Gabe spoke first. Gabe couldn’t help but smell Shawndra’s salacious fragrance. It caught his attention as it trailed behind her stunning presence. Shawndra wore a thin black leather jacket with jet black fur on the collar, fur at the end of the sleeves, and at the bottom of the coat. Shawndra carried a black matching leather purse. She dressed well in her inexpensive clothes. Her dark blue jeans matched a quilted dark blue sweater her mother made for her, and the black pumps that held her feet made her look very tall over Cleofis. Hair pulled up like a scorpion’s tail, in the back, she hadn’t had enough.

“Is your mother here?”

Kissing her passionately on the lips, pulling her in closely while caressing her bottom, made her garden want him even more.

“I said, ‘Is your mama here?!’”, she pulled from him demanding to know before she took things further.

“Naw girl, her and my little brother gone. You sure you ain’t tired of making love, we made love three times last night, and now you want some more”, Cleofis replied after being fondled in return by the aroused seductive black woman.

There was something about him that turned on a desirable switch. It had nothing to do with the small size of his manhood. It was him that made her damn near climax in her panties.

She didn’t even have her bra and panties off before she went down below, making him feel like a well blessed man.

The nude lip gloss she wore smeared into the streak of saliva, and its candy flavor made his pre climax taste better. Shawndra took her time putting her wet warm mouth on the fragile jewels giving him a tingling sensation. When moving back to his fully sprouted front he stepped swiftly out of the pants that rested around his ankles and pushed Shawndra closer to the sofa.

Sitting with his legs open she jerked back and forth for awhile leaving him looking up at the ceiling in a trance. "Shit girl, you gotta stop doing this to me", he moaned. Going down wasn't one of her specialties, but she wanted to get him into it. She was celibate long enough, cutting ties with her daughter's father a year ago. She held her prize possessions for Cleofis. Far more into him, than he was into her, Shawndra would go a long distance to satisfy him. Buying him plenty of clothes upon his release, of course they weren't Versace and other expensive garments, but it was the thought that counted. Cleofis knew he would have to get back on his feet, before he could afford a small portion of the garments that he liked.

"Lay back", he spoke in a sexy tone. Switching positions Shawndra was now in a laid back position on the couch resting her nude brownie complexioned body where so many other women had been. Dropping down to his knee bought him face to face with her moist womb. "Hold on one minute", he said sprinting to the refrigerator for a bottle of cool whip that Ms. Jackson used on her pies. Returning to the womb he was a little frustrated due to the empty container of strawberries that was supposed to go with the treat. This was something the twenty year old always wanted to try, and now would, with only whip cream.

Shawndra's legs rested on his shoulders at the beginning of the procedure until the sucking intensified and she locked them around his neck tightly, sorta flexible she pushed him further into her center with her ankles. "I love you so much", she moaned out before reaching her peak. As the juices flowed out of the pink lips below Cleofis drank from her cup trying not to leave a drop. Her body shook like she was traumatized and she held his head firmly in between her thighs until she just couldn't take no more. When she released him his breathing was rapid. "Dang girl you tryin' to suffocate a nigga." Shawndra giggled slightly at the remark as Cleofis stroked himself gently with his hand before entering.

The head of his soldier throbbed like a heart beat very irritated from jumping up and down in her constantly the other night, but through his comfortness, all the fourplay gave him the drive he needed. The anticipation made it leak through the creases of his fingers and the short wait made Shawndra impatient. "Put it in Cleofis", she said through a moan. No adjusting was done for his sizc, the soaked womb seem to drown him as he worked the middle with her legs resting on his shoulders. Their mouths would meet frequently and their tongues would dance with each other. The more her legs went back further, the more she could feel him inside of her. They looked like a W combined with an upside down W. She moved her legs from the top of his shoulders but still kept them cocked in the air.

Rolling her body with his, her volcano started to erupt again and this time would be more intense than before. Her mouth opened like she had been stabbed with a knife, and her eye lids closed immediately, unleashing a crystal like tear that fell slowly down the side of her face. Opening her watery eyes, she felt like her soul was on fire, nothing could compare to this feeling. She felt like she was in ecstasy, high off of some drug and for a few seconds nothing else mattered in the world.

Cleofis observed a sheer white coating as he slipped out of her by accident. Full of air her center let out a loud similar to passing gas noise when he began to re-enter. He wasn't a stranger to that noise and Shawndra wasn't either but looking at her tears of love made him burst inside of her leaving their juices soaking into the couch. Shawndra was an emotional creature when it came down to making love, but nobody had ever made her body sing the way that Cleofis had.

Fetching a towel to wipe himself, Cleofis looked disgustfully at Shawndra's stretch marks as she strolled naked to the bathroom. The stretch marks swirling around her stomach, hips, and ass was a complete turn off to Cleofis. He hadn't grown to accept a woman for her results due to bringing a child into this world? The marks didn't affect the strong feelings that he produced for her through his hard times during his incarceration. She and her mother were the people that were there for him mentally.

"Where's the tissue?" Shawndra yelled from the bathroom trying to let as much juice drip out of her as possible. "Look fo' it, it's in there." Cleofis put his joggers back on along with a tee shirt. He sat on the couch and waited for her to return into the living room. Shawndra came walking from the back slightly stumbling, Cleofis stared at her with a proud of the job he did look on his face, but he was also ready for her to leave. "I gotta get back to work", she said. I sure am glad, is what Cleofis wanted to say, but instead he said, "Alright baby, I'll be over there tonight." Hurry up he thought in his head as her breast flapped, as she put on her panties. Cleofis was anxious to get out and about, to see what woman wanted to greet him pleasurably. Though his soldier was throbbing dearly he still had some catching up to do.

Calling Gabe to swing back through and get him, Shawndra was almost out the door when he stopped her dead in her tracks, "Ay girl", she turned in his direction, "I love you." The remark made her heart melt. "Love you too."

Cleofis jumped up and peeked through the blinds, watching Shawndra fix her hair with the clip that fell out during their activity. No sooner than her car pulled off, a blue Chevy Caprice pulled up, *"Who the fuck is this?"*, he thought to him self, because it sure wasn't Gabe. The passenger door opened revealing a face he thought would never drop by. "Mother fuckin' Kim!" he shouted. "She got her nerve and she in the car with a nigga." Cleofis didn't want to open the door for her but he was curious to see what she wanted. "What you want", Cleofis asked, swinging the door open, to allow her to enter. "I thought I told you that I never wanted to see you again."

"Cleofis", she spoke in astonishment. "It's really you, you really free. I didn't believe them gossiping hoes at the shop, I just knew they had to see somebody else."

Cleofis stood there observing her features. She didn't look as half as good as the Kim he met at fifteen. Her face was fuller, she bore a nice size gut, and the acne on her face was worse than ever before.

"Where yo' shorty at?", he blurted while she was still gawking at his presence. "Oh, he's with my mama…that's my man out there, some lame ass nigga that be lacing me with paper."

"Why you bring that fool over my tip."

"He's cool, I told him I was coming to see if my first love was out, and he thought it was joking. I guess he think I'm in one of my girls' house."

"Any ways I got stuff to do", Cleofis responded. Kim threw her arms around his neck, and went for a kiss. "Knock if off Nah, I got a woman so you gotta roll", moving out of the way of the kiss and knocking the girls arms down.

"I still love you boo", Kim began, "And I would like a quickie before I leave, if that's not a problem." Cleofis spoke brutally honest, "Hell yeah it's a problem", Kim wouldn't give up so easy she dropped to her knees quicker than a heart beat, pulled his soldier out quicker than his reaction and started bobbing like there was no tomorrow.

"Oh, you don't want none of this bomb head", she asked pulling his helmet out of her mouth.

"No, I told you I had a woman", he replied in a surrendering voice.

"Oh well", she said and continued the job with plenty of experience. Hoping he would screw her brains out once it felt good to him. But Cleofis had no intensions on screwing Kim, and she probably wouldn't be able to jump a ride on one of his desperate days. He felt no love for Kim at all, and enjoyed seeing her continuing her work. He enjoyed seeing her suck Shawndra's nutrients off of him. *A dirty dick, for a dirty bitch*, is what he thought, while she worked for something she wasn't going to receive. "You want this pussy, don't you?" She asked with a thick string of slob stringing from his spout. Cleofis said nothing as he pushed her head back into action.

"You ready homeboy", Gabe asked walking directly in the house. Cleofis shot his pants up quick, and Kim started acting like she was searching for something on the ground. "My bad", Gabe replied, turning to walk out the door. "You straight don't go no where, just give me a minute." Cleofis said with a smirk on his face, trying to hold in the laughter.

Cleofis gave Kim a believable story, she left the house disappointed, but with hope for the future. Gabe turned his nose up very disgusted, at the naïve man who laced Kim with a kiss, when she got into the car. "Ugghhh, that's a nasty bitch", he reflected while Cleofis locked his front door and started towards the car. "You still pushing the old Buick, huh", Cleofis slammed the long door. "Yeah, I still got old Betsy, and I see you still got old Kim."

"Nigga I just got my dick sucked… so, and that bitch was begging fo' some dick she didn't get."

Not everybody knew that Cleofis was free. Some was convinced that they would never see him again because of the murders surrounding his name. Cleofis knew people feared him, and there were people who wanted to kill him as well. And cruising around without a pistol made him feel like he stepped outside naked.

Nervous and confident, Cleofis stopped and checked on quite a few people, they all wanted him to stay but he'd made up in his mind that he was going to hang with Gabe for the day. Cleofis made it his business, to pop up on the dealers that still owed him a little bit of cash. Spooking people in a physical form got him a wad of cash in minutes, as he gave them his up and coming murderous look.

After seeing some relatives they swung by an Italian restaurant, that was close by Kankakee's only mall. "Homeboy", Cleofis replied before Gabe answered, "I just gotta ask you what that pussy like." It took Gabe a second to catch on to the fact that he was referring to Kiara. "It's cool, it's cool but I think I got her pregnant." "Shit, I don't blame you for trying, because if it was me, I'd keep that bitch pregnant, and barefooted."

They slapped hands playfully, "With some flip flops on", he continued after they chuckled together. The waitress bought their food out and Cleofis eyes beamed straight to her ass when she turned around. "Man, boy we gotta get you some pussy, 'cause that waitress ain't got no ass on her while you staring."

"Boy you just don't know when they skinny like that, that pussy be hella wet, and good."

The two shot the shit with each other all day, kicking it hard and enjoying each others company. At almost midnight Cleofis got dropped off at Natalie's.

"I'll hit you in the morning", he said while exiting the car. "Don't do nothing I wouldn't do", exclaimed Gabe.

Natalie opened the door with a fluffy red bath robe on from Victoria Secrets. It immediately caught his attention, he knew there was no bra on under the robe by the way her breast hung, but his eyes were trying to figure out if she had on some panties. Tied tightly, the robe clung to every curve on her body and her hair was down instead of in a ponytail, that he was used to seeing during incarceration. She looked so pretty and she was, "You sure got here quick Mr. Jackson. I was just about to get in the shower", she spoke clean and proper as usual unless around a certain type of crowd. "Well when I called you I was in the neighborhood pretty lady, and with it being night an all I wanted to hurry so you wouldn't be here alone."

"Is that right?" Well you can sit down and take a seat on the couch, I'm fenna shower and I'll be right out…oh and pull them shoes off."

Cleofis glanced around the two bedroom house. *This chick most definitely had class*, he reflected. The house had a china cabinet with plenty of expensive china dishes in it, the rugs on the floor was clean and expensive, the dinning room table set was mahogany, the couch love seat and recliner was Italian made in a creamy vanilla color, and the 63 inch Panasonic TV was a nice sight. The house wasn't big but it was decked out, the chandelier lights set the dinning room off and everything was nice and neat.

Cleofis sat chillingly on the couch and stared into a nearby room that looked like Natalie's, but he couldn't quite tell by the crack in the door. So as the shower water started, he crept in the room to peak. "Ohh that bed is huge", he said to himself. Looking at the massive amount of clothes and shoes, it was fair to say she loved to shop. I know she can't sleep in that big old bed by herself, he reflected bringing his attention back to the bed. The bed was fit for a queen and the only way he got a look was because the draping was open on the canopy bed that Natalie adored so much.

"Cleofis", was what he heard towering over the shower running water coming from the back. "Cleofis come back here!" Pulling her room door the way it was, he flew to the bathroom immediately absorbing some of the steam upon opening the door.

"Jump in with me", she said in a seductive sort of voice. Cleofis knew what time it was, plus he would have a chance to wash his soldier before tending to her. Natalie was a boss freak behind closed doors, and this was something she hid very well from the naked eye. Cleofis thought he knew exactly what he was in store for, but some of the things that were about to happen would come as a surprise to him.

After stripping naked and getting into the shower, Cleofis was instantly erect by the sight of her swollen ass. Watching her lustfully from the back as she squeezed the towel on her left shoulder and the soapy water ran down her back slowly. "You wanna wash my back", she asked. Cleofis responded by grabbing the towel out of her hand. Washing her back gently his eyes just couldn't stay off her butt, his mouth watered as if it was a scrumptious piece of pie that he wanted to eat. When she turned and faced him, he could barely keep his composure, having never seen Natalie's body completely with out clothes. To him it was a beautiful sight. Her breasts were big, but they weren't overly big for her size. Her dark brown nipples were hard as rocks and the water had soaked her long pretty hair. In jail he was getting portions of the cake, but now stood the whole cake with icing, right before his eyes. He thought that she looked so pretty and she tilted her head back to wet her hair some more.

She definitely turned him on more than Shawndra had, and he was both physically and mentally attracted to her. Natalie washed him up almost similar to a new born baby. After washing his back, she hadn't turned him around good before squatting down to put her full sexy lips all over his manhood. Cleofis stood there hands to the side in total shock of her gripping his lower body with a hot and moist mouth. Her giving him treatment as the water hit the back of her hair, this was almost too much for him, and the luke-warm water made everything seem fantastic. The way she pulled on him made him think about when he was a shorty, and was tricking with types that were pro's on blowing on cock. She definitely knew what she was doing.

She then stood straight up, cut the water off and grabbed his hand as she stepped out of the shower. "Girl, what you doing?", Cleofis asked wondering why she stopped the ordeal. "Jus come on silly." They quickly dried each other off, then headed for the bedroom. "Get in the bed and wait for me", she exclaimed with a big smile on her face.

Cleofis did as he was told, and Natalie left out the room, and headed for something that sounded like a basement to him. What is she doing, the thought kept running through his mind. Is she trying to set me up, was another thought until she crept back into the room, wearing a very tight black, diamond cut, skin showing outfit that stopped right below her caramel butt cheeks, which carried a black thong right in between them. She stood there confidently with a black leather whip in hand. "CLOW", was the sound against the dresser as she struck it swiftly. "Girl", Cleofis said in a soft tone, "I don't know if I'm with all this." Her body looked too good in the tasteful one piecc, so cooperation was all he understood. "Come here", she asked sternly with one hand on her hip. "I said, come here." Her wet hair rested gently on her shoulders, and covered up the majority of her chest. How could he say no, just looking at Natalie gave him a rush. She most definitely liked to be in control. "Get in this living room", she yelled as she moved out of the doorway, so he could walk through. "FLACOW" she popped him on his flat behind. "Ah shit", grabbing the sharp pain, the villain felt instant anger, but would not let it show. "Naw, you can't be hitting me on my ass like that." This was all new to Cleofis, the experience was unusual, but his lust controlled his anger. So the will to please Natalie was first.

"Shut up nigga, I ain't even hit you that hard, take it like a man."

Cleofis sat gracefully on the cold leather couch not wanting to blow the mood. Natalie walked over to him like she was some sort of cat woman, and started giving him a lap dance. She moved exotically to the music, she stood straight up and put a dip in her back. The confident freak clapped her cheeks together making her butt talk in front of his face. "Hands off", she shouted, removing one of his hands. The small case of cellulite was looked past, and Cleofis seemed to be hypnotized as he watched her brown booty swallow the thong. Like a swinging medallion he just couldn't keep his eyes off of it. She then stepped up on the couch and shook her fat swollen garden all in his face. She put this show on for very few in the past, this was only done to the people who especially turned her on, and Cleofis was above the few. She wanted to put it on this street celebrity, if doing it right she would be able to cuff him. Natalie felt no women had the gold mine she carried between her legs.

Cleofis drifted his body in between her wide-spread legs, coming from up under like a game of limbo, turning around he watch Natalie grip the back of the couch with her ass sticking out like she was waiting for him to hit it from the back. The gangster wasted no time moving the thong to the side with a finger, and driving his face in between her cheeks. Licking and sucking, his big nose and his small lips was consumed in the wide open womb, he just couldn't help himself and Natalie's feet slid off the edge bringing her to her knees on the coach. Cleofis went to one knee on the floor to level the ass with his face. The more his tongue worked her, the harder she griped the back of the couch moaning from the sensation, and intoxicated by the feeling, her knees imprinted deeper into the leather and his knees imprinted deeper into the carpet.

The loud slurping sound had her so ecstatic as she tried pushing his head further into her cheeks it caught her off guard when his tongue slid to her anus "ssssssss" came out without thought and he went back and forth from hole to hole. "Ah this shit feels so damn good", she exclaimed under her breath, feeling like she was on cloud nine. Her thong was drenched in juices as the sucking came to a halt. He then slid in her doggy style, spreading his legs to level with hers. Everything went slow for awhile as her jet black hair lay on her back, Cleofis had to take his soldier out to bring the sensation to burst down. Something about the way Natalie's hair rested on her back curving in with the dip, just turned him on so much he started grabbing it, pulling it as the speed accelerated, never removing the tight one piece or the thong, he started ramming her. "Harder, harder, harder", she begged as Cleofis pounded away humping almost to a climax before she decided to move to the bedroom where she rode him, bursting at least twice, before he did once and fell asleep on top of him, very worn out and exhausted.

The birds chirped very musically like, as dawn came in a blink of an eye. And the cool morning air made Cleofis maneuver the gigantic cover over both of their bodies.

"Oh shit", said Natalie, "My alarm didn't go off. I know I gotta be runnin' late."

"Lay back down… take the day off", Cleofis replied after a deep yawn.

"Boy is you crazy, I'm not missing work for nobody, so you need to get up and get dressed."

She backed up while moving his arm from around her waist.

"Damn, we must have knocked the cord out of the socket last night."

Cleofis only heard half the statement before he fell back off into a deep sleep snoring slightly.

'Should I just leave him here?', she reflected, but soon changed her thought after thinking about some of the things she might not

want him to see in her house. "Get up!" She yelled, fully dressed and brushing her teeth.

"Alright, alright give me a minute."

Natalie dropped Cleofis off down the street from Shawndra's, totally unaware of his destination. She thought nothing of it.

"Give me a call on my cell at noon", she replied before reaching over to kiss his lips.

"Don't worry I'll call", he spoke with sleep in his voice.

Shawndra finally came to the door after Cleofis pounded a second time. He could tell by the roll of her eyes that she was displeased with him coming in so early in the morning.

"Mothafuckaz kept me out all night", the lie started seeping out of his lips. "Fucking around with Gabe and shit, this nigga had me on the west side of Chicago while he waited on some ugly ass girl."

While he continued on with his lie, Shawndra picked her daughter up out of her bed. She then went to lay her down in her own bed room, making room for the liar. "I ain't playin' baby, this mothafuckin' girl was ugly."

Shawndra waved her hand in an 'I-don't-wanna-hear-it-anymore' style. She climbed back into her bed under the warm covers leaving him talking to himself. Sitting at the edge of the bed, Cleofis let his upper body fallback, gazing at the wall he thought about his next move, 'cause the chump change he carried around in his pocket wasn't gonna cut it, and going back to selling bags wasn't an option. Just then it hit him, have Shawndra or Natalie take out a loan. They both had good jobs, he thought to himself. If he could talk both of them into doing it, it would be a hell of a jump start. Legitimate work crossed his mind on a few occasions, but it soon deteriorated by the sight of seeing the local dealers flossing.

Everything was beginning to take off when Shawndra came through, after Natalie's decline to get him the loan. Shawndra came through without question, taking out a five thousand dollar loan to get Cleofis back on his feet. His position on the Cartels was like a celebrity mingling with normal people. Most of the dealers were obliged to look up and see him on the block. They had no problem making room for him and his crew, which was now called the Capone gang. Cleofis, Berry, JW, Jackpot, Cliff, and Disco all got matching tattoos on their forearms. Cleofis tried to convince Gabe, but he wanted no part of it.

The Capone name eventually would spread swiftly throughout the city, and dealers and gangsters were now referring to Cleofis as Teflon, head man of the Notorious Capone Crew. For right now the crew was only pulling schemes and exercising their gangster mentality among the lame ass hustlers. No serious crime was committed yet, because Cleofis didn't want the heat from the law, he just wanted to get money for now. It was said that the crew possessed an arsenal of weapons, but only shared one knee knocker between the six of them. Ms. Jackson had once again thrown all of her sons' guns away. Cleofis hated having only one pistol. He asked Gabe on many occasions for his, but Gabe having only one himself refused his request, not wanting to be left naked.

Gabe felt the Capone tattoo was very stupid, and an easy way to be identified. Cleofis distanced himself from Gabe to lead the Capone crew. Learning in jail that niggaz looked to him for guidance and leadership. He took what he had and ran with it. In his mind, he felt he was doing what was expected out of him. Cleofis wanted Gabe to eat off his plate, but Gabe had his own plate. But from the outside looking in, it would seem like Gabe was a part of the crew. No one in the crew cared for Gabe except Cleofis and Cliff. Others felt he was weird, too humble, and blocking their friendship with Teflon. And just like jealous little girls, they spoke behind his back like he thought they would.

Cleofis managed to cop a gray 1986 Delta 88 to get him from A to B. And when Cliff started bringing around Kevin a military young man gone AWOL. The opportunity to shake the car for something new presented itself. Kevin possessed a nice piece of cash and looked up to the dominating Teflon, which he heard so much about. Kevin wanted to be a part of the crew, and Cleofis knew just what to do with a square like him. Kevin was blind in a den full of hungry and thirsty lions. Just starting to hustle, Kevin was pinching off a lump sum of money, replacing it with profits from small drug deals. Wanting to invest all of his money in coke, Kevin looked for the right person to partner up with, and when mingling with Cleofis through Cliff, Cleofis eventually made him feel like family comforting him for the sting.

"Ah shit, muthafucka. I told you not to hit me that hard." Cleofis bent over grabbing his forehead in agony and pain. When seeing the dark blood seeping through the creases of his fingers, he went into a temporary rage, knocking Jackpot to the floor with one Punch, his frail body collapsed. "I knew he was gonna hit you too hard", said JW. They were faking a robbery out in the country part of Kankakee. With twenty thousand dollars of Kevin's hard earned money, which he confided in Cleofis to go to the store and cop with. Cleofis had no intentions on giving Kevin shit, he also shot the Delta 88 up with bullet holes to make it seem like they barely got away with their lives.

"I got stuck up", said Cleofis with a convincing look of anger.

Kevin sat in the back seat of the Delta just getting ready to ask about the bullet holes in the car. "Man 'Moe' tell me you didn't, that was all the money I had!"

Cleofis stared at JW, "Would you tell 'em JW, we barely got out alive." JW shook his head in agreement, rubbing his palms on the steering wheel of the car.

"Tell me exactly what happened!" Kevin sternly asked, tapping the back of the driver's seat.

Jackpot sitting next to him in the back seat could barely hold his laughter together, but was still salty about the black eye that Cleofis gave him.

"I went in there to get the shit, and my connect came from the back with a pistol in his hand. I thought nothing of it at first. I thought he was just taking precautions because Jackpot and JW was in the car outside. But the nigga patted me down and took my thumper right", Cleofis glanced to make sure he was soaking up the script. He then continued, "So when he did that, the mark smacked me with the butt of his gun, see." Cleofis turned around showing Kevin the open wound making the story to believable. "I don't know where I got the strength, but I jetted outta there like Carl Lewis… the nigga was on my ass bussin' crazy, tryin' to take my head off. That's how those big ass holes got in the car, and these scary ass niggaz tried to leave me." Before Kevin could reply, Cleofis spoke again, "Look don't worry, 'cause we going back up there and we gonna kill them niggaz. I don't care if I gotta rob every pussy ass nigga in this town,

I'mma get you yo' bread back." Kevin said very little as the reality of him being broke sank in, and was more than he could bear.

"Just give me something to hold me down", Kevin replied in an upset voice while exiting the car. "I got you don't worry", Cleofis assured him.

"This Vic is sweeter than what I thought", he reflected, rubbing his hands together like they were cold.

The Movie Theater wasn't packed like it usually was on weekends. Cleofis and Shawndra held hands in silence as the presentation began. Slouched down in his seat with his cap pulled down to his eyebrows the villain couldn't help but to think about Natalie as much as he tried to shake the thoughts. Dealing with Natalie was becoming an every other night thing. Cleofis would tell Shawndra he was out all night hustling, although Shawndra's heart told her that he was lying, but her mind believed every word of it. She was madly in love with him and cherished the quality time they spent together, even though it became lesser and lesser. "I hope Shay Shay don't give my sister a hard time like she did the last time." Shawndra said concerned.

"Pissssssss, come on now, you know that little girl of yours is something else." Shawndra chuckled at the truth of the statement, "She always wants you, the other night she gonna tell me she waiting up for CJ." She paused as Cleofis giggled, "I told her if she didn't get her little ass in the bed…

"You shoulda called me", Cleofis began. "I would have come in from off the block just to tuck her in bed." Shawndra then smacked her lips and said, "Well I didn't want to disturb you, you know how busy you be." The sarcasm rolled off of her tongue, "You are staying the night with me and Shay Shay aren't you?" Cleofis squeezed her hand tighter saying, "There isn't any other place in the world I'd rather be." Shawndra reached over and kissed him, leaving cherry lipstick on his lips.

"Chirp chirp", was the sound of the car alarm to his pearl white Aurora. He'd dropped half of the sale price in cash and worked out some very low payments. The Aurora made him feel half of how he used to feel back in 96'.

Shawndra loved the car and tried to drive it every chance she got. "Oh baby I just love this car, we should trade, let me give you mines."

"You must be crazy", said Cleofis, bending a corner. Shawndra took the response as a joke, but he was dead serious. "So how did you like the movie Egg Head?"

"It was straight pop belly."

"My stomach not big, but yo' nose is and that's a fact. I know you got teased a lot when you were little", Shawndra said jokingly.

'Hail Mary' from Tupac's 'Makavelli' CD bumped on the factory speakers, and the rays from the street lights gleamed on Shawndra's lower body as they passed them. Glancing at her soft hips in some white jeans, Cleofis reached over for a feel. Shawndra's hips were the attention getter of her figure.

"CJ we almost home", Shawndra said, as she removed his hand.

"Just wait a minute baby, and you need to pay attention to the traffic."

Shawndra jacked him off, all the way to her place, making him feel relaxed. Cleofis wasn't wearing his glasses and she knew he couldn't see well at night, so she ended his touching and started some of her own. They weren't even through her door good before they were out of their clothes and in the bed making passionate love. She loved the way he rough-sexed her. Shay Shay wasn't there so she could scream as loud as she wanted.

Cleofis had just finished making love to Shawndra when Gabe was at the door.

"What you want chump?" he asked jokingly with a scoped rifle in hand.

"Man where you get that from homeboy?"

"Nobody important", Cleofis stepped out closing the door behind him. "Watch this"

They stepped to the edge of Shawndra's small balcony, where you could see the traffic and street lights. Cleofis positioned the twenty-two riffle on the rail, aimed for the light and fired.

"You see that lil nigga, I put that light out in one shot, and I can hit without a scope!"

Making Gabe a believer, he took off the scope and hit the green light. Now, all three of the lights were out, because he shot the other one out earlier that day.

The aim had amazed his friend. *This is a dangerous nigga*, Gabe reflected. *How could he hit them street lights from this far of a distance?* The thought frequently moved through his mind.

"What them prices like?"

"I'll be able to tell you tomorrow morning", Cleofis replied, dropping the rifle to his side.

"Well tomorrow morning it is, and it betta not be no bull shit, 'cause you know I don't like fucking with yo' janky ass."

A second of laughter seeped out, "How much you got nigga, 'cause this some butter I'mma be getting and I gotta have top dollar."

"I know you ain't gonna tax me, especially if you want this bank roll", Gabe said jokingly, pulling out his wad of money.

"Well, if you was a Capone or a Blackstone you could get it dirt cheap like everybody else in the crew, but you a brick." Cleofis chuckled as the words rolled off of his tongue. "And you know I don't like bricks."

"Shut yo' hook ass up nigga, I'll be over here in the morning, then I'll tell you what I want."

After talking to each other in their usual fashion, the friends departed almost always on good terms.

"CJ" The voice had awakened him out of a deep sleep. "CJ", get up and fix me some ice cream." Little Shay Shay asked, pulling up his eyelid with her finger. Shawndra had just picked Shay Shay up from her sister's house. She had never bought any men around her daughter except for Cleofis, Bruno, and of course, Shay Shays father. "A'ight little girl let me get up", his voice rattled. "Oh, and yo' breath stinks CJ." The little girl covered her mouth and nose. The gangster laughed deep and short. Shay Shay had stole his heart the first time he met the smart and pretty little girl. He also had over time started to develop feelings for her as if she was his own daughter. Tugging his hand she escorted Cleofis to the kitchen bringing him past Shawndra who was sitting on the couch watching TV. "Make sure you don't give her a lot."

"You should have gotten her some ice cream -- you see I was trying to sleep." Cleofis didn't know what time it was, but he knew it was early in the morning.

"She wanted you to get it, so I told her to go wake you up." After fixing Shay Shay the ice cream she smiled like a little angel, "Can you come in here and sit down with me and mommy?" Though Cleofis was still mad tired he couldn't say no to the little girl. "I love you CJ", Shay Shay replied before shoving the big spoon of ice cream in her mouth. "I love you too sweet-heart."

The moment brought tears to Shawndra's eyes -- her five year old daughter had never even told her father she loved him. Shay Shay sat very close to Cleofis and she made him feel very proud and awake. "What time is it?" Shawndra glanced at her cell phone, "Almost ten."

"Hmmm I was wondering why she was asking for some ice cream so early, but its not that early. Why you let me sleep late?"

"It's not late, and you know how you be when I wake you up."

Shawndra and Shay Shay were gone. Cleofis and Jackpot had just finished cooking up some coke, stinking up the place with the strong smell. "Teflon what you want me to do with that bowl." Counting every weighted up ounce on the table, Cleofis looked him up and down "We gonna bag it up you dummy what you think that little shit don't sell or somethin, and go see who at the door" Jackpot peaked threw the peak hole "It's that little nigga Gabe you want me to let him in"

"Yeah, and peak at the parking lot to see if Shawndra back yet"

"Naw she ain't back yet" replied Jackpot

"You niggaz wild, I can smell that shit threw the door. The shit smells like butta."

"It is butta little chump." Cleofis said with a big gold link chain with a five point star charm dangling from his neck. The chain rested on one of his silk Versace shirts that he coped back in 96. The crush embedded diamonds screamed for attention "Were you get that at?" Gabe pointed at the necklace.

"Some hype that stole it outta a store, the motherfucka worth ten stacks, I priced it."

"Yeah right!", Gabe responded, tossing his roll of cash on the table. "Count it -- see how much it is then put something on the clock that's reasonable."

After Gabe purchased and left, Jackpot brought Cleofis some disturbing news "It's been something I been wantin' to tell you Moe", Cleofis looked Jackpot dead in the eyes almost making him change his mind "Did you know Bruno fucked Shawndra?"

"You sho or is this some shit you heard?"

"Naw 'Moe', I just now remember him saying it one day when I was with him."

"Why you just now telling me this shit?"

"'Cause I didn't know you was that serious about her, plus I told you I didn't remember. But come on 'Moe' it neva crossed yo' mind that he cracked her?"

"Yeah, but I figured he didn't 'cause I neva noticed anything other than a platonic relationship between the two."

"But you know how yo' cousin was -- that nigga ain't gonna have a chick like that around and don't at least try."

"You right, you right I'mma ask the bitch bout it when she gets back."

"Well just don't tell her I –."

Cleofis cut him off, "Nigga I ain't fenna tell her you told me shit."

"So you fucked my cousin huh?" The words could barely wait until Jackpot exited the premises, "Go to yo' room Shay Shay", Shawndra asked her daughter politely then proceeded to take her coat off. "I know the fuck you heard me talking to you Shawndra -- don't make me fuck you up."

"Why?", she began sort of hysterically. "Why does it matter if I did or not? You weren't my man at the time."

Cleofis swiftly moved directly in front of her. "Just answer the question."

She looked at his hands to see if they were balled up.

"Yes", she spoke with a crying voice. "But it was only once, I promise baby, it was only one time. I wanted to tell…"

"Shhhhhh", his finger covered her trembling lips, "Don't worry about it boo. It was before my time." Looking for a reason to dog her in front of her face, Cleofis now had one. The partial respect he possessed for her was now out of the window. *Damn what bitch didn't he fuck?* He reflected, wanting to smack the shit out of Shawndra, instead he just soaked it up, played cool and left.

After speeding through traffic he arrived at Shanice's house. Cleofis was willing to do anything to get the panties, Feeling his reputation would speak for itself, he was eager to sex Bruno's main squeeze, so that he would have some relief about the agitating news.

"What's up home girl?" he said tapping her shoulder as he walked in.

"Did I tell you to come in?" she said firmly. Shanice was cautious of Cleofis, for Bruno said he couldn't be trusted on many occasions, before his death. "So what's up Teflon?"

"Nothing much", seeing she called him by Teflon, stroked his ego. "I was just stopping by to check you out, just making sure you okay."

"I'm fine, how are you and Shawndra doing", she asked after observing him give her a flirtatious look.

"Not so good, I just found out the bitch fucked Bruno." Cleofis looked to Shanice for a disturbing sign but didn't see one. "All this time I'm thinking she's a good woman, man that shit hurt my heart." Knowing that her and Shawndra was still good friends, he hoped to tamper with her emotions, making her vulnerable for the seductive proposal.

"Well Teflon, as they call you. That's part of having a man like Bruno. I didn't see any woman that could resist him. As long as he took care of home, which he did and still continues to do from the grave, I never had a problem with the affairs. I mean come on now." She looked Cleofis square in the eyes, "The man had women all over the United States, but I was his heart and he was mine. So him fucking Shawndra doesn't surprise me, he probably fucked all of my friends. But Shawndra's a good woman, and he's known her since they were kids. So if you gonna let something like that come between the love ya'll have for each other, that's on you. But Shawndra will always be my friend."

Cleofis sat on a wooden stool in the kitchen, letting the words marinate for a minute, wondering what other angle to try, "I feel you girl, but where yo' nigga at 'cause I know you got one", brushing the back of his hand up against her stomach. "Don't do that." She said strictly, taking a step back. "Well, I have something to do, so I'll holla at you later." Cleofis could see wasn't nothing shaking, and left out the house with a heavy foot.

All of Bruno's property in Kankakee was in Shanice's name, plus the unknown amount of money she kept stashed at her house. It was also said she had some bricks of Bruno's that her brother helped her dump, and get rid of. She wanted for nothing and was very stable, financially. Therefore she kept a high tech security system along with two big Rottweillers. Bruno's other real estate, cars, and other accessories belonged to his aunt, who was a hot shot attorney in Chicago. A few left over accessories now belonged to a multitude of women across the states.

Shanice was bothered by the information, but already suspected it long ago, and refused to let it show in front of a person she didn't trust. *"Oh well, no need to let it get to me, I knew how he was -- even though Shawndra could have let me know"*, Shanice thought as she watched Cleofis pull off through the window.

It was the begging of 1999, as Shawndra stood in front of her bathroom mirror staring at herself. "Why won't he love me the way that I want him too? God I've been more than a good woman to him. Maybe I should've told him about Bruno, but I didn't want to lie to him. I'm ready to settle down and get married God, and I want to know if he's the right man for me." She blew through her lips, "Who am I kidding, God I know he's not for me, but I love him so much." Tears dropped from her eyes, cruising through her mascara, the thought of Cleofis' disrespectful mouth, stern threats, women she knew that couldn't be some kin to him, being up in her house, and the fact that he hadn't spent a night in weeks. All of this was starting to take a toll on the emotional creature. She wiped her tears, and continued to get ready for Cleofis to come and pick her up for dinner at his mother's.

Shawndra paced the floor in a yellow V-neck shirt, with beige Capri's. *"Where is he, we were supposed to be there thirty minutes ago"*, she thought out loud. Plopping down on the couch, she flicked quickly through the channels with the remote. She pulled one of her legs up on the sofa, "This fool got five minutes to come, and then I'm going over to my sisters for the rest of the day."

Picking up the phone, Shawndra called him, but got no answer. After trying the cell phone a couple more times, she gave up. "Fuck it! I'm going over my sister's."

Normally Shawndra's patience wouldn't be so thin, but because she was getting tired of his shit, her tolerance was low. While driving to her sisters she spoke repeatedly to herself, *"This big nose punk gonna have me get ready, and his ass didn't even show up, we'll see about that, the next time he want me to do something for his punk ass."*

Swerving into the right lane, she made a sharp right turn. "I'mma see where this nigga at, who the hell he think he is, standing me up." Racing to his mother's house she was observing very well, because she spotted the egg head shaped villain on the passenger side of a car, while speeding through a block just before his mothers.

Making a complete U-turn, she darted to the side of the still running motor vehicle. Cleofis tried to lay the seat back, but it was too late. She could spot him from any where. "So this is who you spend yo' nights with?"

Natalie was reaching for words when Cleofis found some, "What?!", he yelled like she was annoying him. "What do you want, you always stalking me -- you know I don't fuck with you like that."

"Okay muthafucka, you wanna front huh", said Shawndra as he tried to get Natalie to pull off. "If I'm stalking you, then how come you had yo' face in this pussy the other night, talking about how good it taste?"

"I know she lying", said Natalie, "Is you and him fucking?", she didn't let Shawndra respond, "Cause if ya'll is, ya'll can keep on 'cause he'll neva get anotha whiff of this." She then sipped her Pepsi through her straw as if the situation was nothing to her.

"I don't want his ass either", Shawndra began, "All his little dick ass good for is eating some pussy, and that's it. Oh and yo' shit be sittin' outside on the street."

"Crazy Bitch", yelled Cleofis, "Stop lying on me hoe, Teflon don't eat no pussy bitch", his voice towered into her car. Shawndra sped off uncontrollably, but crying inside. On the other hand Natalie was still astonished by the comments. The cold from the Pepsi froze the back of her throat in an attempt to reply. "You need to check yo' bitches", the car was half way down the block by now. "That's not my ---." Bitch never left his mouth, for his face was greeted with a cold splash of Pepsi. "Bitch you just got pop all over my white Polo shirt." Cleofis could barely control his temper. "Get out muthafucka", she yelled. "You heard me, get out my car." So pissed about his shirt he got out quick, but changed his mind. "Natalie baby, that ain't my Bi-----."

Once again bitch didn't get out, because last nights rain was splashed all over him from the back of her tires as she pulled off rapidly.

"BITCH!" echoed through the neighborhood. "Them crazy ass bitches, fuck both of them hoes, I don't need neither one of em."

Shawndra went home and cried herself to sleep like a baby. Natalie went on to work with an attitude and flirtatious intentions.

After a short period of time, and a massive amount of attempts, the twenty one year old had both women back in the palm of his hands.

CHAPTER 5

Independent Youngster

Kankakee IL 1993, fifteen-year-old Cleofis Jackson walked along side of Gabriel Smith, or Gabe for short, as he peddled slowly on a bicycle. Gabriel being a couple of years younger than Cleofis took to him like an older brother. They had a lot in common at the time. They both liked to sell weed, cocaine, and most of all, they both loved guns at a very young age. Living on the east side of Kankakee, they stayed in the same neighborhood.

Kankakee just south of Chicago was where they both witnessed the drug dealers, thieves, robbers, killers, and drug addicts. They met through Cleofis' younger brother a couple of years ago. Cleofis took a liking to young Gabriel always telling him new things he learned from older teen-agers.

Standing a little over five feet at the time, fairly thin with a large nose that made his eyes seem like they set far back in his face. Cleofis walked with a tough guy strut at a young age, a strut that you would think he was doing on purpose, but through time you would realize that's just how he walks. His father died when he was eleven which had a very devastating affect on his life. His father left behind him and his younger brother Lonzale.

Cleofis' mother was a good Christian woman who loved both of her sons unconditionally. Ms Jackson would take them to church every Sunday as kids trying to make sure they grew up the right way.

Cleofis always had a fascination with guns though, as an adolescent, he would shoot squirrels with a bee-bee gun that he had found. After his father died he grew eager to shoot somebody. Mimicking older troublesome youth, he would pick fights with other kids to see if he was tougher. He being smaller than most kids, his opponents would always underestimate him. Built up with a lot of anger from his fathers death, he would try to release it every chance he got on other kids. Seeing his older cousins with everything he ever wanted made him yearn for wealth, power, and respect at a young age. Cleofis kept a short temper as a youngster. He was always anxious to prove something to somebody. 1993 was a very dangerous time in Kankakee for a young African American. The murder rate was very high. Cleofis would socialize with the killers on many occasions, adapting a gangster mentality.

The gangs that originated in Chicago had a lot of influence on the crime in the small city. They would come from the windy city with their recruits, extortion, and murder bull dog tactics. The gangs would war for drug territory, and respect in the city. The north side being the most notorious for its drug dealing and murder. This was where Cleofis would spend a lot of his time.

Unbridled by his older cousin, Cleofis, was free to sell drugs on just about any block he wanted to on the north side. In Kankakee there were only two projects. The north side projects, called the Durrels, and the west side projects called The Valley. Then there were four drug infested north side streets that was located right by the projects that drug dealers called the Cartels. The Cartels was where the most double crossing took place in the city. This was where anything could happen at anytime. This was also where Cleofis had been coming to ever since he was a pre-teen.

Riled-up about a pistol that his cousin lost, Cleofis boasted to Gabe about what he was going to do about it as Gabe peddled his bike along side of him. "This pussy ass nigga done lost my gun. I'm a make him pay for it. He better have me another strap or some change when we get over here."

"How did he even get the strap?"

"He went in my stash and took it", Cleofis began barking. "Then he went to the party and lost it last night. That was the only strap I had, 'cause I sold the other one. That nigga gonna pay!"

When Cleofis saw his cousin he went into a rage calling him every name that came to his head. Cleofis being only fifteen at the time sized his cousin up that was three years his senior. Gabe rested his arms on his bike wondering what was about to happen next between the two. With spectators starting to lurk around Cleofis swung and connected, for thirteen year old Gabe it seemed like the punch echoed with it sounding so loud. He watched while Cleofis tussled around the grass with his cousin. Both of them using all of their strength to try and over power the other. Gabe with loyalty to his friend said to himself, "If only that wasn't his cousin I would jump in and help him."

Knowing that was family business Gabe stayed out of it. Cleofis wrestled with his cousin until he got tired and didn't want to fight anymore. But his cousin still had a little of wind left and wanted to fight some more, but due to the throbbing of his left jaw he quit also. Afterwards Cleofis and Gabe strolled back to their neighborhood.

"Did you see how I hit that nigga? I damned near knocked his ass out. I know he didn't think that I could hit that hard, he thought he was just fenna to beat the shit out of me. He thought I was playing about my pistol. He gonna act like he didn't want to run me no change for my lost that nigga will think twice before he go into one of my stashes again." Cleofis' adrenaline was still pumped from the fight, when he and Gabe walked into his house. His mother was in the kitchen washing dishes when he came in bragging about how he hit her nephew in the jaw just minutes ago.

His mother told him she didn't want to hear about it. He mumbled a little bit then walked into the living room where Gabe had taken a seat on the couch. Irritated by the aching and swollenness of his hand he returned to the kitchen, grabbing a bowl filling it with ice his hand.

The door bell rang, it was Berry Hilton. Berry was a friend that Cleofis did a lot of illegal activities with, he was also the same age as Cleofis, and had known him longer than Gabe. Cleofis opened the door and put his hand in the bowl of ice as Berry walked in. "What's up homeboy? What's going on wit'chu?", Cleofis spoke casually,

"Nothing much I just heard about you though, on my way coming over here. I see you got your hand in some ice and I don't see no scars on your face, so you must didn't need my help", Berry said with a grin.

"Come on now, you know I'm good with my hands, and I ain't taking no ass woopin' from nobody", Cleofis replied as Berry spoke to Ms. Jackson. Berry came in and sat down on the couch next to Gabe. The marijuana smell traveled behind him from a blunt he had smoked on the way over there. Ms. Jackson was instantly bothered by the smell, "You and your company need to go outside" she said in a very serious tone. Cleofis didn't argue with her "Come on" he spoke directly to his company. They pulled up a couple of chairs from the back yard and sat down in the drive way. It was a very hot and humid summer for the most part. Cleofis had got expelled from the high school on his first day for beating up the principal, so for the rest of the year he had to go to alternative school for kids who can't attend public schools because of behavioral problems. Not to mention that he rarely attended alternative school he was enrolled in.

The summer time came as a relief for him, "No more school", he thought to himself, *"And about time it starts back up again, I'll be old enough to quit"*. Knowing that once he turned sixteen, he could drop out without getting in trouble by law, made him laugh to himself. His mind was set, he wanted to be the biggest, powerful and most feared drug dealer in the city.

His mother would always try to talk to him, and tell him how he was blessed to have a roof over his head. She worked a full time job like most mothers, and paid mortgage on a three bed room house with a garage and a nice big back yard. At thirteen Cleofis and Berry had broken into almost every house on the block. The neighbors furious but with no proof, complained in silence but they always knew he did it: They would almost always ignore Ms Jackson's invitations to her get togethers. Ms. Jackson would eventually find this out years later.

Cleofis would betray anybody if they had something he wanted, he didn't care how close you was to him. And this was something that the people close to him would learn in the future.

Watching his mother getting ready to leave in her car, Cleofis looked at Berry with a grin. "I'm fenna to get me some head, you want some too."

"Hell yeah, I want some! What about you Gabe?" Berry asked excitedly.

"Shit, I'm about to go around here to the crib. I'll get up with ya'll later."

"That nigga don't wanna never get no head with us. Nigga! She ain't gonna be worried about what size you thang is, all she gone want is a couple of these dime bags I'mma give her and she gone suck all three of us up", Cleofis exclaimed with lust on his mind.

Gabe still declined the offer, saying he had something to do at home. Cleofis and Berry went in the house as Gabe walked off. Cleofis then jumped on the phone and called his uncle's girlfriend, a known drug addict. He told her to come over to test something out for him. She said she was on her way. Cleofis then ran to his room in the back, grabbed a shoe box containing cocaine that was individually wrapped, took some out and put the rest back in the box. With sexual activity on his mind he glanced over at Berry. "I ain't got no rubbers do you."

"Nope, I don't got none either, but you sure your uncle's girl gone get down for some work."

"She should, even though I ain't neva asked her about nothing like this before", Cleofis continued. "Come on now, you know this work have them fiends knocking on doors in the middle of the night. If we ain't got no rubbers then we'll just go with out em, it ain't like we never haven't before."

"You know that's right", Berry said before conjuring up an enough nerve to ask a question he already knew the answer to. "Look CJ, Why don't you let me get some of that work so I can start back hustling again?"

"Man! You know every time you get some work you mess it up and that last pack you messed up wasn't even mine. That nigga still want his money every time I see him, but I ain't giving him shit." Cleofis looked Berry directly in the eyes while speaking.

The door bell rang and Cleofis opened the side door with a smile from ear to ear. The tall thin and gaunt woman stood there appearing to be undernourished but still retained a small amount of beauty. Knowing what he had in mind, he told her to come to his room in the back, so they could talk where Berry couldn't hear them. It was in the back where Cleofis made her an offer she couldn't refuse. Before you knew it Berry could hear the loud sounds of his friend being pleased. "Come on back here", Cleofis yelled. Berry went to the back then proceeded to take his clothes off immediately, instantly excited he smirked at Cleofis while watching the woman please him. Berry didn't think Cleofis could convince his uncle's girlfriend.

With Cleofis hand still throbbing, it was difficult for him to enjoy himself so he let Berry have his turn. Going back to the front of the house to make sure his mother hadn't come back. Cleofis picked up his bowl off the table and stuck his swollen hand back into it. After his uncle's girlfriend was done with both of them she made them promise not to tell anybody before leaving out of the door. They both kicked their feet up and relaxed after she left.

A couple of days later Cleofis was on the Cartels making coke sells. He would give his pager number to as many addicts as possible. Making his bags bigger to rid his competition was something he learned from his older cousins. There were many dealers on the blocks, but Cleofis had been there since early in the morning and was now on his second thousand dollar pack. He was a smart drug dealer for his age most of his competition didn't have pagers and they didn't come out as early and stayed on the blocks as long as he did. Every addict that pulled up knew him from being out there all the time, he would be the first one they would choose out of the young dealers. They would pull up and Cleofis would go to the car with quite a few baggies in his hand, make the transaction and the car would pull off. At this age he stayed geared up, wearing a cream Boss hat, with a cream Boss shirt to match and jeans that he got from a local store. Always trying to keep the latest Nikes or Jordan's, he wore a jet black pair of Nikes with his cream outfit.

"When I get done with this pack I'mma have close to two stacks. What am I going to buy myself, some more gear or that big fat herringbone I seen in the store. I think I'm gone probably get the herringbone and grab some of them new Jordan's. It shouldn't even take me that much longer with this last pack. The block's been dumping pretty good today. After I get done, I'll probably have fun for the rest of the day, and go cop in the morning", he reflected.

Cleofis' mother rarely bought him anything. He had been selling drugs for the past three years, and basically bought everything he needed himself. His mother received a social security check for him every month. She gave him the majority of the check, figuring that, that would be all he needed for food and clothes for the month, and kept the rest to pay bills with. She stopped disciplining Cleofis when he was a pre-teen, realizing it was nothing much more she could do. Instead she just prayed and left it in God's hands.

More dealers crowded the block, but by this time Cleofis was almost done with his last package. The crowdedness of the block made him very irritated. He hated how all of the other dealers would run up to the cars all at once, because this would make the addicts nervous and sometimes pull off without spending any money. Cleofis tried to get rid of his last, knowing it was just a matter of time before the police would raid the block and start searching the young dealers for drugs. Cleofis spotted Gabe walking in his direction, as he thought, "I could see if my little homeboy wants a wholesale for the rest of this work." Cleofis reached into his crouch for his package as Gabe approached.

"Say lil homeboy, I gotta nice little wholesale for you if you got the right price."

"And what's the right price?", Gabe asked, feeling entitled to a deal.

"Just take a look at these stones and tell me how much you'll give me for em." Spreading his hand so Gabe could have a better look, he hoped Gabe would say a larger price than the one that was in his head. "You see they boulders, and ain't no nigga out here on the block got no boulders like these. You'll double you money and make a little more."

"They fat but my money a little funny right now."

"Well, give me what you got."

Cleofis wholesaled the majority of what he had left to Gabe. With only a couple of baggies left, he strolled away from the Cartels, counting almost two thousand dollars. Reaching the projects a car cut the corner and slowed down as it came closer. He recognized it was one of his customers off his pager. Cleofis jumped into the car quickly and told the customer to pull off.

"I only got a couple of stones, so how about you let me keep this car for the rest of the day."

"You don't even look like you old enough to be driving and you got to give me more than a couple for this car. I know I been getting my work from you and all, but I could get into trouble if you get caught driving this car", the hype replied honestly.

"First of all this car ain't the shit, so you can't expect me to give you that much for it", Cleofis began loudly, but toned his voice down, "And I'm old enough to drive, you ain't got to worry about me getting you into no trouble. I just want to go check out a couple of girls today, that's all."

After rifting back and forth with the addict they struck a deal. Being only fifteen not only could he drive, but he was better at it than most adults who had been driving for years. You couldn't tell him he wasn't grown. And when spoken to like a kid by elders he could be very disrespectful in return. The car he was keeping for the day wasn't the best but it got him from A to B. Immediately upon driving he picked up Berry, and headed to a local jewelry store.

"Damn CJ, where you get this ride from", Berry asked in fascination.

"This hype that I serve from time to time let me keep it fo' the day", Cleofis responded.

"So that means we about to kick it tonight. Let's go check out some girls, I know where some at, that will let us run a train on em."

"We can do that, but first I'm going to the store to get this big ass herringbone I seen for sale, and its fourteen karats. Wait until they see me step out on the block with my chain, the chicks gone dig me even more."

"You must be trying to get stuck up or something, Niggaz already around here snatching shoes off of niggaz feet, you gone have to watch yo'self. You better buy a strap first", Berry advised.

"I ain't worried about niggaz robbing me, 'cause if they rob me, they better kill me dead. Or else I'm gone come back and kill they whole family", Cleofis replied with a boom in his voice. "Look at how much money I made today, them niggaz out there jealous of me. They be glad when I leave the block, so they can get some money. I done made two stacks today, all by myself."

"Well, give me some 'cause I'm broke, I ain't got a dollar to my name."

"I told you befoe", Cleofis began directly, "I wasn't doing nothing else fo' yo' broke ass since you messed up that last pack. I ain't about to be giving my shit away, you must be crazy."

Determined not to give Berry any money Cleofis continued "Maybe after I buy me a few things and see what I got left to go to the store with, I might give you something." That was just a script to keep his friend from being mad at him. Cleofis had no intentions on giving Berry any money. Feeling good about his wad of cash he strutted in and out of the store with the thick necklace that had a very big charm on it. The reaction Berry gave him was the one he was looking for.

"You wish you was me right now don't you." Cleofis flamboyantly bragged, Berry looked at the chain that carried an uzi gun emblem and looked back up a Cleofis.

"That's bad as hell right there, damn I wished I had me some money, I would buy me one too." Getting back into the car Cleofis patted the brakes a couple of times before starting the engine.

"You got to start hustling like I do and then you can buy the shit I buy", purring the engine he pulled off as he continued. "You got to stand out here long like I do, and get up early like I do. If you quit pussy footing around we could both get some money together, all you got to do is listen to what I'm telling you."

Berry turned his head towards the window looking at the view. Instead of soaking up the advice like a sponge, he was very negligent to the information, and continued to glance over at the expensive necklace that Cleofis wore around his neck. He couldn't help himself, and neither could Cleofis as he swerved into traffic, because of trying to look into the rear view mirror at himself. The car had no air conditioning in it and they both started to complain to one another about the heat. Sweating tremendously in his cream pants Cleofis complained, "I sure wish they had some shorts instead of pants to go with this shirt, 'cause I'm burning up." Cleofis wiped the dots of sweat off of his forehead. If I knew there wasn't no air in this piece of shit, I would have only given the dummy one bag instead of two."

"Shit this leather burning the hell out of my back. Let's go some where there's some shade at or something", Berry said irritated.

"We'll be at the park in just a few minutes", Cleofis assured him. "Just hold fast."

The car was very junky and needed a cleaning inside and out. The leather seats showed a multitude of cuts and holes. The carpet in the car was overwhelmed with filth. The two didn't care as Cleofis punched the gas down a busy street.

Entering the Blue Fairy parking lot they could see it was quite a few teenage girls sitting on the benches. Cleofis was excited about showing his chain off. He parked quickly and jumped out of the car. They went and sat on an individual bench, which gave them a better view of the girls. The loud bump from a car coming into the parking lot made the girls turn their heads in amazement. You could hear one say, "Girl he shaking the ground with them sounds he got in that trunk! Who is that?"

Listening to the girls talk from a distance, Cleofis turned towards Berry then shook his head up and down. "Wait 'til I get my shit, I'm gonna shut shit down when I come through, just watch and see."

Berry laughed briefly thinking to himself. "I'd have to see it, to believe it". He then took a bag of weed out of his shorts, opened it up and poured the weed into some Tops-paper. After rolling it and sealing the weed by licking the paper, he then asked Cleofis for a lighter. Cleofis dug into his long pockets.

"I thought we stopped smoking joints and was only smoking blunts."

"This joint will do for now for me, I ain't trying to get real high 'til tonight. Plus a couple pulls of this gonna have me over there talking to them girls. You got the chain to help you and you geared up. Why don't you go over there and ask them what's up!"

"Don't rush it. The time will come just wait a few minutes. I'm still trying to choose which bitch I want."

"The one in the pink is fine, that's the one I want. I don't know about you CJ 'cause you'll take any one of them hoes. Me, I'm picky, I don't like ugly bitches or straight hoes."

"Nigga you ugly, so how you expect to have a pretty bitch!"

Cleofis could barely get the words out his mouth as he slapped his own leg with laughter, joking with his friend. Cleofis' brown skinned egg shaped head, and horn for a nose, from what people called it from behind his back. Wasn't an eye catcher nor attractive to girls, by many he was called ugly. With his innocent dark brown little boy eyes that when mad would turn into a cold empty breath-taking stare. He had a way of reeling people in like a fish pole, and once he had you, it was hard to break free. Berry, wasn't the ladies first choice neither, and would sometimes drown himself into discouragement from rejection. More than ever he wanted to be recognized as a player of many women.

The group of girls kicked a round bouncy ball back and forth to one another. They were getting tired of watching the basketball game that was taking place a few yards ahead of them. Continuing to kick the ball resulted in the ball drifting over towards Cleofis and Berry after being missed by another girl's foot. One of the girls ran over to recover the ball, when Cleofis got off the bench and grabbed the ball himself.

"Hey, you want your ball back?"

"Yes, thank you."

"Wait a minute don't I know you from somewhere."

"It seems like I've seen you some where before too, ain't you that boy who beat up the principal on the first day of school?"

"Yeah, that's me. So that's where we know each other from, huh? Too bad I got expelled because I would have liked to see you every day. What's your name?"

"My name is Kim, what's yours?"

Light skinned, with shoulder length hair. She wore a pink mini skirt with a black shirt to match, with pink letters in detail on the front. She was a petite young girl. Her looks were presentable a little less then what she looked like from a distance. The little acne on her face clouded her natural beauty but it didn't make her unappealing.

Kim was a semi-popular freshman at the public high school that Cleofis only attended for a day. They spoke a little longer, before both of them inquired their interest in going to the bowling alley later on in the day. The bowling alley was a hang-out for the teenagers in the city, part arcade and pool hall. The bowling alley stayed packed, especially on weekends.

Cleofis and Berry rode around more as the day turned to night. Now rolling the weed into a blunt, Berry took a couple of puffs.

"Where you be getting all that green from, because you always talking about you broke. Every time I turn around you lighting up some green, so you must got some type of money", Cleofis said.

"I thought I told you my sister's boyfriend be hooking me up.

The nigga got that shit by the pounds. Sometimes he just gives me handfuls."

"Do you want to rob that nigga?", Cleofis spoke seriously. "How much green this nigga be keepin', 'cause all you got to do is leave the door open and let me know where it's at."

"I can't rob my sister's boyfriend, he cool, plus the nigga treat me like family. If he wasn't my sisters boyfriend I would be all for it."

"You ain't got to do shit, but act like I'm robbing you too. You acting like you scared or something, I'll drop you off if you scared. 'Cause I don't like scared niggaz around me."

Berry exhaled making the smoke come out of his nose, he coughed a little before saying, "Nigga I ain't scared... of shit." Taking another cough between his statements not realizing the mind game Cleofis was trying to play.

Grabbing the blunt out of Berry's hand, Cleofis replied, "What ever."

After smoking the blunt they pulled up in Cleofis' driveway, both of there mouths were dry and there stomachs felt like they were empty. Driven by hunger they exited the car very mellow, with a feeling good sense about themselves. It felt as if they were gliding to the doorway.

They entered the house with laughter. Berry sat down on the couch in the living room, watching Cleofis as he rambled through the cabinets in the kitchen. After retrieving some snacks, he walked into the living room tossed Berry a couple of the snacks. He then went back into the kitchen and filled two tall glasses with grape Kool-Aid, spilling the Kool-Aid all over the floor and counter he yelled, "Oh shit!", he then went back into the living and sat next to Berry on the couch totally forgetting about the mess he just made in the kitchen. They both gulped down the Kool-Aid holding their glasses with two hands, as if somebody were going to try and take it from them. After scarfing down the snacks Berry giggled loudly "Damn I'm still hungry, why don't you go see if there's some leftovers you could warm up."

Becoming pissed at Berry's laughter Cleofis stated, "Quit laughing so loud, my mom's in the back, you dumb ass nigga." Opening the refrigerator back up Cleofis was unaware of his mother who had just walked into the kitchen.

"Why are you just standing there in that Kool-Aid CJ, what is wrong with you? You done tracked it all over my kitchen floor", Ms Jackson yelled in a loud but demanding voice.

"Oh, Ma I didn't know. I'll clean it up right away, where's the mop?"

Ms. Jackson instantly noticed her son's abnormal behavior. Looking at her son she could see that his eyes were fairly shut, as he tried so hard not to look into her face. She watched as her son pull the mop out of the bucket and start to clean his mess.

Angry by what she was seeing, and not being very fond of Berry put the icing on the cake. She could no longer control herself. "Do your friend's mothers let you come over to their houses and disrespect them like that?" She then got straight to the point, "You so darn high, you forgot you spilted Kool-Aid all over my dog-gon-kitchen. You and that boy Berry, all ya'll want to do is destroy ya'll lives, and where did you get that car from, CJ?"

"One of my friend's Ma! Dang you always trippin."

"Listen CJ, you are fifteen years old, you not even old enough to drive. And I know you ain't got no job that pay big bucks, where you can afford a necklace as big as the one you got on? Stop bringing them drugs into my house, because the next time I find them, I'm going to flush them down the toilet!"

Cleofis stood there mopping in the same spot over and over again while she continued. "I don't want Berry in this house anymore 'cause it's one thing for you to disrespect me but I'm not about to be disrespected by nobody else's kids. Now when you get done mopping that mess up, you and your company need to leave and don't come in this house too late tonight, you hear me?!"

Turning her back towards him she walked to her room mumbling, "I should call the police on ya'll", then screamed, "Don't call me if you get picked up for driving and I'm not going to answer if the police bring you to my door."

They exited the house, jumped back into the car and headed for the bowling alley. Cleofis couldn't help but to think about his mother's face which favored his own, except that she was dark skinned with short black hair and a very broad nose. She also had the sweetest little voice ever, and her resemblance to her son was very strong.

He thought to himself, *She always trippin*'!, as he turned the radio up, blasting Snoop Doggs' 'Gin and Juice' off his 'Doggystyle' album.

The marijuana had worn off a little when they pulled up in the bowling alley's parking lot. He could see the youth staring at his necklace when he got out the car. The parking lot was filled with youth who hung in and outside of the bowling alley. He nodded his head at a couple teens with his eyes still half way open as he pushed the double doors making his confident introduction into the place. There was tremendous amounts of noise that followed throughout the place, from bowling balls crashing into pins, arcade games, and the pool hall that sat off in the back, and also massive conversations. All of these things made him breeze through the crowd very fast and alert. While going into the arcade room he ran into Kim a second time. Not even paying attention as she walked up and caught him off guard.

"Whose necklace you got on? It's probably fake", her curiosity spoke.

"Damn girl don't be walking up on me like that, and my chain ain't fake. You want to see my receipt, and its 14 karat gold."

"Well I'll know if the next time I see you and its silver, it's fake. You must got some money if you can afford to buy a herringbone that big. My cousin's is not even that big!"

"Your cousin is not me, mine is one of a kind..., so how long you been up in here?"

"For about fifteen minutes, but we are about to go in a few minutes."

"Why don't you stay and chill with me, and I'll drop you off at home when you ready to go."

"How you gonna take me home -- you got a car or something?"

"Yeah, my car is right outside, me and my homeboy drove up here."

"I don't know about me riding with you and your homeboy, ya'll might try to kidnap me or something", Kim said worriedly, "I barely even know you."

Purchasing some tokens for the games Cleofis spoke, "Well it's up to you, if you want to go or not. I'll give you my pager number if you want me to." he glanced at her tan colored legs.

"You can give me your pager number and you can buy me something from the concession stand if you don't mind, with all that money I just seen you pull out."

Cleofis smiled greatly, knowing that he pulled his wad of cash out only to get a response.

"Why don't you come and play me in a game or two and I'll get you something to eat when we get done", he spoke smoothly, "And I'll give you my pager number."

They played a couple of games before Kim had to leave. Her older cousins were ready to go. Cleofis tried everything in his power to convince Kim to let him take her home but she refused several times, then she told him he could stop by her house and she would come outside. Cleofis took her up on her offer.

Cleofis and Kim got close quickly in just a matter of weeks. He was keeping his stashes of money at her house under her bed so her folks couldn't find it. Her parents liked him in the beginning. They felt very comfortable with him around Kim. They always let him relax in there fifteen year olds daughters bedroom. The two always snuck and had sex every chance they got. His influence on her was very negative. He always convinced her to skip school, steal, lie, and drink. She would do anything to prove herself to him. When the cocaine was lucrative he would shower her with many gifts, keeping her in the latest stylish teenage garments. Her friends had started to wonder where she was getting all the stuff from.

Cleofis would tell her parents that his uncle hit the lotto, and they believed every bit of it. They would fix him dinner and invite him to their relative's house, her dad took to him like a son he never had in a sense. And Cleofis would present himself like a nice young man, always complimenting them and showing them a huge amount of respect. The whole family participated in the likeness, Kim's cousins, aunties, and uncles. Cleofis would walk into there home as if he lived there, and on occasions when he didn't have an addict's car they would let him use their car to take their daughter to the movies and on other outings.

Kim would also spend a lot of time at Cleofis' house when his mother was not there. His mother was very old fashion and would only allow his company in the living room. The bedroom was definitely off limits for girls. "This is not a motel Cleofis", Ms Jackson would always say. But Cleofis would disobey her every time she would leave.

CHAPTER 6

Big Cuz - The Mentor

Coming close to the end of 1994, Cleofis now sixteen going on seventeen, pulled up in front of Kim's house, and started honking the horn in his 82' Regal. He had bought the clean, burgundy color Regal from his cousin Bruno, for a little bit of nothing about a month a go. Honking the horn some more he yelled, "Damn, I wish this dumb ass bitch would hurry up!" After seeing her step down off of the porch, he made a hand gesture for her to hurry up. Kim barely had the door of the car closed when he sped off quickly.

"Shit girl you taking all day when I'm tryin' to get back to the crib to meet somebody. What the hell was you doing, your hair of something. When I tell you I'm coming you better be ready when I get here." he growled.

"Calm down CJ, I had just got out of the shower and I got dressed as fast as I could, give me a break."

"If you make me miss this nigga, I'm supposed to meet, I'm gonna give you a break alright, a break in between ass woopins, so just shut up 'cause I'm already pissed off."

He raced back to his house driving like he was in possession of a license if he got pulled over. In a rush to meet his cousin Bruno who was already there, Cleofis gunned it down a side street, putting the peddle to the floor.

"Slow down CJ, before you kill us", Kim screamed.

"Well if it's our time to go, then we'll go, I ain't scared to die."

"CJ please slow down. You're scaring me baby, please!" Kim begged again.

"We're almost there now, so you can shut yo' trap up."

Kim stumped into the house while Cleofis jumped in the Cadillac with his cousin, who was just about to leave. Cleofis told his cousin to pull up more into the drive way, so they could discuss business.

"Now that's a stupid ass bitch. She gonna make me beat the shit out of her." He replied holding the rail on the door.

"You don't want to do that little cuz, she will calm down. You probably upset her about something. She's a nice little bitch to have so don't mess it up by putting your hands on her. She a good asset out here in the streets."

"Forget that bitch. I don't even want to talk about her. What's up with the work?"

"We going to make a move on that tomorrow, so just hold your ends 'til then. And I heard you hit the dice game for a lot of paper today. They say you won big. What, hell I'll tell you about them dice games. Stop bringing all that money 'cause when you lose it, like you have before, you gone be paging me. Talking about put me back on."

"You right, but sometimes I just can't help myself." Avoiding a lecture Cleofis quickly changed the subject. "Is the work gonna be butta 'cause last time I got some complaints about it. I had to fatten my sacks up a little more just to get rid of em'. And I'm dry as a bone you need to hurry up."

"Don't tell me what I need to do shorty", Bruno was bothered by the comment. Just stay yo' little bad ass out of trouble, 'cause I been hearing about you and your little crew you be around. Calming his voice down, 'cause he wanted the teen's money, he continued, "You ready to buy these Daytons I got for that Regal I sold you. You sure been keeping that ride clean. It will look better with these Daytons I got."

"I just put some sounds in there that I paid a nice piece of change fo'. It all depends on what you want for em'."

"We'll work something out tomorrow, just page me and I'll have the Daytons in the trunk, you can see them for yourself."

Cleofis exited the luxurious black Cadillac that Bruno pulled up in. He told him peace and proceeded into the house.

Bruno was five years Cleofis senior, very handsome, and had been dealing drugs since 1988. Being his big cousin, plus a mentor, Bruno was always lending his advice to the youngster. Standing not much taller than Cleofis, you could look at him and tell they were of some kin. Bruno was not a flashy person but he did enjoy his fruits from his labor on the streets. Possessing a brand new 1994 Cadillac Deville was his only visual statement, which probably was a tool in the gossip about him being one of the biggest dealers in the small city. He was the reason Cleofis stayed two steps ahead of the young dealers.

Born in Chicago, where he spent most of his life until 88, Bruno came from the windy city with dreams of prospering in the drug trade without worry of extortion. He tried to mold Cleofis until a money making machine, by showing him tricks and ways to get over, that he had learned in the windy city.

Cleofis looked up to his cousin Bruno who showed him the tactics to make his finances increase on the streets. Every time he would listen to Bruno his pockets would get fatter. And just to be associated with Bruno meant you was doing big things. Cleofis would try to be seen with his cousin as much as possible, and at only sixteen his name would come up in some of the local police mouths. Because Cleofis didn't have many run-ins with the police as a juvenile, all they basically knew was that he was the young dealer that

Bruno kept around him at times. They called him "Small Fish" and would question him about Bruno they called the "Big Fish" on occasions when pulling him over. On these occasions Kim was driving the car which was one of the things Bruno instructed Cleofis to always do unless he received a license. And Cleofis would follow what he was told the majority of the time, unless he was in one of his moods where he just didn't care.

Cleofis had purchase two 380 firearms a couple months ago, that he would stare at everyday before putting back into his stash. These were new addictions to his revolvers that he essentially hid from his mother. Sometimes, moving them to different hiding spots, occasionally.

Kim was becoming boring to Cleofis who tried so hard to control every aspect of her life. She was head over heels for him and had become very submissive to whatever he wanted to do. Cleofis would show off in front of her friends pulling out wads of cash and giving them five to ten dollar bills if they asked. They were very astonished by how much money Cleofis would have at only sixteen. This made Kim's friends practically adore him. Always willing to do him favors. And they would cover for him when she would spend a night secretly in Cleofis room.

Kim's friends would often try to imitate her by getting involved with young dealers who had money like that. But a lot came along with being the woman of a hustler who also feels he is a gangster. She never told them about the verbal and physical abuse she received frequently through out the relationship.

Cleofis swung the door open hard, knowing nobody was there but his little brother, he stormed into the house. "I'm getting tired of yo' funky ass attitude Kim, you gone make me hurt you girl." Cleofis grabbed his clothes out his closet as he continued. "Iron these clothes for me while I jumped in this shower, and make sure you iron them right this time."

"You always hollering at me, you don't get to holler at me like you my daddy." She gained up a little courage to say.

"Girl I don't want to hear that shit, just iron my damn clothes now!", he yelled.

Kim ironed his clothes mumbling some very hurtful words under her breath, she felt helpless and stripped of her power as she pressed his pants. Watched by Cleofis' younger brother Kim felt temporarily embarrassed, waiting on him to get out the shower. The shower stopped and Cleofis called her to the bathroom with a mellow tone in his voice. "Say baby, why don't you count this fedi for me?" Kim passed him his clothes and picked the lump sum of cash that lay across the toilet seat. She counted the money till the last dollar, while Cleofis dressed in front of her. "How much is that?" Kim put one hand on her hip. "You know how much it is", she exclaimed. "I don't know why you have me counting this money when you know its sixty two hundred and thirty five dollars. What you about to give me some?"

"You can have some, if you want. I just licked them niggaz on the dice fo' three stacks. Them niggaz was looking sick when I left, kept begging me for they fedi back, I told them niggaz see ya, and I wouldn't wanna be ya."

"This is a lot of money CJ. I don't think I ever counted this much for you. You should put some of this money up instead of spending it on drugs all the time. Kim was making a logical suggestion. Just use half of it for some drugs and the other half put it up. Then when you make another profit put it up along with the half."

"I doubt that I'll do that you dumb girl", He said bluntly. "I'mma use all my money because Bruno likes when I bring all my money to the table. My cousin knows what's best for me. You see how he balling, I want to get it how he got it."

"I hear you baby, but maybe you shouldn't move so fast. Your business is all in the street, I'm only trying to have your back like you got mine." She spoke sweet trying to avoid an argument.

"And that's why I love you girl, but I know what I'm doing" he said after a soft kiss that he planted on her lips. Cleofis had brought her some special cream for the acne on her face that was now clearing up starting to make her look more appealing to the teenage boys who she went to school with.

Kim went to use the house phone in the front of his house, calling one of her friends who came around her a lot. She explained that she was over Cleofis house, and for her friend to get dropped off over there. Hanging the phone up Kim spoke "That was April she's on her way over here, that's not a problem is it?"

Cleofis glanced at his younger brother smiled from ear to ear and replied, "That's no problem with me". His younger brother who was stretched out on the couch knew that, that smile meant his older brother was up to no good. April was one of Kim's friends that would flirt with Cleofis, and she was one that didn't mind asking him for money when she seen him flash it. At the time Kim was very naive about her girlfriends, and there actions around Cleofis. She opened the door for April, at Cleofis' request, April came in and sat down on the love seat.

"I came by your house and you're father said that you had just left. I told you I was coming over, you had me walking over there for nothing" April said.

"I'm sorry, that's why I called you to tell you I was over here Cleofis showed up sooner then I thought."

"What I tell you about calling me Cleofis, I told you I don't like that name. If you don't call me CJ then don't call me nothing at all", he screamed, while putting his belt through the loops of his pants.

"Oh, CJ quit trippin Cleofis is not a bad name", April replied trying to calm the barking dog.

"Look April I just don't like it, please don't call me that. When I get eighteen I'm going to change my name. See your girl Kim be doing that on purpose, and I try not to get mad, but it pisses me off sometimes."

"Well CJ you know this girl love you and you love her. I only wish I could find somebody as good as you. Or like you at least." Kim rolled her eyes while April continued. "Nigga you ballin, and all that money you be having a make a girl crazy. Kim better be glad she spotted you first."

Cleofis smirked a little bit, threw a tape in the radio and responded, "Kim don't know how to handle me, I need to find somebody who know how to handle me."

Kim laughed then jokingly smacked hands with April after she replied. "What you got is not much to handle anyway." Cleofis brother laughed a little too much, which resulted in him sending his brother to his room. Cleofis brushed the comment off saying, "You always screaming at the top of you lungs though."

April reached into her purse pulling out some gin with a bottle of orange juice. “Look what I got. Are we getting twisted today or what?”

“You got your nerve girl. I thought you didn’t like to drink anymore”, Kim replied.

“Well I’ve changed my mind for today, what about you CJ, are you drinking with us today?” April asked with a mischievous look. “Yeah I guess, y’all can kick it with me today, but ya’ll can’t be acting stupid.”

“Boy I know how to handle my liquor, I don’t know about Kim.”

“Bitch, you must be crazy, I done drunk with my uncle and them before and you know they some alcoholics”, Kim lashed back. “Ya’ll two motherfuckers is crazy, I know ya’ll don’t want to drink right now do ya’ll?”

“We can, it ain’t nothing but a thing to me.” April shrugged her shoulders. “Well mix that shit up April, and CJ were some cups at?” Kim couldn’t wait.

Cleofis went to fetch some cups out the kitchen saying, “Ya’ll gonna grow up to be some alcoholics, I’m telling you, ya’ll gonna be some alcoholics!”, he yelled from the kitchen.

After handing them the cups he raced to the back room and fetched some marijuana he had stashed along with some top papers. Coming from the back he continued, “April, you might as well Chief some of this green girl, it won’t hurt you.”

Kim looked at April and emerged her eye brows, “You might as well girl, let’s get fucked up.”

Cleofis watched them as they took sips out of their cups and they watched him as the weed smoke inhaled through his mouth, and exhaled out his nose. The top paper burned slowly, stuffed with green you could hear the popping sound from the seeds. Cleofis knowing his mother would be gone until late at night put him in a comfortable state of mind about the smoking and drinking session that was taking place in her home. His mother would probably curse, which was something she never did, if she knew what was taking place in her house. The Tupac, Thug Life album was setting the mood for the three. Cleofis would rap the words dancing around in a brand new garment, looking at April saying to himself, “I know she want me, I'm a wait 'til they both off they square then I'll see if she really want me."

While drinking and smoking April giggled at the sight of Cleofis dancing. Which was not exactly dancing, but more like two stepping. April stared at Cleofis with a glare in her eyes, as she poured majority gin in a cup, with very little orange juice. Kim sat on the foot stool trying to inhale what she could off the notch of weed that was rolled. Cleofis strolled over to the sandwich bag containing a little more weed, and proceeded to roll two more joints.

"Damn, ya'll drunk and high as a muthafucka. And April you almost done killed the rest of that gin. Pass me that swig in the bottle, I'll drink it straight, 'cause Kim done drank all the orange juice. She barely even had some liquor in her cup."

"Nigga I had some liquor in my cup", Kim exclaimed with a slur in her words, "Shhhh… shut up CJ you need to just leave me alone."

A little time went by and Cleofis found himself lying on the floor with slob dripping from his mouth as he lifted up. He could see that Kim was laid out on the floor also, but was in a coma like sleep due to her loud grizzly bear snoring. Looking up on the love seat, he observed April who was also sleep, but was in a sitting up position. She looked so attractive to him, "She looked better than Kim." Cleofis reflected. He realized this was his opportunity to seize the moment. He crawled on all fours over to her motionless body, put his hands on her thighs and started kissing her neck. April moaned a little bit still not in her right state of mind. He then kissed her lips and leaned back a little to look at her peach complexioned large cleavage area.

He moved to loosen her pants, taking his time while he opened them, he noticed her head turn, from facing the ceiling to a tilt. She also dropped her right shoulder, making him think she was aware of the situation. He unbuttoned her blouse all the way. He was aroused tremendously at the sight of her brassiere that could barely hold her breasts in tact.

The loudness of Kim's snore made everything seem slightly unreal to the intoxicated, but still functioning properly Cleofis. The highness was still heavy on his eyes as he felt the garden between her legs, putting one hand behind her back lifting her body into an arch. He carefully slid her panties down with the other hand. Thinking she would open her eyes in this process, Cleofis smiled nervously wondering what she would say if she woke up. Without a second thought he dove into her garden face first. He shared an experience with her, which was taught to him by an addict that he couldn't resist tricking with a year and a half ago. Performing this form of activity was something he practiced with Kim a lot, that he made her swear along with the addict to never tell a soul. April felt absolute satisfaction, thinking she was in a dream when she awoke to find Cleofis' head in between her thighs. She stopped him by a slight touch on the top of his head. "What are you doing?" she asked.

"Just relax, I won't hurt you", he replied. Her body lifted up a notch off the couch to confirm her friends snoring body on the carpeted floor. She then laid back down, "come on", she exclaimed softly. He continued his garden work a little while longer before taking down his pants, not knowing his younger brother was watching the whole episode through the crack in the room door. His younger brother watched in amazement by what he was seeing. He was a little confused about watching his older brother do garden work.

Cleofis started to penetrate her saying to himself, "I knew she wanted me, I knew it." April laid there, body on fire from the dream that turned out to be reality. She adjusted her body for the entry and showed no remorse of her friend, which was still stretched out across the floor. Her mind state would not allow her to think about nothing but the fire works that were erupting inside her body. Bent off life and the substances that were running through her system, she became excited with the intercourse, pushing the lower part of her body forward while grabbing Cleofis' back. She pushed him to the floor and jumped on top of him. Touching bases with her curiosity, she exotically moved her body like a snake. The feeling from the alcohol made her negligible to the carpet burns she received on her knees due to the fast pace.

April lay on top of Cleofis awhile after the act before putting her clothes back into proper place. She then rolled over closer to her friend and fell back to sleep as if nothing ever happened. Cleofis climbed up on the love seat making this his resting spot, gazing at the two young black ladies until his eyes closed, which only took a few minutes.

Cleofis awoke to see that the two young girls had disappeared. He leaped off the couch and opened the front door and discovered that his car was missing. "That stupid bitch done ran off with my car!" He yelled strutting back to his younger brother's room. He asked "Did you see Kim and April leave in my car?"

His little brother was gone also, paging her 911 he slammed the phone down and gritted his teeth from the throbbing headache which came over him. It was dusk outside as he returned his pages. "Man I been knocked out, these girls done took my car, I don't know if my little brother is with them or not, but I got a nasty hang-over", he spoke lightly into the phone to Berry.

"Damn man you ain't supposed to drink liquor early in the day like that, you supposed to wait 'til night time for all of that. You silly dude, you got a hang-over and it ain't even dark outside yet. You gonna be an alcoholic", Berry chuckled on the other end of the phone.

"Look you square ass nigga, Kim and April got drunk with me too. And I got some out of April while Kim was asleep!"

"You lying nigga, you ain't hit that, I don't believe you."

"Come on, you know I'm a playa. When I say I got it, I got it. And no questions asked chump. Slide by here and they'll probably be here by the time you get here." Immediately after hanging up the phone with Berry, Kim called. "We're at the store CJ, and we got your brother with us, you finally woke up huh?"

"Don't ever leave in my car without telling me, what the hell your problem is? All you ever want to do is go spend some money, that's why I can't never borrow no money from you when I need some."

"I'm sorry for not telling you baby, but me and April had seen these cute shoes, we had wanted to buy a couple of days ago, and you was asleep, so I took the car because I didn't think you would mind. I bought our shoes with the money you gave me. I'll take the shoes back if you want me to, it's really no problem."

"You ain't got to take the shoes back, just get here now!", he slammed the phone down. Rumbling through the kitchen cabinet looking for some headache medicine, the door bell rang, it was Gabe. They greeted with a handshake, "What's up with you Gabe, I ain't seen you in awhile, where you been at homeboy?"

"Just chillin', check this shit out I got." Gabe said with a sandwich bag full of a substance that seemed to be cocaine.

"Where you get all this work from little nigga, you must have hit a lick."

"It look real don't it, but its not, I got it from somebody. They say it's some kind of procaine or somethin'. My cousin says it gives the fiends a quick high."

"Man I think we can make some money off of this, them types be mad but fuck em'. After we get rid of this, we can please them with something better, some boulders of butta, I'mma be getting tomorrow."

"Are we gonna go on the Cartels tonight and sell the work", asked Gabe ready to go and make some money.

"I'm going but you shouldn't 'cause them niggaz a get mad at you over there if you sell some dummies, but me, I'll do what the hell I want. You can work my pager 'cause I already got a few sales on it already, so I'm gonna leave you with my pager and when Berry and the girls get here, me and him will work the Cartels. When they complain just tell them I'll take care of them next time but don't give no refunds back to nobody."

Cleofis dropped the girls off, then him and Berry went to the Cartels. They parked up the street from the drug infested blocks. It was now night time out side and they walked into the darkest area that they could find. Cleofis thinking about what transpired earlier sparked conversation. "That April sure got some good stuff, even though I could barely remember it, being drunk as I was."

"You sure you wasn't dreaming, 'cause Kim will kill you if she find out."

"Nigga, she the one who bought the liquor, she been wanting to give me some of that for the longest. She don't even drink like that but she wanted to get twisted just so she could see what would happen between us. Just watch I'm gone be tagging her everyday. You'll see her at the house."

"Okay, nigga we'll see. I know these types gonna be trippin about they money CJ."

"So! Just let me deal with it."

The block they were standing on was very dark. The street lights were out from the youth throwing rocks, shattering the bulbs. The only light that was provided was the porch lights from the homes. Which were very few, because majority of the other homes and buildings on the blocks were abandoned. You could hear the noise echo the street from the wine heads, drug addicts, and bad children that conversated about a variety of things. The loud barks from unfed dogs would let you know that someone was coming. There was no grass on most of the lawns.

The other dealers that hugged the block spoke casually amongst Cleofis and Berry. Loud talking would be a must among the dealers. When it rarely got quiet you could hear the television sets from the few houses. And in the alley you could hear the sounds of cats fighting over scraps, usually tipping over garbage cans scattering diapers and trash all over the place. This was part of Kankakee's ghetto, the smell of filth and realization of poverty. The police rarely combed the blocks at night, most of them in fear of what was hidden in the darkness. The Durrel Northside projects were at war with some Chicagoans just a distance away from the Cartels, and the word was out to be careful even when standing on the Cartels.

Cleofis jogged from a car after making his tenth transaction he had already been asked about a refund several times, but kept a swift mouth piece for the encounters. Telling the addicts it wasn't his fault then giving them more for free to squash the animosity, was proving to work for the both of them.

An old man returned on a bike upset about the product, he got off the bike immediately, you could tell he was at least in his early sixties with similarities to the famous comedian, Fred Sanford. You could hear the grunting in his voice.

"What the hell is this shit, you little niggaz just sold me?"

"That's what was givin' to us, I know it ain't the Bombay, but I'll give you a little extra for the quality of it, 'cause I know the shit ain't that good."

"You damn right it ain't that good, and you can keep that extra bullshit, 'cause I want my money back. I can't feel a damn thing when I hit that."

"I told you I'll give you some extra but I can't give you that money back."

"Ohhh little nigga you gonna give me my money back! You little niggaz don't want me to act a fool out in this spot, and CJ I ain't even think you would be on this type of shit, all that 'cain' you help Bruno push and you out here selling dummies."

"Look old man them ain't no dummies, it's just bad work, so you can take the bullshit up the block somewhere, 'cause I don't even want to hear it no more."

The old man looked at the other teens on the block knowing he was out numbered if he decided to throw a punch, "You little bastards gonna pay for this shit", he replied. Then climbed on his bike and disappeared in the night. The other teens laughed uncontrollably, not many teens would say anything about the bad for business tactics Cleofis brought to the block. Cleofis had already punished most of them with his fist, as a preteen.

By midnight they'd distributed most of the substance, frustrated from the upset customers Cleofis told Berry, "Let's get the hell out of here. Let's see if we can get into Ben's and drink till we fall out." On the way to Ben's Tavern Berry was bothered by the fact that Cleofis didn't want to stop by Gabe's house to see what he had made.

"You know that little nigga probably done made plenty of money off yo' pager that you let him keep. Why you don't want to stop and see how much he made?"

"'Cause I already told you I'll get it from him tomorrow. He stay right around the corner from me, lil homey ain't going nowhere. Every hype that call my pager gonna tell me how much they spent anyway, 'cause they loyal to me. Gabe is cool and the lil nigga love guns just like me. And if the little nigga try to get over, then I'll beat his little ass."

Berry stifled his conversation, after acknowledging Cleofis confidence in the bright youth. With both of their pockets plump from the late night hustling, they both thought of ways to get into Ben's without being ID'd. Crossing the street on foot after parking the car, they noticed a dark colored Astro Van speeding towards them, then slowing down. The van rolled down a back tinted window, and let about four shots ring out of a small fire arm.

The two sprinted into Ben's, past the door man and into the back where the bathroom was at. Ben who was in a nearby back room when he heard the two's commotion in the bathroom, and went to go investigate. Prone to the loud urine smell in the bathroom, Ben spoke, "I don't know what you boys think you doin' in here, but you little gang bangers better leave my bar right now, 'cause who ever you runnin from ain't about to be coming in here trying to get yo' little asses."

Not able to hear the gun fire due to bass from the music circulating throughout the tavern, old Ben stood there, drowned in the stench from hard liquor.

"Ben this me CJ, you remember me from my Pops don't you?" said Cleofis. Ben adjusted his frown, "Little Cleofis Jackson, boy you look just like your daddy", Cleofis rapidly spoke. "Sometimes I come in here with my cousin Bruno in the day time, I know I'm young but they say this is the spot at night."

"Boy you better be glad I know your father, and yo' cousin, I must not be here in the daytime when you be coming in, 'cause I don't remember you in here. Now if I sell ya'll some liquor, you better know how to handle it and you must go sit down at the table and not at the bar. How much money ya'll got?"

Cleofis reached into his pocket bringing out his successful earnings from the night.

"We got bank, you should know that from who I be with and this ain't nothing to a hustler like me."

Ben knew of the young Bruno, not only from encounters but from the rumors of the large amount of money he was said to have. Unconscious to the younger protégé that accompanied Bruno, Ben had served them drinks several of times before, not caring how old or who the youngster was as long as he was with Bruno, who overpaid purposely on alcohol. Cleofis always knew who Ben was and thought that Bruno knew the same.

"Why you young fellas not at the bowling alley or something?", asked Ben.

"'Cause we like to be with the older crowd."

Cleofis was a little insulted by the question feeling grown all his life to him to mingle with elders was nothing more than putting on a pair of shoes. It was never found out who shot at the two. They didn't see who it was, and it could have come from a variety of sources. Who ever it was, it made him think twice about leaving home without his protection. Due to prior juvenile arrests, Bruno advised him that it wouldn't be good to carry a weapon, more arrests might have resulted in going to a juvenile detention center.

Ben fetched them a couple of cold ones and showed them to a secluded area. The two drank at a small table vibing to the grown folk's music, their cups filled to the rim with suds emerging out the sides. More settled, they kicked back and spoke amongst each other until Ben advised them to leave. The duet finished their drinks and proceeded to leave escorted by Ben to a side exit. Ben noticed a police officer who came in from time to time and didn't want to get into any trouble for serving so he told them to come back tomorrow. The side exit led to an alley "You really got it made every bastard in this city know your cousin's a big shot. Ben said we could come back tomorrow nigga, don't forget about me", replied Berry. "If I go back in there tomorrow you know you coming with me so don't sweat it", said Cleofis. The two wasn't drunk but both was feeling very good when they noticed two legs moving simultaneously from behind some trash cans. It startled the two, "Who the hell is that over there?", Berry yelled as Cleofis went closer to investigate leaving Berry a few yards behind him. To his discovery was a man looking his mid twenties, holding his neck from a cut and choking off his own blood. "Berry hurry up, come quick", Cleofis yelled. With a short but fast jog, Berry stood by the side of Cleofis, took one look at the man almost hidden by the trash cans and said, "Damn! He's dying CJ. What should we do?"

"Go get some help", said Cleofis, "Run back in Ben's and tell them to call the ambulance!" Berry ran back into Bens, Cleofis just stood there over the man while he fought continuously for his life. As the blood gushed from out the man's neck, Cleofis refused to help him, saying, "Help is on the way." The man reached out to Cleofis with one of his bloody hands, Cleofis showed no response, constantly watching the suffering and the pain looking him directly in the eyes. Fascinated with death, the blood shooting out of the man's neck sent chills of excitement through his body. Wondering how long it would take him to stop moving.

Cleofis had witnessed one of his older cousins kill a man at Blue Fairy Park, about a year ago and he still remembered the lifeless body of the young black man riddled with bullets. But he never watched a man actually struggling for his life. The sight would be unbearable for most sixteen year old boys, as the wounded man stopped moving, Berry and onlookers approached the corpse.

"Man CJ he ain't moving no mo', is he dead?" asked Berry. "What you think stupid ass nigga?", replied Cleofis. The two departed from the scene when they heard the siren from the ambulance, they didn't want to be questioned about the condition of the man when they first saw him.

Driving through a stop sign Cleofis started, "I watched that nigga die when you went to get help, it was nothing anybody could do fo' em, somebody cut the shit out his throat!"

Berry shook his head slowly from right to left, "Who ever killed dude probably was in Ben's tonight."

"Probably", responded Cleofis.

The burgundy Regal purred through the streets as the wee hours of the morning took a toll on the teenagers making them shift from different positions to keep awake their sleepy bodies. Cleofis took Berry home then proceeded to Kim's house. He would knock on her window frequently in the middle of the night either for his cocaine stash, or to be let in for the night when his Mom was fussing. But this time he just didn't want to sleep alone, so he parked around the corner then walked to her house.

The next day Cleofis awoke to loud talking and laughter amongst teenage girls. After yawning loudly he thought about what transpired last night while his feet hit the floor. He wondered what time was it, he'd felt like an entire twenty-four hour day had passed while he was asleep. Looking for his pager while rising of the bed he checked his pockets thoroughly, I know this bitch ain't got my pager she probably done called some of the numbers back. Opening her bedroom door he walked casually down the hallway not aware if her parents were home are not, he tip-toed until reaching the noisy den filled with Kim and three of her friends looking at old year books. The four girls' weren't aware of his presence standing in the door way watching them like a hawk. He stood there a couple seconds longer before speaking. "A nigga can't get no sleep with ya'll making all this noise."

"Boy it's almost the afternoon shouldn't nobody be sleeping this late", replied Kim. "What you looking so mean for?"

"I just got up, what you expect me to look like and where's my pager?"

"Oh it's in my purse, I put it on vibrate 'cause it kept beeping, my Ma thought it was mine. You didn't know if my parents was here or not, why you just roaming through the house! My dad would have been tripping if he knew you spent a night."

"Well I figured they wasn't here anyway, and if they was oh well."

Cleofis voice was very deep and rough from the long night sleep. Clearing his throat he glanced at April while Kim went through her purse for his pager. April was sitting next to Makeela who was also a good friend of Kim's, the fourth girl was extremely unattractive to him and he tried his best not to look her way. Makeela was his next challenge that he was contemplating on going after when the time was right. Already conquering April, he felt it was just a matter of time before he had her too.

As Kim returned the pager, April winked at him before saying, "You was snoring your ass off in that room I don't see how Kim got any sleep last night. You sound like a great big old grizzly bear."

"He sure do", replied Makeela. "Kim how did you get any sleep last night?"

"Girl I was knocked out I wasn't thinking about him, he better be glad I let him in 'cause I almost started not to get up out the bed."

"Stop lying you know you was going to get up out the bed for me", bragged Cleofis. "You'll ain't gone believe this shit I saw last night, this dude got his throat cut over there by Ben's, and me and Berry watched him lay there and die."

"Why ya'll didn't call the ambulance?", asked April "You mean to tell me you just stood there and watched him die."

"We called for help but it was too late, he died before they even got there, it was so much blood everywhere man it was tripped out. If y'all would have seen it you could tell it was over for dude."

Cleofis spoke of the incident a little while longer amongst the girls before telling Kim he would see her later.

Pulling in front of Gabe's house he honked the horn until the youngster came out. Gabe hopped into the car and Cleofis pulled off, headed for his house.

"How much you make last night lil homie?"

"I dumped all that shit, they were complaining but they still spent they money. I've been paging you all this morning. How much of that bullshit did you get off?"

Cleofis cracked a long smile as he pulled up in his drive way. "It's a lot of mufuckas mad at me, I got to hurry up and call Bruno so I can get some real shit, one of them hypes might try and kill me."

Watching his friend's facial expression let Gabe know he was for real in a joking way "Man CJ, you think he the type that would really kill us over this."

"Hell yeah 'cause it only gives them a split second high, and with most they don't get high at all. You already know this shit I'm telling you 'cause yo' big cuz told you about it, how do you think hypes feel when they spend they hard earned money on some bullshit!?! The ones that were killers feel like killing somebody."

They both went into the house still speaking about the ups and downs of the situation. Placing his body on the living room couch Cleofis started returning his pages on a nearby house phone while watching Gabe count out yesterday's earnings off his pager. Gabe was light skinned, slim and still growing. Brown eyes, fairly large head with uncombed box style of hair. Extremely handsome, the youngster wondered how much money he could keep for himself, as his friend reassured customers' reimbursement over the phone.

The door bell rung when Cleofis slammed the phone down on the receiver. "Damn I told these hypes I'mma pay 'em back, these mufuckas betta quit paging me with this bullshit 'cause I'm starting to get pissed off", he shouted, then opened the door letting the turtle shaped head Berry into his mother's house, "Man these hype's getting on my nerves Berry!"

Berry in return stated, "Bruno's outside for you and he said hurry up."

Forgetting that he had paged Bruno, Cleofis rushed to his bedroom and grabbed his shoebox that contained some cash. Coming from his room he demanded, "Berry, Gabe give me that che-che ya'll got so I can put it with this, matter of fact we fenna count this shit out real quick." Dumping the money on to the living room floor, they started counting as quickly as they could.

Stuffing seven grand into his pocket Cleofis said, “We’ll keep the rest to go shopping with just leave it on the table I’ll be right back don’t move.”

He could hear the horn from the Cadillac Deville honk as he opened the screen door to leave out. He knew his cousin would probably be pissed about the delay so he picked up the pace going to the car.

“What the fuck took you so long?” barked Bruno. “Didn’t yo’ buddy tell you I said hurry up?”

“I know but I had to count this cheddar to make sure it was right.”

“How much you got little nigga?”

“Seven stacks on the dot, with no dollar bills like you taught me.”

“Damn little nigga I didn’t know you had that much, what you do rob somebody? They told me you hit big on the dice game but I didn’t know it was for that much.” Bruno continued while pulling off, “Toss that bread in that bag behind yo’ seat.”

Cleofis reached behind the seat uncovering a black bulging book bag. Unzipping the book bag revealed a massive amount of cash. “Shit cuz how much money is this?” Momentarily hypnotized by the sight his eyes got gigantic. “That’s a hundred long and with yo’ bread it’ll be that, and seven. Put it in there and throw it back behind yo’ seat, I got to collect a little more bread then I’ll be ready.”

Cleofis did as told, “How can I get that much money? Tell me what I gotta do”, he asked ready to soak up some game.

“Just be smart and stack yo’ paper. You see me, I don’t wear them fancy clothes you wear, little cuz. You see me with these gray colored jogging suits all the time, and in the summer I wear plain tees shirts with plain pants. You’ll never catch me pulling out thousands of dollars unless I’m at a casino, niggaz didn’t even know I had money till they seen me in this Cadillac. Stop spending your money on bullshit, buying all them clothes and shit fo’ that girl. When you buy new Jordan’s you buy her some too, that’s a no-no, it’s alright to get a girl a gift now and then but to redecorate her wardrobe is nuts. Imagine if you save all that money you spend on bullshit, you wouldn’t be able to stuff it all in your pockets. I know you got a lot of customers on your pager but that don't last forever you better do like I told you and stack that money."

"I'm trying, but I be seeing shit that I want so I get it. I ain't never had as much money as I just gave you to go to the store wit."

"I know you haven't", Bruno continued, lighting what looked like a joint. "Patience is the key lil cuz, all you got to do is listen to me and have patience and I'll make your dreams come true."

Cleofis still stunned by the large amount of money he saw listened to Bruno's perception, taking in an earful while watching his big cousin collect more money from the local dealers. Some money was from debtors and some was from people who trusted him to use their money for better deals in return. Cleofis money was for a better deal in return that he usually got and with seven grand he expected a very good one this time.

After making a few more rounds the money could no longer fit in the book bag so Bruno would instruct him to set the money that wouldn't fit on the back seat.

"Let me hit that joint", asked Cleofis.

"Oh lil' cuz, I don't think you can handle this. This ain't your average green. This here, is laced with something."

"Nigga, I'm a grown man I can handle myself pass me that shit."

Handing him the joint Bruno smiled before saying, "That's a mac joint little nigga -- don't hit that how you would hit weed."

"I told you I can handle myself", Cleofis replied before taking a couple of pulls from the mac joint. Taking two more hits he passed it back to Bruno. Hunched over forward he started coughing uncontrollably, hitting his chest with a bald fist trying to regain control of his cough. "Damn…..I could tell…..that shit was different by the way it smelled."

Bruno looked at Cloefis with a stern look, "Don't make this shit no habit understand me, 'cause this ain't no shit you smoke everyday." Sharing the mac back and forth he continued, "Oh and I got those Daytons in the trunk fo' ya, you can get 'em once we get to yo' house, I'll just take it out yo' work before I give it to you."

"How long you gonna be with the work 'cause I got people waiting on me."

"It should be later on tonight as soon as I page you, return my call right away."

"How much you taking out fo' the rims?"

"Don't trip it won't be that much."

Cleofis rolled the last Dayton rim into his house with help from Gabe and Berry. The tires were in average condition and he couldn't wait to put them on his Regal. The high from the mac joint was kicking in but he thought nothing of it as he relaxed on the sofa. Berry and Gabe was waiting on the next move after complimenting him on his rims. They both wanted to go to the local clothing stores and purchase some gear.

"Man y'all I'm high as a kite that shit cuz was smoking got me fucked up. I don't even want to get up I'mma just sit back and chill."

"So what about the che-che 'cause I need me some gear." replied Berry. "You want us to go in the car and come right back?"

"Give me a minute we can all go together, let this high go down 'cause I swear it seem like my hand was just melting. I'm fucked up, homeboys stay here with me till I get back straight."

"Nigga you act like you ain't never smoked green befow, that nigga musta had you smoking some chronic 'cause you sure acting funny", Gabe continued. "You on some bullshit, me and Berry ready to roll!"

With his head in a tilted laid back position the sixteen year old noticed his vision impaired, which drove him into a paranoid state of mind. Gabe speaking to him sounded like no more than an on going instrument he'd heard once in a concert at school. His friend seem to move like the Matrix to him as they switched to corresponding about the dying man in the alley next to Ben's last night. The more they talked the more the sofa felt like it was sinking in on Cleofis, hearing his friend's voices circulate from what seemed to him rampant throughout the house led him to reaching for one of the sofa pillows that he palmed in his hand and laid over his face. His mothers living room set was mediocre with a reasonable inch TV plus a stereo system sitting a nice amount of feet from the set.

The TV seemed like it was blasting as he buried his face more into the pillow speaking to himself in whispers, oh shit I can't even see straight. Abstracting the teen purposely touched the bottom half of his features. Amazed by the submerges of his jaws to his abnormal knowledge propelling to the kitchen sink he tossed water on his face. "Man would y'all just shut the fuck up", he shouted. "You fools gonna drive me crazy with all that talking and turn that loud ass TV down."

"This nigga trippin I'm fenna bounce up out this crib", said Gabe. "When you niggaz leave to go shopping don't forget to scoop me."

Berry nodded his head up and down. "We'll be through there as soon as this fool stops trippin."

Hours later the fatigue of the teen was slight, his high was dying down as he tried to grasp some mellowness from the breeze smacking him dead in the face. Accompanied on the passenger side as Berry drove throughout the city, Cleofis said a little bit of nothing while Berry went in and out of clothing stores leaving him in the car to himself.

Turning on West Broadway Berry didn't even consider picking up Gabe before starting to shop. The lil nigga should've never left.

West Broadway was outlined with shopping centers and the money was burning a hole in his pockets as his friend laid loaded next to him. He ignored Cleofis' mumbles watching him lay back looking unpleased with his condition Berry could tell he wasn't fully aware of the money he was spending and took advantage of it.

"Nigga I ain't that high you slick bastard, I see all them clothes in the back seat I'mma kick.....yo...ass.....soon as this.....high die down you frog face coward."

Berry laughed loudly at the remark. "Yo' hands can't hit what yo' eyes can't see. I was about do fo' some gear anyway, so just sit tight I'll be right back out CJ."

Berry got back into the car as Cleofis reclined his seat some more. "Give me the rest of that cheese", ordered Cleofis. "It probably ain't shit left fo' little homie, but it betta be some left fo' me."

"Shut up nigga you know I left you some", replied Berry, passing him the small remainings of the once lump sum of cash. Berry wasn't exactly scared of Cleofis at the time but recognized him as the more dominating one in the friendship, everything he wanted to do Berry was ready to join him.

Berry was a drop-out as well as his friend, tired of school he rarely paid attention in. His self-esteem was very low, feeling like unequal treatment was done by school mates towards him. Berry put on a front for his friends always masking his sensitive feelings with lies, alcohol, drugs and anger. His mother was strung out on drugs when he was a child, which resulted in him staying with his auntie. Berry's father was out the picture before it could even be painted. Looking for love and affection at sixteen led him to the rebellious teens that he tried so hard to show his loyalty too, under fear that if he crossed them they may disassociate themselves from him.

Just about all Cleofis' cousins were gang members, drug dealers and killers. Majority of his aunties and uncles were strung out on cocaine or heroin. Mrs. Jackson, his mother chose a different lifestyle from the majority of her family. A very loving and tender person she struggled with her relationship with her mother who Cleofis was very fond of. Grandmother Sterling was an old southern lady with southern memories from the south. By many she was said to be an old crazy lady that'll shoot you for walking through her lawn. She was a Grandma that didn't mind contributing to her grandchildren's gangster lifestyles by harboring them when they were wanted, supplying ammunition for their firearms and becoming a safe house for their drug stashes.

Ms. Sterling was very devoted in seeing her grandchildren succeed in whatever they chose to do unless their drug addiction was out of control. She cursed like a sailor and would talk rapidly which often drove her to mispronouncing names and places. Staying on the corner, not to far from the drug infested Cartel blocks, she refused to move. Adapted to the crime wave, she had purchased her fairly large house via illegitimate avenues and was comfortable sitting on her spacious screened covered porch. A very peculiar personality for a grandmother, usually unbalanced, I guess it's safe to say she had a screw loose.

The dark brown wig she wore suited her dark brown skin. Possessing the family tree giving nose she would smile seldom showing her unpolished gold tooth. She had crows feet around the eyes and her face became freckled with age spots. The tomboyish demeanor on top of the thick glasses that sat neatly on her wide plumped nose was a mere glimpse of old age compared to how she looked at bedtime.

Cleofis instructed Berry to stop by his grandmother's house where they walked carefully on the sidewalk avoiding stepping on her grass on the way up to the porch screened door. When they walked in, Mrs. Sterling was just starting to cook dinner, the aroma from the tasteful smell made his stomach growl with hunger as he listened to the grease sizzle from the hot skillets.

"Hey Grandma, what's that you cooking?"

Startled by the unannounced voice she turned around swift. "CJ what have I told you about that boy, you gonna make me bust a cap in your ass, now I told you about walking in on your grandma, one of these days CJ, one of these days." Cleofis smiled a little. "Aw Granny you just want to shoot somebody anyway, I'm glad you cooking 'cause I sho' am hungry."

"Well you and Jerry here can have a seat 'cause it won't take that long."

"His name is Berry Grandma."

"Oh I mean Berry shit! Ya'll know what I mean don't be correcting me now 'cause both of you little niggaz ain't too old to get yo' heads busted. And CJ I know yo' little bad ass got some money, why don't you give yo' Grandma some child."

"Berry spent all the money I had Granny, I started to hit him in his jaw."

"You should of hit that nigga in his jaw 'cause that was money you could of gave me…..now ya'll can go in the living room and sit your little asses down and take them damn shoes off!" she yelled.

CHAPTER 7

Point To Prove

Cleofis cruised the Southside of Kankakee sitting comfortably in his maroon crush velvet interior that was installed a couple days earlier. The seats felt plush as the Daytons he'd just shined seemed to glow while the sunlight hit them. The car was washed thoroughly by his drug addict uncle he gave crumbs of yack to do the job. The Southside was where Kim stayed but he wasn't interested in stopping by her house, all he wanted to do was hit blocks showing off his clean desirable car. This brought a lot of jealousy in a time where you could get shot at, robbed or killed for being at the wrong place at the wrong time.

Cleofis was considering flipping to another gang organization. He was already a Gangster Discipline but loved the fellowship of the

Black P Stone organization. His cousins that were in gangs were mostly Gangster Disciples.

I wonder what motherfuckers would think if I flip to a Blackstone, that nigga Bruno will probably stop fucking with me. Who knows, the Gangstas might try and kill me. It seem like all they do is fight amongst each other while the Stones all see eye to eye with each other.........I wonder if some hoes at Blue Fairy Park today.

Occasionally teen girls would come out to Blue Fairy Park when the killing died down. The park was a killing ground for gangs and dealers. But the girls who had relatives that were associated with the lifestyle hung out there sometimes watching the basketball tournaments or looking for attention like Kim and her click of girls.

The Vice Lords tolerated Cleofis' flamboyant methods, if it wasn't for Bruno who did business with their leader they would have snatched the sixteen year old out of his Regal when riding through their territory. The Vice Lords, Black Stones and Mafia Insane were long time rivals of the Gangster Disciples and when a truce was broke all hell would break loose. Because it was so many Gangster Disciples it would usually take all rival three organizations to go to war unless the Vice Lord's leader called back up from the windy city and that would open a blood bath. The blood baths of the early nineties mostly came from these organizations. The Gangster Disciples was what Cleofis had been apart of since his father's death, and being shot at was not uncommon for him so he would try to stay within his cousins territory at night.

A Black Stones general had extended a hand to him and wanted him to be apart of their organization. The Stones always liked Cleofis, they thought of him as a bright young prospect with an uncanny sense of the dope game. The Mafia Insanes hated him at the time and they would have conflict often sometimes resulting in shootings where he used his Jennings 380 hand gun ferociously. He would practice shooting at a near country part of Kankakee, and became very accurate for a teenager his age.

Cleofis bent more blocks before running into a familiar face. It was Makeela walking down a Southside street with her LA Gears lighting up at the bottom with every step. She was looking seductive to Cleofis with her hair cut short in the front and long pressed in the back. Her maple like complexion, brown eyes, luscious lips and very big butt was what he fantasized about. Never having an opportunity to pursue his lascivious thoughts, but kept her in curiosity by flirting and being generous he now had his chance.

"Ay Makeela", replied Cleofis. "Ay Makeela this me CJ, where the hell you going?"

"I'm going home, I just came back from my aunt's house", she exclaimed softly, approaching the vehicle. "What you doing, just riding around in this nice car?"

"Yeah you can say that, why don't you hop in I'll give you a ride home."

She opened the car door in relief. "Thank you", she said. "Cause I didn't feel like walking past them dumb ass niggaz up the block they always acting stupid."

As Makeela closed the door to the two-door Regal, he spoke confidently. "You like my new interior, don't it just feel good?"

"It sure do, it feels like suede. I love the touch of this type of material. Has Kim felt it yet? 'Cause I know she'll like this."

"Not yet. Her folks been trippin', so we had to give each other some space."

"I thought you had it made over there, shit my Momma don't even want no niggaz at her apartment when she's not there. But shoot, my man always there when she gone."

"Your man real lucky to have you on his arm, 'cause if I hadn't seen Kim first then you'd be my girl and I would have spoiled you."

"Is that right, boy you betta quit talking like that, you know Kim crazy about you."

"Oh she crazy alright, but not about me." Cleofis continued with his eye brows raised high. "She got a nigga she be messing with on the side that she keep secret from everybody including you." He glanced at her swiftly to see if she would buy the lie.

"Poor baby", replied Makeela. "I didn't think Kim was like that. You're a good man you should be entitled to good woman."

Cleofis slowed down in front of Makeela's apartment building, feeling that the time was running out he uttered "I know I'm a good man that's why I'm fenna leave her tired ass alone and find me someone who would appreciate it when I spoil them." Bruno had taught him well on how to play on girls mental. He continued, "Ya'll got something in yo' crib to drink?"

"It's some Kool-Aid in there you can come up and get you some if you want to."

That was all he wanted to hear as he cut his car off immediately silencing the Top Authority rap group that played continuously as they talked.

Upon entering the apartment he asked, "Who all here?"

"Nobody right now but my man will probably stop by he knows I'm the only one at home today", replied Makeela.

"Well Makeela is you gonna pour me some Kool-Aid or do I have to do it myself."

"Take a seat I'll pour you some."

Cleofis didn't want to take a seat observing the massive amount of dirty clothes all over the place, where the hell could I take a seat at in here?

The sour smell from damp sitting clothes flooded his nostrils making him hold his breath in long pauses. Reaching for a stool he said to himself, *"Man that ass is phat",* while watching her bend over to put the container back in the refrigerator and then handing him a dark blue cup. She pulled up a stool and sat down glutting her own cup of Kool-Aid. "What happened to that big chain with the 'uzi' you used to have?"

"Kim silly ass put kinks in my shit that was so big that it couldn't be fixed", exclaimed Cleofis. "I started to get me another one, but I said fuck it." Staring at the dried up cereal that stuck to the walls he hadn't took a swig out his cup yet. I'mma have to come up with something quick, this bitch got a nasty ass crib, look at the fucking carpet I've slept in dope houses cleaner then this.

Spontaneously he tipped some of his Kool-Aid over on his sweater. "Damn how the hell I do that?" Makeela came to his rescue with paper towels off the counter. "Boy you wasted that all over! Take off your sweater. I think we got something you can put on it so it won't get stained."

Cleofis maneuvered his sweater fast, and then dropped his pants. "I got some on my pants too." Makeela bent over patting his pants that were around his ankles fully aware of his crouch that hung above her head. Cleofis stared, in a split second daze at the small top portion of her butt cheeks that showed from her straight envelope folded figure. Looking at the beginning crease in the cheeks he couldn't help but get a erection that came bulging out from his boxers. Makeela accidentally hit the back of her head on the firm sprout, she jumped back enticed by the sight she put one hand on her hip. "You want to do it to me don't you?", she asked very seductively. "You know you do with your slick ass!"

"Yeah!"

"Well come on we got to hurry up before my boyfriend stop by." She grabbed his hand and led him to a back bedroom.

After the ten minute exercise, Cleofis exited the apartment skipping down the second floor stairs. I'm glad I'm out that stanking ass crib I don't think the roaches could live in that muthafucka. He was used to nasty cribs, but not from girls that he wanted to sex. His mothers and grandmothers house usually stayed clean and he could remember one of his mother's sayings. A women who keeps her house dirty is usually dirty herself. He didn't take heed to this saying. While touching his pubic hairs in the car he didn't even pull his hand out good before he was hit with the strong fish like smell. His pubic hairs had absorbed the stink from in between her thighs. "Owwee that bitch pussy stank, I'll never fuck her again, that stinkin' bitch", He yelled, pulling off the curb turning up the Top Authority music that was in his CD player.

Arriving home he remembered that his mother was having a cookout when smelling the barbeque in the air. "Man you throwing down today, I know I can invite some people over."

"Boy you know I don't want none of your friends at my cookout."

"I'll only invite the ones that's good."

"If you do bring some people over ya'll have to stay in front and no loud music, our disrespect towards my guests or your family members that will be here. Do you understand me CJ?"

"I hear you! You won't even hear us."

Getting dressed after showering he put the navy-blue Khaki pants that was stained in the dirty clothes hamper wondering if the stain would come out the Georgetown sweater also. The bitch never went and got the shit to get this out with. Cleofis went through his closet trying to decide on what to wear, the Jobo or the Karl Kani outfit for the day as he rubbed his chin. I think I'll go with the Karl Kani today I probably need to go to Ju Town and do some more shopping..............Bruno gonna have to give me more or something 'cause I know them rims didn't cost that much that nigga think he slick.

The evening came as the front and back yard filled with guests. Among his guests were Berry, Gabe, Disco, Clifford or Cliff for short and James (JW) Wells who was Cleofis first cousin. Also there was Dim, April and a couple more girls they brought with them. All the fellas were Gangster Disciples except for Cliff who they all considered as lame, but Cleofis let him hang around anyway. They all wanted to be around the prosperous Cleofis Jackson that had a nice car, clothes, jewelry, guns and money. They were all the same age except for Cliff and Gabe that were only fourteen at the time.

James Love pulled up in his rosy red drop top Mustang, only eighteen the streets called him Jackpot because of his wealthy family and on top of that he moved weight. James (Jackpot) Love was a Blackstone that would occasionally be around Bruno. Bruno would give him deals on cocaine when the Stones didn't have any. Jackpot was a light complexioned thin young man who respected Cleofis hustle and loved to mingle with the commotion. They knew each other not only from Bruno but from hearing about the others lucrative profits in the streets.

"What's up CJ?" replied Jackpot observing the deepness of the crowd as he approached the front yard. "I could smell that Q a couple blocks over."

"Yeah my momma threw down on the grill today you can go back there and grab a plate if you wanna. You seen my cousin Bruno today?"

"Nope, it's been a few days since I seen him."

"Been a week since I seen the fool and his cell phone is off unless he got the number changed."

Jackpot looked a little worried as he glanced at some of the mean mugs on the Gangster Disciples faces intimidated by the frowns he suggested. "Why don't you come out to the bowling alley tonight, niggaz gonna be betting change on the pool table."

"I might swing out there and bet some che-che that's if they betting enough."

Nigga you know we can bet whatever you want to bet, you know ain't no bet too big for Jackpot."

"A'ight nigga", yelled Cleofis as Jackpot jumped into the Mustang.

Jackpot weighed no more then a little over a hundred pounds, very frail and fairly handsome. He would be easy prey for the wolves that stared at him. James (JW) Wells a dark complexioned loose lip action fanatic crossed his arms right over left saying. "I'll get that nigga! Go on and give me that pistol cuz and I'll rob 'em for he pull off. "

"Cool down JW I'll let you know when the time is right", replied Cleofis. "I'm surprised the nigga even stopped by here by himself, but leave it alone for now. "

JW talked a lot of shit, it seem like his mouth never stopped running always talking about what he'll do to somebody. He stood about six feet, slightly slim with the large family tree givin' nose. Being Cleofis' cousin, JW would always try to play fight with him hoping to prove who was tougher.

Disco was a peach-colored teen that stayed in the neighborhood -- very heavy set with a box hair cut that resembled Gabe's. At the time he was soft spoken and quiet and still attending high school where he gambled repeatedly in the bathroom with other teens.

Cliff was a high yellow kid who didn't even look like he belonged in this atmosphere. Him and Gabe spoke casually in school, they'd known each other since Pre-School. Gabe, including others could never understand why he came around at the time Cliff didn't sell dope or do any of the other activity's the bunch did. And rumors had it he was still getting woopings at age fourteen.

"CJ can you get me a pop, oh and get April one too?", Kim asked.

"Girl, why don't you go to the back and get it yourself." Cleofis had watched how Kim had stared at Jackpot when he was there and was slightly jealous. "Betta yet why don't you ask that nigga you was staring at to get one."

"If he fine then he fine why don't you stop trippin' CJ?", said April. "You act like it's something wrong with looking, my girl Kim was just looking, you act like you wouldn't look at a fine girl if you saw one."

"April you betta learn to mind yo' business, only reason why I ain't fussing at you is because you too pretty, with yo' fine ass", Cleofis tried pissing Kim off.

"If she so fine then maybe she can put up with yo' big nose ass", retorted Kim. "'Cause its plenty of niggaz who want to push up on this."

Gabe looked at Kim and smiled at Cleofis. "Uh-huh, I'll treat her right."

Cleofis slapped Gabe's shoulder in laughter. "Boy you wouldn't know what to do with all that."

"He just might", Kim spoke rolling her neck. "'Cause you sure don't with yo' two minute ass."

The whole front crowd participated in laughter as Cleofis last words seeped out. "Well ya'll might as well just go on and fuck and get it over with", He advised. "And she got some good stuff too." The whole crowd giggled at the jealous remarks finding both individuals funny.

As Marvin Gaye played from the stereo system Mrs. Jackson requested Cleofis take it outside. The crowd ate barbeque and other foods while vibing to the music. Cleofis thought about April and Makeela. "I sure do want to fuck April again that pussy was good, that girl got a bomb in between them legs.....that motherfuckin' Makeela be straight if she soaked in some bath water.....I wonder if I can fuck anymore of Kim's friends....I'mma have to come up with a way to get April when she sober, 'cause the bitch don't drink that much.....fuck it I'm just gonna slide her my number, she'll page me if she want some of me."

Mrs. Jackson walked up to the front yard yelling, "CJ somebody's on the phone for you."

"Who is it?"

"I think it's your cousin Bruno. Ask him why he didn't stop by here."

"Ok Ma. Kim is getting on my nerves, Mom. I'm tired of her mouth."

"Well boy you the one chose to deal with her, so you either deal or you don't."

Obtaining the phone he raised his voice a little, "Damn man I been trying to get in touch with yo' mark ass."

"Hold up little cuz I ain't no mark and I done told you about disrespecting a gangsta. I called to tell you that was some stupid ass shit you and your homey did not too long ago."

"What the hell you talking about?"

"Selling all that bullshit you little niggaz had, motherfuckaz thinking I had bullshit. I don't see why you would try to fuck yo' clientele up like that just for some quick cash. You a stupid little muthafucka, you too impatient, and yo' little ass move too fast. Always wasting your fucking money, little nigga I know everything that go on in the streets, did you forget I'm the head nigga in charge -- Every motherfucka know me."

"I don't even want to hear that shit you talking", offended by Bruno's statement. "I need some more work 'cause you took out to much for them rims they wasn't worth that much and I'm running through this shit you gave me pretty quick. So man you gotta give me something."

"Little nigga I ain't gotta give you shit, didn't nobody get over on your stupid little ass you just always want something for nothing."

"Nigga, you could have given me more for my seven stacks."

"Fuck you, you little pussy ass nigga, I gave you what you was supposed to have and I ain't giving you shit else."

The phone clicked, Bruno had hung up before he could respond back. But he remembered hearing his grandmother's voice in the background. He raced out the front door bumping into his guest to break through the crowd.

Berry could see the displeasure in his body language as he peeled to the car. "Ay, 'Gee' where you bout to go to?"

"Stay here I'll be right back", said Cleofis. "This motherfucka gonna give me what he owes me."

Bruno wasn't a gangster to play around with, gangster meaning nothing to do with a gang but just a person that favored Al Capone with his tactics. Bruno was feared and respected, highly intelligent for twenty one and owned the four unit building he stayed in. Eveybody in Kankakee knew him and a lot of dealers worked for him. The gang leaders didn't fear him, but because his coke was cheaper then a lot of dealers in Chicago, they avoided altercations with him under assumption that the coke prices would remain good. He'd never been robbed like a couple of the other big dealers in the city after demonstrating murder on two teenagers in '92' for just plotting on robbing him, no one dared to try. And a known fact was that he hated stool pigeons and valued to exterminate anyone who ratted on anybody in his crew. Even though he was a Gangster Disciple. The Gangster Disciples gave him his space because they knew Bruno took orders from no one and he saw to it that they had the latest on artillery.

Bruno had his own crew of gangstas who were very loyal to him. He loved to vacation from the small city and a lot of times he would be out of touch for weeks. He looked at Cleofis as a younger dealer with potential to be big if he could stop making dumb decisions. But he didn't respect his gangsta and also thought of him as a wanna-be tough guy.

Bruno was looking puzzled when Cleofis all of a sudden pulled up but immediately broke off into a distasteful look as he neared. Standing in their Grandmother's back yard talking on his cell phone, he quickly told the caller to call him back. "What the fuck you want! I told you I wasn't giving you shit." The Grandmother looked through her back window as the two argued. "You ain't gonna keep talking to me like I'm some bitch", Cleofis spat. "'Cause it ain't no bitch in me."

"I advise you to get yo' bitch ass back in the car fo' Granny be out here picking yo' punk ass up off the ground." Bruno continued, "Nigga yo' nuts ain't big enough to fuck with me yet."

Sounding like he was losing his voice Cleofis was so outraged. "Bruno you bitch ass nigga, I told you I want my fuckin' shit and what you won't give, I'll take."

Letting the cell phone go out his hand Bruno punched him before it hit the ground. Furious at this point he scooped Cleofis and dropped him. "Get up bitch, I told you not to fuck with a gangsta didn't I?"

Cleofis was dazed not thinking his cousin was that strong. Barely back to his feet, he charged Bruno courageously, feeling caught off guard by the first punch. "Motherfucka I'll kill you!", he screamed throwing wild punches, Bruno blocked every one of them then connected with a right punch knocking Cleofis to his knees. With a hand full of his shirt Bruno dragged him with one hand and slugged him with the other as Cleofis tried persistently to get up. "Uh-huh you little bitch.....ass.....punk I don't give a fuck about you." Bruno yelled, beating him bloody.

Grandmother Sterling almost fell coming out the back door. "Now that's enough Bruno you hitting CJ a little too hard, you hear me I said that's enough motherfucka!" Neighborhood viewers was observing the fight and carefully moving closer to be nosy until Ms. Sterling yelled. "I'm going to get my gun I'mma kill both of yo' asses. You motherfuckas is crazy and you motherfuckas that's watching I'm a kill y'all ass too." Some of Bruno's crew that was sitting in the black Deville got out and broke the fight up the best they could. "You better get them sons of bitches off my property…them assholes wanna try an kill each other I'll do it for 'em, shit they think they crazy I'm the bitch that's crazy. Tell CJ to take his ass on home befo' Bruno kill em."

Cleofis wrestled with some of Bruno's crew before stomping off to his car and driving off like a mad man. "Imma kill this motherfucka", he screamed as he punched the steering wheel while in traffic. Flying to his house to retrieve his Jennings 380 he continued to yell looking at his face in the windshield mirror. "Look at my face this nigga fenna pay for this shit I swear he gonna pay!" Extremely teary eyed the thumping of his head put him more in rage. His pride had been hurt and the feeling of embarrassment drowned him. A lot of people saw the beating he just received. This bothered him more than the throbbing of his headache. Wanting to cry so badly, he sucked up everything that leaked out while racing out of his car leaving the door opened and not even close to the curb, parking in front of his house. Half of his guests had left figuring he wouldn't be back soon. Kim ran up to him concerned about the bleeding coming from his face. "Baby, what happened to you, are you okay?"

"Get out my fuckin' face NOW!", Cleofis screamed. "Berry! go get in the car, you driving", Berry ran and got in the car with no questions, not knowing who but knowing they was about to go after somebody. Cleofis cursed all the way to the garage with no care of his mother's guest. Ms. Jackson wasn't aware of her son's actions until he had already rambled through the garage for his stash of guns, and was peeling off in his car.

"Kim, where's Cleofis going too, and what's wrong with him?"

"I don't know Mrs. Jackson, he just went off on me."

"Boy, I tell you, that boy betta learn how to control his temper."

Ms. Jackson had walked to the front yard after being informed of her son's disrespectful outburst, she wondered what his problem was.

Berry wondered what was going on as he watched a drip of blood come down Cleofis' nose. "What the fuck happened to you?"

"Just get me to my grandma's house nigga, quick as you can."

It was like Berry could see the steam coming from the top of Cleofis' head as he watched him close his eyes, biting the swollenness of his bottom lip. His eyes were lit up like Christmas lights, and his brown face was as red as the color.

The 380 was held tightly as Cleofis rested it on his right leg, breathing very hard and fast. His adrenaline still rushed from the lost fight, and rushed even more at the thought of what he wanted to do about it. Wiping the blood from his nose, he noticed Bruno was still at their Grandmother's house, just a block ahead of them. "Pull me right up on this bitch ass nigga", yelled Cleofis.

Bruno had one leg in his Deville, and one leg out, arguing with their grandmother, but when he noticed Cleofis approaching in his Regal, Bruno turned and walked up to the up coming car. Bruno raised his arms in a capital tee stance. "What the fuck you want to do little bitch?"

Their grandmother screamed, "CJ I told you to take yo' ass home now -- go on now."

Everything seemed to go in slow motion for the teen as he swiftly emerged the 380 from the passenger side window, POW! Cleofis leaned out the window more to release more shells, but was halted by the unfortunate jamming of the automatic. He could see

Bruno grabbing his chest in pain while they turned the corner. "I hit that nigga, did you see that! I think I hit him in the chest."

"Man you should have told me it was Bruno you was fenna shoot", Berry said nervously.

"Quit acting like a pussy, just go straight to your house and hurry up."

"Damn man that nigga gonna kill us!", Berry yelled worriedly.

"Just shut the fuck up and drive this car, motherfucker."

"What the hell happened, why you shoot em?"

"I told you to shut up, just get me to yo' house."

Cleoifis was just as nervous as Berry, but didn't let it show. He now thought of the consequences to come behind the shooting. I hope I didn't kill him. My Grandma's probably having a heart attack right now, DAMN! Shit is crazy.

The duet went to Berry's house, they parked the car in the back yard and tensely went through the back door. "Don't be talking loud 'cause my aunt's probably in here sleep. Cleofis' pager never rested, he got paged every five minutes by family members and friends, he eventually put the pager on vibrate, and the more it vibrated the more he worried that he killed Bruno. Taking a deep breath Cleofis trembled slightly while breathing out, not knowing what to do. He started to pacc Berry's bedroom floor, never loosening up on the grip he had on the jammed automatic. Berry was sitting on his small old fashioned like bed, curious about Clefois' next move.

"What the hell you gonna do CJ? You know sooner or later people gone check to see if you over here, and my aunt's gonna trip if Bruno's homies come through here, with drama, she'll probably put me out."

"Just give me a minute to think I'mma come up with something. Rubbing his forehead while pacing he replied, "I can't go over my mom's, they'll probably come looking for me at Kim's. Where the fuck can I go?"

"Wait till night time, then go over Kim's, you know her parents will probably let you hide out there."

"Them people don't even like me like that no more, well I don't know, her mother might let me stay."

The shooting could have all been prevented if only Cleofis would have stayed at his residence but he felt insulted and cheated by someone who made it possible for him to have the things that he had. The shortage of the cocaine he didn't receive was a mere glitch compared to the items Bruno gave him for retail value. Not including Bruno's imperial flag that was posted through the city that unbridled the young teen that he seemed to take for granted. Bruno was the line between a lot of harm being done to the youth, but hot head Cleofis wasn't anybody's bitch and was already eager to prove his gangster to his cousin and others who he envied.

Months passed and Cleofis turned seventeen before he was caught by the law enforcement. Bruno had recovered from a gun shot wound to the right side of his chest. The doctors did not remove the bullet in fear of his life. Bruno did not inform the detectives who shot him, but they knew from the witnesses that were outside at the scene.

Age seventeen had just put Cleofis as an adult in the State of Illinois. He was out long enough to see the New Year, before he got caught going back and forth from relatives and friends houses.

Cleofis declined Bruno's request to help him, in fear that Bruno would kill him if they saw each other face to face. Listening to his voicemails on his pager Cleofis almost called Bruno, but would always think about how slick his cousin could be. "This nigga just tryin' to get me to come out of hiding, so he can blow my head off", Cleofis reflected, listening to the concerned Bruno over his voicemail. Cleofis' last days were spent at Kim's house until Kim's father eventually allowed detectives to search his home. They also found Cleofis concealing the 380 used to shoot his cousin. He left his car with Kim, and his coke and money with Berry. His little brother got the satisfaction of wearing his flashy garments.

In a matter of weeks Berry had blown all of the coke and money. And in a matter of months Kim had some how crashed the Regal with no insurance. But Cleofis forgave her in a letter and also expressed how much he loved her on paper. Berry, he was very upset with, and wanted to beat down as soon as he got out. Sitting in a medium penitentiary Cleofis yelled, "DAMN, I should have known better, than to give that fuck up my money, and yack!"

CHAPTER 8

They Said I Wouldn't Live To See Eighteen

Cleofis wound up doing twelve months out the whole deal, where he took the time to work on his now muscular physique. Maxing at three hundred and thirty five pounds on the weight bench. It was now the beginning of ninety-six and he was eighteen, which he had just turned at the end of ninety-five.

Bearing few prison house tattoos, Cleofis felt at the top of his game, he had flipped to a Black Stone, and had spoke with quite a few wise men in the game. Now craving the need for power like never before, he learned nothing but more ways to be a success in the underworld.

Cleofis had made it in the house minutes ago, Ms. Jackson had came and picked him up from the medium correctional facility. The snow had dried up some, from the sun shinning a lot on the ground. It was cold but not freezing in Kankakee.

Cleofis loved breathing in the fresh air while standing with the front screen door cracked. Mother Jackson was preparing dinner for her now ex-convict son. She hoped that he'd learned from his mistakes and wasn't as troublesome as he was before. It was pretty much still outside, no wind blowing and not very cold with it being the early part of the year. You could tell this was a day that people tried to take care of all their business in fear that the next day it would be freezing outside.

Cleofis could see Gabe coming from around the corner. Also, he could hear a person riding what sounded like to him mo-ped. He knew the sound from anywhere due to his love for them in his early teens. He said to himself, *'I wonder who around here riding a mo-ped, it's too cold for that, I bet you it's somebody from the neighborhood I know. My little homey Gabe look like he got taller.'*

Opening the screen door Cleofis stepped outside walking with a New York Knicks jersey on with no shirt under it letting his broadened arms show along with his built bulging chest. With his tough guy strut Cleofis greeted Gabe with a pleasant nod.

"Dang CJ! You sho'll got swoll boy, what the hell was you lifting?", replied Gabe.

"A little something something, nothing major compared to the niggas I met in the joint, what's happening with you though, you still hustling?"

"Every now and then, but this school shit be knocking my hustle. I still get a little money." Cleofis felt a cold breeze that made him feel like he was shirtless. The rush from being free exceeded the cool weather. Feeling like a caged bird that was finally set free, the teen spoke inspirationally, "Well you know you need to stay in school 'til you graduate because the streets got no love out here. So many niggas in the joint for their homeboys ratting on them, it's pathetic. But if you really serious about getting some money I'll put you down with me, and trust me I'm fenna to get plenty of it."

Gabe stuck his hand inside of his pullover Nike coat, "I know you got to be cold in that little jersey you got on, 'cause I'm cold and I got on a pullover."

"Shit nigga this work out weather, in the joint. We'll be on the yard shirtless in this type of weather." Knowing it was nippy outside Cleofis still boasted about being ok. Gabe was curious about the rumors he'd heard about him flipping to another organization. "Niggaz was talking about you flipped to a Blackstone, I was like naaaaaa, not my homey he'll never do no shit like that."

"It's true lil' homey, I'm all well now. I couldn't fuck with that GD shit no more, I was already thinking about it before I got locked up." Showing a five with his right hand and turning it into a bald fist, he hit the left side of his chest powerfully then continued. "Even though I'm a Blackstone I'm still a gangsta like Capone, please believe it my nigga. You should come on home and be with the Stones too."

"Nigga is you fuckin' crazy?! I'm GD 'til the world blow, I ain't no mothafuckin' pancake." Gabe had raised his voice a little being offended by Cleofis remark.

Cleofis bragged about his gang and the qualities they had over other organizations until Cliff drove up on the mo-ped he'd heard, "You know it's too cold to be riding that mo pad, look at your face all red, your nose running and shit. Let me ride that motherfucker real quick, I'll bring it right back." Cliff let him see the mo-ped, astonished by the build Cleofis had become, he was tongue tied, "Dang …….. You …..Got big", Cliff replied, handing over the moped. Cleofis had no intentions on coming right back, he sped off. Cliff won't see this bike for a few hours....I'mma drop in on Kim, I bet she don't even know I'm out yet.

Speeding up Fairmount Street the wind made tears roll to the side of his face, going so fast he barely caught a glimpse of what he was passing. The cold wind freezing his hands, face and upper body was becoming too much to deal with. Damn I'll fuck around and freeze to death before I make it over there. Shuddering at a stop sign he thought of turning around but the thought of pleasure upon his visit quickly controlled that contemplation.

Now at the peak of his height Cleofis was five foot four and would never get any taller then that.

The gang's weren't as bad as they were in the early nineties. '94 would mark some of the last gang organization killings. Now in '96 it wasn't uncommon to see two gang members of a whole totally different organization getting money together. Kankakee wasn't on count anymore, meaning the leaders of the Chicago gangs didn't receive dues and drug money from the city. Because Kankakeeans couldn't handle their positions given to them by high ranking Chicago gang members.

Kankakee became an open city, meaning anybody could do what they wanted and associate with who they wanted. Chicago organizations tried to reach out to Kankakeens in '96 but would always have complications with collecting money from the drugs that were fronted. The Kankakeens that Chicago trusted in would screw up the money and this would result in disappearances of Kankakeeans that were never seen again.

Kankakeeans couldn't be controlled. Half of them had no honor for nobody unless it was a very known Chicagoan in the organizations, the other half just didn't want nobody telling them what to do. Kankakee's felt they was smart but Chicagoan's felt they were smarter, matter of fact Chicagoan's felt Kankakeens was slow to the game. In reality most were but there were a handful of exceptions. Kankakee dealers' rarely invested there finances into legitimate businesses such as car washes, restaurants, and real estate like Chicago dealers did.

Cleofis drove the mo-ped up into Kim's front lawn, put the kick stand down and parked it. Opening the screen door to the porch he took his time trying to be as sneaky as possible. I know my Boo gonna be surprised to seem she probably gonna break off into tears seeing me fresh out an all. Entering the main entrance his heart beat fast from the anticipation. Man the front doors wide open Kim's buddies must be in this piece. Walking further into the house there she was, Kim on the couch cuddled up with, from the looks of it a man. Cleofis stopped in his tracks, and just stared at the two from a side angle. They didn't even notice him standing there. The two were more focused on a movie that played from the VCR. The joy on his face was stolen and the sight of the man palming Kim's butt made it seem irreplaceable.

"Damn bitch I been gone a little over a year and you already got some nigga in my spot, huh?", he yelled. Kim's eyes got as big as bowling balls, she scrambled for words while the man put his hands up in the air, in a I-want-nothing-to-do with it fashion. Kim feeling like lightening had struck her in the stomach, backed up off the guy and managed to respond. "We just friends, ain't nothing going on CJ, I promise you." She took a hard gulp that seemed like she was swallowing a distasteful food, while looking at his muscular physique, thinking to herself, "Damn he big, and damn I'm in trouble."

The man looked relieved when Cleofis stated, "Look homie, you got to go, Kim a holla at you some other time." The man replied, "Bye Kim", as he stood up and headed for the door. "And don't come back nigga!" Kim knew she was in trouble, as she stuck her hands out in a please-don't-hit-me position. *He had smacked her and scuffed her up before, but God only knew what he'd do now*, Kim thought. All the love letters they wrote each other flashed in his mind, trying to keep his composure, he yelled, "IF YOU NOT FUCKING HIM, THEN WHAT WAS HIS HAND DOIN' ON YO' ASS – What, you didn't think I saw that did you?"

"It's not what it looks like CJ, you got it all wrong."

Cleofis' mind went blank after hearing the explanation, furiously choking her was when his mind started thinking again. "Nasty, bitch, I knew you didn't love me." Cleofis continued while choking her harder, "All them fuckin' letters.... All them fuckin' lies... bitch I oughta kill you." His voice got hoarse as he yelled more while putting his knee in her chest, and smacking her repeatedly. "You ain't nothing but a hoe, just like yo' friends." Kim's light skinned face was red as ketchup. She grabbed his striking hand long enough to yell. "What about my friend Makeela you fucked?! Huh, what about her? Yeah I found out you snake ass nigga. Bitches always run they mouth's when you stop fucking with 'em." Smack! Smack! Smack! Cleofis continued the beating, now more pissed off by the discovery of his cheating. "So what, you funky ass bitch you out here fuckin' and probably sucking."

"I ain't did shi...... with no .... Nigga", Kim replied while Cleofis choked her some more. He then grabbed her now cut short black hair in his hands and pulled her off the couch. Dragging Kim back and forth through the house, slapping her on every part of her scalp because she was rarely moved her hands that covered her face. Cleofis hadn't even thought what if some body was in the two story house. The control he felt he had over Kim, putting his hands on Kim again while in prison just went out the window. "Is somebody here bitch, you can hear me hoe, I said is somebody here?! No, she cried, "My parents are out of town, please stop hitting me CJ, you gonna kill me." Letting out a loud grunt, Kim yelled, "Let's talk CJ if you love me, you'll stop hitting me so we could talk." "Okay talk", he replied. Kim let her guard down with her body shaking continuously and reached out to hug the middle part of his body, when he cold cocked her with half-balled fist that sent her flying back down hard hitting her head on the tiled floor. She screamed on ear splitting scream that could break an expensive glass, grabbing her head as if she'd been shot in it. She yelled, "I hate you, I hope somebody kill you bitch... wait 'til I tell my cousin, you gonna be a dead muthafucka, you punk ass bitch they gonna kill yo' punk ass."

Kim climbed back on the couch in a daze, balling up in a roll slightly weeping due to the throbbing of her scalp. Cleofis felt a little sorry about the last strike but still felt she got what she deserved. Sitting on the couch next to her he tried to be a little affectionate by putting his arms around her rolled up figure. "I'm sorry for hitting you that hard but I love you and it pissed me off to see another man touching yo' ass.....you all I got", he exaggerated a little with that one. "I never knew how much I loved you till I was locked down in a cell. I know I got a mean way of showing it, but you know I love you girl." At that moment Kim raised her head from beneath her arms with a look of submissive emotion while he guided his hand to the covered up private areas of her body. Kim relaxed a little as he tried French kissing her holding her lips together as tight as she could she finally gave in.

Man I sure missed him even though he wooped my ass I still love him no matter how much I try not too...he sure been working out with his sexy ass, I bet you he could hold me in the air while he giving it to me...where did he get those tattoos done they look professional to be done in prison...I wonder did he fight a lot in there. Oh well, I'll think about that later after he done tasting my flavors. Kim felt like she was in a sexual trance as she exploded before he could even get into his garden work good. *No this motherfucka didn't just make me cum that quick...owweee I can't even stop myself from shaking damn! I'm fenna tell this nigga I'm sorry for what ever I did.*

While a lot of teens in '96 wasn't into oral sex Cleofis performed it frequently on Kim from '93 to the beginning of '95 when he got caught. Cleofis knew tricks that some old folks didn't know. The addict that taught him showed him all the right spots and how to find G-spots without asking. He had a real gift when it came down to satisfying women this way.

After the episode he laid there in between her thighs, both fully nude spread-out on the long average looking couch just vibing off each others presence. They kicked it reminiscing about the past, conversating about the present and thinking about the moves they could make together in the future. Cleofis also thought about his next move on the street with no car, no pager, no money, and no drugs. Shit! I'mma have to start from the bottom. Wondering if Bruno was mad at him another thought hit him. I'mma have to watch Bruno that nigga don't forget shit and he most definitely ain't forget that bullet that's still in his chest.

Cleofis went looking for Berry not as cold as he was before due to a coat Kim found in her father's closet. Now all he had to worry about was his face and hands. With every intention on staying at Kim's until her parents returned from vacation, he laughed loudly at the thought of Kim begging him to stop beating her.

Flying down River Street on the way back to the eastside neighborhood, he shivered from the frost bitten elements traveling on his uncovered face.

He drove the mo-ped up his driveway and parked it by the garage. It had been a while since he'd been gone so he figured Cliff probably walked somewhere to chill.

Entering the side door, he hadn't closed the door behind him good when Mrs. Jackson replied, "Foods been done CJ where you been? That boy Cliff was waiting on you to bring some bike back, do you have his bike?" Cleofis sat down getting ready to pig out on a long awaited dinner. "Yeah ma, I parked it by the garage he'll see it out there", he ate a little bit before asking her the question that he wanted to ask when he was on the run. "Say Ma…what you do with my guns?"

Mrs. Jackson sat down across from him at the kitchen table and looked him square in the eyes. "I got rid of those guns -- that wasn't nuttin' but the devil making you collect those life takers. I hope you don't pick up anymore guns 'cause next time you might take a life and the Lord will have a hard time forgiving you for that. You must keep your temper under control -- stop being so much like your father before you make a mistake that can't be replaced. Get back into school CJ, become something in your life. And repent your sins for these are the last days. Through the grace of God your cousin Bruno survived that shot, and through the grace of God you only got a tear for what you did. I know he beat you up but he still loves you and he forgives you for what you did to him." With a very sincere facial expression Mrs. Jackson continued. "Now leave them drugs alone, for you shame God and please the devil every time you sell one of those little bags to somebody, I raised you better than that, and no matter what you do, I will always love you."

There was a moment of silence before Cleofis uttered. "I love you to ma and I've listened to everything you've said, sorry if I hurt you in any kind of way." Mrs. Jackson hugged her son, as she did the many times when he came through the prison gates. She squeezed tightly, she couldn't believe he'd gotten so big. Finally her nightmares about what she heard they do to young men in prison had come to an end. She could know get a good night's sleep knowing her first born wasn't fighting no men trying to take his manhood.

THUMP! THUMP! THUMP! THUMP! THUMP! Berry was at the side door knocking like the police. Cloefis turned the knob swung the door half way open and gave Berry a vicious stare. "You got a lot of nerve… all that you messed up, nigga you lucky you my homey else I'd pound yo' face in." He let him in as he continued, "You knocking like you the police or somebody and no I don't wanna hear yo' lame ass excuse about that fedi you fucked up."

"Look CJ I know I fucked up but …"

"You two better watch y'all mouth in this house", shouted Mrs. Jackson who wasn't quite in her room yet.

"Sorry Mrs. Jackson", Berry apologized loudly. "Let's go outside so I can holla at ya."

"I came looking fo' you after I left Kim's, you was no where to be found."

"Probably 'cause I was trying to find a ride over here, and how the hell you come looking for me?"

"On that mo-ped sitting by the garage, man I was freezing like a motherfucka on it -- that little motherfucka go fast though."

"They say you flipped Blackstone."

Cleofis hog-spit in the grass before replying. "Yeah and… if motherfuckas got something to say about it then fuck 'em. I had to come to my senses 'cause GD wasn't doing nothing for me.

Berry gazed at a passing car. "But GD is what we always been."

The sun was setting when the two got dropped off at Kim's. Cleofis was upset with Berry about the money that was lost, but knew Berry would come in handy when starting from the bottom. The thought that Bruno might front him some coke to get back started crossed his mind, but he felt no obligation to apologize for the shooting.

Kim had some house guests, two of her little cousins thirteen and fourteen year old girls that ran away from home. Kim promised not to call their mother but eventually did and let her know where they were and they staying for the night. Their mother was happy the girl's were out of her hair saying, "Keep them little hoes, matter of fact keep them forever." Both little girls had bodies like adult women, and Berry smiled like a lion seeing its prey. "Man them little motherfuckas thick", he whispered to Cleofis who was sitting next to him with his shirt off. The little girls admired Cleofis' body saying to Kim. "Dat nigga got a nice body!" Kim frowned her face a little and replied, "Y'all some little fast ass hoes and you all not sleeping in my room tonight. Oh and Berry you got to leave when we go to bed." Cleofis quickly responded for his friend, "My homeboy can spend a night over here if he wants too."

"Well he better sleep in one of the rooms in the back 'cause he ain't sleeping in the living room with these little fast ass girls." Kim was dead serious, "And if I even sense something that nigga got to go."

Berry was disturbed by her remark calmly interrupted, "Be easy Kim you act like you don't know me or something, girl ain't nobody gonna touch yo' cousins, I don't even get down like that."

"Well forgive me if I sound mean but them little hoes is fuckin' and they won't be fuckin' in this house."

Cleofis kicked his shoeless foot up on a foot stool. "Shut up Kim don't nobody want yo' little cousins, go in the kitchen and get us something to snack on."

Ring! Ring! Ring! Kim picked up the phone on her way to the kitchen.

"Hello."

"Put my little cuz on the phone."

"Who is this?"

"Who it sound like?"

"CJ the phone fo' ya", Kim yelled in the living room.

"Who is it?"

"Why don't you come see?"

Cleofis glided to the kitchen with no knowledge of who was calling him over Kim's.

"Who dis?"

"Yo big cuz, I heard you was home."

"How you get this number?"

"Come on nigga this me you talking to."

"Well how you know I was over here?"

"'Cause you fresh out so you gonna go were the quickest nut at. Come holler at me outside I'm in front of the house."

Cleofis paused for a few seconds. "A'ight let me throw my shirt and shit on."

Remembering what his mother said about Bruno forgiving him put him a little at ease. When nearing the red Neon, Bruno was sitting on the passenger side, Cleofis stood by his window, bent down in a squatting position, he cautiously observed who was driving before conversation.

"So how long you been out little cuz?"

"Since earlier today, trying to come up with some fedi to get some new clothes." Cleofis thought he'd tell him about the situation to see if he'd contribute to helping.

"Well why don't you get in and I'll have Shawndra run me by my place so I can get you some money." Bruno was referring to Shawndra Coleman someone Cleofis hadn't met yet.

Cleofis flew into a hesitant mode for a few seconds. "Cool, I'll ride."

Bruno lit up a blunt as Cleofis watched him carefully from the back seat. Shawndra introduced herself seconds later. "I'm Shawndra and your name is..."

"CJ", Cleofis replied. "Do I know you from somewhere?"

Shawndra glanced at him in the backseat. "You don't look familiar to me, you look a little young."

Being that it was dark in the car Cleofis couldn't see her vividly. "I may be young but mentally I'm an old man."

Pulling hard on the blunt Bruno cut in, "Damn little cuz you tryin' to mack or something? You don't even know if this my girl or not."

Cleofis smirked a little, "I wasn't tryin' to mack, I was just getting acquainted."

Bruno passed the blunt to Cleofis. "I'm just joking. This like my sister right here. Me and her go back like ten years from when I used to fuck with her little sister in junior high."

Bruno sometimes used Shawndra Coleman when making out of town pick ups. She would travel down south with him to see one of his connects and he would then send her back by herself on a plane, greyhound, train, or rental car. Most of the time she carried a duffle bag full of heroin, for heroin is were Bruno got majority of his money from. This was something he never revealed to Cleofis, all Cleofis knew was his cousin carried a lot of weight on the cocaine side.

Bruno would pay Shawndra well for the risky trips she made, furnishing her apartment with expensive furniture, paying her rent months in advance, buying her a brand new Neon and showering her little daughter with gifts. But she wasn't just his runner, they'd also knew each other from his involvements with her sister. Bruno and Shawndra called each other brother and sister. And Bruno held a great deal of respect for her, she was trustworthy, didn't run her mouth, and was a down ass chick. Cleofis had never seen her with him before but that didn't matter Bruno was known for keeping substantial people on the low.

Bruno hopped back in the car and threw a wad of cash on the back seat. "That's four-fifty cuz that should be enough to get you some clothes and shoes."

Cleofis hit the weed slowly and put the knot in his pocket. "Good looking out, I sure needed it."

"No problem little cuz we still family no matter what happened, I still got love fo' ya."

Cleofis felt the high kicking-in when he thought, *'What if this nigga put somethin' on this weed to get me fucked up so he can take me somewhere?'* Getting slightly paranoid he spoke mercifully. "Man cuz I was on some wild shit, I just blacked-out I wasn't even thinking, when you kicked my ass I lost it."

Bruno chuckled like a wolf in sheep's clothing. "It's all good, gangstas react, then think later. That's all you was doing, 'cause it's in your bloodline. But me, I'm a gangsta that'll think, then react more vicious than Al Capone. You have to be a thinker out here in these streets. So what you want to do now that you out?"

Cleofis coughed, clearing the herb out his throat, then tapped Bruno on the shoulder, and when he turned around said, "Get rich and never stop till I do, matter fact I'm out here till I get a million."

Bruno turned towards Shawndra and smiled. "At least he wants more than these niggas on the block."

Returning back to Kim's house Cleofis instructed her it was time to go to bed. Kim's bedroom was now in the basement, she'd moved down there for more privacy. With three rooms upstairs and one room downstairs, she declined the downstairs room because of no door. The basement was carpeted, clean and had a spare bathroom.

Cleofis was now high as a kite and was anxious to go for round two in the bedroom as he guided Kim down to his front telling her to go slow. Kim looked up at him with a requesting look before blurting. "Let me know when you getting ready to….."

"Ok damn! I know just don't stop…..shit girl you wasn't doing it this good before I left."

The great sensation made him wonder in the back of his head was she doing this to somebody else while he was incarcerated, but the pleasure soon soothed his thoughts.

Cleofis woke up in the middle of the night. His bladder felt like it was about to burst and Kim's snoring irritated the hell out of him. Strolling up the basement stairs he heard moans and semi-strong breathing. He felt he'd use the bathroom up stairs to check on Kim's guests and his. To his discovery, Berry was butt naked with a pair of legs on his shoulders, with his back turned towards him stroking in and out of one of Kim's underage cousins on the couch. He noticed the other cousin was sleep on the hard cold floor. "Fuck me Berry, fuck me!" Kim's little cousin moaned as Cleofis crept closer for a better look. The two didn't even notice him stroll past them to the bathroom.

Unzipping his zipper he laughed to himself, '*Homeboy in there killing that pussy, that little girl must got some fire*'. Trying his best not to pee in the water, only on the sides, he crept out the bathroom, driven by curiosity and aroused by the noise. "You got room for two little girl?" The two jumped up, covering themselves. "Homeboy you think she can handle both of us?"

Berry, relieved that it was Cleofis talking and not Kim exclaimed, "I don't know? Ask her?" he replied, as he tried to catch his breath.

Dropping his already undone pants, Cleofis moved in closer and whispered, "I will tell Kim if you don't."

When Cleofis started to stroke the little girl, Berry got impatient. "Damn CJ, you just gonna take the pussy from me, huh?!" After seeing Cleofis was ignoring him he climbed further up on the couch and proceeded to get lower body treatment. The little girl had her hands full with the two, being that she had never 'tossed' before, this was a new experience. Their wish was her command as she indulged out of fear that Cleofis would tell Kim and it would get back to her mother.

The next morning Cleofis was out and about in Bruno's Cadillac Deville. Bruno requested he take the car to go shopping. The grey leather interior felt relaxing as he bumped the latest Scarface CD, hearing, "I never seen a man cry tell I seen a man die", gave him an instant rush, a feeling like he was ready to harm someone.

Passing by his house he noticed Gabe leaving the premises. "Hop in little homie", he insisted. Gabe was still in shock of his change to another organization. "What's up pancake?" Gabe jokingly replied getting in the Deville. "Bruno let you push his ride hu?"

Cleofis giggled phony. "Yeah…..little nigga you gonna stop it with the pancake shit fo' I beat yo' ass. You my little homey but I'll fuck you up if I have too."

Gabe looked out the window and said, "Shhhhhiiit, nigga please."

Cleofis was thrilled at the sixteen year old barking, but felt he wouldn't bite if in a tough situation. He respected the fact Gabe wouldn't never backed down from him in a tongue battle, but felt he wasn't taking the hustle game serious at the time. He often was bothered by Gabe when it came down to hustling 'cause Gabe hustled his own way and Cleofis wanted it his way. This would lead to a tug-of-war, where both would eventually drop the rope and go the other way displeased that the other wouldn't give.

Cleofis parked at a K's Merchandise store where they sat in the car riffing for a minute.

"Me and Berry tossed the hell out these girls the last night! I'm still drained from the shit, this little bitch was taking dick like a pro." Cleofis exaggerated about two girls. "I tell you boy! I'm fucking everything that move."

"I wish you would have come and got me, I could have showed ya'll some things."

Bruno blew air though his lips. It ain't nuttin' you can show me, I been fuckin' ever since I was two." Gabe laughed at the statement while Cleofis continued while exiting the car. "They said I wouldn't live to see eighteen little homie", sniffing in the fresh air, Cleofis continued. "But I made it. I'm here -- ain't nothing they can do to stop me."

Upon entering the store they went straight to the back where the gun section was. Browsing at the collection of fire arms through the glass, you could hear Cleofis' excitement. "All these motherfuckers raw! But if I had to go with two I would probably say the gray knee knocker and the black knee knocker." Knee knocker meaning, nine millimeter automatic.

"That gray one is raw", exclaimed Gabe, "I'd love to have one of them."

"You can have one if you hustle hard like me and get you somebody with a gun card to get you one."

"Whatever nigga, I hustle hard. I could buy one right now."

"Uhmmmm, sure you can", Cleofis responded with laughter.

CHAPTER 9

Manipulation, Murder and Money

The scent from the blunt was unusual to Gabe, watching Cleofis blow out a small cloud with one hand on the steering wheel. Disco and JW was accompanied in the back seat of the eighty four Malibu, as they cruised passed the south side bridge at night. The Kankakee River that glittered with golden yellow streaks from the lights up above, and stank bad from the fish smell, made Cleofis feel there was no place like home. The crossing of the train above the viaduct they went under, blew a loud horn that spread throughout the south side.

It was roughly spring time and Cleofis already copped him a Malibu from a local drug dealer who lost it in a dice game. The Malibu was nothing to brag about, green and very ugly. He felt the Malibu was a step towards a dream car. Cleofis was getting back on his feet thanks to Bruno. He was in charge of a dope house on one of the Cartel blocks that Bruno stopped by every other day to collect from. The cool air blew through the vents form the outside due to the no heat in the car. "Man it's getting chilly in this motherfucker", replied Disco, "You need to get yo' heat fixed CJ."

"Nigga as fat as you is, you should neva get cold, you big ass grizzly bear", Cleofis responded. The whole car chuckled except for Disco who didn't find it a bit funny.

"Nigga I ain't all that fat", Disco exclaimed while Cleofis passed the blunt to the back seat.

"Why the fuck, Gabe ain't 'chiefing', that nigga always acting like a square."

"Nigga I ain't no motherfuckin' square, I'm just cool that's all", Gabe exclaimed.

Gabe didn't smoke weed, cigarettes, or drink like the rest of the crew. He learned at an early age his body had a low tolerance and wouldn't take a chance of being out of his state of mind. Gabe could hear JW inhaling the weed deeply when asking, "What kind of green is that? That shit smell different." Cleofis looked at Gabe and blurted, "That's hash little homie, it ain't that much of a difference." Cleofis didn't smoke and drink as much as the people he kept around him. He liked to be sober a lot so he could observe the people around him, watching their every move. When the blunt was basically gone Cleofis yelled, "Ya'll some stupid motherfuckers I ain't smoke none of that shit, I fooled ya'll dumb asses."

"What this fool talking about?", JW said, tapping Disco on the leg, Disco couldn't even respond because of the high, "What I'm saying is I never inhaled that shit, I was just faking you niggas out, 'cause I knew y'all smoke it if I did. I'm surprised you dumb niggas couldn't tell, nigga I wasn't fenna to smoke no hash."

The two was so high, all you could hear was mumbles, "You wild….. I'mma stop messing with you", JW managed to get out a few words. Cleofis laughed continuously taking his hands off the wheel to clap, very amused by what he'd done. Gabe tried not to laugh but was sucked in by Cleofis tapping him on the arm saying, "Them some stupid ass niggas, them niggas gonna be dope fiends one day… they always tryin' to do what I do."

Cleofis enjoyed pushing people to see how far they would go, and then make a fool of them. Master at instigating he could be a real shit starter at times, this would sometimes quench his thirst to see violence.

Bruno's four unit apartment building was located on the south side needed its grass cut badly, Cleofis thought, walking up to the building. Gabe was waiting in the car patiently for his return.

"Looks like that grass needs to be cut", Cleofis insisted while Bruno shut the door behind him. Walking more into the luxury furnished apartment his eyebrows rose when seeing the seven individual kilos of coke on the table. "One of them niggas outside was supposed to cut the grass yesterday, I'mma stop payin' them little niggas in advance", Bruno barked. "I bet you ain't neva seen this much work in yo' life." Cleofis looking dumb founded replied, "Shiiiit, what's them bricks?"

"Yeah little nigga, seven barely cut bricks, and don't tell nobody you seen this shit either."

"Oooh, cuz you know I don't run my mouth like that", Cleofis explained when Bruno took a seat from Shawndra who was focused on the Oprah show. "Hey Shawndra. What's up?"

"Nothing", she replied, "Just watching this show about these poor people in Africa on Oprah. I was telling Bruno just the other day that y'all more like brothers then cousins."

"Yeah, right", Bruno responded, "that little nigga ugly, he don't look nothin' like me."

"Don't say that, dude not ugly, don't talk about yo' cousin like that."

"I don't pay the nigga no neva mind Shawndra, 'cause he always talking shit."

"I heard you been into it with those Latin Kings over there", Bruno replied, "Leave them crazy Mexicans alone, before you start some shit."

"They the ones been fuckin' with us, I didn't say shit to them Mexicans. Every time they ride by, they throw up gang signs and shit."

"Them the ones that stay around the corner now, huh?"

"Yeah, and every since they moved around the corner from the Cartels they been starting shit with everybody."

"Well I'm probably gonna have to swing through there and holla at them Kings, 'cause they ain't fenna bring that bullshit in our neighborhood. On the other hand I should let them get yo' ass fo' flipping Blackstone", Bruno continued jokingly, looking in Shawndra's direction. "This nigga been GD since I could remember then he gonna go to the joint and flip."

Shawndra declined to laugh at Bruno's clowning session, as he stuck his hand under the couch to retrieve a brown paper bag filled with powered coke to give to Cleofis.

"Now that should be six ounces, remember to only put a quad on each one. Bring my fedi off top, and if you have any problems cookin' it, call my cell phone."

Cleofis caught the bag as it was thrown to him saying to himself, *"This nigga always trying to front when somebody around. He wouldn't even have no bitches if it wasn't for his money. Clown ass nigga, he wasn't talking shit when I shot his mark ass in the chest. I would've killed his punk ass if the gun didn't jam."*

Cleofis was leaving out the door when Bruno yelled, "When you get on little cuz, get you some real estate. It don't cost that much to invest, when I get the rest of this cheese this nigga owe me I'mma buy another four unit building. And another thing don't get the real estate in yo' name, later cuz."

Cleofis shut the door and breezed down the stairs, angered by Bruno's statement he wondered about Shawndra. *"I wonder if he hittin' that 'cause she don't neva act like the other chicks I see him with. They talking that brother and sister shit, he probably is hittin' that. That chick bad, if I had her I'd settle down and stop cheating, I see how she be looking at me, I'mma get her one day"*, he thought to himself.

Shawndra Coleman bore a brownie like complexioned skin tone, 5"8 about one-hundred and sixty pounds. She was twenty four years old at the time, very thick, but stout young lady. Beautiful big brown eyes, a mediocre strand of black shoulder length hair, skin a little rough for a woman, and she wore inexpensive clothes from K-Mart or Wal-Mart.

The Malibu passed loudly through the gritty north side streets. It needed a new muffler and because of the noise this was a dangerous move when traveling with six ounces of powder coke. The chances of them being pulled over were high, but Cleofis didn't care. They drove to a north side house where Bruno's trusty chef, Bones greeted them with open arms. Bruno let the chef know they were on the way and advised him to be ready to cook.

Taking the melted down coke out the microwave then pouring it on a cutting board where they hit it with an ounce and a half of baking soda was the goal. The chef whipped the melted coke with a wooden soup spoon while Cleofis watched like a father when his child is being born, excited by the smell, turned on by the creamy cake like batter. Gabe sat wondrously in the other room as he watched Cleofis from a distance seem to reach an orgasm as the dope hardened into a thick vanilla shaped cookie. It was one problem, when they weighed the cocaine, it didn't weigh what was expected, Cleofis then called Bruno to notify him of the shortage and with the chef witnessing the shortage. Bruno lowered the front price of what he wanted back. Cleofis sold Gabe a nice little bit for the money he had. He dropped him off and headed to the Cartels.

After chopping the coke up in twenty sacks, Cleofis distributed it amongst his friends and some of the teens on the block. Cleofis would often stop and converse with the only white family in the neighborhood, which consisted of a mother and her two sons. The oldest son sold drugs and would occasionally purchase them from Cleofis. The young son was only eight years old and was just as bad as the black kids in the area. Little Toby would be out at night riding raggedy big wheel up and down the block.

Finally, after beefing back and fourth with each other, Cleofis wanted to prove a point to the Latin Kings. He had it up to here with their disrespect, including the rest of his friends. It had rained before dusk, the moisture brought in a visionless fog, where you couldn't see anything but what was right in front of you. Cleofis charged by the opportunity to creep the Mexicans, wore a wool hoodie with the hood over his head tightly and clutched an automatic pistol in the sweater pocket. Hopping on a youngster's mountain bike, Cleofis peddled gently by his self as he neared the corner where the Latin Kings were. The fog made Cleofis feel invisible and he was in a sense until he was right up on you. He could see the headlights of a car backing into the

Mexicans driveway. His hand twitched and he started to have second thoughts before pulling out blasting but his will to destroy somebody took over. "Fuck it", he said, pointed the gun in the direction of the car he heard Mexicans exiting and squeezed the trigger. Buck! Buck! Buck! You could hear the Mexicans running for cover. Cleofis let three more shots go before disappearing into the fog.

As he got further down the block he could hear the Mexicans returning shots and speaking in a non English language. Cleofis peddled faster hurrying back to safety it was an exciting moment until hearing the sound of the artillery they had. "What the hell they shooting at, sounding that damn loud. I would sure hate to get hit by whatever that is", Cleofis reflected, riding faster.

Little Toby was dead -- it spread like wildfire threw out the city. All the local dealers knew of the little white boy that hung around the little black kids. Toby just happened to be riding the big wheel up and down the street when a bullet struck him in the chest. What a shame, Cleofis didn't even have knowledge of the news yet. Off into a deep sleep on his living room couch Bruno banged on the front door until Mrs. Jackson let him in. "What's wrong Bruno is everything ok?" she asked. Bruno couldn't look her in the eye when he uttered. "Everything's fine Auntie, just need to talk to CJ real quick"

"Ok nephew I'll be back in the room if you need anything" she said with a smile.

After hearing Mrs. Jackson close her bedroom door, Bruno smacked Cleofis in the jaw. "Wake up killa, you got yo' self in some shit now!"

Cleofis instantly rose up with his hand cocked back ready to swing until acknowledging who it was. "What the hell wrong with you hitting me that hard?"

"Little Toby dead cuz…motherfuckas saying he got killed last night. And the Mexicans saying they didn't do it, who ever was shooting at them musta hit the little white boy and niggaz on the Cartels already spitting yo' name out their mouth. But I covered fo' you I said you was with me last night. Some niggaz saying they seen you on a bike though."

"It wasn't me 'cause I don't even have a bike."

"Don't lie to me, because I already did my best to cover for you, so yo' best bet is to give me that pistol you used so I can get rid if it. The way people talking right now 5-0 might want to question you and you need to be trying to come up with a story."

"What could I say?", Cleofis said worriedly but seeming like he'd not yet grasped the fact that he killed an eight year old boy on accident. "It was an accident I didn't see any kids out side, it was to foggy fo' anybody to be outside all I was trying to do was tag one of them Kings."

"Shhhhhh", Bruno exclaimed. "Keep yo' voice down you know auntie got satellite dishes fo' ears." Bruno then sat down right next to him on the couch. "What the fuck was you thinking? I told you to leave them Mexicans alone but you neva listen. Know look at this shit, they not gonna let this rest till they find out who did it and it was a little white boy too, pissssssss", he blew through his teeth. "Them detectives' fenna turn them Cartels up side down till they find some answers."

"What should I do, leave town, hide out, WHAT?!"

"Who all know you did this shit?"

"Disc, Disco the one I was with before I jumped on the bike to go over there."

"Well cuff Disco, keep him close to you don't let him out yo' sight, make him spend a night, every night if you got too. Continue to go out and about like nothing happened, don't hide out 'cause then them niggas gonna know fo' sho you did it. Matter of a fact, I'm fenna to go snatch Disco up right now, and bring him to you, sit tight I'll be right back."

Bruno came back fast with Disco and had spoke with him on the way over there about keeping his mouth shut. They sat him down, questioned him about who he'd spoke with about the incident, but Disco swore no one. Disco suggested people only assumed it was Cleofis 'cause how he would go off the rocket when the Kings drove by disrespecting. Disco also insisted nobody on the Cartels had been questioned about the murder, the Mexicans didn't know who was shooting at them and if they did know something they wouldn't say. Bruno replied very harsh and simple, "If I find out you ran yo' mouth I'mma kill you, and if I can't get you I'll get the closest thing to you."

This remark had Disco's fat pudgy face, shook up. He was shaking so badly, he couldn't even stand still.

Later that day the Mexicans moved out the area realizing somebody wasn't playing with them, and also 'cause of the heat from the authorities. The authorities never questioned anybody off the Cartels. They figured it was the Kings rival the Satan Disciples. Cleofis made Disco stick to him like glue, not wanting to take a chance of him straying away, and gossiping amongst friends. Cleofis thought to himself, *"I should just kill this nigga, 'cause like Bruno said if they snatch him up all he got to do is say my name and I'm outta here. I do got love fo' this nigga, we do go back far, but I'll knock his shit back if I have too"*

Disco stuck to Cleofis for a month, this is when Cleofis started to case up. Always making Disco spend a night at his house or telling Disco he'd spend a night at his house also. This bought the two closer together, Cleofis even manipulated Disco to steal from his uncle who was a dealer.

"Man go on and take the shit, next time you go back over there, if he find out so what, I'll get Bruno to holla at em, Disco gone and get the shit so we can get out on the block and dump it before the night over with." Cleofis talked him into it and didn't mind the fact Disco would be betraying his uncle. Cleofis didn't care, all he seen was dollar signs.

On several occasions he'd manipulate his friends, even his cousin James Wells. "Take that weed from yo' brotha he won't do shit, plus you know I'll have Bruno talk to him if he trip. The nigga don't give a fuck about you, the nigga will buy them bitches shoes before buying you a pair, and yo' shoes talking, they so old. Leave the door open I'll get the motherfucker myself", Cleofis said.

With Cliff, "You say yo' step-pops got money in the bank right? Then if he do, then take his safe, the money he got in the bank a cover that. Shit, you know how much we could do with that fedi boy! I'll be able to put you on, the right way."

With James Love, "I was always a Stone in my heart nigga, I just was misguided as a youngster, but me and you with that change yo' parents got, you outta let me hold you fo' ransom, make them pay a hundred thousand and go get us some work and take over this town, you say they don't help you right?"

With Gabe, "Yo' brother in law, I know he got some fedi, or some yack. Next time you see something with yo' own two eyes, page me and I'll come through and stick both ya'll up. Then we'll split it once you get from around the nigga."

With Berry, "I'll kill Gabe sister and her kids, nigga I don't give a fuck. If I go in that house and she don't want to tell me where that fedi, I'll kill everybody. You feel me nigga, 'cause you gonna come with me if I go."

Cleofis tried to manipulate everybody he could, most fell for it but the one's who was strong minded would refuse his offers. To get to the top Gabe was one of them, who didn't believe in betraying his loved ones, or betraying anybody for that fact. Gabe believed in, *'y'all leave me alone, I'll leave y'all alone, don't cross me and I won't cross you'*. Gabe was a man's man, is what they call it in the mafia, meaning honorable man of his word. A man you could trust, one who was dependable, and most of all a man who wasn't a snitch. Not necessarily thorough like De Niro, in Heat but trusted like Meyer Lansky to Lucky Luciano.

Gabe liked Cleofis aggressiveness, determination and his hustling mentality. Cleofis could take nothing and make it into something, make the impossible possible. But Gabe also thought Cleofis was to demanding, to loud talking, too controlling and too flossy. Especially in possession of a large amount of money. Gabe didn't want the shine, he wanted the money and to play the back field while getting it. Berry, James, JW, Cliff, and Disco all wanted whatever Cleofis wanted. Cleofis recognized that Gabe couldn't be dominated at a young age. Even though Gabe breezed around him Cleofis couldn't treat him less than a man or disrespect him, and not expect to get disrespected back, but that didn't stop Cleofis from trying.

Cleofis hated the independency of Gabe, the leadership he had, and the fact he wasn't dependent upon him like the others. Gabe would refuse the help and neva really liked to be fronted cocaine, if he couldn't buy it with some money, Majority of the time he'd wait 'til came across some.

Cleofis and James (Jack Pot) Love was becoming more in tune with each other, considering Cleofis changed to Jackpot's organization. Jack Pot had money and Cleofis liked him around, plus a lot of girls were attracted to the handsome drug dealer. Once on the verge of letting his crew stick him up, Cleofis now used Jackpot for more recognition in the drug trade. Jack Pot enjoyed the attention that came from Cleofis, and would scoop him up in his drop top Mustang randomly.

Gabe was the coolest one out the crew, Disco and JW was the bark but barely bite type of niggas, Cliff was the quiet one, Berry was the down for whatever one, Jack Pot was the scared one and Cleofis was the grimy one.

The Cartels was dumping normally, and Cleofis was still in charge of a crack house for Bruno. This is where he made Bruno's money and his own, along with lucrative schemes on the side. What ever the crew would come up with, from sheistyness, Cleofis would sell first before making Bruno's money, which was something Bruno was well aware of, but said nothing about. Bruno wanted Cleofis to handle some business on the dog food side, meaning heroin, but wasn't dumb by far and was very intellectual, street wise, and could be as nice as he wanted too, with intentions on killing you. Cleofis didn't know he was playing chess with a master and Bruno, had his way with a valuable piece.

'If shorty could only be straight up with me, I'll put him on his feet, so he wouldn't have to be in the Cartels', Bruno thought. Missing his home town Chicago, where they operated out of buildings instead of streets and houses all claimed in around each other. Bruno really didn't need the money from Kankakee, even though it did come in handy, especially his heroine spots on the south side. He sometimes would travel getting rid of his dog food, and yack in other cities. Milwaukee, Rockford, Joliet, Gary, Chicago, Aurora, St Louis, Bloomington, and Chicago Heights were just some of the places he made moves in. He would usually save the left-overs for small Kankakee, not wanting to turn his back on the dealers that was in his family, who would always have sob stories about losing money to a variety of things. Yack was another meaning for cocaine but sometimes used as the meaning for a certain brand of liquor.

Cleofis was pissed because Bruno gave the ok for an out-of-towner to do business out of the same house. The out-of-towner named Muddy was black and crisp, with clean white teeth that would be the only thing you could locate him by in the dark. He had low cut nappy hair and wasn't even as tall as Cleofis. Muddy was from Chicago with a jazzy mouth piece, he was in debt to some dealers up north and fled down to Kankakee in search of Bruno. Bruno extended his hand to help Muddy to pay his debt by letting him sell the coke he came down with, then re-copping from him for a helpful price. Muddy was very grateful, but looked at Cleofis and his crew like they were new-comers, feeling like his way of hustling was more superb, and he had tried to speak to Cleofis as if he was a silly little kid.

Muddy was no older than Bruno, with a very thin figure, known to the streets as toss around weight, no more than one hundred pounds. He flashed his money frequently throughout the day. Cleofis was tired of his bragging and most of all, his mouth. Muddy would politely insult them saying, "You slow ass niggas down here got it made and I like this spot ya'll keep, this looking fairly straight compared to where I come from." Cleofis would smirk and shake his hand a little mumbling, "Ohhh if this nigga don't stop with that slow callin' shit, I'mma rob his bitch ass, and tell him to go tell Bruno that."

Plus Muddy was taking from Cleofis' money from the side, always cock blocking on the routine sells, and the bigger Muddy's wad of cash got, the more Cleofis wanted it for himself. Cleofis was starting to hate the sight of the black crispy man.

The crack house was two stories with a basement for the trusted smokers. The downstairs was filthy. The carpet was cruddy, with a bunch of spots from spills, dog piss, and moist dirt. Three bedrooms, small kitchen, small bathroom, small living room, and the couches smelled like ass, orange, yellow, and very decrepit. They were probably made in the early eighties or late seventies.

The mice would come out and play as if this was their home. Nothing was ever in the refrigerator, aside from liquor or pop. The two rooms downstairs were empty, except for the one that had a spot stained mattress on the floor. The twelve inch TV in the living room was ancient and barely kept a picture. They would have to dangle a close hanger that replaced the antenna. Who knew what color the carpet originally was? The basement floor was covered with wet spots, mildew, and feces from the dogs down there. Cleofis had set up a bunch of cheap chairs for the smokers.

The upstairs was Cleofis' domain which he kept clean, with only one room upstairs along with the only bathroom in the house, the upstairs was like a suite compared to the rest of the house. Containing a queen sized waterbed, nicely quilted covers, thirty-two inch modern TV with entertainment center including VCR and stereo. The bathroom was usually clean and decorated in red thanks to the hood rats he kept in and out the house. If caught with hood rats coming out the house he would rapidly reply. "They're here for the guys."

This particular night Kim was upstairs with Cleofis. Muddy and another dealer name Marvin was downstairs along with Berry, Disco, and JW. Marvin was basically unliked, just like Muddy. Marvin was average height for a man, ashy dark skin and had a slow right eye.

Kim, laying under the covers with a tee shirt and some of Cleofis boxers on, complained about the condition of the house. "CJ, you need to make them niggaz clean up down stairs, how could a person even conduct business down there with that smell, let alone sit on them nasty ass couches, them friends of yours down there is nasty…ugh! It makes me want to throw up every time I come downstairs."

Cleofis, sitting with a three day worn Polo outfit on at the edge of the bed trying to adjust the VCR to play Menace to Society, was irritated by the comment. "What the hell do you expect it to look like down there, this a feinds get high spot, them niggaz don't care how this house look as long as they get paper they cool."

"Well make one of them feinds clean up for some work, or something 'cause I'm tired of coming over here with it looking like this and smellin' like that."

"A'ight boss lady I'll have somebody take care of it first thing in the morning so shut your trap and take a nap."

When Menace to Society went off Kim was out like a light, and Cleofis couldn't hear any movement downstairs so he went to investigate. Everybody was asleep on the nasty couches. Half of them had their mouths hanging open like they wanted something to crawl down their throats. Berry was sitting on the floor with his back to the side of the couch and his arms in the sleeves of a Texas Long Horns pull over coat. Look at this sleeping beauty, he reflected. Disco, JW, Marvin and Muddy were all crashed on the couch. It was a lady feind knocked out in the room with the stained mattress. Nobody was in the basement except for the dog, and Cleofis now stood over Muddy watching him sleep like there was no tomorrow. I bet this nigga got some fedi stuffed down in them shit stained draws of his, I should teach this nigga a lesson about that smart mouth of his. I'mma kill this ugly motherfucka. At that thought he headed to the kitchen retrieving a very thick garbage bag. He paused for a minute while looking at the black crispy man with his head hanging off the arm of the couch sound a sleep. Owww this motherfucka ugly! He positioned the garbage bag to smother him. Wanting to know how long it would take him to stop breathing he wondered, *"It shouldn't take him that long to stop breathing once this bag is over his face...I'm a turn this TV up a little just in case he get loud. Cleofis continued to think while kneeling down on one knee beside Muddy's head. If he breaks out my hold I'll tell him I was just playing, what the fuck can he do"*

Cleofis swiftly covered Muddy's face with the garbage bag squeezing harder like a python every time Muddy took a breath. "Uh huh let me hear that mouth now", he savagely whispered. Muddy yelled but the sound was snuffed out by the thick black bag.

Muddy grabbed Cleofis' shirt after reaching for his face. Gripping for his life, you would probably have to pry his hands loose. With Muddy gasping for air Cleofis pulled with all his strength with his hands crossed over each other clutching the ends of the garbage bag in an X shape. Watching Muddy's legs kick their last kicks he spoke in another evil whisper, "Die motherfucka die." He was having flash backs of the man who was dying from a cut throat in the alley next to Ben's. This made his grip even tighter as Muddy hyperventilated rapidly then slowly into a non breathing state.

Not sure if Muddy was dead when he stopped moving, he squeezed a little longer to make sure the suffocation was properly done. With every vein in his body popping out including the ones in his head, the hate he possessed for this man turned him into a vicious monster with his heart racing fast. He looked and felt possessed by a super natural being as he sat on the floor breathing like a devilish beast. If anybody who was sleep had woken up at this moment, the very sight of Cleofis would have frightened them into a terrifying death.

"Get your ass up", he spoke with a stern voice kicking Berry in the leg.

Berry opened his pretty girl eyes, "What nigga?!"

"Help me carry this nigga outta here befo' somebody wake up?"

Cleofis had already gone in Muddy's drawers, stole his cash and stuffed in his pockets. While doing this, he came to the conclusion that he wanted to drag the body to the dumpster in the alley and burn it, hopefully into nothing but ashes.

"What the fuck you talking about? What nigga?", asked Berry.

"Jus get cho' ass up and help me, and hurry up?!" Cleofis riffed as Berry hopped up. "Go get a couple sheets out that closet in there."

They wrapped Muddy's lifeless corpse up into several bed sheets and drug him out the back door heading to the dumpster in the alley. "Make it look like we carrying some old clothes", exclaimed Cleofis. He looked around cautiously, as they neared the dumpster. Berry started to panic, "What if somebody see us?" Cleofis struggled to get Muddy's upper body higher into the air. "Nigga just help me put him in here I'll take care of the rest."

The sound of the body hitting garbage bags in the dumpster sent chills down Berry's spine. Returning into the house he watched as his friend grab gasoline from the basement and raced back outside.

It was like Cleofis could feel every drop that came out the gas can, moving very fast he accidentally dropped the can in the dumpster. Damn …..Oh well the can, can burn with the nigga. Lighting the match was becoming a hard job as it seem like none of the matches were any good. Down to his last few the spark finally turned to fire and he dropped the match on the gasoline doused corpse.

Cleofis jetted back in the house, then Berry announced that he was going home. He tried to convince him to reconsider, but his mind was made up. "Go on home then pussy, but you better not tell a soul. Promise me you'll keep this to yourself 'cause people are gonna wanna know what happened to dude when they can't find him."

Cleofis thought that by setting the body on fire it would burn to ashes. He never stopped to think that somebody would call the police about the smoking dumpster.

Cleofis built up the courage to go upstairs and try to go to sleep like nothing ever happened. His body was tired but his mind was thinking about the consequences of getting caught. He looked like a zombie on the edge of the bed trying to make himself believe he was dreaming. Finally after fighting to stay awake from paranoia, his upper body collapsed onto the cold surface of the water bed. It was only a dream, it was only a dream, it was…only…a…dream.

Awakening to Kim's concerned voice. "CJ get up, CJ get up I think somebody dead in the dumpster, police all over the place in the back." He felt like he'd only closed his eyes for a second. Unconsciously he still felt like it was a dream, gliding out the bed strolling down the stairs followed by Kim. "What is you talking about Kim, who in the dumpster and where?"

"Look out the back window you'll see!"

Cleofis looked out the back window in surprise of the large crowd of people in the alley with homicide detectives, police, and the coroner. Everybody that slept in the house was outside.

"Shhheeiiit what's going on out there? I see everybody and they Momma outside somebody must be dead."

Pacing out the back door he strutted to the crime scene. Trying to break through the crowd he looked Disco's way. "What the hell going on out here?"

"Somebody in there, they say they burnt so bad they don't know who the nigga is."

"Damn, somebody in the dumpster." Memories from what happened last night came to him, though he was still in belief that it was all a dream as he stepped under the orange crime scene tape.

"Who's in there?", he asked a detective by the name of Diamond.

"I don't know you tell us", Diamond replied. "Nobody seems to know who he is, why don't you take a look if you got a strong stomach, but I warn you it's not a pretty sight."

As Cleofis approached the dumpster the flashbacks became more vivid. The burning smell made him hold his breath as he stood on his tippy toes to view the body. Closing his eyes shut tightly, then opening them, reality hit him like a head on collision. "That's Muddy", he said in a low shaken up tone.

"Who did you say that was?"

Cleofis hesitated to repeat those words again. "That's…Muddy!"

Detective Diamond took out a hand sized tablet and jotted the name down, "Muddy who? What's his real name?"

"I don't know", Cleofis explained feeling like all eyes were on him. "I neva knew his real name."

Cleofis felt like vomiting not just at the sight but 'cause he was at the scene of a murder that he now came to terms that wasn't a dream, he really killed Muddy. He felt like he was in a momentary spell when Detective Diamond asked, "What's your name fella… You hear me what's your name?"

"CJ", he uttered, before saying, "I got to go I'm getting sick."

The white clean cut detective took a mental picture of his disturbed face before he walked off. The corpse was a gruesome repulsive sight that many wouldn't have the stomach for, and could spoil a person's appetite for a week. Diamond wondered how could anybody tell so quickly who the corpse was. "It got to be a connection", he said to himself.

Kim was standing in the back door way waiting for Cleofis to return into the house.

"Baby what's going on, why that white man was all in your face?"

"I don't know, they was asking me did I know Muddy's real name."

"That's Muddy in that dumpster?" She asked frightfully.

"Yeah that who it look like to me."

"Stop lying CJ, he was just in here last night. You're scaring me baby are you for real?"

"Quit acting stupid! Do it look like I'm joking?"

Some days went by, Cleofis got the word from Bruno that the Detectives wanted to question him about Muddy's gruesome murder. They had already questioned Disco and JW. And were now looking to question him, Kim, Marvin, Berry and the drug addict lady whose name the house was being rented in.

Cleofis paced back and forth while Kim sat in a chair at his house going over what to say when being interrogated.

"Look Kim fo' the last time, tell them pigs you got out the bed and went to go get something to drink out the refrigerator, then you seen Marvin carrying something that looked like sheets out the back door."

"But I didn't see him carrying anything at all I was sleep, CJ you want me to get in trouble?"

Cleofis rubbed his temples with his hand. "If you would just listen to me with yo' silly ass, I'm trying to tell you if you don't do this fo' me they gonna try to lock me up."

He had already paid the drug addict to say she seen Marvin dragging something wrapped up in some sheets out the back door and he knew with Kim saying she seen almost the same thing that would bake the cake. And when they questioned him he would say, "I could feel the cool breeze from the back door upstairs when it shut", then put the icing on the cake by saying Kim told him what she saw when climbing back in the bed with him.

Det. Diamond was not pleased with Cleofis' half way cooperation during questioning, Diamond wondered why he wouldn't sign a sworn statement, and they'd already picked up Marvin for the murder, compliments of his two allies. But they had everybody's statement in the house except his. Cleofis' hostility made him a prime suspect in Diamonds eyes.

"Am I free to go 'cause I already told you I ain't signing shit."

"Ok Mr. Jackson you're free to go but don't stray too far now?" Det. Diamond insisted.

Bruno had advised Cleofis if anybody knew him and Muddy was beefin' with each other he'd be the prime suspect. If it wasn't known to everybody that they didn't get along he would have kept his mouth shut and advised the same for Kim. But he was panic stricken, and conjured the first eluding story that came to his head.

"Motherfuckaz betta quit putting my name in that shit!" Cleofis shouted, standing on the sidewalk in the Cartels. Some hood rats was gossiping when he over heard them saying his name in connection to the Muddy murder. Gabe stood on the side of him pondering about what the hood rats was chit-chatting about.

"What the hell they yapping about CJ?"

"Man some 'ol bullshit, niggaz gonna quit saying I had something to do with that!"

"Watchu talking about?"

"That's dumpster shit with Muddy, motherfuckaz trying to say I helped Marvin do that shit?"

"Fa real?"

"Yeah I'm fo' real. Motherfuckaz should know I ain't that evil, Marvin killed the man, then set his body on fire, I don't get down like that. I was knocked out when Kim woke me with the shit so how did I have something to do with it."

Cleofis strolled down to the end of the corner speaking back and forth with Gabe. He had bought an Orlando Magic bubble inflated pullover coat, a bunch of Polo gear and another knee knocker to replace the one he accidentally shot the little white boy Toby with. All these purchases came from the money out of Muddy's drawers, the rest went to Kim to put up. He knew Kim had a guilty conscious, he wondered how could she hold her water about accusing an innocent man. But the fact that she really didn't know who did it, but suspected Cleofis had something to do with it, relieved the egg shaped head villain.

Bruno pulled up in a black Grand Am. "Get yo' famous ass in the car", he barked.

"I ain't famous nigga, if anybody famous it's you", Cleofis began as he shut the car door. "I'm tired of selling bags I want to sell weight."

"You ain't gonna be selling shit if you keep up the stupid shit, 'cause I know you had something to do with that dumpster shit and what the fuck was yo' reason behind it, I don't know. The streets is talking, you better watch yourself Muddy's family called me asking me to find out who killed him, they want some answers they want revenge. Slow yo' roll young nigga 'cause ain't too many real niggaz out here in the field, most of 'em dead or locked up. I'm the last gangsterfied ass nigga left in this city that got weight, all the rest of them niggaz is bitches they only slang to who they not scared of and most of 'em wont sell you shit unless it's day time. So if something happens to me the niggaz that's gangsterfied won't eat unless they go to Chicago."

"Fuck that nigga family if they come down here I'm ready fo' war."

"Little cuz, you ain't neva been to war, war is dangerous 'cause not only you got to watch ya back from niggaz why you getting fedi but you gotta watch out fo' 5-0!"

"Man! Forget the police ain't nobody stopping me."

"Well check this out killa, I got a lick fo' you but you got to do it exactly how I tell you, No fuck ups. It's this nigga that owes me some change in Chicago, I'm fenna go see 'em soon if he ain't got my change I want you to tear the nigga off and I know where he keep his stash at."

"How much he owe you?"

"Fifty stacks. Now listen you must be super careful 'cause this nigga got power."

"You know I'm with whatever cuz, but who is the nigga?"

"It's best you don't know, but this lick will put you exactly where you want to be. You'll be a six figure nigga but you got to be focused 'cause this nigga won't stop till he kill you. And he got a lot of niggaz under his chain of command, so if I give you the go ahead don't fuck this up."

"Damn! He must be a hellafied nigga, I'm wit'chu cuz and that's till the death."

Bruno knew by now that Cleofis was officially a loose cannon and probably thought of him as the right man for the job.

In more days to come Cleofis had influenced his whole crew to flip Blackstone all except for Gabe who angrily replied. "If you don't get the hell out my face with that bullshit, I'm GD or nothing you pancake." Cleofis would laugh Gabe's out burst saying, "You still my homey no matter what nation you is so ain't no need to yell lil' homey." He kinda respected Gabe's loyalty to his organization and never lost a day of sleep over his decision.

Kim was reading the Kankakee Daily Journal when Cleofis walked in. Bruno was outside waiting for him to fetch some cash from the stash spot.

"What you doing reading the paper didn't I tell you about being nosy?"

"We need to talk CJ and I mean now. Come down to the basement 'cause my father's upstairs."

Following Kim to the basement he was irritated when he began. "What is it now and grab that change out that stash so I can give it to this nigga outside."

"Look at today's paper CJ."

He glanced at the paper saw Marvin's name charged with Muddy's murder then threw the paper back in her face. "So what the fuck you showing me that shit fo'? The nigga did it, so what's the fuck to talk about."

"What if he didn't do it CJ, what if I sent an innocent man to jail, it could have been Berry, he's the one who left."

He grabbed her by the throat swiftly. "Shut the fuck up about that shit, Berry didn't do it. Marvin did it and if they want you to come to court just repeat what you said in your statement", he loosened up on her neck. "Look baby this is important you must keep everything we talk about to yo'self nobody can ever know that you lied or they'll try to put that shit on me."

"But why CJ…why would they think you did it?", she questioned with water in her eyes.

"Look I don't got time for this, get that change so I can bounce I'll holla at you tonight", kissing her on the cheek, his last words before leaving was. "Trust me your doing the right thing."

Berry was on the Cartels when Cleofis got dropped off he stayed away from the blocks since that murderous night.

"Who was that Bruno that just dropped you off?"

"Yeah I paid him off, so everything I make now is mine shit! I'm tired of pushing these bags."

"You know I'll help you with whatever!"

"Nigga only thing you'll help me do is lose some mo fedi, you wouldn't be able to stay on yo' feet if you was born on them silly ass nigga", he continued. "And that dirt we did them pigs probably gonna question us again so tell me exactly what you told 'em nah."

"I told you all I told em, was that everybody was sleep when I left. Then he got to talking about this crack spot shit and some other bullshit about how they know we all sell yack out the house. I told the man we don't sell drugs then the mark just laughed at me."

"Well they think Marvin did the shit fo' some reason so fuck it if they don't ask nuttin else about it then just forget about it."

"Man! I ain't gonna lie I just been able to get a whole nights rest. What about you?"

"I slept good, that nigga wasn't my homey so fuck that loud mouth Chicago nigga."

The following Sunday Cleofis and Berry had just arrived in Maywood, a suburb of the Westside of Chicago. The weather was shitty in the middle of May. Kind of windy on the ride up north in Shawndra's Neon that blew with the wind. Bruno recruited the car for Cleofis and supplied them with a cell phone to wait on his call. Cleofis live wire friend tucked a baby knee knocker in some hidden compartment on the passenger side door. They did a hundred all the way there eager for the lick, Bruno was now positioning him to do in case of excuses for no payment from an unknown person with power.

Bruno and the cronies of his cruised around the Westside of Chicago while Cleofis and Berry waited in a middle class neighborhood in Maywood down the street from the home of the target. Bruno had instructed them that the target stayed with his wife in a middle class Maywood neighborhood, if he gave them the ok. They was supposed to knock on the door, portray them selves as religious people, then when she opened the door, tie her up and ransack the garage where the stash of drugs was at. They both were clean cut casually dressed with a bible on hand, they'd done everything Bruno advised them to do. Bruno knew the wife went to church faithfully and would open her door to young men posing like religious prospects. But as Cleofis sat waiting on Bruno's call he remembered. Shawndra got some spark plugs in her glove compartment. I could probably break the window without anybody hearing it and just sneak in the garage. He looked at Berry. "Give me them spark plugs we saw in the glove compartment.....break 'em up into little pieces 'cause we might can just sneak in the garage without the bitch even noticing we in there."

"What, you don't want to try the religious trick?"

"We can, but why tie her up and take the shit if we don't have to. The garage ain't attached to the house, it ain't like she gonna hear us, fo' all we know the bitch could have company."

"But didn't you say Bruno said don't nobody be at this house but dude and the bitch?"

"Yeah, but fuck what Bruno said he ain't the one taking the risk feel me?"

"Yeah, I feel you, it's whatever with me you know I'm with it."

Thirty minutes flew passed and the duo's patience was running thin. The neighbors were starting to observe the two sitting doing nothing and Cleofis feared that sooner or later they'd call the police. The house they were watching was two stories of wealth with a three car garage and very neatly cut lawn.

"Whoever dis cat is, he got some fedi just look at the house."

"It is raw how much you think he paid fo' it?"

"Some hundreds of thousands just look at the neighborhood its beautiful around here, who ever he is he probably got more change than cuz."

"You really think so, shit I don't know if he got mo change then yo' cousin how much change you think yo' cousin got?"

"Put it like this nigga I seen him with ten bricks and 200 stacks one time", Cleofis exaggerated before seeing a tall petite lady dressed in a business suit step out the targets door.

"I ain't got to see that bitch up close to tell she bad", said Berry.

Cleofis was pumped and ready for the lick speaking more, he complained, "I wish this nigga hurry up and call so we can know something."

The garage door went up and the wife backed out in a tan colored Jaguar.

RING! RING! RING!...RING! RING! RING!

"Yeah."

"Take care of that now and be careful!"

"Aight later."

This was the call they were looking for as he watched the wife pass them glancing into the Neon. "Fuck! The bitch is leaving", Berry yelled. "What the hell we suppose to do, just break in, in this neighborhood?"

"Nigga I'm a do it, just watch my back and hand me them broken up spark plugs." Cleofis growled as he pulled in the drive way. "Give me that bible and that pistol I'mma see if somebody there first."

Walking up to the front door of the house like it was nothing, he was concealing his nervousness good from Berry. What if some niggaz in here or what if it's a big ass dog in here? Ringing the door bell for the third time he got no answer. He turned and looked at Berry giving him the eye meaning watch my back I'm going to the garage.

Cleofis just couldn't stop staring at the size of the house. He knew it was better not to look suspicious so he had to be quick. Breaking windows with broken up pieces of spark plugs was something they did as kids when breaking into cars to steal. Spark plugs lowered the sound to almost nothing when shattering a window.

Cleofis cracked the only window to the garage and gracefully pushed it in. Throwing the Bible and the pistol through the window, he slid his short bulky body in, almost hitting his head on the concrete floor. To his finding was a gray older model station wagon, he looked around with his hands on the trigger and his eyes bucked for a minute. *Dang this a big garage.* His eyes scowered it from top to bottom. The garage was empty besides the station wagon and some cardboard boxes. Cleofis knew he didn't have all the time in the world so he went through the boxes quick, threw a broken piece of spark plug at the Station Wagons driver side window, pushed the cracked glass in like the garage window, unlocked the door, pressed the trunk switch when entering the car, and went through the inside of the car before checking the trunk.

Moving his way to the trunk, two big blue bulging duffle bags sat there all alone, nothing else in the trunk but them. Oh shit I think I found the stash. He unzipped one bag and was immediately hit by the raw powdered cocaine smell. Opening the bag more his eyes filled with excitement. Shhhhhhit cuz wasn't lying.

Cleofis didn't even check the other bag, he zipped the first up and headed for the cleanly broken out garage window with both bags. He thought he was dreaming when he first open the bag filled with ten kilos of raw coke. Not knowing how many was in each bag, just anxious to get off the premises, he picked up both bags after throwing them through the window before himself. Berry quickly opened the trunk of the Neon so Cleofis could load the bags in when all of a sudden the wife was turning on to the street and zoomed behind the two, blocking them in with her Jaguar.

Cleofis had to think fast. *'Ahhh shit this bitch blocking our way out'*, he thought about ramming the Jaguar with the back of the Neon, but came up with a better plan while listening to the woman yell out her rolled down window on the cell phone calling her husband.

Closing the back door to the Neon, Cleofis obtained the baby nine out of his pocket pointed in her direction and barked. "Move bitch before I kill you", she pulled up so they could back out. "Don't shoot that lady", Berry requested with nervousness in his voice. The wife made a U-turn in the yard and began to follow them in Neon. "If this bitch keep following me I'm gonna kill her", said Cleofis then without a thought the Neon halted, he opened the driver's-side door let off a couple shots and sped off being no longer pursued by the wife.

"You think you hit her?"

"I don't know, but fuck it, she ain't following us no mo'."

Getting back to Kankakee was a sigh of relief for both of them always feeling like somebody was following them on the highway and thinking the light of day they would never see of being pulled over by law enforcement had them on the edge of their seats. They went straight to Cleofis' house from the highway.

Coming through the side door followed by Berry he was glad Mother Jackson and his brother was still at church. .

"Open them bags up Joe"

Joe was another meaning for homey or homeboy.

"Hold yo' horses let me make sure nobody here." Cleofis checked the house then returned to the living room were Berry had dumped the two bags onto the floor.

"Damn nigga you mo' impatient den me."

"Look at this shit, we fenna ball 'til we fall."

"Nigga you only getting what I give you it ain't like you did shit, plus I gotta give Bruno his cut before anything."

All together it was fifteen kilos of raw coke and five kilos of heroin. But the two didn't know what the heroin was that was wrapped in aluminum foil individual wrapping. The fifteen kilos looked just like the ones Bruno had on his table they were barely cut, Cleofis could tell by the thickness and the overwhelming smell it was some of the best powdered coke money could buy. He heard Bruno speak about how they use a mix to put on powdered cocaine to make it more when it hardens. The only mix he heard of was baking soda but had made up in his head that this was the mix Bruno was talking about.

"What the hell is this shit that's in these foil thangs?"

"I think it's that mix Bruno was telling me about, we'll just put that shit to the side, matter of a fact, we gonna tell him we hit fo' 5-keys of coke and 5-keys of this mix shit and stash the rest."

"You gonna stash ten bricks! What if yo' cuz find out?"

"He won't motherfucka if we keep our mouths closed", he barked with his eyes full of greed. "Plus he don't know what was in there all he know is some shit there."

"So how much can them bricks be sold for?"

"I think I heard Bruno say twenty-seven… twenty- eight stacks one time, but I'll find out exactly."

"Look at all this shit", Berry screamed joyously. "You gonna be a rich nigga, you better hit me with some of this shit."

Trying not to show his erupting excitement Cleofis replied. "I got you just be cool and keep yo' mouth closed. We gonna have to be as smart as can be, that nigga Bruno knows everybody, so we gonna have to be super careful, feel me?"

"I feel ya, but where you gonna hide all this shit at?"

The cell phone rang, it was Bruno calling to check on the two. "Put them ten back in the bag take them to Kim and tell her to put the bag up. Here go the keys hurry up and go 'cause this Bruno calling right now. And come straight back", said Cleofis before answering the cell phone.

"Yeah what's up?"

"Y'all cool, y'all made it back safe?"

"Yeah we cool man stop by here and check these ten thangs out", he was lying through his teeth.

Bruno cut him off before he could say anything else. "Don't talk like that over the phone you forgot what I taught you, now just be cool, I'm on my way through there and don't touch shit."

Cleofis let Bruno through the front door saying to himself. *Shit! I told Berry to come straight back.* Before Bruno could say anything Cleofis spoke about the aluminum sealed wrappings.

"What's this shit, that mix you was telling me about?"

Bruno opened the middle one that was already cut open a little bit. This some motherfuckin' dog food. He said to himself. This little nigga don't even know what this is…I'mma just tell him its some bullshit mix.

"That's some mix little cuz, that bullshit they put on yack." The lie came out so natural. "Give 'em to me and I'll get what I can fo' em." Bruno looked Cleofis in the eye to see if he'd take the bait that he unconsciously put on the reel himself.

"Go on 'head cuz, how much you think we can get fo' em?" Cleofis asked. "And what about these five bricks."

Bruno glanced at the five bricks of coke and because of the value, he knew what the heroin was worth, he almost told him he could have all five bricks. "Give me all this shit I'm a cook it up give you two and half bricks and give you half of whatever I make out of the bullshit mix. You cool with that?"

"Yeah I'm cool with that", he said naively. "But how long it's gonna take you?"

"Nigga I'm fenna to take care of that right now." Bruno headed for the door with one of the blue duffle bags.

"Ohhhh, I forgot to tell you I might have shot that bitch."

"What Bitch?"

"His wife or whoever that lady was who tried to block us in."

"Well if you did then fuck it, the nigga shouldn't been holding out on me anyway, if you done did his wife he done took two loses that mean I'm one up the nigga", Bruno laughed monstrously. "That's a beautiful thing…where is Shawndra's Neon now?" He stood halfway in the screen door.

"Oh Berry went to go scoop Disco up, I told 'em to bring his ass straight back."

"Well when he get back park that car and don't drive it no more, chill out fo' a minute I'll be straight over here when I get done. Oh! And good job lil cuz you fenna be on ya feet."

Tuesday afternoon Cleofis and Kim sat down counting cash on Kim's full sized bed. This was Kim's graduation day, she wouldn't walk the stage until later in the evening.

"Nine hundred and sixty, nine hundred and eighty… a thousand, baby what are you gonna do with all this money?" Kim asked while putting the thousand next to the already counted thousands. "This eleven thousand dollars you got here and I know it's more to come."

"I don't know yet, but I'mma keep putting this change up till I come up with something."

"So what am I getting fo' my graduation day?"

"Shit! Kim you barely even made it", he said jokingly. "As much as you used to skip school, but I'm proud of you girl. Here take this stack."

"CJ you fo' real you givin' me this thousand dollars for my graduation?"

"Yeah you better hurry up and spend it fo' I change my mind and take it back."

Kim hugged him tightly around the neck and kissed his lips. "Thank you baby, I love you so so much!"

Cleofis felt good about giving her the thousand dollars knowing in his head that it was much more to come. He gave Berry nine ounces and told him to do what he wanted with it, Berry complained for more but realizing he's never had nine ounces before stifled everything.

The ten-kilos was still in Kim's possession in the other blue duffle bag, under her bed in her basement room. Cleofis sold some weight to get the quick eleven thousand he'd just counted with Kim. He still had a key load and twenty-seven ounces left from the two and a half bricks hard, Bruno cooked up and gave to him. It had been two days and Bruno gave him no word on the heroin he thought was bullshit mix. Cleofis put the thought in the back of his head. I don't care cuz can have that bullshit mix even though he probably made some fedi off it.

Cleofis' plan now was to sell the rest of his hard cocaine in twenty dollar bags and try to sell as less weight as possible. Twenty dollar bags would see to him getting every penny off the cocaine making sure they were super big to kill the competition would work. But all them twenties would take a lot of patience in this small city. He had given very good deals to fatten his pockets with the eleven, but now ten-thousand due to his gift to Kim. He'd brought the latest pager and cell phone from the mall.

A red Ralph Lauren Polo tee shirt with black Ralph Lauren jeans along with black and red Jordan's was what Cleofis sported, running into a beautiful mixed girl at a Dairy Queen on the eastside. She was Vietnamese and black with a buttermilk radiant smooth skin tone favoring Catherine Zeta Jones a little bit in the face, cute baby like dimples hazel brown eyes and sandy brown curly baby doll hair. She had her hair pulled back in a pony-tail held together by a pink scrunchy with the baby doll side burns showing. Her body was a little over petite about an inch taller then Cleofis wearing pink polyester and cotton shorts meeting half way between her knee and thigh with a matching short sleeve shirt. She wore no make-up just natural beauty and the baby oil on her flesh glistened making her look tempting to any man like a ripe apple greeted by the early morning sun. Pink and white Reeboks with ankle cut socks, gold ankle bracelet, a gold wrist bracelet, and a small gold chain with a half of a heart-charm emblem. Her shorts hugged her rear end showing you her panty line. Cleofis almost crashed in traffic trying to pull in the parking lot craving to introduce himself to this particularly materialistic Pocahontas.

She paid for her ice cream then returned to a white ninety-five, Infinity Q45 that he coincidentally parked next to. In his muffler roaring Malibu, this young lady was undeniably gorgeous.

With a streak of confidence he spoke, "Excuse me Miss, but I couldn't help but notice you have all that ice cream and none for me."

She had a senseless look on her face when she said. "I don't even know you so what I look like buying you some ice cream?"

Watching her bend over to put the ice cream in her car he thought to himself, *Damn!*, before replying, "You could get to know me if you not scared of a hustler baby, by the way what's your name?"

"The names Angie, but I'm not interested in getting to know any hustlers."

"Well Miss Angie, they call me CJ and any and everything you do fo' money is a hustle. You must not be from around here 'cause I never seen you before and if I would have, I'd surely remember."

Angie felt like he was a nerd trying to be down. She nearly laughed in his face when he spoke about hustling more then likely she felt he was a wanna-be. Putting her seat belt on, she explained. "No, I'm not from around here. I'm from Wisconsin. I'm just here for the summer helping my aunt out." Getting a better look at him she realized he wasn't her type as she tried to end the conversation. "Look I don't want this ice cream to melt before I get to where I'm going, so I guess I have to go."

"Well why don't you take down my cell phone number and give me a call if you want"

Angie grabbed a pen and searched her glove compartment for a piece of paper not wanting to be mean she quickly took his number down then started to back out.

"Who let you drive their car?", yelled Cleofis out the window.

"Nobody! This my car", replied Angie, pulling out then pulling off.

Cleofis was glad she was gone because he didn't want her to know that was his car with the loud noise from needing a muffler.

CHAPTER 10

June

Three times the Fun. Three times the Action. Three times the worry.

Cleofis could hear the wave's splash up against the shore from the passing boat while pulling into the Riverview High-rise apartments in his silver ninety-five BMW 740i Sedan. He purchased the silver over black leather luxury heated-seat vehicle from one of Bruno's Chicago buddies for 25,000 in cash. He fell in love with the car the moment he'd saw it and made the Chicagoan a cash-for-car-and-title offer. He still had plenty cocaine left and hadn't touched the 10 kilos under Kim's bed yet. The BMW was in Kim's name which was a big mistake when you are not being faithful to the woman you're in a relationship with.

Angie had called Cleofis a couple of weeks ago because she was bored. She thought she'd tossed his number in the garbage but discovered it in her car before cleaning it out. Cleofis had come to the conclusion that she wasn't going to call him and had almost forgotten about her before receiving the call. Angie didn't think a short phone call would lead to a long interesting conversation. She liked his personality and they would speak frequently throughout the two weeks until she finally invited him to her aunts top floor apartment at the Riverview High Rises on the south side. The high rises gave an incredible view of the Southside River brushing up against the back yards of middle class houses at night. The building stood clear over the trees right at the edge of the Kankakee River. Cleofis hadn't yet seen the view that would make him feel so on top of the world.

Just stepping out the car the night air comforted him immediately. Browsing around the parking lot looking for familiar cars before noticing Angie at the front entrance preparing to let him in the double doors, Cleofis felt subdued knowing he rarely seen anybody around the high-rises when passing them by vehicle.

The Riverview High-rises was a retirement home for old folks like Angie's auntie, she'd come from Green Bay, Wisconsin to help out.

Cleofis hit the alarm on his car before stepping into the clean old folks smelling building were the air conditioners hummed the same tune hanging out a multitude of windows.

"Hey, how you doing I'm glad you was waiting' fo' me 'cause I forgot what number you told me to press."

"Hmmm so that's your car you in huh?"

"Yeah, I told you I brought me a BMW, you must didn't believe me."

"Oh I believed you, I just didn't think it was like my fathers, my father has one just like it."

"Is that right, yo' father must got some taste", he replied as he stepped off the elevator at the top floor following behind Angie.

Angie was wearing some plaid pajama pants small white tee shirt and some yellow tweedy bird houses shoes. Her mother and father were surgeons in Green Bay, Wisconsin. Oldest out of three kids she was still spoiled by her father, who brought her everything she wanted. She came from a very wealthy family and had a very good heart always willing to help somebody.

Eighteen years old on her way to a university college after summer, she was also anxious to take a breather from her cheating college basketball star boyfriend.

A very intelligent and game conscious lady she loved her boyfriend who she gave her virginity to but was fed up with his cheating. Even though she was in Kankakee to help her aunt, she was hurt and vulnerable and Cleofis was the only man she gotten to know since she'd been in Kankakee. She had a couple male cousins that showed her how to get to the grocery stores around the city but for the most part she rarely left her sick auntie since she'd been there.

Cleofis followed her through the small apartment and on to the balcony where she arranged two lawn chairs with table. He couldn't help but step to the edge, grab the rail and with no fear of heights rest the upper part of his body on it. Being at the very top of the high-rise on the balcony he gazed at the moon, stars and the river down below. The river seemed to sparkle at his presence. Feeling like he was on top of the world for a minute he was high off the no limitations he planned to go through to accomplish millionaire status.

The view took him to his own little world, perfectly sober he felt like he could fly wondering what was his destiny on earth, Angie startled him.

"Pretty nice view huh?"

Turning his head to the right his shoulder covered his face from the nose down. "Yeah I didn't think this small city could have such a nice view from up here at night" he was being himself around her but controlled his filthy mouth in awareness for the young manner-able lady. She's got to be one of the baddest bitches I done seen. He snapped out of his momentarily day dream. "Where's yo' auntie?"

"She's in her room sleep I just checked on her."

Cleofis turned around and leaned up against the sturdy rail facing her. "I don't mean to meddle in yo' business, but I don't see how any man could cheat on a pretty thing like you." Angie blushed a little as he tried to dazzle her with his compliments. "If you was mine I'll treat you like a princess."

"I have my father to do that and besides, I'm not looking to be in a relationship with anyone at this moment. I wouldn't have a problem with being friends with you 'cause you seem like a cool guy."

"All you got to do is give me a chance Angie and I'll change yo' mind."

"Anything's possible but I'm still in love with my ex and when I get over him I don't think I'll be getting involved with anyone else like that again."

"Maybe you right baby girl but to me it's worth a shot."

Cleofis didn't want this gorgeous young lady to know he dropped out of high school his freshmen year so he lied to her about that and a few other things while stretched across the lawn chair, feeling like an untouchable hustler.

Meanwhile Bruno's toes curled from the enjoyable blow job he was receiving from Cleofis' girlfriend Kim. He had sexed her many times when Cleofis was in prison feeling like it was partial payback for the bullet in his chest. Showering her with money until she gave him the sex, Kim had it bad for Bruno after the first episode and he would be the one to teach her how to satisfy a man orally.

With his seat reclined in a white and black Jeep Grand Cherokee he guided her head up and down. The no teeth feeling on top of the sound had him close to a climax within minutes. Kim used no hands throughout the majority of the process, she knew he was about to burst when the grip he had on the back of her head got tighter. "Don't stop" he moaned, bursting like a pipe, she gagged momentarily leaving none to drip or leak. "Shhhhit Kim" he replied softly as she sat up straight and rested her body in the seat with a smirk on her face very proud of the job she had done parked in the back alley of her house. While performing the job she would often look up not knowing when Cleofis may pop up, this started to irritate Bruno, that's why he guided her head hindering her chances to take a peek.

A few minutes flew by, Bruno then tried to slick Kim out some information, he had already slicked info out her before with out her even conscience of his game. He knew just how to play her because she felt she had game. He would tamper with her mental wounds from the dirt Cleofis done to her, cunning her out of everything while still making her feel intelligent. This was one of the rawest ways to slick somebody out info by making yourself seem slow and making them seem smart.

"Lil' cuz been taking care of you, he got yo' ass spoiled rotten, that nigga must got a lot of fedi now huh?"

"Well you know he got the game from you, that motherfuckaz pockets be fat, I don't know where he get all that cheese from?" Kim was lying through her teeth about not knowing where the money came from, but Bruno figured she was anyway and played along.

"How much cheese the lil nigga be getting 'cause I'm probably gonna have him invest in this real estate I'm fenna buy." Bruno was also lying threw his teeth he'd just felt Cleofis had held out on him from the lick and wanted to know if there was more.

"I helped the nigga count forty stacks before he bought that BMW that's in my name, and that motherfucker still got some work." Kim ran her mouth some more as Bruno studied everything coming out of her mouth, separating the truth from the lies.

"I love CJ, but he's a dog ass nigga, and I hear and see too many things, until he's faithful to me, I'mma do what I wanna do." Bruno's stocky body slumped over to look for his loud ringing cell phone, as he listened to Kim's last statement before finding it, he chuckled to himself, "with his little dick ass", she ended.

"Hello!"

"Yeah, what's up cuz, this me, you in town or you m-i-a?"

"I'm m-i-a", Bruno lied to Cleofis, "I'll probably be back in the morning, what's up with you."

"Shit, over this bad bitch crib, just stepped back in her spot fo' a second, but cuz this bitch here, nigga you'll go crazy if you see her."

Kim could hear Cleofis voice but couldn't make out everything he was saying to Bruno, knowing Kim could probably hear Cleofis, Bruno pushed the phone up closer to his brown face.

"I'm tryin' to crack this bitch."

Kim could hear Cleofis clear as day now, but she said nothing, she opened Bruno's pants back and started slobbing his manhood again, making it firm while moaning a little on purpose, hoping Cleofis noticed her moan.

"Damn cuz, that bitch sound familiar that I hear in the back ground, who is that?"

Bruno couldn't really speak as Kim tried her best to deep throat him, "Na'll… cuz… you… don't know her."

"Oh nigga you must be getting yo' dick sucked", replied Cleofis, Kim's face flashed through his head but he shook it out quickly, convinced Bruno was out of town sexin' some chick he'd never seen before. Bruno heard about the loss from fellow buddies out of Chicago. Speaking on more then what Cleofis returned from the lick with. He figured Cleofis pulled more of the lick than what was split, but had no proof. Bruno already had slicked Cleofis out of the extremely profitable heroin, but wanted more if there was more. Kim spoke reckless but never mentioned the ten bricks that rested under her bed.

Bruno was salty, Cleofis wasn't depending upon him like usual but briefly came to the assumption of Cleofis falling off his feet, and then resorting to him for a jump start. Kim was so pissed by Cleofis on the phone she offered to blow Bruno all night, he declined after his second climax, which took a whole hour to accomplish.

Bruno rolled down the window so they could get some fresh air, the moisture form their body motion seemed to dry up, when greeted by the night air. They both took a breather said a few words to each other, then departed.

Kim's tired body and throat floated in her house wondering what chick Cleofis was trying to sleep with. It crossed Kim's mind to do quite a few things with the ten bricks after hearing Cleofis unfaithfulness over the eaves dropping ear, but slowly forgot about it as she fell into a routine coma like sleep.

Cleofis and Disco bopped their heads slowly, to the Isley Brothers that played in Ben's Tavern. Seated off in the cut the disco lights along with a drink of Courvoisier made Cleofis valor to dance with the fully grown. Mirrors flooded the walls of the dance floor, and the cut up brown leather on the top of the stools emerged as grown folk got up from the bar to dance. Cleofis gave Ben a crispy hundred dollar bill, when entering with Disco, Ben was becoming prone to Cleofis' late night visits and gave him the red carpet treatment. Ben had a dark complexion, with gray hair sticking from the sides of his baseball cap. He had an average size frame, except for a massive beer belly, enjoyed seeing the under aged young man have a good time, plus the extra money didn't hurt. The wooden dance floor was unpolished and the thick faded black carpet at the bar was begging for a cleaning, snapping his fingers, moving to the rhythm Cleofis was determining which solo grown woman he'd grind on the dance floor. When he told a little white lie, "Remember that chick Angie, I was telling you about, that's my bitch now."

Disco's fat face jiggled, while he was worn out from a much needed rest. "Nigga pleeeease, you know Kim ain't having that shit."

Angie was not Cleofis bitch, but Cleofis was determined to make her his and didn't mind convincing other people that she was. Disco hadn't even seen her yet, but already had a well painted picture of her in his mental from Cleofis.

"Kim's yo' bitch! And she yacks all the time about if she can't have you no one can. Plus the bitch been tellin people ya'll gone have a baby."

"Get the fuck outta hear 'moe', that bitch on the shot, and I'm the one who take her to her appointments, so the only way she gonna get pregnant is if I tell her not to take the shot, and I'm not fenna to just leave the bitch alone, but she got one more chance to fuck up.

Disco looked at the glossiness in Cleofis eyes, from the tipsiness. Lifted his drink off the table and drifted it over to meet Cleofis glass. He cheered him and responded sarcastically, "What ever you say 'moe'."

Moe was a term Blackstone's used to embrace each other, a term that was frequently said in a conversation between Blackstone, but could also be used by a person greeting a Blackstone. Oh well moe, twenty of 'em moe, or stone run it was some of the expressions used when they carried themselves with pride, and drowned themselves with dignity.

Cleofis spotted a woman in her middle thirties with a wide, but not overly sized ass, her dancing reminded him of a penguin of some sort, her face was full and round, and her lips regularly pointed out in a kissing shape, she wasn't far from dark skinned, her hair was cut low on the sides, and slicked back all together, made her face seem bigger than what it really was. The full figured woman motioned for Cleofis to join her on the dance floor as she brought her rump down to the ground and back into the air rump first.

In a very suave way, Cleofis two stepped his way towards her joining her with a clap, and a spin, feeling very pimpish about himself he spoke boastfully, "How does it feel to be in the presence of a young rich nigga." She gave him an invitation for seduction with her eyes then turned around and backed her rump up on him not saying a word to Cleofis, but he could tell she loved every minute of him grinding her from the back and front as if they were having sex on the dance floor.

Disco watched in fascination at his egg-headed big nose short friend he just couldn't get over how grown he acted carrying himself like a mid-30's adult and the adults treated him like a mid-thirties adult. Disco was mature for his age but was no different from your average 18-year old street hustler mind. Disco knew Cleofis was a leader and he was ready to follow him all the way to the top. Feeling like Cleofis did whatever he wanted when he wanted and nothing ever happened to him made him a firm believer in his friend's choices.

"Fuck!", Cleofis yelled. "Watch them teeth baby girl", the penguin shaped woman released his man hood out of her mouth and said "I'm sorry it won't happen again." Cleofis pushed her head back towards his waist. "Just keep going baby girl you fuckin' up the mood."

Disco sat in the back seat of the black leather plush interior of the BMW tripping off his friend while watching him ride around being pleased by a mid thirties women he'd just met in Ben's. He just couldn't believe how his friend could spot the promiscuous in a woman old enough to be his mother and bring it out of her within minutes. Maybe it was the BMW or the fresh new garment. *'Cause it definitely wasn't the looks,* Disco thought in the back seat to himself while getting aroused by the sucking sloppy sound.

"Want some pussy?" Cleofis asked Disco directly then tapped the lady on her shoulder and said. "You don't mind if my homey get a crack at that, do ya?" She popped Cleofis man-hood out of her mouth like a blow pop before saying. "One at a time sweetheart yo' friend will get his chance."

Disco didn't know his friend was paying for the pleasure Cleofis made it seem like she was doing him off his reputation. When pulling into Cleofis driveway the round faced lady jumped in the back seat and started taking Disco's pants down while he got out the car and went into the house to grab some cocaine for a sale he forget about.

Retrieving the cocaine from his bedroom Cleofis stopped in his mother's room before leaving out slipping a wad of twenties into her purse for some brand new furniture he heard his mother telling a friend she wanted. Mrs. Jackson always refused the drug money but after he left her no choice she would shamefully take it finding it hard to turn such a large amount of money down repeatedly.

Returning outside Cleofis could see nothing in his car for the window was all fogged up from the sex. The back window rolled down and Disco threw out a semen filled condom. "What the fuck?" he yelled, going around to open the driver's-side door. "You better get out here and pick that shit up nigga, my momma gotta go to work in the morning" Disco opened the back door sweating' like an NBA basketball player and breathing like a winning track star. "Calm down moe I'm fenna get it" reaching down to pick up the condom Disco was heavily embarrassed when Cleofis screamed. "Man what the hell is that smell, my fuckin' car smell like ass you motherfuckaz is nasty y'all gotta walk fo' that shit." Disco thought he was playing, until he gave him a look that could stop a horse in its tracks. "I mean it, both of y'all get the fuck outta here now!" Disco and the penguin shaped lady mumbled several curse words as they got out and closed the doors and began to walk to a destination.

The beginning of the next day was drama for Bruno. Kim left a pair of her panties in his girlfriend Shanice's Jeep Cherokee on purpose. Stupid bitch Bruno reflected on the night before while listening to Shanice complain. "Lying ass dog these ain't my panties, so what bitch you had in my truck last night, huh Bruno you hear me talking to you?"

Shanice was his main squeeze and though he had a lot of women, she was the one he truly loved. And anybody with sight could see why, she was a light skinned fashion statement very pretty. Bruno laced her with everything she wanted. Knowing it was about due for him to spend some of his massive amount of cash from the lucrative heroin trafficking. He walked calmly out of her house as she continued yelling about the panties and called Cleofis on the cell phone.

"What's up lil' cuz were you at?"

"About to pull up in front of Kim's crib and see what the fuck she want."

"Clear yo' day out, bring that little bad bitch you was talking about and let's go shopping in downtown Chicago today."

"That sounds cool I'm sure ol' girl'll be down. Man! Cuz I was over her spot last night and I didn't even know them high-rises had such a raw view of the Southside"

"Nigga that ain't shit I'mma show you some places in the city that's gonna blow you and that chick minds. So bring some doe cuz we gonna have us a ball."

Cleofis ended the call strolling into Kim's house. "What the fuck you want girl, paging me 911 why you didn't just call me on the cell phone"

Kim looked down at her feet shaking her head wanting to say something about the conversation she heard but would never be able to explain being around Bruno that time of the night. "I just missed you that's all…come get in the bed with me let's take a nap"

Cleofis slightly serious replied. "Girl it's to early in the day fo' that nap shit plus its fedi to be made."

Cleofis figured Kim wanted some sex so they tongue-kissed their way to her bedroom in the basement were they had hot sweaty sex for a half an hour. Laying naked under Kim's sheets he requested, "Go get me a drink of water boo I'm thirsty and see if y'all got some snacks too." While she was upstairs he noticed her small phone book slide half way from up under her bed anticipating on looking through the little book he came to a quick decision. Flipping through the book he seen a lot of nameless numbers one in particular stood out, Bruno's pager and cell phone number which was also nameless.

What the hell is this niggaz number doing in her phone book, nasty bitch probably fuckin' him. I should ask her about the shit but fuck it I'm tired of this hoe anyway.

He questioned her about the numbers but after she gave the explanation that was expected he said very little. The first thought was to beat her but for some odd reason he turned the other cheek figuring he had no proof. That voice he'd heard over the phone with Bruno last night sounded so much like Kim's. *I wonder was that her.*

He thought, leaving her house then stopping over Travis townhouse that was on the Southside.

Travis was a tear off artist, coke cooker, gun and bullet proof vest seller. He was the type of person who would study drug dealers' everyday movements, and when the opportunity presented itself Travis would break into where ever their stash was at. Cleofis knew the banana complexioned tall figure from Bruno. But Bruno no longer dealt with Travis because of his back stabbing ways. Cleofis low on cocaine needed somebody that would cook a couple keys of the powdered coke and keep it out of the detection of Bruno. Travis had some how got a hold to two knee knockers with the twist, meaning silencer. Cleofis was determined to make a deal for the two weapons, never seeing a gun with the twist on it ever before except for in the movies made the items seem essential to him. Willing to pay anything Travis wanted, they struck a deal for the two weapons including a bullet proof vest for a fronted half a brick of powder coke which Travis would have to pay a little over 75% back. Cleofis didn't want to front this much coke out, but Travis begged to be put back on his feet and Cleofis wanted the two knee knockers with the twist more then anything. Travis would also be obligated to cook Cleofis coke for free. They slapped hands as he assured him his return would be short.

"Don't be all day", said Travis.

"I won't, just don't sell them straps", replied Cleofis.

Cleofis was on his way to Shanice's house to meet Bruno accompanied by Angie that he convinced to come to Chicago after a variety of refusals. He had already taken care of his business with Travis and stashed one on of the weapons under the passenger seat Angie rested against. He had filled a brown paper bag with cash and gave it to Angie to put in her purse.

The AC was damn near putting Angie to sleep when they heard the siren of a police car behind them demanding them to pull over. It was Sergeant Fox the head of the Kankakee metro enforcement group a task force made specifically for the drug dealers in the small city. Fox was a white prejudice, racial profiling low down dirty metro police officer who abused his authority every chance he got. The task force mostly rode around in a jet black Crown Victoria with tint on all the windows. The six foot slim very hairy, similar to Wolverine looking officer had a chip on his shoulder. He was very dedicated and divorced three times do to his first love which was his job. Fox who really looked like X-Men's Wolverine in the face, usually kept his long dirty beer smelling hair in a pony tail. And his long beard was a part of his psychotic look. He'd adapted the name Fox from his glowing dark fox eyes and uncanny sense of the right time to catch a dealer with a bundle of drugs.

With no probable cause other than rumors and being black in a last year model BMW, Fox approached the luxury vehicle with his right hand on his pistol and other hand motioning for the driver side window to come down.

"License and registration please?"

"I don't got a license, but she does", he pointed to Angie. "I got insurance though!"

"What's your name and birth date?"

"Cleofis Jackson, I'll be nineteen at the end of the year."

"Cleofis Jackson…I finally get the pleasure of meeting you, could you step out the car for me please?" He stepped out the car as Fox continued "Is your license suspended Mr. Jackson?"

"No I just never went to get em."

"Step to the back of your car, put your hands on your hood and spread your legs", he did what Fox ask while praying he didn't want to search the car and find the mag with the twist under Angie's seat. "Anything in the car like weapons or drugs Cleofis?"

Cleofis took a hard swallow before uttering "No sir."

"You've seem to make a pretty big name for yourself at a young age Mr. Jackson." He spun him around after overly fondling his crotch, looked him square in the eyes and asked, "Tell me the truth, is there anything in that car before I search it because if I go in there and find anything I'm a make sure you get the maximum punishment for whatever it is."

"I told you sir there's nothing in the car." Cleofis expressed with a convincing face.

Back in the car Angie's heart was beating fast as she said silent prayers after discovering the nose of the mag coming from under her seat. She gracefully pushed it back under the best she could with her ankles praying that it didn't go off.

Cleofis returned to the car with a warning for having no license not knowing that he not only was relieved, but Angie was relieved as well to know Fox was just bluffing about the search.

"Why do you have that big old gun under my seat?", she asked as they pulled off.

"Oh I'm sorry about that", he could see the uncomfortable look on her face. "That's somebody else's."

"Well can you get it from under my seat please?"

He reached down under her seat grabbed the weapon and put it under his seat. "That gun is not coming with us is it?"

"Naw girl, we jumping in the car with my cousin, that's staying in here."

"I hope that's not your cousin's gun that were about to go to Chicago with is it."

"No Angie its not, don't worry everything will be alright!"

Angie somehow believed Cleofis because even though she knew he was a hustler she never thought he could be the bang bang shoot 'em up type of guy. He had a way of presenting himself nicely around the naked eye to many he wouldn't harm a fly and was nothing more then a warm hearted loving person.

"Damn!" Cleofis honestly replied entering Shanice's house followed by Angie. "Cuz you doing yo' thang ain't you."

Bruno and Shanice sat on her bright leather couch counting money out of two big black garbage bags spread across the glass top of the table. It was a gigantic pile of money. Cleofis thought it was probably a million. Never seen that much cash in his life he was anxious to know how much it was as him and Angie took a seat on the snow white leather seat.

The whole living room was decked out in white, white carpet, white beautiful curtain drapes, a big white expensive polo bear rug with the head on the end. This was a living room where they both had to take their shoes off before entering. Cleofis didn't want to touch anything because everything seemed so super clean and new.

Shanice's house was a place you could eat off the floor it was so clean and comfortable.

Cleofis glanced over at Angie to see if she was in the same breath taking moment as he was. Sitting directly across from Bruno and Shanice, his mind suddenly turned cold after noticing Angie was trying to avoid looking in the direction of the huge wide pile of money.

I should kill Bruno and his bitch right know take all this fedi and buy me a house with Angie in another state. This got to be a million dollars, I know this nigga counting this shit in front of my face on purpose he knew I was bringing Angie with me the nigga always trying to show off… But dang this nigga really rich. Cleofis thought to himself, smelling the stink of the dirty drug money.

"How much dust is that cuz? About a mill"

"Not quite" Bruno answered with a nonchalant body language. "It's turning out to be a little over eight hundred long."

Cleofis whistled softly "Shit I'mma just start calling you king pen."

Bruno slightly irritated by the comment heard a horn honk

"Shanice go get the door that's my sister" meaning it was Shawndra. "Wait till you see my ride lil cuz, I just had Shawndra go get it out of storage"

The ride was a '96 Carolina-blue S500 Mercedes Benz, and Cleofis fell in love with it on sight, him and Bruno stepped outside so he could take a look at it.

"Man cuz we rolling out in this, what kind of Benz is it?"

"This a 500 edition. The kind you hear Tupac raping about on his CD. So nigga you ain't gotta picture me rolling 'cause I'm rolling nah."

Cleofis laughed a little. "So we rollin' in this right?"

"Of course nigga what you think I had Shawndra go get it for." Shawndra had gone into the house with Shanice and Angie.

"That's a bad bitch you got in there boy you better keep her from around me 'cause I'll spoil that bitch outta your arms what is she mixed with?"

"She Vietnamese and Black, I'm trying to get the pussy."

"Fuck trying to get the pussy you need to cuff her if she ain't no runner. I hope you brought plenty change to trick off 'cause I ain't givin' yo' ass nuttin."

"Nigga I don't need your fedi I got plenty from selling bags"

"Ahhh, that's how you been getting all that change" just then Shawndra stepped out the door.

"I like her CJ, she seems like a much better young lady then Kim."

"Yeah I know, hopefully you'll see me with her all the time.

"Shawndra this little nigga don't know what to do with that."

"Maybe he does Bruno how would you know? I heard about your little episode last night. "

"And I'mma tell you like I told her I don't know whose panties them was"

"Sure you don't", Shawndra replied sarcastically.

"So that's why we taking the shopping trip", Cleofis began. "You done fucked up with Shanice now you gonna let her shop till she drop", he laughed uncontrollably barely able to get out his words. Bruno's just shook his head thinking about the realization of it being his bitch if he only new.

Bruno stuffed eight hundred grand back into the two garbage bags on the living room floor, and took the differences which was a hell of a lot for the shopping. Shawndra took both bags of money to an unknown location for Bruno, and was to reunite with him immediately upon his entrance back into Kankakee.

Cleofis was wearing a old one fifty hat he found in the corner of his closet in mint condition one fifties was hats with leather, suede, snake skin and different types of clothes they mostly bore a band-less watch with the right time on it in the middle front of the hundred and fifty dollar hat. The colorful cap blended in well with his Chicago bulls jersey shirt blue jean shorts and jet black Jordan's.

Angie was wearing a badge skirt with a matching short sleeve dressy three button up top, some matching elastic sling back heels, and her beautiful hair rested on her shoulders.

They both sat comfortably in the back of the luxury Mercedes as Bruno drove and Shanice chilled on the passenger side. Bruno put in some Al Green in the CD player and fired up a blunt. Shanice turned around glanced at Angie then requested Bruno to put the blunt out. She could tell by the disturbed look on Angie's face that she didn't like the atmosphere but felt she would be out of place to say anything.

"What's the problem Boo? This my first blunt today."

"I don't think CJ's friend back there like it."

"How you know I didn't see you ask her" Bruno looked in the rearview. "You want me to put this weed out pretty lady?"

"Could you please. Thank you", Angie said respectfully.

"See told ya next time you'll learn about my womans intuition", replied Shanice

"Pisssssss whatever."

Cleofis had rested his head on Angie's shoulder and felt to envisioned to say anything he thought to himself. This Benz is way more roomer then my car. Man cuz really rich I ain't never seen interior this color, fuckin' sky blue… this nigga clowning too much. I hope I have at least a quarter mill when I dump all this yack then I'll show this nigga a ride he only seen in his dreams. I need something like this to fuck Angie because she already used to BMW's and shit maybe if I spend enough change on her up here I'll get the pussy.

The foursome went in and out of the downtown stores in Chicago. Bruno spent cash on Shanice like there was no tomorrow dropping thousands of dollars at a time. He might not have worn fancy clothes but he had a lot of them at a variety of women's houses. He was familiar with a lot of New York popular clothing lines that Kankakeeans knew nothing about. Some he could find in Chicago's downtown stores others he would purchase when visiting New York. He would only wear his expensive garments when stepping out to clubs out of town looking to catch another beautiful woman. His style was very distinguished and for a minute you'll think you was dealing with a dirty rock then would be astonished when realizing you've found a valuable diamond with its own unique sparkle when wiping off the dirt.

Bruno would be imitated by many but never duplicated by any. And through Cleofis' growing greed, jealousy and envy at the age of eighteen he still wanted to be like his cousin Bruno.

Cleofis copped Angie a red mink jacket and plenty other expensive garments trying to compete with his cousin but Bruno bankroll was just too big. Angie continuously tried to refuse the gifts he bought her but he insisted on her to take what he was giving her with hopes of sexual activity soon. They all went to Michael Jordan's restaurant, the navy pier and to the Lake Front. The Lake Front was a beautiful view at night for a small city young man that never really been no where outside of Kankakee.

The later it got Bruno wanted to stay in his home town for the night and suggested it to Cleofis.

Cleofis finally got Angie to agree after long persistence but she was angry with him feeling like they had this planned all alone.

The first hour at the Hampton's was irking Angie 'cause she didn't want to be there and for a minute Cleofis had made up in his head he was going to take her stuff back in the morning. Him and Bruno both paid for suites at the Hampton Inn and Cleofis was feeling edgy when Angie's mood changed tremendously. Before giving up on trying to sex her he reminded her about her ex cheating on her. After Angie sat and thought about it for a while her mood did a total flip. Her boyfriend had hurt her so she sexed Cleofis all night making him wear a rubber that he did not want to wear. Angie in some weird way felt she was paying the cheating boyfriend back who called her everyday since she arrived in Kankakee.

Cleofis felt like he won the lottery and tried to please her every way possible. It was only so much he could, for Angie only required the missionary position and refused it any other way, she also repeatedly checked to make sure the rubber was on. This most definitely wasn't a usual episode for him but he eagerly made the best out the situation. Cleofis figured she finally came to her sense s about all the money he spent and was ready to give him something in return not knowing her decision came from pure retribution for her broken heart.

On the ride back Bruno let Shanice drive. "So little cuz when you think you'll be ready to make a move?"

"Soon, very soon."

"You sure you gonna be straight 'cause all that change you spent on your girl back there might of set you back."

"Look man, I worry about you and I'll worry about me" Cleofis replied nonchalantly after a deep breath. "And by the way what you gonna do with that spot 'cause them people done been there twice."

"I'mma let you have it for now, that's if you want it, I'm sure you and yo' little crew can finish burning it up."

Cleofis didn't like that statement and could see Bruno was in one of his fronting moods. But that wasn't the case, Bruno kept track of Cleofis' expenses and figured his money should be low along with cocaine even if he was bagging it all up he knew Cleofis wouldn't sell that many bags.

Cleofis stared at Angie's cute small triangle shaped lips and just couldn't believe what happened last night between the two.

"Dang y'all sure is quiet back there, you ok? Angie my little cuz didn't hurt you did he?"

"I'm ok, but thank you for asking."

"She's probably still tired I know I am", replied Shanice.

"You all didn't get no sleep or something?" asked Cleofis.

"How could I, your cousin act like he couldn't stay on his side of the bed."

Cleofis giggled slightly and Angie smiled until he released. "I didn't get much sleep neither"

Angie swiftly kicked his leg, and butted in, "I don't know why you didn't, I slept well last night." Angie didn't want everybody in her business.

Shanice dropped Angie off at the high-rises upon their arrival. Cleofis helped her carry the bags of fancy clothes up into the apartment, and then requested they get up later.

Shanice went into her house where she exited the vehicle, letting Bruno take over with Cleofis moving to the front seat.

It was now just Cleofis and Bruno. Cleofis basked in the attention they got from block huggers who did double takes at the two cruising by slowly. His BMW didn't get this much attention, the Mercedes had from the youngest to the oldest women staring. He really felt high and mighty riding with his king pin status cousin.

Bruno had never ridden around Kankakee in his Benz before. The Benz was for flossing out of town but he felt since it was about to go back in storage it was okay to give the streets a taste of his fine automobile. Both cutting back on their cell phones from not wanting to be disturbed, Cleofis now shared the feeling of importance, recognizing his message box was full just like his cousins.

"Sooooo little cuz I know you tended to that last night!"

"Nigga I stayed in her like it was a crack house where all the feinds had thousands."

Bruno chuckled, "No wonder why you ain't get no sleep man, lil cuz she's a keeper you feel me." Cleofis nodded his head yes as Bruno continued, "So I guess you through with that little rat Kim huh?"

Cleofis shrugged his shoulders while his right arm rested half way out the window. "More den likely."

Bruno turned the already low Daytons Family Music down a little bit. "Good 'cause she ain't shit and you don't need that slut."

"What you fuck her or something?" he asked very smoothly.

"Well you know me lil cuz, how could I turn it down."

The car got silent except for the low playing Daytons Family Music. Bruno was waiting on a response, when he didn't get any. He smirked on the left side of his cheek knowing Cleofis loved Kim and was very bothered by the information.

That's what the lil nigga get, always working with his heart, Bruno reflected. "Damn cuz, I know you ain't salty at me over the lil bitch?"

Cleofis said nothing but shook his head from right to left trying to cover up his anger.

He merely said, "I'll holla at you later." When being dropped off at his BMW that was still parked at Shanice's house. Bruno replied, "Don't tell the bitch I told you", as he slowly pulled off.

Cleofis was now furious, as he jumped into his car and raced over to Kim's house. I knew she fucked him. He shouted out loud, weaving his way through traffic.

Cleofis flew past Kim's warm greeting mother at the door, went down into the basement where Kim was laying on her bed talking on the phone, and started whaling on her. "What did I do?" screamed Kim.

"You fucked Bruno, you nasty rotten bitch", he yelled. "And bitch I know it ain't no lie!"

Kim's mother could hear the commotion going on beneath her feet, she ran down stairs to find him beating her daughter like a man.

"Get your hands off of my daughter", she yelled, clucking him upside the head with a near by lamp.

Cleofis came to his senses, reached under Kim's bed, grabbed the blue duffel bag full of coke, and headed for the door.

Cleofis pulled quickly in front of the Riverview High Rise entrance, called Angie on his cell phone, gave her the duffel bag when she came down, and told her to put it in a safe place. He then parked his car in the parking lot and waited for Berry to pick him up, who he'd already called on the way over there. He thought Kim's mother had called the police, and didn't want to take any chances of being stopped with a concealed weapon under the driver's side seat.

Berry pulled up beating some Mc8 out the trunk of his early eighties box Chevy. He was near broke after buying the Chevy. He jacked most of his money off and was now looking to Cleofis to put him back on. "What's goin' on Moe?" asked Berry

Closing the passenger side door, Cleofis replied, "Nothing just drive." Not wanting Berry to know what just happened, he acted as if everything was all good.

Bruno knew Cleofis would beat the shit out of Kim, and figured this as the ultimate revenge for her leaving her panties in Shanice's truck.

The early part of July wasn't turning out so good for the villain, he'd took a two brick loss from law enforcement that discovered the bricks in a broke down Ford Tempo located by Travis' crib. No one knew who tip the cops off but the cops were observing and watching the Tempo in hopes of Cleofis returning to retrieve the bricks.

Cleofis couldn't do nothing but accept the loss and he sure wasn't going to try and steal the coke back from the cops.

Travis was in serious debt too, Cleofis had fronted him a brick and hadn't received a penny of his money.

Cleofis was losing money left and right from the dice games to the expensive Versace garments and the daily tricking on hood rats. Also the money that he gave Angie to keep a smile on her face, she wasn't attracted to him and deep down inside he knew that. She'd never gave him anymore sex after that night at the Hampton's and was playing his dumb ass for every dollar she could squeeze out of him.

Cleofis had purchased a drop top Chrysler Sebring in cash that he had painted a burnt orange with 18 inch chrome wheels, he'd also got his 84 Malibu painted a candy color red, with red and black interior, coped him a Ninja motorcycle that wasn't cheap and got his BMW switched over in Kim's name.

After all the spending he only possessed a little over a hundred and fifty thousand in cash, that was stashed at Angie's until he could find a connect. Very low on cocaine he rented a house stationed down the street from his mother's. He watched Bruno like a hawk knowing he was fully aware of the bricks that he with held from him. But half the time Bruno was out of town closing a deal on some real estate, snatching up every piece of property he could.

Kim was still very salty that Cleofis dropped her like a bad habit, and went out her way to hate on him every chance she got.

Berry, Disco, Gabe, Cliff and JW were all still pushing bags, but Gabe pushed enough to get him a late eighties Buick.

Cleofis was becoming more repugnant to Gabe's independency even though he had more then him at the time, he was still pissed that Gabe didn't need him like the others.

He and Jackpot kept in touch. He would give Jackpot player prices on yack telling him to keep it on the low from Bruno.

Even though Cleofis didn't have what was expected he was practically enjoying his flamboyant ride around the city on his Ninja bike with Angie holding his waste and resting her chest are on his back. "Hold on baby girl", he said before speeding recklessly through the projects.

Angie screamed at the electrifying experience, while her long beautiful hair blew in the wind, her back had an arch in it and her butt stuck out with the small shirt raised up in the back. You could clearly see her pink Victoria Secret panties, then an inch below the Levi dark blue jeans seemed as if they were made for her figure.

Cleofis wore his Florida Marlins baseball cap straight to the back with a small tilt to the left, Marlins button up jersey with jean shorts to match. His Rolex along with a small linked chain with a marijuana leaf emblem sparkled, and his egg shaped head always looked funny when the baseball cap was to the back.

"Where you taking me to?" asked Angie. Cleofis pulled up slowly in front of a town house. "Just chill for a minute I'm final' see if this nigga got some change for me", he put the kick stand down, turned off the Ninja and marched up to Travis' door leaving Angie waiting in the hot scorching sun.

"This me open the door", answered Cleofis before Travis let him inside a house filled with guests sitting on the couches watching two other guests play a video game.

"I told you I'll call you when that lick come through."

Cleofis motioned for him to go into a back room cutting his loud excuses short. "Look Travis I want my money", he yelled after shutting the room door behind him. "I don't know what the fuck you take me for."

"Hold on 'moe'." Travis used hand gestures. "Don't come over here on that tough shit, because I told you the business when you came here with that little nigga a few days ago and what you saying I owe you is way too much, what about all the bricks I done cooked for you?"

Cleofis, could barely keep his sanity, "I'm a come by this motherfucka tomorrow and if you ain't got my bread we gonna have a problem."

Travis interrupted, "'Moe' I ain't scared of you so you can save them bullshit ass threats, if I ain't got it I ain't got it."

Cleofis ended the conversation saying, "A'ight nigga", very smoothly but evil at the same time before Travis could say more.

On his way out he noticed somebody let Angie in. "Didn't I tell you I'll be right out."

"Boy it's too hot to be waiting for you on that bike."

They got back on the Ninja then skated to his eastside neighborhood, stopping by his two bedroom house he was renting, they jumped into his drop top Sebring.

Flying back past the projects in the burnt orange drop top with the top down made he felt superior and he enjoyed every bit of it.

Gangsters, thugs and dealers all couldn't help but to stare at the 18 year old doing his thang.

Cleofis flossed like there was no tomorrow forgetting the teaching that was taught to him by elders in the game. Everybody knew he had money some even thought he had a meal ticket. He would brag about the lump sum of money that was kept in his pockets he was living for today and refused to see tomorrow doing things as they came to him.

He tried his best to make a spot in Angie's heart but she continuously kept her guards up. He repeatedly showed her respect, though his frustration from no sexual activity was taking a toll on him.

What Cleofis didn't know was that Angie was still very much in love with her cheating boyfriend who was still begging over the phone everyday for her to return. Angie never condoned a relationship with Cleofis, but after the Hampton's he told everybody who seen her that she was his women. Which she considered him as only a good friend but his woman is something he believed, and convinced others also.

Sergeant Fox and the rest of the drug enforcement group wanted Cleofis bad. The minute he got the drop top, Fox pulled him over just to take a Polaroid picture of him in it, wanting all the police in the city to know that the burnt orange drop top Sebring was a drug dealer named Cleofis Jackson.

Fox was also a good associate of Homicide Det. Diamond who informed him of Cleofis being a suspect in the Muddy murder.

Cleofis still ignored the heat and rode around with Angie on the passenger side as if he wasn't the number one drug dealer the Kankakee, law enforcement was after.

"Seems like you and that guy Travis was angry with each other… how much money do he owe you?"

"Too much baby, if it wasn't for him and this other loss I took I would have been able to make up for all the spending I did this month."

"I hope you learned your lesson, stop buying all those clothes and jewelry. And how many cars do you have?" Cleofis smiled blissfully while she continued, "Just think of all the money you spend on materialistic things, and you painted this car for what, more attention. I'm not trying to tell you what to do but you need to tone it down a little." Cleofis slightly rolled his eyes moving his head in the opposite direction from her. "What if you get caught then what?

He cut her off by turning up The Ambitions as a Rida, by Tupac off, The All Eyes on Me CD. She was blowing his fairly good mood with the speech.

He bopped his head strongly, pulling up to a stop sign rapping the words. "I want deny ya I'm a straight rida you don't want a fuck with me, got the police busing at me, but they can't do nothing to a gee!"

Shawndra drove up next to the loud noise vehicle, "Turn that racket down!"

He looked towards her direction and turned the music down a little, "What you say girl?"

"I said turn that racket down", Shawndra slightly laughed then continued. "Must you serenade the whole neighborhood?"

Cleofis laughed at the funny statement, "Girl you must ain't got nothing to do. Were my cuzo at?"

"I don't know. You know how your cousin is."

"Secretive as a motherfucka", they replied at the same time.

"Hey Angie how you doing I see you still with this bad boy."

"I'm not exactly with him, he just won't leave me alone", she jokingly replied but was dead serious.

"Ha ha so funny but anyways I got a TV you can have, this hype came through with two and I already got two so I'm probably gonna use one for the other room at my house. So you can have the other one if you want it, it's a pretty nice 19 inch TV."

"Yeah I want it, when can I come get it?"

"Today or tomorrow it don't matter."

A car honked its horn from behind Shawndra, Cleofis looked the driver with a wait 'til we get done talking look, and continued his conversation when Shawndra yelled. "I'll just stop by later I know were you stay at."

Cleofis could see the driver lip boxing through the rolled up windows. "Fuck you too motherfucka", Cleofis yelled with his finger in the air.

"CJ", Angie spoke concerned. "They didn't do nothing wrong they just wanted to get by in traffic."

"So! And don't tell me what to do."

"Calm down I'm not trying to tell you what to do. If you gonna be trippin' you can take me to my aunts."

"You the one trippin', just like every time I try and touch you down there, what the fuck is the problem I know you trying to follow by your religion and all, but damn you already gave me the ass."

"You know what Cleofis, just take me to my aunts, right now!"

She had put the religion story on him the last time he tried to sex her but it wasn't the religion she just didn't like him like that and usually kept a high maintenance attitude when being in his presence. She was becoming mind wrecking to him, always trying to figure out a way to get her out of her panties again.

Damn didn't I put it down at the Hampton Inn? Him trying to get sex from her was a turn off, that she could never turn on and she felt she'd already evened it out with her cheating boyfriend, and was starting to miss him like crazy the more she heard his voice.

Cleofis spotted Gabe at Ben's on his way to drop Angie off so he pulled into the parking lot to talk business, stalling her demands to go to her aunts.

"What's the buz lil homie?" Cleofis spoke, stepping out the drop top.

"Nuttin just waiting on this hype to come through", Gabe exclaimed, sitting in his Buick.

"Hold on a minute 'Joe' I gotta holla at you about something I'll be right out."

Cleofis spun up into Ben's, slammed some money on the bar table, took two sots of tequila and spun back outside like it was nothing hoping to relieve some of his distraught towards Angie.

"Looks like that hype is late."

"He'll be here. So what you gotta holla at me about?"

"I know you don't like getting fronted, but I was willing to front you the rest of this little yack for a nice price and you already know its butter."

"Well just stop by my moms crib later on and well see." Cleofis then jumped into Gabe's passenger seat. "What's up you got something else you wanna holla at me about or something", Gabe asked.

"Naw I'm just stallin' this bitch 'cause she wants to go home."

Cleofis sat there acting like he was conversating as Gabe looked past his shoulder telling him everything Angie was doing.

"She getting mad den a motherfucka 'Joe'. You betta gone over there before she get out and walk."

At the end of Gabe's statement Cleofis could feel the tipsiness creeping up on him from the shots of Tequila.

The motor from a van pulling up parking on the side of his drop top sounded all too familiar, when he acknowledged it was Kim's mothers van, but Kim's mother wasn't in it, it was Kim and three of her loud mouth female cousins.

Cleofis noticing Gabe's customer was approaching the car, he stepped out, slid to his drop top as Gabe pulled off and didn't get his hand on the handle of the door good before hearing. "Herpes spreading motherfucka… that little nasty dick of yours is gonna fall off one day", replied one of Kim's cousins from the van window.

"What you say to me?" Cleofis yelled before hearing her practically repeat herself. "Fuck you bitch with yo' big beastly looking ass trying to throw salt in a nigga game." He was too embarrassed by the dark lady's comment and was almost about to pull off when she jumped out in a challenging stance. "Get out the car motherfucka, I got your bitch, you might scare Kim but you don't scare me, get out you big nose motherfucka", she screamed.

Cleofis paused for a second then excited the vehicle before he could even get out the car, the beastly woman started punching him, being hit by the second or third punch blew his tipsiness back to a sober state of mind. "BITCH", he said strongly when socking her in the eye with a balled-up fist knocking her on her back as she held her aching eye. "Aw hell naw", was the words that came from the van as Kim and two other cousins sprinted out of it. Kim ran to Angie's side and started flooding her with punches as her three cousins rushed Cleofis.

Cleofis laid both of the two girls out with wild hard punches along side of their first cousin that ran up, then moved swiftly over to poor defenseless Angie's aid and body slammed Kim so hard you could here something crack.

One of Kim's cousin's boyfriend pulled up, saw the girls laid out in a daze and was ready to bring the drama to whoever, but when he saw the riled-up Cleofis with the temper of a raging bull the boyfriend greeted him with a hand shake saying. "Good job 'Moe' these hoes need a good ass whoopin'"

Cleofis gave him a cold stare before replying, "Aight 'Joe'." Then jumped into his Sebring thinking, I don't even know that nigga, as he pulled off rapidly.

Angie was screaming a variety of curse words, he had never heard her curse, he knew she was extremely upset.

He said nothing to Angie on the ride to the high rises. I can't believe Kim told her cousin I had herpes, was all he could think about. I know Angie probably heard them hoes, damn! Those bitches just messed up my chance of some more pussy.

Cleofis had picked up the non curable STD from an eighteen year old when he was fifteen since then he'd been continuously raw dicking everything that came across his path. He'd passed the disease to Kim only so far, basically only able to spread during outbreak. He sexed her one day with his irritated penis and brought her into his incurable world of genital herpes.

Cleofis tried to forget about the STD, but when he forgot an outbreak of the disease would remind him. Going to the clinic was embarrassing after the first couple times so he stopped going.

He advised Kim to never tell anybody about the secret they shared between each other but Kim loved him and exposed his secret to her friends out of jealousy of Angie. She even told her friend April who she had no clue was involved with Cleofis. April didn't take Kim's statement serious, figuring she was just jealous which she was but also took it as player hating considering Cleofis was through with her.

Kim didn't even know that his cars were in April's name along with Mrs. Jackson. Kim and April were very good friends it hadn't come out yet about April's fling with Cleofis.

April was a play by the rules chick, she played her position and never asked for another one, her time with him was whenever it was convenient for him. She never complained, never asked too many questions and was a great listener when he chose to blow off some steam.

"Coming with me?" Cleofis asked.

"Sure", April said then grabbed her purse out of her living room.

Cleofis let the top up on the drop top while heading back to his eastside house.

"Let me tell you about your silly ass friend. Her and her cousins tried to jump me."

"For real, I thought you were through with her?"

"Shhhit I am she won't leave me alone, her and them ugly ass cousins of hers."

April laughed at his comments. This was one of the qualities he liked about her, she always seemed to be interested in what he was saying unlike Angie that he couldn't wait to get to her aunts due to her constant demands for an explanation before she got out the car made him more madder at Angie, who wouldn't meet his request for pleasure.

He'd dropped the yack off to Gabe after giving him a steal on the front price and was now back at his house with April.

Cleofis watched April from his Maroon leather couch as she flipped through his stereo disc changer looking for Toni Braxton's latest CD.

The bottom of her peach complexioned butt cheeks showed from her light blue jean daisy dukes that cuddled her rear end. "Got it!" April found the Toni Braxton CD.

You sure do Cleofis thought, contemplating on a seductive move. He really appreciated her devotion to her spot on a team filled with all sorts of females and to show his gratitude he dove face first slurping her up like biscuit with gravy while listening to Toni Braxton's, You're Making me High.

After a long intensified event Cleofis laid with his hands tucked behind his head in his full sized bed. April laid next to him positioned on her left side looking straight at him, she could tell he was in deep thought. Murder was what was on his mind. Never blown anybody brains out before. He went over and over in his head of what it would be like to blow Travis' brains out.

Thinking about the Scarface scene, when he kills dude in the car, after telling him no wife no kids, would it be like that he thought. He'd been anxious to plug somebody since purchasing the two knee knockers with a twist from Travis and from the looks of it Travis was begging to be his first candidate.

Cleofis had a gun in every room in the house including the bathroom you never can be to safe, he would tell his friends. He also bought the gray and black nines that he and Gabe saw at K's Merchandise when he first touched down.

They watched 'Juice', 'Boys N Tha Hood', and 'Jason's Lyric'. And Jason's revenge for his bloody brother Josh would be the last scene he would see before falling asleep.

Cleofis was awakened by a knock at the front door. "Who the hell knocking on my door?" he said out loud, covering his face from the rays of sun light shinning through half closed blinds.

He opened the door after looking threw the peep hole and seeing that it was Shawndra. She stepped into his sex smelling house with quite a smirk on her face glancing at his early morning erection. "Hmmmmm, somebody must have made you happy in your sleep."

He put his hand in front of the bulge, reached into the linen closet and put on some jogging pants over his boxer's only body. "Shawndra, if I didn't know better I'd think you wanted this young swoll nigga."

"You may have a nice body but I don't think you can handle a women like me I'm not none of them little girls you run around with."

Cleofis picked a small bit of mucus out his nose. "Ohhh really. From what I hear, your baby daddy been tripping like a little ass boy."

"Aw that's nothing, his insecure ass think I'm fuckin' Bruno, when I told him Bruno and me are like brother and sister. I don't look at him like that, and I don't think he looks at me like that.

"I don't see how", he spoke, retrieving the 19 inch TV from out the kitchen. "Cuz be a fool not to want you."

"Just hand it to me I'll carry it out to the car", she requested, fully capable of carrying the TV by herself.

"You think you could run me somewhere", he asked, holding open the front door so she could exit with the TV.

"Hurry up I'll be out in the car waiting." She answered.

With murder still on his mind he flew back to the bedroom, lifted up the mattress He grabbed one of the automatics with the twist, threw on a tee- shirt, some shoes and headed for the door, being careful not to disturb April's nude sleeping body. He had his mind made up if Travis didn't have a portion of his money he was going to kill him and nobody was going to hear it.

"I'll be right back", he replied to Shawndra. He could see Travis looking out the blinds on his way to the door of the town house. The automatic had almost slid down his waist when he tightened the string up in the jogging pants.

"I told you I'll call you man! You ain't gotta keep coming through here like that", Travis irritated hissed, standing in the doorway.

"Let me get something to drink I'm thirsty than a motherfucka."

Cleofis noticed Travis had company immediately upon him moving out the door way to let him in. Some nobodies that was playing the video game paying no attention to anything made him pause for a second.

Watching Travis fetch him some Kool-Aid everything seemed to go in slow motion. He trembled slightly as he exhaled through his nose, if Travis would have looked him in the eye when opening the door he probably wouldn't let him in, for Cleofis eye lids opened the window to his murderous soul. His stare was so cold and empty like there was nothing there.

The partial nervousness made his body seem to beat like a human pulse and the dots of sweat on his face was nothing compared to his sweaty palms.

Travis, with his back turned to Cleofis said, "I think it might be a little sweet", but the words seem to come as a blur and the room seem to spin like a merry-go-round, the upstairs bath water ran and every sound seem to echo.

In a blink of an eye, he pulled the long nose attached 17 shot knee knocker from his waste. The guest sitting on the couch with his back toward him was the first to get it. Creating a low repulsive CLUNK! when entering the back of the man's head, then exiting out the front. As the shell jumped out the chamber the man's body flew forward leaving spatters of gruesome brain fragments on the curtains.

Cleofis wasted no time turning towards Travis to fire, but Travis was already in motion to throw the cup of Kool-Aid in his face. When the Kool-Aid splashed on his shirt and face, the silenced pistol let off a round piercing through Travis left shoulder.

He wrestled with Travis who was fighting for his life, bear hugging his waist with all his might, pinning him to the back of the couch.

Cleofis then elbowed the blood shooting shoulder like a WWF wrestler, and stood over him as he crawled on the good shoulder trying to take cover behind the end of the couch.

Cleofis sighed with relief. Damn I thought I'd never get this nigga off me. CLUNK! CLUNK! CLUNK! Was the dull sound of the bullets injecting in the back of Travis' skull. How brutal was he, he even kicked him for the tiresome wrestle he put him through.

Cleofis was ready to bounce when he heard the running bath water upstairs cut off. "Ay! What ya'll doing down there", someone yelled.

He panicked for a couple of seconds, wondering what to do. *"How many niggaz in this house?",* he thought, then some words gradually came back to his anxious to leave mind. No witnesses, no case.

Cleofis hit the stairs feeling like Jason off a horror movie. For a second the witness stood at the top of the stairs in a pause with a towel wrapped around his nude body trying to figure out what Cleofis was coming up for. But then he ran and locked himself in the bathroom after noticing a pistol in his hand.

Shooting two rounds through the lock on the bathroom door, uncovered the nude man with his towel around his ankles holding his hands out trying to block the bullets. "Please CJ not me, what did I do, stop…"

Cleofis let off three rounds CLUNK! CLUNK! CLUNK! The bullets seemed to go through the victims hands never reaching the head. The twist gave the weapon a tweet like sound with every shot and the villain felt he nailed his target after releasing four more rounds. "Ssssssss" the rapidly breathing victim expressed from the holes in his hands but yet nothing in his bobbing and weaving skull. Cleofis was becoming frustrated as he put his left hand on the three fingers of the right, held the nose laced nine steady, and then pulled the trigger with his index finger. CLUNK! CLUNK! CLUNK! One bullet pierced threw the victims cheek, one hit the wall, and the other ripped through the middle of his forehead, leaving another splatter of brain fragments on the wall.

Cleofis flew down the stairs astonished by another noise coming from a door cracked bed room. It was a hype, with half of his body out a broken window when Cleofis kicked open the crack door. He pointed the empty hammer slid back nine. Click! Click! Click! But nothing came out as he saw the bottom of the hypes feet, then heard the heavy landing of a scared to death addict. The hype was in the bedroom getting high when he witnessed him kill the two guys downstairs through the crack in the door, and when seeing Cleofis head upstairs the hype went for a drastic get away. Knowing no one would live to tell the story in that house.

Bo Pete was his name and Cleofis identified him while looking regretfully out the escape window. "Damn that's that motherfuckin' Bo Pete", Cleofis raced out the front door of the townhouse not even closing the door all the way, Shawndra damn near wanted to pull off when seeing bloody shirt Cleofis trying to stick the long mag in his waist, jogging towards the car.

"GO! GO! GO!" He exclaimed wanting to catch up to the scared for his life Bo Pete.

"What the fuck just happened?" Shawndra asked while watching Cleofis pull the bloody tee shirt off.

"Nothing", he replied. "Just hit this block up here."

Bo Pete was entering a Southside Amoco. "Go to the gas station", he yelled wondering how Bo Pete sprinted there so fast. Cleofis wrapped the murder weapon up in his shirt and told Shawndra to be cool as he hopped out to speak with Bo Pete. Fuck! I shoulda brought that other mag.

Bo Pete ran dead smack into Cleofis coming out the gas station door. "Ma, ma, ma, man CJ I ain't see shit, please don't kill me", Bo mumbled.

"Shhhh keep yo' voice down", Cleofis replied planting his hand on the man's trembling shoulder.

"Look Bo if I hear you told on me, you dead and if I can't get you I'll get the closest thing to you. Nah yo' best bet is to lay low, and get in touch with me so I can take care of you. You won't have to worry about looking for your next high 'cause it will always be there."

Bo shook his head like Pinky off Pinky and The Brain. "Ok CJ please just don't kill me!"

Cleofis repeated his cell phone number to Bo Pete several of times before spinning back into Shawndra's car.

"Look! I'm finna take you home CJ 'cause I don't know what you just did but I'm scared."

"Be cool, stop driving fast, do the speed limit before you get us pulled ova."

"What the hell just happen CJ? Why your shirt all bloody. Tell me what's going on!"

"Look! I don't got time to explain right now, take this shit and I'm finna go in the house and change pants then bring you these jogging pants."

Cleofis switched pants quick and shot back out to the car. "Burn these, you hear me? And burn 'em good, I'm talking about until there's nothing."

Shawndra took the bloody Kool-Aid stained clothes, then went and did what she was told. Something in the back of her head told her he just killed somebody and to run as far away from him as possible. But she loved the electrifying experience and felt like a get away driver for an up and coming gangster, unaware that a triple murder just took place and she was the accomplice to a lethal injection crime if found guilty.

Shawndra waited at her apartment for his phone call. Finally the call came.

"Hello!"

"You burned them clothes like I told you? "

"Thhh, I took care of that, but where are you?" she sounded very concerned. "What am I supposed to do, what if somebody seen us? I'm scared!"

"I'm dropping somebody off, just calm down, don't go anywhere in that car, I'll stop by there soon as I get done."

Cleofis dropped April off and stopped by Fresh Fades and Hair Do's a local barber and hair salon. His eyes seemed to light up like light bulbs when everybody looked at him walking in. But it was just his guilty conscious and a head rush from the previous massacre.

He had wiped the dots from his pouring sweat glands before entering and tried to pull himself together the best he could.

The cold steal of the Tech9 rubbed up against his six pack with the barrel tucked under some jean shorts covered by a 49ers jersey. A hair cut was a little over do and George was the best in town. He could cut and line your hair with such delicacy. A small amount of rumors was spread about the married man, and some believed they were true even if he was married to a woman. Cleofis for some odd reason wanted a haircut minutes after the triple murder. He'd trained himself to act normal like some of his older cousins after a slaying. The motto was if you got away clean why not come out and act as if nothing happen.

He had told April to stash the three body carrying weapons at her house, she thought nothing of it and he went and obtained the chunky Tech9 to feel secure.

"Hey CJ how's your mother doing?" asked George.

"She's fine. How many more heads you got 'cause I'm kinda in the rush."

"I'm just about through with him. You can climb in the chair next if your paying extra."

He pulled out his knot. "Everybody got their price I see. As much women hair you do down here, you shouldn't have time to cut no hair."

George was a soft spoken guy, kind of feminine to the average eye. A handsome man that befriended a lot of females that walked into Fresh Fades and Hair Do's. Always full he wouldn't normally take walk-ins but since he stayed down the street from Cleofis and known the teen half of his life it was ok.

"Just a nice low cut fade as usual!"

"I got you. Life must be treating you good huh, 'cause that's a nice automobile you riding in." Cleofis smirked as George continued. "Tell me the truth how much money you make a day?"

"Not much", Cleofis answered, as George pushed his head down and cut the back of his head.

The hair falling off his head on to the apron tickled, grazing his ear while dropping and his small brown weasel like eyes, glanced up at his surroundings. The noise from the small TV that set in the corner was smothered out by men sports and women gossip amongst the two parties that waited their turns. "Turn it up." someone yelled. Everybody in the shops attention was on the TV that showed an all too familiar townhouse on the news.

"We interrupt this program to cover a brutal triple murder that took place in Kankakee, not even an hour south from Chicago. The neighbors say they heard nothing, but the bodies of the three young men were discovered by a family member of one of the men who says the door was half way open. Two of the men have not yet been identified, though detectives haven't came up with much of a motive for the three executions. They are looking to question a suspect who exchanged threats with one of the young men just yesterday."

Cleofis reached under his skirt and clutched the Tech9 strongly as his eyes scowered the room. George hadn't started to line Cleofis head yet when he jumped on the cell and called Angie. The news cast said they would have more on the story later, Cleofis prayed Angie would come straight there. Very shook up he knew someone must have informed the police of him and Travis arguing. "Dang CJ you made me mess up your lining", replied George. The sharpness of the liners caught Cleofis off guard while thinking of a place to lay low. "I'll fix it when I get home", exclaimed Cleofis, tossing some money on the chair and jetting out the door to meet Angie who just pulled up.

Detective Diamond had questioned Cleofis intensely for 17 hours before letting him go. Cleofis was now laying low at his mothers, while he walked around the house clutching a grey knee knocker. His mother's house felt a little safer then being down the street at his own, plus Mrs. Jackson wanted him close to her after recognizing the police wanting to question her son over the triple murder. Mrs. Jackson feared that if the family of the victims found out her son was a suspect they might come after him just off assumptions. The triple murder spread through out the small city rapidly everybody was talking about it, the city hadn't seen such a murder since the early nineties and no one knew who did it. Many said it was a professional hit man and others spoke of all sorts of tales.

"Now Cleofis must you walk around this house with that gun in your hand son?"

"Ma, I ain't taking no chances people already gossiping just 'cause I got questioned!"

"Boy…yo little brother stays in this house too, and I will not have him seeing his big brother walking around the house with a gun. So you better put that thang away."

He said a little of nothing as he went to his exactly how he left it bedroom, Mrs. Jackson figured he'd be back sooner are later.

Disco was sitting on a stool in Cleofis' room wanting so badly to ask what happened when he began. "These motherfuckas beat me damn near the whole seventeen hours. Talking about ya'll some cold blooded killers, them pigs say, you couldn't have pulled these murders off by yourself Mr. Jackson. Man 'Moe'…every time I said I want to talk to a lawyer they smacked me in my mouth….. 'Moe' these motherfuckas made me taste blood, I wanted to kill somebody about time they got through with me. Then came the Bruno questions, you and Bruno supply this city, you and Bruno this, you and Bruno that, blah blah blah, where you get your cars? Where you get your clothes, just tell us who was with you and we might be able to save you from lethal injection."

Even though Cleofis never said anything to hurt himself he was shaken in his shoes, and on a few occasions felt like confessing thinking Bo Pete possibly got scared and came forward. If only the detectives would have held him longer he would of sang like a bird, but his release only reassured more confidence of an almost clean get away.

"What happen in that house 'Moe'?" Disco got up enough courage to ask.

"What the hell you mean what happened, nigga I don't know, I wasn't there, I really don't know what them people talking about."

Disco could tell he was lying but declined to question his outburst of an answer. He could see it in his eyes Cleofis most definitely had something to do with the murders.

Shawndra had put her car up in storage paid for by Cleofis, and was driving her baby daddy's car. Upset with Cleofis for not renting her a car she missed his calls on purpose and was told repeatedly by Bruno to avoid the hot headed teen. "That nigga with that cowboy shit gonna get us all pinched, them white folk's ain't finna let that murder go unsolved. What the fuck he pop the other two niggaz for, I tell you the little nigga gone crazy, stay the fuck away from him Shawndra 'cause he ain't gone last long", Bruno stressed to her.

Cleofis started to live his days as a paranoid man only coming out at night and always wearing the bullet proof vest he'd got from Travis. He'd cruised to a deep part of the Kankakee River and tossed the nine with the twist used in the triple slaying.

Angie was still unaware of the horrible things he had done and thought nothing of it as she waited in her car as he disposed of the murder weapon. Once he heard the splash from the night time quiet river he was very sure the gun was sinking to the bottom of it. A small weight was lifted off his shoulders knowing the weapon was sitting at the bottom of the river.

187 would sometimes appear in his pager and if it wasn't that, then phone calls from unknown people breathing hideously, and making death threats. He dreaded calling some of his pages back, and finally cut the pager off after calling back the mortuary.

CHAPTER 11

A 100 Thousand Dollar Bounty

"I'mma push dis nigga wig back on sight and leave his ass right where I find em… Cleo or whatever the lil bitch name is shawty."

The country loud mouth man wasn't aware that the target he was sent to kill was staring him right in the face. Gillmen was his name and he was brought in from Tennessee to collect on the hundred thousand dollar bounty that was put on Cleofis' head by family members of the townhouse victims. Tall and lanky long wool like hair, his face out like one of the Simpson's with gold covering the top front of his mouth and country then a motha.

Gillmen once stayed in Kankakee and had a reputation both places for being a ruthless thug. And Gillmen brought a couple ridaz from the south to assist him in his search. Well in his twenties the country accent carrying man knew Berry from when he was a little boy and spoke to him like they were close family.

Cleofis standing observably right there as Gillmen study spoke about him to Berry, not knowing that the Cleofis he was looking for was positioned next to Berry, and getting nervous.

"Damn! Motherfuckas really want me dead that bad... they don't even know if I did I or not", Cleofis thought. Swallowing uneasily, Cleofis studied the features of the man never taking eyes off him with his hand twitching debating whether to kill the obnoxious hit man as Berry pretended to embrace him.

The out-of-towner had spotted Berry leaned up against a car speaking to his unknown target, and decided to stop to rift with the all grown up Berry. Gillmen's goons waiting in his car made Cleofis control the nervous cowboy that wanted anxiously to come out. Tapping the handle of the gun covered by his shirt Cleofis' inner cowboy was becoming more nervous and ampt, a very dangerous mixture as Gillmen stepped back to his candy painted car.

"Let me know if you see that nigga Cleofis… I mean it Man it'd be somethin' in it for ya, stay cool lil soldier." Gillmen threw the peace sign up as he rode off.

"I thought you was finna pop that nigga", Berry began while driving Cleofis to Gabe's crib. "Dude must don't know you, he must think he looking for a soft nigga and who the fuck finna pay a hundred thousand dollars for your head?"

Irritated by his friends dumb question Cleofis replied, "They fuckin' family dummy if they families combined their money together who knows how much change them people can come up with. I'm telling you man, I don't wanna kill nobody but the first nigga who try me I'mma body his ass, that's on Blackstone!"

"People really think you did that shit", Berry spoke trying to see what he could squeeze out of his friend that he knew without confession took some part in the massacre.

"Come on 'Moe'", Cleofis explained, tapping Berry with his left hand. "If I would have done that shit you would have been there with me. Now I could kill a nigga or two but three niggaz….that was a hit man. Travis always was ripping somebody off left and right ain't no telling who killed them niggas, but niggas ain't finna start saying I did."

Something about his eastside neighborhood seemed to ease the dangerous situation that almost got hectic minutes ago.

Cleofis hadn't found a connect yet and had been out of yack for awhile and was roughly peeling off the once little over hundred fifty grand at Angie's. He had a little over a hundred grand left and was now coming out and about during the day. Trying his best to stay with a crowd of armed villain's, Cleofis was tricking, gambling, paying for expensive hotel suites, dining at high price restaurants and living expenses. And when he paid for pleasure he paid for everybody that was with him, this fella was taking tricking to another level in the small gossiping city. Not to forget greasing Bo Pete crack head palms, he wanted to kill him but was still trying to figure out how to maneuver from around true accusations set forth by family members blaming him because he was questioned.

Det. Diamond told mournful family members that Cleofis Jackson was a suspect in the triple slaying and that was all some had to hear especially Travis' big brother and his now going crazy mother.

"Let me get something out ya little homie", Cleofis asked demandingly. "Boy you know you sure hustle slow. I would've flipped that shit twenty times by now."

Gabe rolled his eyes at him as he counted out the money. "Look nigga I ain't the one who wanted to be fronted you basically forced the yack on me-

"Nigga please", Cleofis said humorously cutting off. "You saw that front price and you jumped at the opportunity to fatten your pockets, you bricks always trying to bullshit a motherfucka."

Gabe smiled, caught up on the presence of his so hard to get up with friend. "Just take the money you hook ass nigga and don't come over here trying to front me no mo yack", he jokingly continued. "Start answering your phone scary ass nigga, I ain't the one who is at you."

"And nigga if you was you'd be a memory like a lot of others", Cleofis sounded partially serious before stepping out of Gabe's crib. The slick talk would be something they'd do a lot in the future.

Cleofis phone rang right before Berry dropped him off at his rented house on the eastside.

"Who the fuck is this?"

"It's me Shawndra, boy you okay. 'Cause I've heard so many things."

"I'm straight just some gay ass nigga keep calling my phone talking gangsta and shit, but don't never want to say who they are. I thought you was mad at me."

"Naw its just that I felt you could of least helped me get a rental car, then you start being out of touch but anyways, I was just calling to make sure your okay."

"A'ight moe", Cleofis threw the bald fist up to Berry as he pulled off and then responded. "You ain't gotta worry about me Shawndra I'll be aight, but thanks for your concern." He glanced around his spot outside, approaching his candy red painted Malibu that was pulled up in the driveway.

"Where my cuz at, I know he gotta know I been trying to get in touch with him, and don't tell me you don't know 'cause I seen you driving his Cadillac."

"I seen him a couple days ago he's been busy I'm sure he'll get in touch with you." Cleofis looked at the hood of his Malibu in shock of dead man keyed in it. "Motherfucka!"

"What? What's wrong? Everything okay", Shawndra sounded very concerned

Cleofis didn't notice the approaching vehicle coming from down the street, the vandalism had his attention. "Some motherfucka done keyed my Malibu, ain't this a bitch. See, this is what I'm talking about."

He didn't even finish the sentence before spotting Travis' mother clutching a pistol trying to aim it at him out the window. "Shit!" He yelled, dropping the phone and dashing to the front part of the car to take cover.

Crouching down he fully retrieved his mag when hearing the lady scream. "I'mma kill you, you bastard, you killed my son!" She slowed down for a second but eventually pulled off after Cleofis never showed himself. "Damn! I don't wanna kill that lady", he said to himself, very shook up from the encounter he forgot to grab his phone all he wanted to do was get in the house where he felt safe.

It took Cleofis awhile but he finally found what he thought was a connect, spending majority of his money he was now stuck with some bullshit cocaine and knew of no way to find the Chicagoan who sold it to him.

Cleofis was very pissed and tried to take it out on whoever let him. "What's this shit you telling Cliff about he need to stay out the car with me you know something I don't know, motherfuckaz at me and you ain't tell me who."

Gabe had told Cliff to watch his back when riding with Cleofis, but Cliff with his loyalty to Cleofis ran back and repeated everything Gabe said. "I was just telling dude motherfuckas be talking-

Cleofis didn't let him get another word out before hanging up in his face. "Niggas always runnin they mouth like bitches", he expressed as he began to weigh up some of the bullshit coke he purchased.

"I told you about that little nigga anyway Moe'", Berry looked at Cleofis sitting across from him and Cleofis then continued. "That's your homeboy Moe'. The nigga ain't even Blackstone like the rest of us, even Cliff right here is all as well."

Gabe regretted giving Cliff any advice. He flew to Cleofis house and honked his horn for him to come out. Cleofis came walking out with a displeased look. "What the fuck you want?" Cleofis closed the car door and Gabe pulled off. "All I told the nigga was to watch himself, come on nigga if I knew who was making threats I would've been told ya."

Gabe learned right then that if something was said, Cleofis' cronies would go back and repeat it even though him and Cliff known each other since they were in pre school Cliff was still a wanna be and instead of soaking up the advice, the lamb relayed it to the figure he wanted to be.

"It ain't nutting man I'm just trippin off this bad yack I got that I can't find the nigga to reimburse me for. I'm a keep going up north till I catch this Vic and when I do I'mma put him on the news."

It was a moment of silence before Gabe replied. "I hope you stay heated 'cause niggaz dirtying your name quite a bit out here. Man it seem like we all so grown now we barely holla at each other."

"You the one choose to do your own thang, and I ain't mad at you for it I just wish you would listen to me sometimes… I got more game den you little homey I know you think you know it all in that big head of yours, but you still got a long way to go to reach my level."

Gabe chuckled at his friend's comments. "You might got mo money then me but I got a raw way of doing shit-

"Yeah ok", Cleofis cut him off. "Only thing you raw at is that dick you keep shoving in that mosquito looking ass girl you in love with." Gabe didn't laugh at that remark. "And for these niggaz. It's like cuz once told me, niggas 90 percent talk 10 percent action. Trust me they don't wanna see me turn the heat up", Cleofis looked at Gabe for an agreeable response. "Whatever you say Pinocchio with that nose of yours you betta never start tooting powder you'd probably O.D."

"Ha ha ha Stone run it, you goofy ass nigga", Cleofis remarked with a vividly phony laugh as he jumped out the car and went into the house.

"What that nigga want?" asked Berry. Cleofis sat down next to Cliff, "Nuttin, trying to explain and shit. I wasn't tryin to hear that shit though, I told the nigga he betta watch his mouth." He lied for no reason at all making them believe he checked Gabe when in reality he explained his grumpiness.

"Now how the fuck I'mma get rid of all this shit. You say everybody in the projects and at the Cartels know its bad right?"

"Right Moe', I say wait till you catch up with that nigga, then you'll be straight", Berry suggested.

"Nigga I've been got…mafucka, what part of that don't you understand, that nigga ain't finna pay me my change I doubt if I ever bump into the mark again. This is a loss I'm just gonna have to accept for right now, and Chicago one of the biggest cities in the world. That nigga got plenty spots to go. I'll get 'em in the future, right now I'm worried about making my change back."

"Only way I could get rid of some of the shit was to give it away dirt cheap." Berry loudly replied.

"Why don't you call and see how Disco doing with the shit?",

"I already hollered at 'em, he saying the same shit?"

Cleofis cell rang in the middle of the discussion.

"Who is this?", he said irritable by the interruption.

"Who it sound like, how many women do you have calling your phone?"

"Oh!" Cleofis said when realizing it was Angie. He then strutted to his room and closed the door behind him. "What's up wit'chu?"

"Nothing much I been thinking about you."

"Oh you have, I'm surprised at that, as much as I been by your aunts looking for you and I guess your cell is off. How did it get like that when I bought you a gang of minutes?"

"Talking to my folks from Green Bay and stuff." Cleofis suspected the minutes was gone because of her ex and his suspicion was right. "I need some money sweetie", she said with a soft warm voice.

He felt like a 'John' who was sprung on a piece he only had once. "Why you always want some money what about what I want."

"And what's that sweetie?"

"You know what it is, I don't gotta say it!"

"You know what CJ that's alright you can keep your money I'll get it from somebody else." Those last words made Cleofis want to cooperate with Angie's request, but they also made him pissed off.

"Well fine then bitch go get some from that nigga you be yapping with on the phone", he yelled viciously. "Gold digging motherfucka!" Angie had already hung up the phone though and put him in a worse mood.

Cleofis turned his rented eastside house into a crack spot and since the house was in April's name he didn't worry about being charged if raided, unless they found drugs on his person.

This dumping went on for a couple months and the villain sold weight and bags dirt cheap. He sold his Malibu, motorcycle and the pulled over every time the police seen it, burnt orange drop top Sebring. All that was kept was the BMW that April drove around unless he needed her. He sold his belongings trying to make up for the big loss with just about none of the bullshit yack left he got word Bruno was in town and was at his Southside apartments that he owned.

Cleofis knew Bruno would probably be busy when coming into town, everybody wanted to see him for business, pleasure, and some just to be in his presence. Bruno was most definitely too big for this little city and he knew it, that's why he stayed away from it much as possible.

"Long time no see, Americas most wanted", Bruno humorously said. He was coming out of the front entrance when Cleofis pulled up. "I thought you probably be dead or in jail by now."

"Nigga you see me, I'm here and ain't hiding from a muthafucka. I was hoping we could do some business if you ain't still ducking me."

"Little nigga ain't nobody ducking you", Bruno said sternly. "I just wasn't about to let you bring heat on me, them people already know you my cousin, they wasn't fenna try and link me to that bullshit. It's good you still alive though, but I'm not surprised especially if you learned half of what I taught you", Bruno folded his arms in a discomforting way. "So what business you wanna holla at me about?"

"Nigga it's serious business, I gotta bag full of fedi and I thought you might have some butter."

Bruno took offense to the statement. "Motherfucka I always got some butter", he growled. "How much you got?"

Cleofis copped some coke from Bruno that was fantastic. Keeping the majority of it at his mother's, house he would only bring a couple ounces at a time to the spot. Him, Disco and Berry dumped hard out the rented house. But when they got raided no one wanted to take the two ounces under the couch case, so Cleofis put it on April and signed a statement on her.

The task force went and picked April up immediately, booked her into the county and charged her with the two ounces hard.

Fox and the rest of the task force knew the cocaine was Cleofis' and couldn't see why April didn't want to make a statement on the man who put her behind bars. Fox made sure they put her bond at the maximum 15,000 for not ratting on Cleofis. April was sick, but Cleofis promised her he would get her a lawyer, get her bond lowered, and then bond her out. This is when he went to the law offices of Mark Galante a half white and Italian lawyer.

Short, pop bellied with jet black hair slicked to the back and favored Richard Nixon. Mark Galante was a wanna be Mafioso who wanted so badly to be in the mob but didn't have enough gut so he sat around his office in his fancy suits barking at his secretary's, convincing them he was part of some organized crime element, which he never represented a mobster in his life and didn't know any.

But Mark was a good lawyer who got down to the bottom of things when representing his clients. At the time when you paid him, he would really go to bat for you.

"And what brings you to my office today Mr. Jackson?"

"I heard you was a good attorney that really cared for his clients."

"Well you heard right Mr. Jackson, but some people like to take my kindness for a weakness", leaning back in his leather desk chair heavily, he swung from right to left then leaned forward resting his forearms on the table. "So who's in trouble a friend of yours or something?"

"Naw", Cleofis began. "She's more then a friend, and I need you to get her bond lowered?" He then pulled out five stacks and set it on the mahogany desk remembering what his cousin taught him. No one dollar bills when doing business. The five thousand dollar roll had nothing under a twenty in it. "Just get her bond lowered and get her the best deal possible", he finished demandingly.

Mark Galante went into the courtroom and took care of business getting April's bond lowered to 7,500 and would of got her out on recognizance if it wasn't for the amount of cocaine it was.

Cleofis bonded April out the same day her bond was lowered. He wanted to try to see if her bond could be lowered more the next court hearing because 12,500 dollars was a lot of money to be losing, but changed his mind in doubt that she'd hold her water for long.

Cleofis sailed to Grandmother Sterling's house, still alert of every car and person that went by him. Going to take his grandmother some money and pick up his bullet proof vest he felt like every body was watching him as he yielded at stop signs, slouching down in his BMW, observing the block huggers with a cautious eye.

"Hey! If it isn't my favorite grandson", Mrs. Sterling greeted honestly. "You know Grandma will pay you back."

Cleofis knew his grandmother was telling a tale as usual. "Here grandma", he peeled off a few dingy c-notes. "Thank you grandson you always take care of grandma, that stingy ass Bruno and the rest off 'em don't give me shit, they think my social security cover everything."

"Vmmmmm, vmmmm", his cell was vibrating when Mrs. Sterling stuck the notes in her bra and suggested, "You could pull your self up a seat if ya wanna I'm 'bout to cook" Ending her last word with a lot of saliva in her mouth.

"You wild motherfucka! Go and have Berry come bond me out 'cause you know you wild!"

At first he didn't recognize the voice, but knew who it was once she finished her sentence.

"You trick ass nigga gonna put that shit on me, huh…I seen yo' signed statement motherfucka and I still didn't tell on your ass. Aw hell naw, I ain't finna do your time motherfucka."

"Tone yo' motherfuckin' voice down", he said monstrously. "Look bitch I already been to the joint you got a clean record so don't trip I'mma make sure you get probation." He cut her off before she could butt in. "If I didn't give a fuck about you I wouldn't have got yo' ass that 10,000 dollar lawyer and paid your high ass bond", he was exaggerating about the cost of her lawyer.

"Naw CJ", April spoke vengefully. "One of ya'll gonna go down there and take that case."

"What you gonna do bitch tell on me or something", he asked viscously, but worried.

"I'mma do what I gotta do", was her last words then he heard the dial tone.

"Now I done told you about that cursing, don't nobody curse in this mutherfucka but me and your grand dad, God rest his soul."

Cleofis brushed his loud talking granny off and headed out the door. Forgetting to grab his bullet proof vest he didn't remember until he got down the street and around the corner. *Damn I forgot my vest.*

Circling to head back to his granny's, he wanted to hurry to his moms to move the coke just in case April snitched him out to the police, but on the way back to Mrs. Sterling's he was suddenly surrounded by police cars. Bo Pete done ratted me out. Was the first thing that came to his mind with a knot in his stomach and a dry mouth. This is it. I should just come out blasting cause I'll neva see the day light again. He quickly changed that thought when seeing the big automatics the cops had drawn. "Get your fucking hands in the air", yelled the officers. He put his hands in the air after pushing the mag back under the seat.

Cleofis thought it was over once he was down in the county but was much relieved when being told he was charged with the pistol before releasing him to Mrs. Jackson who posted the 10,000 bond with his money.

April reported the BMW stolen being that it was in her name, and the eager police couldn't wait to catch him driving it.

She then cancelled the insurance on the car and set it on fire in front of his rented house that she took out of her name.

Loss after loss he was taking, and tried to call Angie who was off in college but got nothing but a request to never call again, she was back with her basketball star boyfriend and didn't need falling financially Cleofis anymore.

Moving some of his items down to his mother's house with Berry he was very salty, and bit his lip frequently thinking about the previous losses.

"Man Moe,'" Cleofis replied hopelessly. "I can't win for losing in this rotten motherfucka."

"All we need to do is go set up shop in the projects Moe' and everything'd be gravy in no time, fuck them niggas out there, we gonna have heat for any nigga that say something slick", Berry sounded confident. "I got your back!"

"Well, we gonna roll with that then and I got butter so the feinds can't deny me. Just make sure you watch my back 'cause that nigga Gillmen still in town."

Cleofis started making frequent trips to Mark Galante's office, giving him money to take on his weapon and auto theft case, but most of all they were starting to get to know each other.

Mark heard about Cleofis' growing reputation and took a liking to the young hot head. Wondering how someone so young could be the prime suspect in such brutal murders. "You're a modern day Al Capone", Galante would say making the restless teen grin from ear to ear.

Cleofis loved when Mark compared him to Al Capone and he was becoming obsessed with Al Capone, taping his pictures up on walls of his bedroom at Mrs. Jackson's house.

He put an iron foot down in the projects giving competition the murderous mean mugs, most were shocked to see him out in the middle of the projects making bag sells with Berry, but hustlers wasn't stupid they knew he still had weight and was trying to make up for losses.

He kept his hands on and off the trigger of a black knee knocker bulging out his back pocket giving niggas a look like I wish you would try an collect on that hundred thousand dollar bounty.

For days Cleofis had no trouble but Berry told him, Gillmen saw a picture of what he look like and was said to come to the projects to collect on the bounty soon.

Cleofis watched his surroundings like a hawk using his ears for running foot step sounds. Berry made the transactions and Cleofis fronted a couple dealers ounces promising trouble if late payment.

Autumn had the trees stripped of their leaves, covering the ground making plenty of hiding spots for cocaine. The hood rats were out on the benches looking for the ballers to come through, and hypes was trying to sale anything once they ran out of their money.

The hood rats crowded more then usual, they knew Cleofis was Bruno's little cousin and that he had plenty money. The ones Cleofis hadn't sexed yet, all wanted their turn to see if they could get him sprung so that he could take care of them.

Cleofis glanced at the hood rats often, calculating which one he was going to tend to after a long day of hustling.

The spaces in between the project houses were where they posted up at, Cleofis covered the back, Berry covered the front.

Berry was counting the earnings when Gillmen pulled up. “There they go!” yelled Berry.

Cleofis drew his mag before turning around. Somebody was driving when Gillmen opened the door behind the driverside and began exiting the vehicle. “CLOW! CLOW! CLOW!” He greeted him with bullets before he could get out the car good, followed by his goons. One bullet spun Gillmen back into the car going through his shoulder. Trying to get back into the car Cleofis ran forward putting holes in the back door he closed in desperation to escape the hell of bullets.

Gillmen’s goons didn’t return fire. Cleofis didn’t give them a chance, striking Gillmen also in the back and leg. The Chevy pulled off as fast as it could, Cleofis emptied his clip on it, still tagging it as it jetted down the street. “Looking for me motherfucka?” he yelled as his last shot busted out the Chevy’s window. “Skirrrrrrrr”, was the last thing you heard from the Chevy tires burning rubber turning the corner far down the street.

Taking the empty clip out putting in another, Berry startled him with his yelling. “Come on ‘Moe’! We gotta get the hell outta here!”

Cleofis pointed the mag at Berry then exhaled deeply. “Shhhit ‘Moe’ I ain’t no who you was”, all the shooting had Cleofis jumpy and paranoid.

They jumped in Berry’s box Chevy and hurled to the fastest destination.

“Shawndra”, Cleofis spoke very jumpy, walking into her place unannounced. “I need to talk to you?”

“Boy I know you done lost your mind walking up in here”, she replied as she sat on her couch with female company, thinking it was her baby daddy at first until she payed attention. “What’s wrong? You ok?”

Waiting until she closed the door behind her to her daughter’s bedroom he responded. “I need to hide out here for a little bit”, looking at her not sure face he continued. “Please Shawndra just for a little while?”

Shawndra blew threw her nose. “Alright, but did anybody see you come here?” Cleofis shook his head no. “Well let me go in here and dismiss my company and what do you want me to tell that boy that came here with you?"

"Tell 'em I'll get up with him later."

Just like that Shawndra was there for Cleofis and in a way looked at him like the bad ass little brother she never had.

Cleofis fully trusted Shawndra mostly because Bruno trusted her, and Bruno didn't really trust anybody. Bruno would say Shawndras one of a kind, and loved her like a sister. And in a sense Cleofis was trying to impress Shawndra with all his ruckus he kept up. And in a weird way she was impressed by the dangerous youth.

Every law enforcement in the county was searching for Cleofis, the charge was attempted murder. Gillmen ratted him out after being convinced by Travis's vengeful family members to put the youth behind bars. They swept the streets for a couple weeks until finally cooling off questioning everybody they felt was associated with the wanted man.

Berry and Disco were dumping his yack where ever they could in the small city and he'd sent them by to collect money from the project hustlers that he fronted the ounces to, but they all gave sob stories when in reality they just didn't want to pay the soon to be captured fugitive.

"Motherfuckaz finna pay me my fedi or get they shit pushed back", Cleofis explained to Jackpot who was taking him to the projects to collect. Nobody expected to see Cleofis while he was on the run, so when he pulled up in a sporty pick up truck with Jackpot, hustlers was shock. "Where the fuck is my fedi", he spoke like a starving beast. The hustlers was froze in a state of shock of him breathing down there necks. "Run me what the fuck ya'll got in ya'll pockets, NOW! You motherfuckas thought ya'll wasn't gonna see me again huh?", he stated bravely as the hoods emptied there pockets. "I know ya'll got more then this, don't make me get out this truck, 'cause I'm telling you, one of you niggas gone be laid out on the pavement"

The wanted figure seemed imperial, barking orders from the passenger side of the sporty pick up truck with the window rolled all the way down. "I'mma send Disco through here tomorrow and ya'll betta have the rest of my fedi 'cause if I have to come back through this bitch its gone be a murder, you hear me?" They all nodded understanding him perfectly.

It was the end of the night and Cleofis had just finished counting some money out that he was gonna have Shanwdra take to the lawyers in the morning. He'd spoke with Mark Galante several times over the phone and Mark promised him he could get the best bond possible for him.

"You sure this lawyer is good", Shawndra asked when walking out the bathroom into the kichten that was connected to the livingroom were he was stretched out on the couch.

"He's straight", he replied, glancing over at the tall stout brownie complextioned woman with a pink cotton pajama two-piece outfit on. Dang if she would just let me smell that. He thought as he hoped she would sit down to watch some TV before going to bed. He had put baby oil on his upper body hoping to catch her attention with his muscular physique.

He'd caught her attention as she poured a glass of water, but she wasn't about to let him know that. Opening the refrigerater to deposit a cold jug of water, the light gleamed on her person, making her thin cotton pajama paints slightly sheer sending Cleofis into an arousal panic. "Good night CJ", Shawndra replied gently, walking out the dark kitchen and past the hormone jumping villan.

Cleofis watched TV, playing with himself until he fell into a sinful sleep.

Shawndra laid in the dark with her pillow between her thighs tightly, until she fell into a lustful sleep wondering if the appealing young man could satisfy her.

Cleofis headed for Kim's house after many disturbing nights of Shawndra's baby daddy stalking and beating on the door in the middle of the night. He and Kim would talk frequently on the phone about how they missed each other and Cleofis came to terms with the soft spot Kim still had in his heart. She was his first love and he still loved her, she was the only woman he made love to so far.

After perpetuating his drug trade he was down to 42,000 after collecting debts, money from accomplices, giving the lawyer more money, and finishing up on his last batch of cocaine.

Taking 40,000 to Bruno in hopes of getting fronted what he bought. The villain stumbled upon a big dice game with Bruno and an assoicate, shooting a thousand and betting a thousand.

When Cleofis came through the door Bruno had just about wrapped things up, winning over 20,000 of the man's money.

Cleofis stood there and watched his cousin break the angry but silent man. Kim was waiting outside in her mothers van for him to return.

"Go to yo' vault nigga", yelled Bruno after winning the man's last thousand. The man stormed out the house bumping recklessly into Cleofis on the way out.

"Damn cuz that motherfucka is pissed, if he wouldn't have lost so much change I probably woulda popped his ass for running into me like that."

"Anyway, what you want America's Most Wanted?" Bruno spoke humerously, sorting through his pile of money. "I see you won't leave that hoe alone, huh!"

Cleofis laughed the remark off not wanting to show attitude before asking for his favor. "This forty grand right here, front me what I buy."

Bruno shook his head, sitting up on his knees on the carpet, pulling his designer sweater sleeves up. "I tell you what, I got 60 stacks right here, get down and try to win it. If you win you'll leave up outta here with a 100 grand, and if you lose you'll leave up outta here broke 'cause I ain't fronting you shit", Cleofis glanced at the thirty thousand and wanted so bad to say no but was tempted by the opportunity to be a six-figure nigga again.

Cleofis dropped down with confidence winning two grand through the gait. "Pass on his ass", he spoke firmly to the dice. Bruno watched him pass a couple more times before craping out. "Nah it's my turn little nigga", the dice clicked in his hand with a unique sound and the blunt smelled like it was laced with something to Cleofis. He literally hated the way Bruno acted as if the money was nothing throwing the dice like a humble crime boss.

Bruno observed the mag sticking out of Cleofis hoodie pocket and knew instantly if he broke him it would be a problem so he stroked him slow passing on the impatient fugitive with style.

"Foe lil Joe or big ben to help me win", he bragged when making his point after picking up on a side bet. Bruno was now running through Cleofis' pockets shooting craps picking up four grand a wop from point made and side bets. "Damn can I get a shot in this motherfucka?" Cleofis expressed loudly starting to suspect the dice were tricks he checked them thoroughly only to come to the conclusion that Bruno was hot.

Cleofis wanted to quit while he still possessed closed to 20,000 but just couldn't snap out of the tables turning spell.

Finally Bruno crapped out, Cleofis glanced at the 10,000 he had left and yelled. "Fuck it, shoot it all, make me or brake me", his hands were nervous when picking up the dice to throw them and Bruno smiled because he knew scared money usually didn't win.

"Shoot lil nigga you ain't said nuttin' but a word you cur." The word cur pist him off before seeing the snake eyes he threw on the dice. "Poor baby", Bruno said to get under the youngsters skin.

Cleofis bit his buttom lip, closed his eyes, then opened them to the all too real reality. "Mothafucka", he yelled as he reached for his mag but Bruno beat him to the draw brandishing a big forty five that rested on the side of the couch where he couldn't see. "What you reaching for, you not swifter then me little punk, I was poppin niggaz when your father was alive, matter of fact, we did a caper together."

Cleofis seen the look in his eyes and that his hand didn't twitch.

"I shoulda killed you when you popped me in my chest lil bitch", Bruno snatched the mag out of his hand. "You was gonna rob me or something lil nigga?"

"Naw", Cleofis said in a soft scared for his life tone. "Man cuz I'm broke and I need yo' help, please don't kill me", he begged for his life, staring down the big barrel of the forty- five.

"If it wasn't for your momma I swear", Bruno shook his head looking him directly in his eyes. "I would of killed you the minute I raised this mag, now get the fuck outta here for' I change my mind, and if you get on some bullshit behind this I'll put a real bounty on your head and you won't be able to handle the motherfuckas I send at you."

Cleofis left out of there uncivilized, sick, and mentally hindered wondering how Bruno got the drop on him so fast. Feeling stripped of his gangsterness and naked from no protection he said nothing to Kim all the way to her house. She asked what was wrong but by the look of his body language she quickly resorted to silence.

When he curled up in her bed he continued his silence feeling powerless and in a weird way wanting to be caught by law enforcement.

"I'm down lil homie", Cleofis expressed in a distress tone night's later. "I'm struck and I need your help, you got some change you could spare."

"I don't know", Gabe began. "I been really tryin' to stack my little change. How much you need?"

"Whatever you can spare, beggers can't be choosers", he was trying to put some money together to go with the two grand he had left. He knew he gave Jackpot deals and was hoping he'd returned the favor.

"Where you want me to bring it to?" asked Gabe willing to help his friend.

"You know where I'm at", he spoke assurily. "At my first loves house call me when you get outside the door and she'll come and get it."

Cleofis called Gabe back after he left to express his appreciation for his help, Gabe felt like that's what friends were for, contributing to a friend that he felt was genuine. This made Cleofis look at Gabe in a whole nother way creating more of a brotherly love for him. "I like the way lil homey just came through for me, no questions asked", Cleofis said to Kim. "That's a real nigga!"

CHAPTER 12

Bless My House

Natalie was awakened by a slight tap on her leg coming from Cleofis' finger.

Half asleep, she yawned and turned her head in the opposite direction paying no attention to his paralyzed body lying next to her.

Why do he feel like playing with me in the middle of the night like this, he know I gotta go to work in the morning, she reflected.

Turning around to tell him a piece of her mind, the look in his wide open wartery eyes told her something was terribly wrong. "What's wrong baby?", she asked scarcely, but no words came out of Cleofis' mouth and the tapping on her leg continued.

Lifting her head up off the pillow to observe him better she could see something was holding him down for his body was imprinted deep into the bed. *Am I dreaming*, she asked herself. What is holding him down, glancing back at the scared look in his eyes she broke out into a loud cry. "What's wrong, Cleofis baby, talk to me. I don't know what to do?" Feeling the presence of a supernatural being, every hair on her body stood straight up. "God please help me", she yelled with her knees to her chest and arms wraped around the lower part of her legs.

Burying her face under her arms she continuously prayed whole heartedly until an earful scream came from the other room. "Dasia", she said sprinting out of the bed. Basically busting down the door, Dasia clung to her like a magnet. "Mommy there was a man in my room with a flash light in his hands", the eleven year old said. Scared half to death her heart pounded rapidly, the little girl was traumatized as she trembled from head to toe. "Who ever you are leave this house now! Can't you see my daughter's scared", she yelled through sobs.

"Natalie!" She turned quicker then a speeding bullet. It was Cleofis looking just as terrified, breathing rapidly from the encounter. "Boy what's in this house", Natalie screamed in tears. "I don't know", replied Cleofis. "Something was holding me down, I couldn't get up!" Natalie looked at him still hysterical. "We are not staying in this house for the rest of the night, we going over my cousins!" Cleofis growled at her decision, not wanting to show he was scared of anything. "You ain't goin' nowhere", he barked then brought his voice volume down. "As long as you prayed, we'll be straight let's just go back to bed, let Dasia come in here with us." Dasia sqeezed her mother tightly, "Momma I don't wanna stay in this house... please momma, please?"

"She said she saw some man in her room with a flashlight", Nataile spoke to Cleofis without responding to her daughter. "Well let me see", Cleofis scoured the room with his eyes. "I don't see anybody in here, See Dasia", Cleofis' hand scrawled the room. "Nobody's in your room, but you can come sleep with us."

"Can we leave the light on?" asked Dasia. "Yeah we can", he took a deep breath through his nose heavily. Cleofis was more than happy at the girl's request, but refused to let it show.

Natalie barely got any sleep, she stayed up 'til it was time for her to go to work in the morning, Cleofis and Dasia was knocked out like a light, both snoring like they were in hibernation. Cleofis now had a key to the house and stayed there anytime he wanted to. Natalie had become like Shawndra she didn't care if he fooled around as long as it didn't get back to her. She loved her slot on his team of women because she knew she was number one at the time.

Cleofis was later found guilty at the end of 98 for the gun and stolen vehicle case, but Mark Galante got him another appeal, which freed him on the same 10,000 bond posted when he first caught the case, every time the state thought they had him he would slip through some tiny hole and come from up under it.

April was hiding out after receiving a lump sum of intense probation and community service, Cleofis sent word that if she didn't change her flimsy statement about him stealing his car from her he would have her killed. April was terrified and only came outside to do community service.

In a two story section eight house on the Southside of Kankakee, James (JW) Wells was becoming tired of his mother lecturing him about keeping drugs out of the house. JW was quick tempered and simple minded, and to prove he was a killer, pumped through his veins like his cousin Cleofis, at young age, but he was now 21 as well. He wanted to be respected and feared like his cousin, everybody knew the Capone crew was nothing without its leader.

JW was down for whatever though, not very sharp up top, and scared of no man.

Mrs. Wells, the sister of Mrs. Jackson was a fairly dark colored woman, with a gray hair for every other black one in her head, and also carried the gene, giving nose gene that was passed to her son. Divorced, she kept her last name instead of switching it back to Sterling. She didn't want her son staying in her house as long as he continued to sell drugs, but how could she refuse her youngest out of her only two children a place to stay. Tall and slim, she sometimes smoked premos, where the tobacco is laced with coke. She was worried about being kicked out of her section 8 if the task force raided the house.

"I'm telling you James if somebody come to me saying they watching this house again you might as well take your shit and get up outta here, 'cause I'm not about to risk being tossed out on the street for you. You are a grown man, and frankly I'm tired of taking care of you!"

"Don't nobody take care of me like the Capone's", JW began after slaming a roll of cash on the table. "You don't trip when a muthafucka givin' you money do ya ma?"

"Young punk please, who give you money when you come in this house crying broke after you done spent your little money in da street, and just who the fuck you think you scaring?" she said sternly while finishing braiding a braid in her head. "Let me tell you something", her boney booty scooted to the edge of the kicten chair. "You don't pay not a bill in this bitch, so until you do I'm the only one who can curse in this house."

"Bitch! Who you think you talking to", came from his untamed tongue. "I don't need you or any other muthafucka, you the one a borderline crackhead." James began breaking things in the house snatching anything that came across his path, blowing through the place like a tornado. Mrs Wells fumbled with the phone. "Uhh huh you big bad motherfucka, when the police get here I bet you paying for everything you broke."

JW stormed out the house slaming the door behind him after hearing her exaggerated 911 call.

James (Jackpot) Love sat at the kitchen table of Melissa's apartment baging up some pretty intensified coke. His nose kept sniffing and his finger tips was numb. "I'm telling you", Melissa began in a high pitch. "That Cleofis ain't no good baby and I don't want him over my apartment anymore." Rolling his eyes Jackpot gave her an exasperated look. "Why", he asked, dropping 7 grams in a sandwich bag and tying it up. "The nigga like my brother and he got my back no matter what nigga it is."

"I know you think he's your friend baby", she hugged him around his neck and pressed her brown face up against his. "But that dude is trouble I can sense it plus niggaz wanna kill him for those townhouse murders they say he did." Her lips never stopped flapping as she shifted to massaging his shoulders. "I just don't want nobody to kill you trying to kill him, 'cause it's always the innocent by standers that get hit…the man is evil, can't you tell and look at the way he talks to you like your one of his hoes or something and you're older then him. And why the fuck you get that stupid ass Capone tattoo on your arm don't you know that's on there for life?"

"Of course I know", his voice began to rise as he removed her manicured soft hands. "That's my nigga for life. You always yapping about shit you know nothing about. And the nigga can come over here all the fuck he want to."

Melissa stood with both hands on her hips on the right side of him. She hoped he would at least compromise with her about the situation, and after that she would give him more sex then he could handle, but at the sound of him telling her he was welcomed anytime immediately changed her mind.

The silk turquoise pajama top dropped down to the beginning of her knocked knees and her little brown chicken legs seemed very fragile. Melissa was a decent looking lady who'd been with Jackpot on and off for two years. And was becoming tired of the way the Capone crew was running in and out of her apartment.

It was time to give her a break, he reflected, bagging up his last quarter ounce. Jackpot had fell off during Cleofis' incarceration and not living up to his childhood giving name was ridiculous, so as he tried to pick up the pieces. Cleofis got out and offered him a place at his dinner table where he promised a full money meal for loyalty.

"This nigga the one who put me back on my feet, why you downing him? He the reason why all these bills caught up around here, why your car didn't get reposessed. This nigga you yappin about, make it possible for all the Capone's to eat when didn't nobody wanna give me shit, this nigga stepped up to the plate when nobody was there for me. You know how my momma is about giving me cash, she wanna keep all that money for herself so fuck all that bullshit niggaz say about Teflon that's my guy and I'm ridin with em."

Melissa walked heavily footed out of the kitchen, making sure he was done talking before she walked off. "Well Mr. Teflon wanna be", she screamed from the other room. "Don't say I didn't warn you, so when the nigga get your ass knee deep in some shit don't bring the drama to this apartment."

"Fuck that nigga", Shawndra stated cruely. "Gabe, I'm nobody's fool and I don't know who that nigga think he playin' with but I'mma show his ass", she had pulled up to the side after seeing Gabe standing in front of his mothers. Gabe now stood by the driver's door listening to the broken heart women that he'd gotten to know through

Cleofis. "Now look Shawndra, CJ still loves you he just be busy in the streets makin that bread for you to spend." Gabe took a shot in the dark not knowing if Cleofis gave her money or not.

"Please! That nigga don't give me shit and I'm tired of his silly little threats, like that mean something to me 'cause come tomorrow I'mma get me a gun card and I dare the nigga try to pull it, the bitch ass nigga still owe me money I ain't none of these lame ass punks on the street I'll take it there with his ass!"

"Just calm down", exclaimed Gabe trying to lower her voice. "Everything will be cool just give it a minute." Rolling her neck in his direction she was becoming frustrated with his humbleness. "Give it a minute…shhhit I've gave it long enough I'm not finna continue to share him with Natalie, this motherfucka done got me pregnant, so now all I want is the money he owes me so I can take my 2 kids and get on with my life."

Gabe knew she really didn't mean half the stuff she was saying but her being pregnant was a surprise to him, 'cause she definitely wasn't showing yet. "What girl Natalie?" Gabe played with her intelligence. "The only girl I know him for being around is you."

"Okay motherfucka, you think I'm stupid", she looked him dead in the eyes. "That's what's wrong with you young niggas, y'all thank y'all got so much game. I'm twenty-seven almost twenty-eight years old, believe me you can't run the bullshit on me… and see I don't know why your friend keep playing with me, with the dirt I know on his ass they'll lock the nigga up and throw away the key." Shawndra was letting her heart do the talking instead of her brain, which told her maybe she should keep her mouth closed. But Gabe never went back and relayed any of these messages to Teflon, 'cause he knew how it was when a women got upset, they would say things they really didn't mean. Though Gabe wondered what it was that was so incriminating, he also figured Cleofis probably shot his mouth off too many times around the chick. Because Cleofis loved to be glamorized as an untouchable killer.

While followers mimicked Teflon, Teflon mimicked Bruno, basking in the shadow of the legend, trying to talk and act like him few observed this and these few was amongst Bruno's loyalist, they started to get a whiff of the gangsters roll in Bruno's murder. No matter how hard he tried he just didn't have the gift Bruno was born with, and Bruno's name would continue to ring in the mouths of true gangster ballin ass niggas, that still thought of him as a young stupid little boy with a lot to learn.

Cleofis hated his cousin for sexing two of the women that he cared for but on the flip side of the coin he admired him, and missed him a lot. Sometimes wishing he never let the information slip to the Chicagoans who already suspected Bruno had something to do with the loss, but just didn't know exactly where to locate him. He was now starting to realize the things Bruno did for him in his teenage years. This was the man who gave him all the game he could handle at a young age and shielded him from people who wanted to murder him. Regret started to drench the gangster, but he shook it off for what was done was done it was no changing it.

Pulling up in front of Natalie's, he could see that she was home when she was supposed to be at her second job, what this woman doing home, he reflected as he closed the door to his now eighteen inch Assassin chrome laced rims on his white Aurora. He hoped she wasn't inside packing after the strange encounter that took place in the middle of the night.

The loud laughing was hearable once his feet touched the steps that led to the porch screen door. Shutting the porch door quietly behind him, he wanted to sneak up on Natalie. Snatching the door open the laughter immediately stopped. "Don't stop talking and laughing now just 'cause I'm here", he started after recognizing that it was female company she was entertaining. "Why aren't you at work Mrs. Knowles?"

With a nigga I know you didn't questioning me look, she went on and let him feel like the man. "I called off today is that a problem chief?" Natalie and her company giggled after Cleofis stated, "No problem", like he really was her chief.

"This my girl Mandy, Mandy this big nose Cleofis." Natalie swung her arms from right to left introducing them. Mandy, Natalie's overly sized friend wondered if this was the Cleofis that the streets spoke so much about.

Very cute brown full face, weighing over three hundred pounds, acted tuff like a gangsta, sold coke like an average hustler. Mandy was a scared little girl inside, she had three daughters, loved to smoke weed, drink and gossip. Being around hustlers all her life just like

Natalie the two had a lot in common, though Natalie chose the legitimate road.

"So this the fella you talk so much about huh?" Mandy spoke out loud to Natalie making sure Cleofis heard her. "He's kinda cute where you find em?"

Natalie laughed a little bit at the sarcastic question. "Oh, I found him on some silly little girls' front steps looking so harmless so I couldn't help but to bring the little puppy home." They both broke out into chuckles holding their stomachs.

"Y'all gonna quit with the jokes", Cleofis replied, pouring a glass of water. "Cause if I'm a male dog then what that make you?"

Natalie rolled her eyes and turned her neck from the direction of the kitchen. "Ok Teflon or Capone…whatever your name is today." The reply from Natalie instantly let Mandy know this was the oh-so talked about gangster who headed the infamous Capone crew. A promiscuous look shot across Mandy's face. *My, how I would love some of that meat…I bet you the nigga a ruff rider, s*he reflected licking her lips.

Natalie never peeped the lustful look in Mandy's eyes, for she followed Cleofis to her room to see what he was doing. "What you about to do?"

Bending down to fetch a shoebox from under the bed he glanced up at her. "Taking care of some business why you ask?"

"I was just asking 'cause I thought you might wanna spend the day home with me after what happened in the middle of the night I've been kinda scared to be in this house alone."

"Your friend in there, make her stay 'cause I got things to do and people to see", the last words came out with a smirk knowing he wanted to stay but wanted her to sweat him.

"Look", she spoke begging. "Why don't you take care of your business and come back and chill with me' waiting for his response she continued. "And Mandy in their is a hustling ass female and I told her she could probably cop some stuff from you at a better price then what she's getting now."

"Nah that's yo' girl, I don't know her well enough to sell her yack and how much she spends anyway?" Wondering if it was a thousand or better to make it worth his while.

"She cops an ounce at a time, sometimes two." She blurted out not knowing if she was right or not.

"Well I'll holla at her after I make this run, just tell her to stay put."

Shawndra was on her way home just leaving from picking up Shay Shay at her mothers. Shawndra's mother Mrs. Coleman was a warm sweet person with what looked like a frown but was her natural look. With the same brownie complexion of her daughter, Mrs. Coleman was becoming worried at the age of fifty remembering when she helped Shawndra's long gone father get away with a murder back in the early seventies. The past was hunting her like a horror movie. The more she asked God for forgiveness the more she felt she wasn't forgiven. Feeling a need to confess to feel cleansed, she always thought about this option but would always change her mind after reflecting on the old cancer days that lay ahead of her. She didn't want to spend those days behind bars.

Shawndra could smell the marijuana aroma before she got to the door good. "Cleofis", she stated after busting open the door. "You been in here smoking weed?"

"Naw that was that stupid ass nigga Disco that just left, I told 'em to put the shit out", he replied honestly.

"Well you know I don't like Shay Shay coming in contact with that stuff so I would appreciate if you tell your friends to leave it outside ok?"

"Don't come in here with that shit Shawndra, 'cause I ain't in da mood!" A herpes outbreak was starting to take place in his mouth which was starting to make him very agitated. He'd had outbreaks in his mouth before but this one was the worse. Having passed the incurable STD to Shawndra, she gradually accepted it, for her love for him ran deep.

Natalie was lucky so far some how she hadn't caught the disease yet.

Kim had it since she was a teen in her mouth as well as down there just like Cleofis. She accepted it as a teen, thinking her and Cleofis was going to be together forever just like Shawndra recently thought.

But after Shawndra realized herpes was a disease she would have to deal with alone, it did nothing but add to the stress.

Kim and Cleofis didn't let the disease stop them from performing oral sex on each other. Young and naive they had already been fairly warned about the conditions of oral sex when carrying the disease, but their hormones wouldn't allow them to stop and they both paid dearly for it during the outbreaks in their mouths.

But since Shawndra caught the lifetime STD in between her thighs she refused to catch it in her mouth so a blow job was usually out of the question.

Shawndra mumbled under her breath for a few seconds wanting to tell him a piece of her mind but didn't want to run him away. "And what are your plans for this baby, 'cause I hope you didn't think I was playing when I told you I missed my period last week"

Cleofis clenched his jaws together inflating his jaw bones and flinched his eyes tightly. "Would you just let me be please? Shawndra just let me be?" The words came out very mean as he sat distraught trying to shove the McDonalds down his throat without irrupting the multitude of herpes.

"Ok fine I'll let you be!" She shook her head slightly taking Dasia to her room trying to hold back the tears that was building.

Later that night after spending some sex time with Natalie, Cleofis couldn't do nothing but return the favor to this overly-sized woman performing a blow job out of this world. "Oh shit I'm bout to cuuuuum!" The words came out through a moan.

He exhaled slightly, trembling as he burst in her mouth and the sucking never stopped 'cause she drank everything like it was protein.

Getting his limp soldier back up for the occasion, she released then glanced up at Cleofis. "I bet you ain't neva had your dick sucked like money making Mandy just did?"

Cleofis giggled for a second. "This ain't gone get back to Natalie is it?"

She gave him a silly look with her largely shaped eyes as she struggled to get her pants off. "Boy of course not, is you crazy. Me and Nat go back since we was teenagers", she laughed very stank like.

"This was some of the best head I ever had", he reflected, watching Mandy's legs seem to grow bigger once out of her tight pants.

With no intensions on sexing her, Cleofis stopped over Mandy's house on strictly business after realizing she was gone from Natalie's house. But the situation was turning out to be business and plenty of pleasure.

Never the one to refuse a blow job his irritated tongue now curled at the top of her love below overwhelmed with returning the favor. The fact that the big women was very clean made it no problem for him to give her the come back treatment. After this they sexed in the positions they could and Cleofis shot back to Natalie's where he curled up in the bed and called it a night.

Cleofis usually didn't watch porno's this early in the morning but after rambling through Natalie's closet after she left out for work, he was curious to know if this girl was more of a freak then him.

Sitting on the plush couch in the living room with his maroon silk boxers on, the way the porn star deep throated the other porn star was starting to turn Cleofis on. Ding Dong, the door bell rang as the silk boxers felt so good up against his crotch that he started touching himself.

Who could it be at this time of the morning? Grabbing a mag that rested underneath the couch he walked to the door knowing it couldn't be danger but took precautions anyway.

It was Makeela's mother he'd saw a couple houses down yesterday and told her about the quality of the coke he had. Makeela's mother was a crack head that he'd forgotten the name of.

She knows better then to come over here. "I don't do business over here pretty lady you have to go to my spot and they'll hook you up!"

"Don't be like that CJ", she began, scratching her head full of rollers. "I've always let you in my place when you was in there humping on my daughter." Seeing that she made him grin she continued. "Plus I got this trick down here and I need to get a dub to get him started, he a honkey too, with a roll as big as your dick."

"Oh really", Cleofis replied after a brief laugh, making his mind fly back to lustful thoughts, he looked the women up and down while poking his head out the screen. "Come on in, but don't make this a habit 'cause I don't do business here."

The skinny women breezed in the house, stunned at the way it was furnished. "Whoever the chick you fucking with sure has taste", she yelled to Cleofis who was in the other room retrieving an ounce to break a crumb off of.

"Here you go", he said, setting the crumbs down on a table that set right in front of the porno showing on the big screen.

"I see you like watching flicks huh", she began as she dropped a twenty on the table and picked up the nice sized crumbs. "Them white girls on here don't know nuttin about sucking no dick, I'll show you how to suck a cock for the right price."

Looking at the black womans jaw structure he could tell she could probably gobble a soldier, glancing back at the action on the big screen gave him no second thoughts. "Here", he said braking off another piece of the short ounce. "If you make me cum quick I'll give you more!"

The woman jumped down and completed her job in less then 5 minutes. Cleofis didn't think that this unattractive crack head with early morning slab still in between the cracks of her mouth would make him climax so quick, she was almost as good as Mandy was last night. Giving her the extra piece on the way out the door, The woman returned again and again bringing hundreds of the white tricks dollars. Running through an ounce and a half in bags in the matter of 3 hours Cleofis got scared the neighbors would notice and sent Cliff to the domain just in case they wanted more coke.

The horn of the jet black Suburban SUV honked for Cleofis to hurry up. Shawndra rented the roomier, windows tinted in the back, sports utility that Jackpot sat in the driver's seat of impatiently.

"Hurry up nigga, the game done already started", shouted Berry that was seated behind the empty passenger seat.

Cleofis took his time reaching the vehicle, having just put a pistol and an eighth of a key under his Moms barbeque grill in the back yard. "What I tell y'all niggas about rushing all the time, the slower you move the more you see", he began to lecture but was cut off by JW seating in the third row in the back.

"Man we don't wanna hear that shit, just close the door, so we can go catch the football game."

"Listen to this punk here", Cleofis glanced at Disco that was seating next to JW. "Always gotta get smart."

"Nigga you get smart too", Berry butted in before JW could respond. Sitting behind the drivers side Berry spoke up because he felt Cleofis was always speaking to somebody like he was their daddy. But JW was starting to take things serious, already feeling like he was being paid very little for the risk he took. "Cuz I'm broke", came out right before Jackpot turned the radio up. "And why is that", Cleofis snarled, cutting the radio back down. "Cause you took all my fedi. Everybody else get left with plenty why I get left with crumbs?"

"Nigga you get what everybody else get", the boomness rose in his voice. "I can't help it you trick your change off on them runners."

Jackpot ended the soon to be argument by turning the radio back up loud. Bumping the latest Master P CD, the six man crew felt royal in the brand new 99 SUV. The smell of newness traveled through their nostrils until Berry fired up a blunt. One ride around the city in the clean black suburban would start gossip about the Capone's having a new wip.

"Don't come in here with none of that weed fellas", stated Shawndra as the whole Capone crew piled up in her living room.

"We'll be sure to spark a bee up", said Jackpot with a laugh. For some reason Shawndra was in a good mood and was showing a lot of hospitality. Popping the crew popcorn and pouring them drinks, she catered to them with a bright smile. "Where's that little bad ass daughter of yours", asked Jackpot.

"She's with her father."

Jackpot couldn't help but laugh. "You mean her daddy, I seen you at the movies with last night."

"Yeah, that's the one", Shawndra replied going along with the joke.

"Keep playin' here, and you gonna get you and your baby daddy whacked", Cleofis said with a serious face, sitting on a footstool.

"Ha ha ha Cleofis you ain't gonna wack nuttin but your meat", the whole crew started laughing at the remark coming from Shawndra.

Cleofis said nothing for a minute, not taking it personal as she thought he would. "What I done told you about calling me Cleofis, everybody calls me Teflon and that's what you will call me."

"Naw, 'cause if I'mma call you something besides Cleofis it'd be big nose Cleofis", entertaining the laughing crowd she carried on. "And another thing if you come in this address after twelve at night the top lock will be on the door, which you have no key for, killer."

The way she was talking to Cleofis tickled the fellas damn near off the couch, maybe it was because no one really spoke to him that way or maybe it was because they wanted to instigate like he did in their affairs.

Whatever it was he fell into a mute and had a too serious look on his face as the commercials was over and the football game was back on.

Jackpot fell of into the kitchen conversating with Shawndra about the past. Jealousy covered Cleofis' face, though there was nothing to worry about Jackpot knew her much longer and was just having a friendly conversation. "You need to put something over your legs", barked the gangster. "You walking around here in them shorts and shit everybody in here know you got ass."

Shawndra cut her interesting conversation short. "Ain't nobody worried about my ass but you and these shorts is okay, you act like they all hiked up in my ass. Are these shorts showing too much fellas?" She walked out the kitchen and stood in front of the TV screen, they all responded no, while trying to control their stares at the wide hipped shiny dark brown legs that stood in front of them.

"And the last time I checked my name was on the lease here. "She spoke in a stride back to the kitchen. "Not yours Mr., so I think you got the wrong place 'cause Shawndra Coleman stays here not Natalie Knowles."

"Girl leave that man alone", Jackpot began. "You gonna get yourself hurt with yo' crazy ass, just go put on something 'cause I don't wanna see you two fight."

"I'm not putting on a motherfuckin' thang", she cursed rapidly. "That nigga don't pay no bills in here, matter fact all he is another bill for me, the nigga betta start flying straight or that's his ass."

Jackpot wondered what she meant but didn't let it alter his thoughts. "Say Shawndra why don't y'all two just get married?"

"Nigga please he betta marry that bitch he spend his nights wit."

Cleofis couldn't help but to hear her voice slightly smothered out by the loud football game. "Shhhhhhh, can you'll keep it down lady's" he started. "Since you wanna sit and yap like a girl, that's what a muthafucka gone call to ask for from now on."

"Oh come on Moe it ain't nuttin like that", Jackpot's voice rose just enough for Cleofis to hear it.

JW sat uniquely silent, salty about the lint in his pockets and jealous of the close friendship between Cleofis and the others. I'm his motherfuckin' cousin, shit! I should have more then every nigga in the crew.....and look at this nigga Jackpot…soft ass bitch made ass nigga. His thoughts wouldn't stop rambling. I bet you the nigga put a nice stash in auntie's back yard.

He thought no more for the rest was history. "This game ain't about shit they getting they ass kicked, I'm finna go get me some pussy", came out his JW's mouth as he stood up making a excuse for his departure.

"Bye big nose number two", said Shawndra jokingly, watching him walk out the door.

It would seem like nobody noticed his departure except for Shawndra, but Cleofis was fully observing his cousins strange actions, noticing he only joked with Shawndra and said very little to everyone else.

"Aw hell naw", boomed from Cleofis lips. Lifting the barbeque grill up, there was no cocaine or pistol. *My momma must have found it*, he reflected, not wanting to panic right away.

"Did you move somethin' from under the barbeque grill", asked Cleofis not excusing himself for busting into the conversation Mrs. Jackson was having with a girlfriend.

"Boy don't you see I'm talking to someone. And no, but I seen James back there, I thought he was with you."

"Motherfuckin' bitch ass JW, I'll kill em", the words sprang out as he closed his mother's side door. Mrs. Jackson blew it off knowing her Christian company just heard the disrespectful remark.

"Man I'mma kill this nigga", he started, jumping into the waiting vehicle.

"Who and what the hell you talking bout?"

"That nigga JW just took a quarter key and that mag from out the back yard." Lying about the amount of coke, which was only an eighth of a key. The whole crew looked stunned.

"You bullshittin' right?" came from Berry sitting behind him.

"Nigga I ain't playin, the nigga pulled this shit 'cause he feel like a motherfucka owe him some shit. But that's cool though 'cause I ain't wacked a motherfucka since 96."

While the Capone's were riding around strapped up looking for JW, JW was in a secluded crack house deep on the Southside out of reach.

"Is it butta?", an old staggering blood shot red crack head asked.

"Test it out and see old man", JW spoke confidently. "And after you smoke that chunk I want the next ten sales that come through."

"Well that determines on if I gotta re-cook this shit or not youngster", the old man replied, taking his glass pipe out his drawers. So anxious that he almost dropped the stain covered thing on the floor. The nappy headed old man thought nothing of the offer figuring the coke couldn't be that good.

The end of the pipe sizzled barely as the flame from the lighter melted the uncut cocaine being inhaled by the old man. Exhaling through his nose, the old mans head jerked back like a cobra, his mouth watered tremendously, his eye lids open wide like a surprise, and his mouth made his words come out tangled.

The response brought a vivid smile to JW's lips already knowing the product was butter. That's what that bitch ass nigga get, I ain't even got a place to lay my head at and this nigga's everything is in my pockets. JW blazed up a Newport. "BLING, BLING", his cell phone was blowing up he didn't want to answer it 'cause it was only a couple minutes left on it, but he decided to anyway.

"You gone return what you took motherfucka", an all to familiar voice growled on the other end. "And don't try to act like you don't know what I'm talking about 'cause my old lady already saw you nigga!"

"So what", JW began viciously. "You bitch ass niggas think some body scared of y'all, I want you to try a stunt with me, I bet you want live to talk about it", the phone went dead and Cleofis had hung up and there was nothing left to talk about.

Mrs. Jackson had just arrived at Natalie's house with Pastor Evens. Natalie didn't want an entourage so she told Mrs. Jackson to only bring the pastor.

"How you doing Natalie", asked Mrs. Jackson upon entering.

"I'm livin'. How are you?"

"I'm fine", answered Mrs. Jackson.

After the Pastor and Natalie introduce themselves, Pastor Evans expressed his concern about the feeling he had when entering her house. He told her how he could feel the presence of evil upon entering, then they immediately started praying.

After prayer Mrs. Jackson wiped tears from her eyes. "My son is the one bringing them demons into your house", she gracefully said. "Nothing will come in no more unless you invite it, so if that means keeping my son out your house that's just what you'll have to do."

The three hugged each other very tightly then Natalie went into the kitchen and got the dinner she prepared for them.

The three started to eat after blessing the food and Pastor Evens carried on conversation about how good God is. The late forties, dark complexioned, sorta tall handsome looking black man reminded Natalie of what she once wanted for a husband.

"I'm glad you called", Pastor Evens began. "Cause some people let the demons come in and just take over their house. Now what are you going to do 'bout Mr. Jackson?"

"To be honest Pastor Evens I really don't know. I'm pretty sure I'm pregnant and I haven't even told him yet."

"You're pregnant", Mrs. Jackson's eyes watered as she reached over to touch Natalie's hand. "Honey the best thing to do is pray for my son and if he doesn't want to act right then I'm always here to help you raise my grand child." Mrs. Jackson was becoming very emotional, for the news of a grandchild overwhelmed here with joy. Taking her glasses off to wipe her eyes she continued sternly. "Give him a little time to change and if he doesn't give him an alternative."

Looking in Mrs. Jackson eyes Natalie could see she meant the drugs, murder and his other main squeeze Shawndra.

"A man can only do what you allow him", Pastor Even's started. "Once you show a man that you mean business, he'll either see things your way or leave you completely alone, trust me I know." Pastor Even's covered Natalie's thoughts right when they crept in her head. "And if you worried about being alone, you won't be, 'cause God is all the man you need. Sing to him after your done praying, God loves it when we sing to him, not only does it make him happy but it makes us happy as well."

Walking into Natalie house Cleofis was surprised when seeing Gabe sitting in the recliner and her sitting on the sofa across from him. Most importantly it was night time, what was his friend doing over here.

Pissed off about the no luck search for JW, his eyes scrunched instantly. "What the fuck is he doing over here when I'm not here?" The words came out fast and furious.

"Cleofis", Natalie stood from the couch with a smile. "Me and Gabe is brothers and sisters", before he could speak she continued. "Remember when I told you my father has a lot of unclaimed kids, this is one of them. No bullshit I just spoke with my mother and she even knows about it."

Cleofis stared at her for a second, took the frown off his face then replied without a smile. "I wouldn't claim his big head ass either if I was his daddy -- just look how big the nigga head is!"

Gabe didn't laugh at that remark too much, realizing they probably wanted to be alone he left without saying much to his friend.

"Your mother and Pastor Evens came by and blessed the house today and it's some leftovers in there from the dinner we had."

"Girl why did you call my mother?" his voice towered over his urinating, taking place in the bathroom. "You already prayed for the house, there was no need to have church in the house."

Hearing the sprinkles from the last drop of pee, she wanted to tell him that it was because off him that the unusual experience took place but quickly changed her mind. "Cleofis", she said before he responded buckling his belt buckle. "I'm pregnant",

"You what?" zipping his pants up he stepped back into the living room where she was sitting. "Did you just say you pregnant?"

"Yes and I don't know what to do!"

Cleofis gave her a sharp look. "What do you mean you don't know what to do, I've always wanted a son?"

The joy in his voice made Natalie happy and secure. They made passionate love, both of them pregnant now I can fully control both of their lives. He reflected during intercourse. For Shawndra's pregnancy it was anything goes but for Natalie this was clearly what he wanted at the time. Natalie kept him on his toes, she never got boring, and he treated her with more respect then Shawndra.

Natalie could arouse him no matter how many chicks he'd been with in a day -- his soldier would always stand at his best.

Just about every hood rat in Kankakee County wanted to bed the gangster and Natalie bedded him mostly every night.

Fornicating was becoming an addiction for Cleofis sleeping with at least 3 women a day then returning to Natalie's or Shawndra's bed.

"Happy birthday baby", Cleofis replied with a dozen roses and a small wrapped up gift in hand. Shawndra accepted the roses managing to crack a smile even after seeing the expensive tennis bracelet in the small black box that was wrapped, she still showed no excitement. "What's wrong baby, I know you ain't tripping is you. Girl shake that shit off this your 28th birthday you should be happy you lived this long."

"What's that supposed to mean?", she said looking directly at him.

Cleofis chuckled, for he was only trying to get a response. "Nothing…nothing but dang can I get a thank you."

"What you want me to tell you thank you for getting me pregnant when I told your little dick ass to start using a rubber."

"Please, you the one wanted to get pregnant by me, you know I don't use rubbers."

"Yeah and that's why I got a disease I can't get rid off 'cause you don't use rubbers… you know what, matter fact I don't even want this shit." She threw the roses and tennis bracelet across the room, knocking down a picture of her and him.

"I bet'chu betta find that bracelet, I just spent an arm and a leg for." grabbing her arm she yanked away. "You think I'm playin' wit' you, I said you betta go get that

Shawndra's room door slammed before his last words could get out.

RING, RING.... his cell phone brought him to a halt right when he was getting up enough nerve to kick her bedroom door in. "It betta be important nigga 'cause I'm in the middle of something."

"Rest yo' soul", Berry took a pull from a blunt then began on the other end. "I just seen dude over on the Southside, dumping like a motherfucka and they say he got some boulders."

"Why didn't you tag the bitch ass nigga?", Cleofis spoke in a hollow whisper, stepping into Dasia's room.

"'Cause nigga I was gonna wait on you."

"A'ight, well get ready 'cause here I come, be coming outside soon as I pull up."

Ending the call he wanted to get back to Shawndra but murder quickly seized his thoughts. "When I come back that fuckin' bracelet and them roses betta be picked up", he yelled loud enough for her to hear him. "I ain't playin", was his last words before slamming her front door.

JW sat cautiously in a raggedy wheel chair with a gee pack in his lap, sorta hidden by some leafless bushes in front of an apartment building. To a person on the outside looking in they would think he was paralyzed. With one mag tucked under the bottom of his shirt and another in the bushes he was ready for drama.

I could have sworn that was Berry that drove past about a half a hour ago. So I know that pussy muthafucka done went back and told that nigga. Peaking through the branches of the bushes he could see two approaching fellas on feet striding from a north east angle. They were quite a distance but because he was on his square he peeped that tuff guy strut from anywhere. One of them niggaz is Teflon. Came to his mental, as he grabbed the other mag out the bushes. Without hesitating he rolled the wheel chair forward fully revealing himself from behind the bushes, not even giving the dual a chance to get close he jumped out the wheel chair blazing the two big automatic weapons. “What! You bitch ass niggas want some of this”, he spoke almost as loud as the automatics that was blazing.

Caught off guard Cleofis and Berry hauled ass feeling like they were ambushed.

If JW would have been a little patient he could have waited until they got closer and probably wounded both of them, for the bushes helped camouflage the cowboy.

“Hurry up, hurry up…you ain’t get hit did you”, Cleofis said nervously, closing the door to the getaway car.

“Naw I’m straight”, replied Berry, closing the other door.

“Man…that nigga crazy”, Cleofis, broke off into a nervous laugh. “Shhhhit cuz didn’t even give a nigga a chance to get close…I see the nigga ready for war.” The reality of him almost getting killed by his mother’s nephew that he came to kill sort of tickled the gangster.

He laughed like a mad hatter as his adrenaline started to come down. “I’m fenna go over Natalie’s, take this car some where and stash it.”

“So that’s it?” Berry started, “We ain’t gonna go back through there and lay that nigga down?”

“Man you know how hot that area is, it’s probably crawling with them people right now. Just put the car up and we’ll try again tomorrow.”

Cleofis went into Natalie’s house and curled up in the bed for the rest of the day and more than likely dreamed of an ambush for his cousin.

CHAPTER 13

Two Women In Love With The Same Man

"So this is where he sleeps", said Shawndra glancing around Natalie's apartment, she just moved into deep on the Southside.

"Yes this is where he sleeps when he's not at your house", Natalie responded politely.

Shawndra snooped through Cleofis' cell phone while he was asleep, found Natalie's number and gave her a call. Not even two minutes into the conversation Natalie suggested she stop over her place, so far the two was carrying themselves like ladies, wondering what the other had to make of the man they both loved, be involved with the other.

"So what made you call me?", asked Natalie sitting on her plush recliner chair.

"I was just wondering if Cleofis told you I'm three months pregnant with his child", Shawndra took a seat on Natalie's cozy couch.

Damn! She's the same amount of months as me. "No he hasn't told me that!" Natalie shifted her back in a chair with a puzzled face.

"Well I thought you should know…I don't know if I'm keeping it or not, but I guess I better make up my mind quick."

Trying to figure out if she was going to tell her the same news Natalie tried her best to relax her nerves, not a bit prepared for the information she just received. "So what do you expect me to do?", she flicked her hands.

"Help me pay his dog ass back for the way he's treated both of us."

"He treats me just fine, I know he's not perfect but a man gonna be a man", Natalie spoke honestly.

What does she have that I don't? She doesn't look that fine, so why is he choosing her over me?, Shawndra thought as tears started building in her eyes.

Natalie stood up very arrogant like and passed her the box of Kleenex that was sitting by the arm of the recliner. Shawndra didn't take the hospitality well. Who do she think she is I'm not a baby, I can get my own tissue if I need it. "Well I guess ain't neither one of us gonna be seeing him then, 'cause after I give this information to the police, his ass is a gone-er", she grunted as she sniffed her runny nose. "They gonna lock his ass up and throw away the key when I get finished with his ass."

"Well do what you gotta do", Natalie shrugged her shoulders and simply replied, now wondering what could this woman possibly know for a fact about Cleofis to send him away for good.

"I just don't know what to do", Shawndra's sternness turned soft. "I'm tired of him mistreating me all I ever did was be a good woman to his ass", she started crying like she knew Natalie all her life.

This woman is really heart broken, there's no telling what she might do, thought Natalie. "You don't need him", she began trying to convince her to leave Cleofis alone. "Besides if it's not me it would be somebody else 'cause that's how men are", she was being honest about some of her past experiences. "His little ass only twenty-one anyway and you what, almost thirty, use his young ass just like I use his ass only for cash girl I'm thirty years old what I look like getting all rolled up over a nigga that can barely buy alcohol."

Shawndra listened carefully. She don't even care about his stupid ass. She wiped both of her eyes with open hands. I would never get him for his money and his stupid ass fucking with a bitch that is.

The way Natalie carried on as if she didn't care about Cleofis at all brought Shawndra to the point where she didn't want to hear it anymore.

Standing up tall and making sure there was no more signs of crying on her face, she left ashamed she couldn't keep her composure in front of Natalie, but if she only knew Natalie went in her bed room and let just as many tears loose as her. Feeling like Shawndra would always have a part of the man she was pregnant by and loved with all her heart.

Natalie stumbled to the bathroom, lifted the toilet seat and dropped down to her knees feeling like she was being gagged, the desire to throw up overwhelmed her as nothing but slob and mucus came from her mouth.

Pull yourself together. She coached herself mentally. Don't let this man break you this is exactly what he wants, is to see you like this. With that thought she got up, pulled herself together and started to get dressed.

The apartment she moved in was kind of spacious after having second thoughts about purchasing the house she stayed in on the Westside. This was temporary until she found her another house. Hating to go from a house to an apartment she made the best of it.

As soon as you walked through the door you was in the thick carpeted floor living room, with a very small space for a dinning attached. You could see the hall way the minute you walked in that led straight to her daughter bedroom but before you reached that, a bathroom was to your left and Natalie's room was on your right. The kitchen was before the hallway began, normal tiled floor not very big at all, but enough for the residents who stayed there.

Cleofis was juggling around the 10,000 mark after taking the eighth of a kilo loss, two and a half months ago, paying Mark Galante to make sure he stayed on the streets, paying his car note, pussy bills and his fetish to keep plenty of artillery, he was becoming a frustrated man.

JW hadn't been seen since the failed ambush Cleofis and Berry tried to do that almost cost them their lives, but it was rumored that hc was broke, back around the hood, and ready to kill the first Capone he saw on sight.

The main reason behind the stand still is that it was a drought and the cocaine that was floating through the town was no good. When Chicago caught hell Kankakee caught the pain. The cocaine the Chicagoans had that was butter they wanted an arm and a leg for, so if you wanted butter for a decent price you would have to make a long trip down south or to the west coast, and don't too many hustlers want to deal with that risk.

Besides that you would either pay the price or sit on the money you had until things blew over. While doing this the average person would pinch off their money for this and that, when the smart thing to do would be to pay the expensive price and tax customers on your own prices.

"Man I'm telling you homeboy fucking a bitch in the ass is the business", Cleofis spoke proudly on the passenger side of Gabe's car. "Start by sticking your thumb in the booty hole first, then"

"Man I don't wanna hear that shit", Gabe cut him off not interested in hearing anymore.

"For real homey try that shit one time and I bet'chu like it."

"Tissssssssss, please my dick going in two places and that's the pussy and mouth, I ain't never fuckin' with the booty hole."

"Shheeeiiit nigga you don't know what you missing, get you a bitch who ain't never tried it before, it's like breaking in a virgin. I'm telling you try that shit with Kiara and she'll be climbing up the walls."

"I'm straight. I'mma do me and you can do you." replied Gabe as they were arriving on the Southside.

"Ay, pull over up here and let me out", seeing Shawndra's car parked, but still running over her mother's house, he was stopping by to check up on her. "Hold on a minute, I'll be right out", said Cleofis.

Shawndra was coming out her mothers as he was about to come in. "We need to talk", she spoke very direct. "Come on let's go sit in this car and you can tell Gabe to leave 'cause you fenna talk to me."

"Damn! What the hell wrong with you", he asked, following her to her car and signaling for Gabe to leave." What the hell is it now Shawndra?" he closed the door and she started up the car.

"I told your bitch I was pregnant…she sounded like she didn't care about it at all and she told me all she was using you for was your money, with your stupid ass." Cleofis just shook his head, rolled his eyes and blew deeply out his mouth. "Why don't we go over there so all three of us can sit down and talk", Shawndra began to pull off when his rage started.

"Don't take me no where you stupid ass bitch", Shawndra had already backed out into the street, when he opened the passenger side door. "Didn't I tell you I ain't going no were with you", he spoke very harsh through clenched teeth.

"FLACOW!" The loud noise seemed to break the sound barrier. Cleofis knew that noise from anywhere, he hurried up and closed the car door as the noise split the air again. "Get us the fuck outta here, NOW", he yelled snapping her out her state of panic.

The face in the rearview was a dark colored one with rage. "Shit, JW", he managed to blurt as they sped off still being targeted by three more loud gunfire's were one struck the right side door. "Ill kill you and that bitch!" Cleofis could hear him yell from a distance as the car flew down the street.

"Who the fuck was that?" Shawndra yelled not even fully through her front door yet.

"That's JW pussy ass."

"That's who I thought you said, what the hell you and him into it for" she asked, still very shook up from the encounter.

"Remember when I told you the motherfucka stole a pistol and some yack from me. Well I ain't seen him but one time since he took it, and that was almost three months ago."

Shawndra closed her eyes and took a deep breath. "Do you know if I wouldn't decided to back outta my mothers driveway we probably both would be dead."

"I know, I know…this bitch ass nigga want a war." Cleofis paced around speaking viciously. "Well that's what I'mma give his ass and don't worry about your backdoor 'cause I'mma pay fo' it."

Cleofis reached for the cordless phone with one hand and clutched a mag with the other but before he could pick it up off the receiver it was ringing. It was Shawndra's mothers and relatives making sure she was ok. "I'm ok ma, I'm ok", was the words that came out of her mouth as he stood there listening.

In a way Cleofis was kinda glad Shawndra's mind was completely off paying Natalie a visit.

"What you say, the police wanna question Cleofis", she repeated from Mrs. Coleman's mouth.

"Fuckin' bullshit", Cleofis whispered figuring they would want to question him anyway this was his reason for not going back on the streets immediately to take revenge. Plus JW had kinda shook him up. That had to be a 357 sounding that loud. This was the second time JW brought it to the gangster and Cleofis made up in his head it would be the last time.

Cleofis snatched Shawndra's jogging pants from around her waist, all the emotion along with the fact he wanted to make up for the way he'd been treating her turned him on. Shawndra grabbed her jogging pants that he'd only managed to snatch down to her thighs with one hand keeping the cordless phone to her ear she tried to stop Cleofis from pulling them all way down but Cleofis seeing the opportunity to get her back in order used all his force to pull them down.

Moving her panties to the side he dove face first. "Na uh", she said trying to move his head and cover up the phone while her mother spoke faster then a fast forwarding tape. But he'd backed her up against a wall knowing she could not with stand the pleasure from his tongue. Cleofis eventually made her relax her legs some, and she now rubbed his head instead of pushing it away. If it was anybody else talking her ear off on the phone she would have simply hung up in their face, because it was her mother she tuned her out and pushed the lower part of her body forward. "Ok momma", she said through a moan after realizing Mrs. Coleman was through talking.

The phone hadn't even hit the floor good and it was ringing back to back, everybody wanted to know what happened, but the two didn't answer their calls.

The love making was long, passionate and very emotional, afterwards they relaxed on her silk bed spread, fully satisfied sexually they ignored the phone that still rang from friends and family.

Cleofis knew the silence wouldn't last long so he began to brace himself for the intense conversation.

"So what are you gonna do? 'Cause if you gone continue to deal with Natalie I'm through and I mean it Cleofis."

"Here we go again", he blew under his breath. "Do you hear me bringing up the fact that you fucked Bruno", he tried to lay the guilt trip on thick. "And turned around and fucked me, his first cousin."

"Don't even go there motherfucka", she sat up on the bed as her lips thinned in anger. "We done already discussed that and I see you wanna continue to let some shit bother you that was before your time."

"But damn the nigga fucked you and your sister, where did your so called morals fall into play at."

"Look you little boy I was young and when you young you make mistakes."

Cleofis could tell he struck a nerve. "Well I don't want no baby by you, and you gonna get an abortion-

"Nigga I ain't getting shit", she began as he jumped up and started to dress. "I'm keeping my baby so an abortion is not an option."

"Ok bitch", he replied cuffing the bottom of his pants and tying up his shoes. "You gonna make me whack yo' stupid ass."

Shawndra disregarded the routine threat, "What! You want me to get rid of my baby so you and that bitch Natalie can live happily ever after." Cleofis approached the front door as she trailed behind him holding the silk sheet over her nudity. "And all that bitch want you for is your money." BAM! The door slammed in her face but she wasted no time opening it to get her last words out. "And we'll see how long you be free after I go to the cops. YOU BITCH ASS NIGGA!" The words seemed to store in his mental as he strolled down the street using his cell phone.

This bitch gone make me whack her ass…that shit Jackpot told me was right, that bitch really will talk to the police. The option of turning around and going back to beat her ass crossed his mind but immediately deteriorated when Jackpot drove up.

"What's up 'Moe'?"

"Nuttin' man, just this silly ass girl, take me to my dog crib."

"Cool, now what the hell happened at Shawndra's momma house?"

"That pussy ass nigga JW, almost whacked me and Shawndra."

"So that's who it was huh…you know I heard that stud was back around the hood yapping about what he was gonna do."

"I swear if the bitch wasn't trying to take me to Natalie's house we'll both be dead. That's on my dead daddy wherever I see this nigga at I'm whacking 'em."

"I feel you but what the fuck Shawndra was trying to take you to Natalie's for?"

"'Cause she done went over there telling Natalie she pregnant and shit and I guess Natalie didn't tell her she was pregnant too, but she did say a lot of slick ass shit to her."

"You hollered at Natalie yet?" Jackpot cracked a smile when asking.

"Naw, every time I try and call the bitch she won't answer so fuck her I ain't fenna sweat the bitch. But dig this remember when you told me Shawndra said some shit about she'll fix me or something like that?" as Jackpot shook his head in agreement he continued. "Guess what this bitch gonna say when I left out her crib." Jackpot gave his full attention. "We'll see how free I'll be when she talk to the police."

"You bull-shitin' right?"

"Do it look like I'm bullshitting. Moe, this bitch could get me the death penalty if she talks."

The seriousness in his voice and the look in his eyes let Jackpot know he was humorless about the situation.

"Sorry I never told you but that was when I was in my teens, Shanice…and I never thought you was getting serious with him until it was too late", Shawndra spoke honestly but in shock of the secret some one disclosed to Shanice.

Shawndra needed someone to talk to after all the drama with Cleofis so she flew to Shanice's house in hopes of a shoulder to cry on, but found herself with some explaining to do. "So who told you about me and Bruno anyway", she felt a little on defense.

"Who you think?" said Shanice "That jealous little man of yours, the one everybody's soooooo scared of. And check this, the nigga even called himself trying to push up on me."

"For real", Shawndra replied as her stomach seemed to tie in knots. "That's why I'm through fuckin' with his little dick ass. This nigga had the nerve to tell me I better get a abortion or else he gonna whack me... please girl I told that big nose fucka we'll see who he whack when I tell the police about some of the shit he done did."

"You shouldn't told him that", Shanice replied, hoping she was smart enough not to say such things.

"Why not? I ain't scared of that punk motherfucka. I got a gun just like he do." she lied. "And between me and you I think that bitch had something to do with Bruno's murder."

"What you mean he had something to do with Bruno's murder?" Shanice asked with tears building up in her eyes.

"From what I was told, him and Bruno robbed some dude in Chicago for some weight and Cleofis got salty at Bruno for something and had somebody tell the niggas where they could find Bruno." Shawndra freely spoke now that she had all of Shanice's attention. "To my understanding the niggas didn't know if Bruno had something to do with it or not, but that low down dirty snake confirmed their suspicion. How do you think Bruno had all that paper? I mean he's always had paper but.

Shanice stuck her hand up, not wanting to hear anymore. "I don't wanna hear no more girl, just the thought of it pisses me the fuck off."

"Who wip you pushin?" asked Cleofis, taking a seat after opening his front door for Gabe.

"Aw, that's a rental your girl got for me."

"My girl who?"

"Shawndra chump, why?" replied the cocky Gabe.

"Look little nigga my girl ain't fenna be renting your' ass no cars, hear me?"

Gabe had asked Shawndra to rent him a car and she agreed 'cause she was cool like that, but also agreed 'cause she knew the news of her renting him a car would piss Cleofis off.

"Quit trippin you hook ass nigga you", Gabe playfully jabbed him in his chest. "And where your wip at nigga?"

"Parked", Cleofis said as he stood up playfully sizing up his home boy. "You don't want it, trust me", he flexed his chest muscles through his snug shirt. "Don't make me fuck around and put your ass in a cemetery." He looked playfully serious.

"Nigga! You a high powered coward." Gabe didn't get the remark out good before the two was full of laughter.

"Talk to me."

"I almost had you homeboy", a voice growled on the other line. "But I'll get 'em next time."

"Man what's up with you stealing from the brothaz like that", asked Jackpot in an assertive tone after realizing who it was.

"The brothaz", JW began viscously. "If it was brothaz I wouldn't have stayed so damn broke all the time why this nigga ride around all high an mighty

"Naw that ain't true man", Jackpot interrupted, glancing out Melissa's front window. "Moe always made sure we all had food on our plates you just on some bullshit."

"Fuck you, you stunt dummy ass nigga, and tell that bitch ass nigga if he don't bring his ass out in da open I'mma kill that bitch and make 'em come out."

"I ain't nobody's stunt dummy and I ain't no message boy. And if you feel I'mma bitch then come holla at me."

"Pisssssssssssss, nigga I'm on my way, and when I get over there don't be scared to come out."

"Trust me I won't", said Jackpot.

"Stop honking that motherfuckin' horn", Cleofis yelled, locking the screen door to his mother's house. "Don't never pull up in front of here honking a horn, dumb ass nigga."

“I ain’t know”, the fear stricken Cliff replied. “Where we off to?”

“Just drive ‘til I run into somebody with some yack.”

Cliff kept Cleofis Aurora when the gangster felt it was too hot to be in.

“Why the fuck you ain’t put no gas in here moe?”

“I was about to, before you called sayin come right away.”

“Shhhit I told you come right away ‘cause we need to find some yack. The nigga Gabe just left my crib with a bankroll he was trying to spend. Man I swear if we find some yack for a decent price we’ll be on a brick in no time.”

“I know but this drought shit got everybody bullshitting”

“Tell me about it, and Berry locked up in the county on some bullshit and I wanna cop at least one time before I bond him out.”

“What’s the nigga bond?”

“Five stacks and I can’t leave Moe in that starving ass county.”

The twelve months in prison at seventeen and the 2 years in the county jail he spent for the attempted murder on Gillmen almost broke the villain. And he now made the smartest street moves as possible not wanting to be trapped in a cage again.

Just the very thought of the cage had toned the once wild fella down a notch. Saying he was going to whack somebody was becoming boring to street niggas and was becoming a mockery for women. His reputation was all he had and when you constantly bark you must bite a few times also.

No retaliation had come behind JW’s recklessness and niggas was starting to assume Cleofis wasn’t a threat.

Berry was locked up in the county jail at the time when Cleofis needed him the most for he felt Berry was the loyalist out the Capone’s even though he wasn’t good with money.

Attention Mr. Jackson, don’t bother sticking your key in the door because both the locks have been changed. And the 5,000 dollars you had over here is with who it belongs to and that’s me. You can consider the money payment for the 5,000 loan I’m still paying off that I got your punk ass and a start up for some baby clothes. I hope you and your gold digging bitch Natalie have a nice life so you can stay out of mine.

Oh and don't bother kicking my door in because I just had one of the top of the line alarm systems installed…compliments of you. P.S. Don't you just love me?!

"BITCH", Cleofis shouted as he tried to stick his key in the hole. Balling the letter up, he threw it to the concrete.

Something told me to get that changed before I left.

Shawndra was bluffing about the alarm system but he declined to try her bluff especially how nosy the apartment tenants were, and besides that she wasn't at home anyway.

I'mma give that bitch a couple days to cool off, after that, the bitch better have my money.

JW circled the block, Jackpot was in a rusted out hoopty looking for the very appearance of Cleofis. Figuring he was somewhere waiting patiently to kill him he circled around a couple more times.

This bitch ass nigga got nuts. JW noticed Jackpot standing in front of Melissa's apartment building.

Pulling over to the side he parked and got out not wanting to jump the gun he wanted to get closer to Jackpot before he started shooting. It was quite a distance between the two, and JW glanced in every direction while approaching.

Jackpot stood there with his hands in his pockets and with a blink of an eye he threw them in the air. "Look moe", the freight ness in his voice began. "I ain't come out here to try and kill you I came to talk to you."

JW eased his grip up on one of his pistols that hung on his waste. "Talk about what", he asked, constantly glancing around to see what angle Cleofis would come from.

"I ain't got nuttin on me 'Moe'", Jackpot said loudly, walking in a small circle lifting his shirt up. "I told ya I just wanna holla at cha."

Jackpot basically repeated himself as the puzzled JW walked closer to him. "Well if you wanna holler at me come jump in the car", he spoke still trying to make up his mind whether to blast him or not.

The two entered the hoopty and rarely took their eyes off each other. JW drove around the neighborhood so he wouldn't feel like a sitting duck. JW figured he could over power the thin Jackpot if he tried anything.

"You don't know that nigga like I do, he my first cousin and ever since we was little the nigga tried to get over", JW started trying to explain his reasons for his actions. "The nigga kept me flat broke, I ain't even have a place to stay. Who the motherfuckas taking the risk, us that nigga wasn't on the Cartels like we was all night hustling."

"I feel you, I feel you but moe is the one who makes it possible for us to tip on certain blocks. I know shit ain't the greatest, imagine how I feel you know I've always had fedi but shit is fucked up for me too right now."

"That's because y'all letting that nigga run the show, fuck that nigga we don't need him to get money, all the nigga do is trick off with these scandalous hoes."

"You right, you right", Jackpot agreed after thinking about Cleofis tricking. "'Moe' can be bogus sometime, you just gotta know how to get yours without being noticed.

"I hear you", JW interrupted, "But me I just took my shit 'cause I got tired of hustling for Shawndra and the rest of these hoes. I'm telling you we need to team up kidnap that bitch Shawndra, get that little money and tell that nigga it can go down however he want it.....with your clientele and this spot I got on the Southside, we'll be paid in no time and we can split the shit straight down the middle.

"What bitch house you just come from?" Natalie replied as Cleofis entered her apartment. Ignoring her comment he walked past her and went to her room to change his clothes.

Natalie got up off the couch demanding an answer. "I know you hear me", she continued. "I guess you gonna take care of mine and Shawndra's baby huh, and who ever else you raw dicking",

Giving her a sharp stare he responded. "I told you already that if she is pregnant it ain't mine so why the fuck you keep sweating me?"

"'Cause why would she lie like that, you know you been fuckin' her so it's a strong possibility that it is your baby."

Putting on the latest red and black Fubu wear he was becoming agitated. "Look Natalie I told you the business so you can think what ever you want to think."

"Well I know one thing, like I told you before, whatever Shawndra knows about you she seems like she's ready to tell."

"That bitch just yapin", his cheek bones rose in agitation. "She don't know shit about me", rubbing some Cool Water cologne on his shirt he was ready to leave. "The fellas outside waiting on me, I gotta go."

"Before you go it's one more thing I want to tell you", she said very directly, completely tired of his mess. "It's either gonna be me or her so make up your mind before you step foot back in this residence, or I'll make it up fo' you." With her arms crossed she gave him the most serious look she could before he left out the door mumbling under his breath.

CHAPTER 14

Who did it?

"Shawndra's dead!", shouted Natalie through the phone.

"Yeah did you know her or something", said George on the other line.

"Who killed her?" Natalie's mind was racing. "Do the paper say anything about a suspect."

"Naw girl they say they don't have a suspect yet", eager for an answer George asked again. "Did you know her?"

"I knew of her", she said, pacing her living room. Rubbing her hand across her troubled face she just couldn't believe it. "Where was she?" At first her words didn't come out right. "I mean where did this happen?"

"It says on Brifman and you know how dark that road can be at night." George continued as he noticed her silence. "It says a man driving on the road discovered her body slumped over against her window shattered door at 1:30 in the morning.

Detectives say she was shot twice in the head while her seven year old daughter lay asleep at home with no one there."

Please God tell me he didn't. She was now sitting on the sofa with her legs shut. The more George read the more she wanted to believe it wasn't true. She sorta tuned George out for a minute, for the feeling Cleofis had something to do with this crawled all over her skin.

"Front page, beginning of the summer, it ain't even that hot yet and these niggaz already acting a fool girl. But that's some low down dirty ass shit to do a female like that, ain't it…Natalie…Natalie you still there?"

Opening her eyes to the harsh reality the second calling of her name snapped her out of her daze. "I'll call you right back", she replied ending the call instantly. There was only one thing on her mind -- she needed to hear from Cleofis.

Natalie was listening to his cell phone ring for the second time. I just need to hear his voice, I'll know if he did it or not by the sound of his voice. She said under her breath. But Cleofis never answered his cell phone she tried several more times before slamming the phone on to the receiver. Her gut bore a strange feeling in it. She wasted no time hitting the streets to try to find out more.

Gabe had just received the unbelievable news and was on his way to see Cleofis, what did he mean by it's a lot of bullshit in the air, Gabe reflected, flying in the rental car that Shawndra rented for him days ago.

Kiara was on the passenger side questioning the credibility of the information. "I don't believe its true do you?"

"It's gotta be true 'cause the nigga sounded real weird."

"You think he did it?"

"Shiiit I don't know but I'm fenna go over here and find out."

Gabe just couldn't shake Shawndra's face out of his head, not the kind hearted Shawndra he'd came to know could she be dead, murdered at that, everything just seemed unreal.

"Man what the fuck going on? Is Shawndra really dead?" Gabe began before Cleofis swung the door open good. He could immediately see something was unusual about his friend.

"Shhhhh, come down to the basement", Cleofis said in a hollow whisper.

The residence was unknown to Gabe he'd never been there before and had serious second thoughts about going down to the basement with his strange acting friend.

"You didn't bring nobody with you did you?"

"Kiara, she's out there in the car waiting on me", Gabe said, following him down the basement steps. All sorts of thoughts flashed through Gabe's head but he trusted his childhood friend.

"Next time you come holler at me don't bring a soul, you hear me?" Gabe nodded in an agreement as he continued. "Somebody's trying to kill me, I think its Travis bitch ass brother Chopper, the motherfucka whacked my Boo last night and you know she was carrying my seed."

"You think its Travis brother?"

"I don't know for a fact yet", Cleofis replied giving Gabe a ready to kill whoever did it look. "But I'm just laying low 'cause niggaz already putting my name in the bullshit already…come on man I ain't that cold hearted to do that to my unborn seed." He tapped Gabe shoulder as he was talking to him, this always made Gabe agitated but he brushed the feeling off for his ear was taking in as much as possible. "Homeboy, niggaz done brought out the beast in me, soon as night hit I'mma put me a nigga in the cemetery that's on Blackstone." He hit the left side of his chest harder then a male gorilla with a bald fist that formed before impact.

Gabe could see the vengeance in Cleofis' eyes and volunteered his assistance if needed at anytime before departing from the unknown residence.

Natalie stopped at a local gas station to purchase one of the last Kankakee Daily Journals left. She just had to read the story herself. Shawndra Coleman's murder was selling an enormous amount of papers and was becoming the topic of discussion amongst Kankakeeans.

Natalie was trying to read the newspaper and drive at the same time when Mandy called with expected news.

"You know they saying your boy did that to Shawndra right?" said Mandy.

"I figure people would be saying that anyway with his reputation and all", Natalie began speaking into her cell phone while still trying to read and drive at the same time. "And look at these gossiping mothafuckas jumping to conclusions already."

"Mmm-Hmm until you know for fact don't listen to what comes out of nobody mouth."

"I know, I know but let me call you right back."

Natalie ended her call because she couldn't help but notice the massive crowd of people around a house she just drove past, so she circled the block and went to be nosy.

The homicide detectives, along with the task force were amongst the crowd where they had somebody face down on the ground with their guns drawn.

Who is that? She thought, driving slowly pass the scene. As the lead detective pulled the young man off the ground Natalie slammed on the breaks and the car behind her almost crashed into the back of hers. "Gabriel", she yelled.

Her half brother didn't look too happy as Detective Diamond walked him proudly to an unmarked car, she could tell he was very angry and argumentative.

"What the hell is going on?.....Why are they arresting my brother?"

Little did she know they were arresting Gabe for suspicion in the murder of Shawndra Coleman.

Putting an APB out on the car she rented, authorities quickly saw the only lead they had on this case, being driven by a black male that they identified as Gabriel Smith.

Natalie stopped over a couple family and friends houses before returning to her apartment.

The whispering coming from the kitchen scared her and she almost turned to run out her door until recognizing one of the voices. "Cleofis that's you?" she spoke casually.

"Yeah it's me Nat."

Taking a deep breath she walked to the kitchen to see who he had in her apartment.

Observing her angry look, he explained before she could say something. "He was just stopping by." Knowing she wasn't too fond about people she didn't know in her apartment, he continued. "This my homeboy Jackpot I always be talking about, but anyway baby let me holler at you back in the room for a sec."

He followed her to her room where she wasted no time getting straight to the point.

"Why are people saying you killed that girl Cleofis?" Natalie crossed her arms staring at his facial expression.

"Fuck if I know", his eye brows dropped down in anger. "I ain't have shit to do with it, motherfuckas always putting my name in some bullshit when they just picked Gabe up for it, so why the hell ain't nobody yelling his name."

"So that's what they was arresting him for?"

"Yeah he the one who was last seen with Shawndra from what Jackpot told me, and he got caught driving in her rental car."

"That boy wouldn't do nutting like this, he don't even seem like the type." Her face went into a confused tear building look.

"Please, I know a lot of killers that don't seem like that type."

"Well if people saying it's you it's probably dangerous for you to be over here around me and Dasia."

"Look Natalie", Cleofis began frustrated by her comment. "I told you I didn't do it so fuck whatever people say as long as I didn't have shit to do with it I don't care what they say."

Cleofis took his hand and wiped away the tears of concern that ran down her cheeks. She didn't know what to think as she buried her face into his chest and he rubbed the back of her head. "I want that Jackpot dude to leave, I don't trust him, somebody could be trying to kill you and you know who it is."

"You right", he now rubbed the upper part of her back. "But I ain't worried about no nigga."

"I know", she emerged from is chest and replied. "But our baby needs a father."

Though she felt very bad about Shawndra and her seven year old daughter, in a jealous and selfish way Natalie liked the fact that Shawndra was now out of her way for good.

After long and intensified questioning Gabe was released. Detective Diamond was very pissed that Gabe wouldn't sign a statement of any kind. He truly believed Gabe was lying about half the stuff that came out his mouth. They had no evidence to charge Gabe just 'cause Shawndra rented him a car didn't mean he murdered her. They must have asked him about Cleofis who they sometimes referred to as Teflon at least a hundred times. The more questions they asked the more they realized Gabe wouldn't cooperate with them if he did know something.

"Man I been trying to get back up wit'chu since that day you had me come to some house you was at", said Gabe.

Putting his finger in the air Cleofis told him to hold on a minute. He was trying to finish up on a phone conversation that had become intense. "A muthafucka even think about doing some shit to my 'og' I'll walk up and blow niggas shit back in broad daylight everyday", said Cleofis, clutching a big black 40 caliber in one hand. All the fuss caught Gabe's undivided attention as he sat down on Mrs. Jackson's couch surprised to find Cleofis at his mothers.

"Yeah aight…yeah", was the last words out of Cleofis mouth before hanging up the phone.

"Man I'm telling you", he started. "If a nigga even look at my Moms in a wrong way I'm whackin' him."

"I feel you 'cause I'm tired of people saying I did the shit and talking shit about what they gonna do when they see me. All the girl did is rent me a car and now I'm supposed to have had something to do with her murder."

"If I was you I wouldn't even pay no attention to that shit, 'cause all motherfuckas gone do is talk, who ever whacked her a talk about it soon, and soon as they do I'mma put him six feet deep." Cleofis replied, cocking the hammer of his mag.

Nobody knew for a fact who murdered Shawndra Coleman but the police prime suspect was Cleofis, and they looked at Gabe as an accomplice. The street was speaking all sorts of things, Gabe did it, Cleofis did it, the whole Capone crew did it, niggas that was trying to kill Cleofis did it, and Cleofis and Gabe did it together. Rarely mentioned was James (Jackpot) Love or James (JW) Wells.

Jackpot turned himself in to the court in the middle part of the summer, where he made an agreement to except six years in prison for drug charges he was out on bail for.

JW was lying low since the murder and was barely getting any sleep at night. He was trying to wait patiently for the discussion of the slaying to die down.

Cleofis or Teflon which he was usually called, once again struck fear into street niggas for a murder many say he did and got away with. Teflon always gets away with it, they can never pen nothing on him soured throughout the street corners and households. In the rich and middle class parts of the county his name rang, who is this monster, tax-payers would say.

Teflon had even caught the Mayor's attention, when are you going to get this killer he said to local law enforcement. Every law enforcement in the county waited on the go ahead to go after him. The Feds was trying to get involved in making a case against the never charged with a murder man. Women spoke about him with total fear in their voices. Killing a woman was rare in Kankakee, and a lot of people felt Cleofis had crossed the line. One hundred percent sure he didn't do the murder Cleofis was now on a whole other level whether he did it or not, damn near every body was scared of him.

Hood rats slept with him out of fear and decent women wanted nothing to do with him out of fear. The amount of respect he received was imperial and the name Teflon, become infamous in a way he never imagined. People who never saw him pictured him to be a big black ugly scary man.

"Don't let 'em in your apartment no more. Don't answer his calls. I don't care if the nigga your' half brotha or not I think the nigga had something to do with that you understand what I'm saying?"

"Mmm-Hmm", replied Natalie fully understanding that he meant Gabe had something to do with Shawndra's murder. "Where are you?"

"Taking care of some business, just make sure you do what I tell you 'cause I don't know whose trying to kill me", said Cleofis into his cell phone before ending the call.

To smooth Natalie's hurt and frustration Cleofis bought her a Thunderbird. He felt this would help make up for his cheating with Shawndra. Natalie gladly accepted the gift and followed his rules about staying away from Gabe.

Gabe couldn't understand why his recently discovered sister was avoiding him. Cleofis started avoiding Gabe also, but the distance didn't bother Gabe he just felt his friend needed some time to himself.

"I don't give a fuck how ya'll get it, but ya'll better not come back without it!" The anger in his voice built, as he expressed his demands to Cliff on the other end of the phone. "Find my car nigga I don't care if you and Kevin gotta steal one to find out who stole my shit!"

Cliff and Kevin were calling from a payphone in St. Louis, Missouri. Cleofis had let the two drive his Aurora to the southern city to cop some coke with the small piece of money the crew had left. But when the two went inside a gas station somebody stole the car. With only cop money in their pockets the two was ready to return home.

"Kevin said you can have his car 'til we can buy you a new one", Cliff exclaimed.

"Where is Kevin's car?", asked Cleofis fully aware that Kevin owned a drop top Chrysler Sebring like the one he had back in 96, but was a different color. Cleofis had always wanted another drop top but still wasn't cool about the loss of his white Aurora he was still making payments on.

"His wife has it, but it's in his name. He says the car is yours soon as we reach town."

Cleofis wasn't really holding Kevin responsible but since he was with Cliff he for some strange way felt like he was. And because he feared Cleofis so much he wasn't going to take the chance of tangling with the mad man, plus Kevin wanted so badly to be called a Capone.

How giving could he be? -- He'd been tricked out of 20,000 dollars, now he was giving away his only car and Cleofis didn't give it a second thought while accepting the offer.

CHAPTER 15

It's Funny How Things Turn Out

The sky was baby blue with bright orange streaks at the bottom due to the setting of the sun, and the hot air stood still without a breeze. Cleofis leaned cautiously back into the seat of the midnight blue Sebring Kevin gave him. With the Convertibles, top down he waited patiently at a red light when a white Q 45 pulled along side of him. Glancing into the car he honked his horn. "What's up girl?"

The driver knew who he was right off back. "Cleofis", she spoke turning her radio down. "How you doing Boo?"

The word Boo came as a shock to Cleofis, it wasn't like Angie to use such words.

"Hard to get Angie! I thought you moved back to Wisconsin?"

"I did move back I'm just down here visiting for the summer." The light turned green as she was talking.

"Where you about to go?", she asked while they drove alongside of each other. "Over my mom's house", he rapidly replied. "Well I'll stop by there soon as I come from the gas station", Angie said. *Yeah right you lying ass bitch*, Cleofis thought while nodding to her reply as she turned off.

Cleofis never entertained the thought of Angie coming to his residence and when she rang the door bell it surprised him dearly. "Come on in", said Cleofis. Never for once forgetting the way she treated him in the past. "I see you still got that drop top, what'chu do get it painted another color."

"Nope that's a whole other car", Cleofis replied. He never glanced at her for more then a second, though his curiosity to know what she wanted came to mind.

"Can I talk to you in private", asked Angie. "Yeah come on", he nodded for her to follow him.

Cliff and Disco sat on the couch gawking at her presence, wondering what they were going to the back to discuss.

Gabe was just about to turn around and leave when Cliff cracked the door open.

"CJ in here?"

"Yeah he in the back", said Cliff.

"Damn ya'll act like ya'll can't hear me knocking on the door", Gabe replied. Someone had told Gabe that Cleofis was saying Gabe killed Shawndra. Maybe this was the reason Cleofis distanced himself from him, Gabe thought. But why would he say I did it? The determination to ask him immediately halted when hearing the loud moans coming from a dark back room. I wonder who them nigga back there tossing, probably some nasty runner, Gabe reflected.

"Homeboy!" Cleofis voice shouted from the back room. "You wanna piece of this?"

"Naw I'm straight", Gabe yelled loud enough for Cleofis to hear him. Taking a seat on the living room couch, Gabe wanted no parts of the toss action that was going on in the dark back room.

When he was younger it was his own insecurity, but now he'd heard the rumors about Cleofis having herpes and wanted no parts of a woman he touched.

What was left of the Capone crew came strolling from the back room, all three sweating. Especially Disco, was sweating enormously. Cleofis plopped down on the couch next to Gabe with a vindictive smirk on his face. "You should of came back there." Cleofis tapped Gabe's leg and continue, "She givin' head an all and she ain't no runner!"

"Who is she?"

"You'll see when she comes from the back."

"I want my money Cleofis", Angie said softly as she walked from the back.

"I gave you the fedi what you can't find it."

"Naw I can't find it", Angie's voice rose angrily. "Because one of yo' friends stole it."

"We ain't no thieves", replied Disco.

"You heard em. Besides you earned every penny of it why would they take it", said Cleofis.

"You know what Cleofis, I know somebody took it…so that's how you do business", Angie said loudly.

"That's how you always did business with me. I only treated you like what'chu are", his face struck a frown. "A gold digging bitch!"

"That's ok, that's…ok", she replied as she began to exit out the front door.

The laughter flooded the living room. "You did all that fuckin' and sucking for nothing", was the last words Angie heard before she slammed the door.

Gabe couldn't believe his eyes, he never thought in a million years Angie would be getting down like that. "What was that all about?", asked Gabe.

"Nuttin' much that bitch played me in the past and she just got played", Cleofis said happily. "Ah Cliff toss me that loot."

Angie's boyfriend in Wisconsin got into some trouble with the law, and Angie's parents wouldn't bail him out. Angie came to Kankakee in hopes of catching a baller that was willing to drop a lot of cash for the ass. But what she found was Cleofis who'd she'd juiced out of plenty of cash in the past, only 'cause he felt she would eventually be his woman. And after Cleofis heard her sob story about how she needed some money it was only right to convince her to sell her body, then have Cliff sneak the cash out of her purse and coldly admit to it.

"Damn ya'll gave her all that bread", said Gabe, glancing at the lump of cash cliff passed Cleofis.

"Yep, two stacks and if Cliff wouldn't have snuck it out her purse I would have taken it from her anyway…can you believe I used to buy that bitch minks. Diamonds the whole nine, and the bitch just gone run off and leave me like that, when I'm in the time of need. Fuck that hoe, I had to treat her ass."

The villain slapped hands with Cliff, still directing his attention to Gabe.

"Bitch must have thought I was some suck a duck."

"Well look", Gabe began changing the subject. "Mufakas saying you said I wacked Shawndra."

"Stupid ass nigga what I look like saying some shit like that. How the fuck could you even concoct some shit like that in your head", Cleofis howled.

Gabe didn't know weather to believe him or not by the hostility in his tone, he declined to challenge his answer.

"Jaaaaaaaaames", Shawndra Coleman's screams woke JW up out of a cold puddle of sweat. Shawndra's murder appeared in his dreams so much that he regretted going to sleep.

Sometimes he would go days without rest, for the murder played in his mind like it was on repeat. It was like he could see her face clear as day and it was driving him nuts.

I said I was sorry he shouted, hoping God would forgive him. Sitting on the edge of a stained mattress trying to catch his breath, he realized he just wasn't built for the murder he had done.

Lighting fire to a Newport the killer was glad just to be awake.

"James Wells", a white mans voice spoke from the direction of the doorway where Detective Diamond stood alongside of another

Detective. "We would like you to come down to the station for questioning", said Det. Diamond.

"Who let you in, how did you get in here?"

"The front door was wide open plus we could have gotten a warrant anyway. Just throw on a shirt and let's go."

That bitch always leaving the door open, he reflected about his mother.

All sort of things started running through his head as he rode in the back of a homicide car. What possibly could they have, 'cause I know Jackpot couldn't ratted me out. JW thought as they pulled into the stations garage.

"So who pulled the trigger you are James Love", asked Diamond sharply.

JW hadn't sat down in the chair good before being hit with dozens of questions. What were you trying to kill Teflon for, do you know Gabriel Smith, do you really think James Love is not going to cut a deal with us, did you used to be apart of a crew called the Capones, if you tell us everybody that was involved at least you'll see the light of day again.

JW answered nothing and responded to nothing for he knew the best thing for him to do was keep his mouth shut. But when Det. Diamond showed him the statement of the person who was accusing him of murder it threw the killer in rage. "I DON'T GIVE A FUCK WHAT HE TOLD YOU, I DIDN'T KILL THAT GIRL."

During the questioning of JW, Cleofis was preparing to leave town and was taking Makeela with him. "You got your shit?"

"Yeah I got it", said Makeela as she hopped into the Chrysler.

The US Army had finally caught up to Kevin he'd been AWOL so long some how he thought the government forgot about him. He told Cleofis where he could make the payments on the car and said you might as well just have it, like Cleofis didn't look at it that way anyway. With close to three grand in his pockets Cleofis headed for St. Louis.

St. Louis was where a couple of his relatives stayed and would be a great place for him to start over again. All the pressure from Kankakee was starting to drive him crazy. He was getting tired of looking over his shoulder, though he tried to maintain his fearless presence, his sub conscious was taking over, driving him into a paranoid state of mind.

Makeela had come a long ways from when she was Kim's friend as a teen. After acknowledging some of the embarrassing things people said about her and her nasty apartment she started keeping herself extra clean. And made sure her mother's apartment was as well.

"So how long we gone be down there?", Makeela asked, reaching over touching his hand. "I know you're tired of people saying you killed that girl, but who cares what they say 'cause I know you didn't do it and people who think you did, fuck em. They need to be questioning that low down dirty ass JW, because if you ask me I think he did it."

"It's between JW and another nigga I got in mind but when it comes to surface everybody'll see." A minute of silence occurred. "I used to love the shit out of that girl and I wish I could have adopted her daughter but I knew her people would have been trippin'. Every time I think about little Shay Shay being with out her mother it drives me crazy and whoever done that shit probably scared to death of what I'mma do when I find out."

Makeela stared at him as he cruised on the highway, the emotion he showed made her proud to be next to the ghetto celebrity, and she showed her gratitude by slowly rocking his mike on the high way.

"I'm a kill yo' brother", JW growled in Lonzal's face. "The bitch ass nigga gone make a statement on me, you tell that nigga he dead", he continued, sticking his finger in Lonzal's face. "Go tell him that, you pussy ass nigga."

It was like Lonzal could actually see the steam coming out of his cousin's big family tree giving nose. Scared to death he said nothing and as JW left, he started to worry about his brother because he new JW was capable of doing exactly what he said. Plus everybody knew he had shot at Cleofis and Shawndra. He probably the one who killed Shawndra and now fenna try and kill my brother, the terrified Lonzale thought.

Lonzal Jackson was nothing like the man his brother had grown to be. Lonzal worked, went to community college, and came home to their mother who he had the up most respect for. I guess you can say he was a square.

JW thought he would never see the streets again when Det. Diamond showed him a statement signed by Cleofis Jackson. But the detectives wasn't quite ready to charge him yet so they let him go after long questioning and told him not to drift away far.

JW took the close call as a blessing, thinking they could have locked him up until they gathered all the evidence.

His yearn to kill Cleofis was now more extreme than ever. All they would have to do is get a couple more eye witnesses that seen me shoot at Shawndra's and Cleofis' and they can book me, he thought.

After looking for Cleofis for a day or two he caught wind of his relocation to St. Louis. So he decided to jump on the highway not only to go after his cousin but to dodge further encounters with homicide Detectives.

In a rental car driven by an associate JW felt more relieved, the further he got away from Kankakee.

DMX's, I Can Feel it Coming in The Air Tonight played from the CD player and relaxation covered his body as he thought of his next move. As the driver accelerated to over a hundred on the dash he briefly closed his eyes to vision the future. And all of a sudden he heard, "Aw shit", and opened them swiftly. The driver was trying to pass a semi truck that must have not seen them passing on the side causing them to drive into the far side of the road, the driver panicked. Almost getting side swiped, their attention was to much on the semi truck to observe the very thick steel railing that lay before them.

Immediately upon impact, the head on collision with the rail sent both young men flying through the windshield. The driver didn't fly too far but JW was thrown way over to the other side of the highway where he wasn't dead yet but a passing SUV trampled the little life that was left in him.

One minute he was relaxed and the next his life was snatched just like Shawndra Coleman's.

Cleofis wasn't back in Kankakee for two minutes before finding out it was a warrant for his arrest. Somehow Mark Galante told him the wrong court date. He'd been in St. Louis for 2 months and was only back to visit Berry who was fresh out of jail and to make a court appearance.

St. Louis had been good to Cleofis, he had a good paying job, him and Makeela had an apartment together, and he'd put everything behind him. The only people he kept contact with were his mother, Grandma Sterling, and Natalie whose stomach was growing bigger by the day.

Missing the gun and auto theft case the judge issued a 10,000 warrant. And once again law enforcement combed the streets looking for him.

JW's two month old death was barely missed, but seen as what goes around comes around. And also made fellas start using their seat belts when thinking about the horrible accident.

The summer time was gone and Cleofis decided to stay in Kankakee to hustle up on 10,000 for his warrant. And who could be better for a partner besides Berry. Berry, fresh out and broke was more then willing to make some money. Residing in an eastside neighborhood he grew up in, Cleofis discovered an up and coming crack spot. In no time the spot was ran by him and Berry.

Dang I wish this girl hurry up, Natalie reflected, waiting on Mandy to come outside. They was about to go grocery shopping with some food stamps Mandy hustled from some hype.

"Damn Nat you ain't gotta be so impatient I was coming…that little girl of mine think she fenna lay around and not wash a dish, she must be out her rabbit ass mind." Mandy took a pull from a square she just lit. "So you seen yo' baby daddy since he been back."

"Yeah I seen 'em once or twice…but I ain't fenna be sweating the nigga especially since I heard he was staying with some girl while he was gone. Whoever she is, she can have him 'cause a bitch make plenty of cash to take care of Dasia and this baby I'm fenna have."

"Don't tell me he stopped lacing you with cash."

"Naw it ain't that, it's just that I'm not fenna depend on him fo' nuttin!"

"I feel you about that…have you gave him some since he been back?"

"Yeah", Natalie said regretfully. "But all he was trying to do was fuck me in the ass."

Mandy broke off into a giggle before Natalie continued. "Naw I don't mind it every blue moon but that was all he wanted to do. Girl my ass still sore as we speak."

Cleofis stretched across Natalie's couch comforter waiting on her return from the grocery store. He knew Berry was holding down the new dumping spot as he relaxed flipping through the channels on Natalie's big screen. His mind started thinking about his two cousins Bruno and JW when someone knocked at the door.

Cleofis tip toed to the blinds to see who it was. It was George and at first he wasn't going to open the door but when remembering he needed a haircut he gradually let him in. "Natalie's not here, but I need a haircut you think you could hook me up."

"Yeah, let me go grab my stuff out the car real quick."

"Oh and George", said Cleofis before he ran to the car. "Don't tell nobody you saw me over here."

"Awww you know you ain't gotta worry about nothing like that with me."

Natalie could barely turn the door knob with all her groceries in her arms. Cleofis was laid across the couch the same way he was when she left. "I wish yo' ass didn't have a warrant…'cause you should be the one caring all these groceries."

"If I didn't you'd still be waddling yo' fat ass in the house with the groceries", he smiled then jumped up to help her put away the food. "So what Mandy was yapping about bay?" bay was short for baby.

"Nothing important, she told me to tell you she needed an ounce."

"Let me use yo' cell phone so I can have Berry get right on nat."

Handing him the cell phone she replied, "So I see you cut cho' hair."

"Naw I didn't, yo' faggot ass friend George stopped by here and did. He call himself fenna wait fo' you, I told that fag he better just stop back through."

"Why did you let him in anyway? I didn't want nobody to know you was here", replied Natalie not wanting her friend George to know who she was involved with.

"George ain't gone say shit, I been known dude since I was a shorty. Trust me he ain't gone tell nobody I was over here."

"So thaaaats who your baby daddy is?", said George.

"Yeah, I'm ashamed to say but that's him", she responded into the phone.

"I been knowing him since he was a little kid, so you've hit the lotto now huh?"

"Shhhit he don't got money like people think he do, and it's hard for him to make some when he got so many people against him. I didn't wanna tell you who he was 'cause so many people misunderstood him and on top of that I know he a dog so I figured you'd probably heard some female or two discussing his name at the shop."

"Yeah, yeah I have heard his name a lot, but people refer to him as Teflon and it's a lot of police that really hate him."

"Hold on a minute somebody on the other line", said Natalie

"Who is this?"

"This Mandy girl, tell yo' baby daddy to watch himself 'cause they say Bo Pete setting niggaz up."

"Who?"

"Bo Pete, Teflon knows who I'm talking about just make sure you tell em?"

"Alright whatever."

Cleofis was rotating with Berry when his cell phone rang. "What's up bay" he spoke after looking at the number of the caller.

"Mandy just called talking about some dude named Bo Pete was setting people up."

"Straight up!"

"Yeah she say he done already set up quite a few people so be careful."

"A'ight bay I'll hit you back."

The news tied a knot in his stomach, how long would it be before Bo Pete snitched about the murders. So far the task force had brought in fifty drug dealers, many of which were associates of Cleofis and what was left of the crew. But for some reason old Bo Pete never mentioned the triple murder.

Cleofis still couldn't chance it, with that thought of the electric chair along with associates pleading for somebody to reach out and touch Bo Pete. Cleofis had no choice -- the witness/snitch had to go.

"Man 'Moe' I'll wack the nigga fo' you, just show me where he at", said Berry anxious to prove to his friend that he could kill like him.

"It's gone have to get done one way or another", said Cleofis. "Cause now my life on the line."

Bo Pete was sighted coming out of a north side house a few times where he occasionally checked on his crackhead girlfriend. Cleofis caught wind of the location through dealings in the street.

"Na look, he over there right now", exclaimed Cleofis, handing him a black 40 Cal. "Don't try to wack the nigga from a distance, make sure you get right up on him."

"I got'chu moe', I got you."

"Listen", Cleofis stressed loudly. "Don't talk just listen. Don't empty yo' clip on the nigga 'cause you never know who around him got a mag. And if that crackhead bitch got her kids with her make sure you don't hit none of the kids." Berry shook his head looking Cleofis directly in the eyes when he was conversating with him.

"Whatever you do, don't toss my mag and make sure he inna car when you tag em, so he can't go no where. D-O-A 'moe', this nigga gotta be dead when 5-0 get there, don't fuck this up", He said aggressively. The two built a permanent with there thumb and index finger's, then threw up the five before hitting their chests with such pride and dignity.

Bo Pete was coming out of a small brick house with his girlfriend and kids. No sooner than his feet touched the pavement he was looking around nervously. His eyes were bucked and his hair looked like it hadn't been combed in ages. You could tell paranoia kept him awake at night and this hand was prepared to reach for his waist as he helped put the kids into the back seat of his girlfriend's car.

Cleofis dropped Berry off on a side street and went to go wait in a near by alley. Berry ran up on the vehicle seconds after Bo Pete got into the drivers seat. "FLACOW! FLACOW! FLACOW! FLACOW!"

The four shots were like music to Cleofis' ears as he drove with a light foot on the gas to scoop up Berry. "My nigga", said Cleofis, hitting the steering wheel. Bo Pete caught all four slugs trying to protect his girlfriend and kids.

With his adrenaline pumping, Bo Pete excited the vehicle and pulled out a gun. Attempting to raise the gun in the direction of the runaway assassin, his body dropped heavily onto the concrete. With in minutes he was dead and his girlfriend held him in her arms screaming louder than the sirens from the ambulance.

"You hit 'em right?"

"Moe that nigga gone, I made sho I hit 'em good!"

"Well see, well see", replied Cleofis as he drove as far away from the scene as possible.

When Bo Pete's murder was finally confirmed to Cleofis he laughed very sinister like. No way was he ever going to go down for the triple murder. The $10,000 warrant for a gun and auto theft was something he could deal with but going down for the triple murder was not an option.

Shawndra was gone, and he just saw to it that Bo Pete was killed. These were the only two witnesses who could get him convicted him of the massacre. So the weight that was lifted from Cleofis shoulder was a ton, which gave him relief. All fifty of the drug dealers Bo Pete set up were released with all charges dropped. The streets praised Cleofis for the job him and Berry did. And dealers that once held animosity towards Cleofis now bowed at his feet making him feel welcomed after the public crucified his name with the Shawndra Coleman's murder. Cleofis still was struggling to make that $10,000 mark selling bags wasn't moving fast enough and selling ounces wasn't entitling him too much of a profit.

Berry had become fearsome after committing his first murder and wasn't taking any shit from anybody including Cleofis. And Cleofis could see it in Berry's eyes after pushing him jokingly down a couple of stairs.

Berry quickly retrieved a chrome 380 and threatened Cleofis to push him like that again. Seeing that Berry was no longer a follower

Cleofis laughed the incident off and embraced the gunner as an equal. But Berry was far from the killer Cleofis was. He still was not a thinker or a mastermind like Cleofis.

By the end off '99 Cleofis was arrested along with Berry who was concealing a firearm and police impounded the drop top Chrysler Sebring. Cleofis had only hustled up 7,000 dollars which wasn't enough to bond him out for 10,000 dollars. So Cleofis had Natalie give the seven grand to Puncho, a rising drug dealer from the Durrel Projects who guaranteed he'd bond Cleofis out after he flipped the seven grand a couple times. But no sooner than Puncho received the cash he started having some bad luck of his own, which led him to avoiding Cleofis' calls from the county jail. Cleofis figure he didn't have to be a brain surgeon to know Puncho had jerked him out of his seven grand and didn't plan on paying him shit.

CHAPTER 16

2000

"All that fuckin' cheese I done gave yo' ass, and you gone dodge my calls. with chow bitch ass, what you think I can't touch you 'cause I'm locked up", Cleofis growled into the jail house phone.

"Calm down Cleofis", said Mark Galante. "Just calm down fo' a minute."

"Naw motherfucka, you calm down. I done been in this bitch fo' five months. You phony ass mobster you was dodging me when I was on the run, and you been dodging me since I been in this hell hole."

"Now wait a minute Mr. Jackson, I don't owe you anything. I did everything I could with the finances you gave me."

"You the reason why I'm in this mutherfucka." Cleofis raised his voice, "If you would have told me the right court date I wouldn't even be in this place." Mark was trying to speak but Cleofis words towered over his' "Keep playin' these silly ass games and they gone find yo' ass slumped over in yo' car."

"Look you need to quit talking like that over the phone, 'cause you know they record these conversations." Natalie butted into their situation after listening silently over the three way.

"Hell naw, 'cause the only reason why this bitch picked up the phone was because he didn't recognize the number", said Cleofis. "You know how long I been tryin' to get in touch with this bitch?"

"Cleofis there's no need for name calling, believe it or not, I did not know you was trying to contact me", replied Galante

"Yes you did, you cock sucking faggot. I sent a message through plenty of people, including my baby momma and the only reason why you answering her phone is 'cause she got her number changed."

"Now wait a minute Cleofis", Galante tried to converse

"Naw, you wait a minute, if you don't get me outta here by my next court date I'mma have yo' ass wacked. Hang the phone up bay, I'm through talking to this honkey!"

Natalie clicked the scared to death lawyer off the three way while he was scrambling for words.

"Boy you know that lawyer ain't gone do nothing but go to them people", replied Natalie as she breast fed their new born baby.

"No he ain't, because he knows if he do he'll have to look over his shoulder all the time."

"Ok if you say so."

"Just trust me, I know what I'm doing. Now click over and call that nigga Puncho I was telling you about."

Natalie dialed the cell phone number wondering what Cleofis was about to snap on Puncho about. She knew the short, fat, and dark skinned Puncho from all the times he tried to holla at her. She had considered hollering at Puncho before she became aware of the tension between him and Cleofis.

"Bitch ass nigga, where my chips at?", Cleofis barely gave Puncho a chance to say hello. "What'chu think I'mma be in this mufucka fo' ever."

"Teflon", Puncho shouted into his cell phone. "Who the fuck you think you talking too. Nigga I'mma gangsta, I don't care how many bodies you dropped. I done went to war with the best of em."

"Nigga it ain't gone be no war with me", you have one minute remaining said the operator. "You know how I get down, I don't miss."

"Me neither."

"Okay killer, make sho you keep that change 'cause you gone need it fo' you and yo' mommas casket", Cleofis said sarcastically.

"Cleofis", yelled Natalie after clicking the three-way off. "Cleofis", she yelled again but his call had already expired.

Turn around my son was the last word Cleofis heard before waking up out of a realistic dream. His heart was pounding out his chest as he gained conscious. In his dream Jesus had told him to turn around while standing at the pearling gates. Everything in the dream seemed so real to Cleofis and he dropped to his knees in prayer mumbling. "God please forgive me, God please forgive me?"

Berry glanced down at the pleading friend of his and shook his head don't this fool know he already doomed, all the repenting in the world wouldn't make up for the dirt he did thought Berry, laying on the top bunk.

The two requested to be cellmates upon entry. But now they both could barely tolerate the other so they rarely said anything to each other. Berry was finally coming to terms that Cleofis didn't give a shit about nobody except himself, and that he only helped people to benefit off of it in the long run. Cleofis hated the dumb stuff that came out of Berry's mouth and the way he acted like he couldn't think for himself. Cleofis felt Berry's weakness along with his insecurity showed the more he opened his mouth expressing his sensitive side.

Not quite through with his prayer, a guard was opening their cell. "Cleofis Jackson", yelled the young white guard. "Chief's requesting your body down stairs, so wrap your prayer up, and let's go."

Cleofis snarled at the guards demands as he rose to his feet what could they possibly want down there, ran through his mental. The dream he'd just had, had him in an edgy weird repenting mood. But when homicide Detective Diamond along with other detectives wanted a hair sample he flew off the handle.

Punching, kicking, and biting doing whatever in his power to avoid the authorities from taking a sample of his hair. When they finally restrained him and got a string of his hair they put him in the chair. The chair was a ground floor room wear they strapped inmates into an uncomfortable seat, where you couldn't move at all. And would leave you there for hours until they felt like letting you out. Body parts would fall asleep and plenty of spots would start to itch but you couldn't scratch or hardly shift your body to avoid discomfort.

Once again Cleofis was drawing himself in shame, all the money he had ran through and he couldn't even make bond. It seemed like he only got incarcerated when his finances was very low, and the detectives was starting to piss him off.

Very irritated and worn out from being strapped into the chair all day he return to his cell to find Berry on the shitter. "Damn man put some water on that shit", replied Cleofis ready to have a serious conversation. "Hurry up nigga, yo' ass got the whole deck cutting up." Inmates on the cellblock laughed loudly agreeing with Cleofis' request. But Cleofis was in no playing mood. "Them fuckin' detectives still tryin' to hang this Shawndra bullshit on me. I'm tired of this shit every fuckin' body know JW ass killed my Boo." Cleofis started as Berry flushed the toilet. "I need you to make a statement fo' me", Cleofis voice dropped to a hollow whisper. "Tell them fuckin' people Jackpot was plotting with JW to wack Shawndra just say the nigga told you he was gonna do it."

"Man Moe'" Berry began with a sorry to disappoint you look. "I got love fo' ya but I ain't gone be able to do that, 'cause I don't get down with making statements on people."

"Shhhh", Cleofis put his finger over his own lips. "Keep it down moe. Look, it ain't snitching, it's just throwing the attention on somebody else 'til I can figure out who's out to get me."

"I hear you", Berry rubbed his upset stomach, "But I ain't with it and you can't convince me otherwise."

"Motherfucka", Cleofis moved in just an inch from his face. "I still got that gun you wacked Bo Pete wit, so if I go, you go, got it killer." Giving Berry the nastiest look possible.

Berry just fell back in silence already regretting what he would have to do to Jackpot to keep this turn coat friend of his from disclosing his roll in Bo Pete's murder.

Though they had their differences up until this point, Berry would of gladly did life for his childhood buddy, that's how strong his loyalty was for him. But Cleofis was showing another side of him. *How could he threaten to give him up to the cops, is the nigga just bluffin' 'cause snitching ain't in my vocabulary*, thought Berry.

Cleofis had Berry right where he wanted him. Berry would have no choice but to do everything Cleofis asked, play puppet to a puppet master who was loosing control of himself. Berry thought serious about trying to beat Cleofis ass or smoother him to death in his sleep.

Physically over powering Cleofis would be difficult for Berry since he never won any of there fights when they were kids and trying to smother Cleofis might result in a fight to the death that Berry wasn't prepared for, so the thoughts diminished as quick as they emerged.

Det. Diamond took a sip from his hot Folgers cup of coffee. Sitting at his desk he sat the hot cup of coffee down, picked up Berry's statement and leaned back in his chair as he glanced over it. Slick son of a bitch, Diamond said to himself as Fox walked into his office.

With an overwhelming smell of cigarette smoke, Fox rubbed his hands through his wild hair. "You wanted to see me?"

"As a matter of fact I did", Diamond replied. "I wanted to know if you could use some of your informants to find out some information for me." Fox took a seat as Diamond continued. "I believe I can solve the Shawndra Coleman murder if I could turn some of these people I believe Cleofis Jackson has bribed to make statements into telling me what he offered them, or did they just do it out of fear."

"I thought that Wells dude that got killed in a car accident was responsible",

"I believe he was along with James love and Cleofis Jackson. Now quite a few people had made statements against Mr. Wells including Cleofis, now that Mr. Wells is dead you have quite a few people making statements against James Love, like this Berry Hilton fella who was also apart of this crew they called the Capone's lead by Cleofis. Now we know for a fact there were people in Shawndra's car at the time of the murder but we also think there was a third person driving a getaway car that was waiting for them."

Fox scratched his wild and un-groomed beard. "Well how would James Wells and Cleofis be working together when James tried to kill Cleofis on at least two separate occasions just before the girl was killed."

"I know, that's one I can't figure out yet, but I strongly believe Cleofis took part in this girl's murder not just because Mrs. Coleman believes he did it but because there's been plenty of Shawndra's friends and relatives who spoke about the way Cleofis use to threaten her."

"So have Cleofis made a statement on James Love", asked Fox

"Not yet but I believe he will. Why would a person convince others to make statements on people if he wasn't trying to cover his own ass in the process. Since when does convicted felons volunteer to make signed statements on things they just heard, half of these people are crack heads and drug-dealers. I believe Cleofis gave the drug addicts some crumbs to come forward and manipulated the dealers." Diamond stood up and took a seat on his desk moving closer to Fox to let him understand the seriousness of the situation. "Were dealing with a criminal, who's never been down for any of the murders he's committed, now he wasn't the one who killed that drug addict five months ago, but I believe he had it done. My sources tell me the addict was in that townhouse back in ninety six, but he some how got away. These sources have actually heard the addict describe the triple murders. So I'm thinking maybe Cleofis waited for the right time to strike considering the public would think someone the addict set up had him killed."

"I believe it's possible and it's a shame this son of a bitch a probably be getting out soon", said Fox

"Yeah you shoulda seen how the low life acted when we wanted a hair sample from him, if he didn't have anything to do with Shawndra's murder I don't see why he would act so violently."

"That's 'cause he's a fuckin' animal", Fox started. "I would have shot the dirt bag back in 96 if a rookie wouldn't have shown up to the scene. The way he used to ride around here in that drop top like nobody could touch him, pissed me the hell off."

Diamond cocked his head back, he wanted Cleofis Jackson, but he wanted him by the book and some of Foxes' comments brought his mind to some of the rumors he'd heard about Fox's dirty activities in the streets.

Though Fox made plenty of drug busts, and shot a couple criminals it was rumored some of the busts came up empty so he placed his own narcotics on dealers and that one of the criminals he shot didn't even have a weapon until Fox place one in his hands.

Even though Sergeant Fox was one of Kankakee's dirtiest cops, his help was efficient in homicide investigations due to his dedicated involvement in drug busts giving by informants that kept him posted on the latest.

Giving a list of names to Fox, Det. Diamond strolled back to his chair. "See if you can scare up some of those names, its gotta be one on there that a tell you the real reason they volunteered information on the two James'."

Out of all them murders, this asshole trying to nail the nigger for one he didn't do thought fox as he exited Diamonds office, what a crock of shit he drew further in thought, balling up the list and throwing it into a garbage can.

Mark Galante got the state to drop the stolen vehicle charge and brought Cleofis a sweet deal for the firearm that was found in the car. If he hadn't been sent to prison at age seventeen, the gun charge would have been a misdemeanor. But, because he was a felon, being caught with a gun meant doing some more time.

Cleofis had been dealing with this case since 96 and was ready to get it over with. Even though Galante had successfully appealed his end of 98 conviction Cleofis didn't want to fight the system anymore. It was known that the BMW was his vehicle and it didn't belong to April who falsely claimed he stole it. The state would count the five months as ten months and put Cleofis on parole for twelve months. So once again the villain was released onto the streets, but with a year of parole on his back.

The cold air conditioning from Puncho's 2000 Cadillac Deville blew heavily in Cleofis' face. With all the windows rolled down you could hear "Enemies Give Me a Reason to be The Last Motherfucker Breathin", from one of Tupac's choruses off his latest album.

Cleofis raped a little bit to the verse. "Woke up with fifty enemies plotting my death", he felt he new exactly how it felt to be Tupac.

Phat Farmed out from head to toe, Puncho's Deville made him feel like he was in a airplane flying through the sky, sorta how he felt when being in Bruno's S500 back in 96.

Puncho found Cleofis before Cleofis could find him. He gave him 3,500 dollars -- practically begged for peace, and told him he could ride around in the new Deville until he came up with the rest. But Cleofis wanted more for his long wait and broken promises so his mental constantly was at work on a plan to get Puncho back.

Why kill him? He's more valuable alive. Puncho was becoming Cleofis' stunt dummy and he didn't mind it 'cause he wanted to live.

Cleofis was treating him less than a man, taking full advantage of the fear in Puncho's heart.

The niggaz in Puncho's circle wasn't no push-overs and they hated the way Puncho allowed Cleofis to treat him. They were waiting anxiously for Puncho to give them the ok so they could out Cleofis on ice. Most of them were from Harvey, Illinois and could care less about Cleofis' reputation on the streets.

But for the most part the two acted like the closest of friends, who would ever think they made such vital threats to each other. Plus Cleofis' parole had him leery about making a war move, he knew a crew of gun slangers were behind Puncho and war would be risky with him being on parole. So the best thing to do would be to pluck the chicken as many times as you could without it taking notice.

"You not fenna keep fucking me in my ass", said Natalie, cooking dinner for days ago released Cleofis. "For real boy I ain't playin' that shit hurt last night."

"Didn't seem like it hurt to me", he replied as he stepped out of his Phat Farm shoes.

Just coming in from hitting some blocks he couldn't wait to jump back in the Deville and hit some more. Just like before his five month incarceration all he wanted to do was sodomize her, and it was beginning to completely turn her off.

Putting her chopped up potatoes into a skillet, Natalie leaned against the kitchen counter and folded her arms. "So tell me Cleofis, how long have you had genital herpes?"

"Huh", Cleofis said with a puzzled look on his face.

"If you can huh, you can hear. How long did you think you was gonna keep on screwing me before I got it."

Natalie found out she contracted the STD around the time Cleofis got locked back up. But she still loved him and felt as long as it wasn't HIV they could get through it. Her love for him was deep, vivid, wounded and dangerous because of the lack of trust in their relationship.

"I was gonna tell ya, but I thought you would try and leave me", he replied shamefully. "I caught the shit from a white chick I let suck me up when I was a shorty…I'm sorry boo." Cleofis looked for some sign of sadness as the screams from little Cleofis Jackson Jr. erupted from the backroom.

"Go get cha son, 'cause that little boy ain't fenna keep interrupting me."

Cleofis breezed to the back to pick up the little bundle of joy that looked identical to him. Little Jr. stopped crying once cuddled inside of daddy's arms. "Man this little nigga spoiled."

"I know", said Natalie. "He just like you, he always want his way."

Putting the infant on his shoulder and patting him for a few seconds. Cleofis quickly tried to converse before Natalie brought the disease back up. "Man boy, I wish you wouldn't have been on leave 'cause them guards treated me like shit in that county. And all your friends either don't work the floors no more, or quit…look at me Boo I done lost a lot of weight."

"Well let's just hope it's from lack of eating and not another incurable disease", she hissed. "For now on I think we should use rubbers 'cause I'm not fenna deal with anything else, you hear me."

"Mmm-Hmm", he said sharply under his breath not wanting to discuss it anymore. Usually he wouldn't let her talk to him in such a bossy way, but he clearly understood she had a right to be angrier then she appeared.

The crowd of eight seemed to glow under the beam of the street light as Gabe parked and approached. Shooting craps, hustlers glanced over their shoulders to see who was coming, noticing it was Gabe they turned their attention back to Puncho who was passing on the dice.

Gabe could see Cleofis standing over the crouching flock of gamblers with a mischievous look in his eyes. He hadn't said much to Cleofis since he questioned him about being accused of murdering Shawndra Coleman. And since then Gabe had heard more disloyal slander that supposedly came out of Cleofis' mouth. Gabe wasn't the type to believe he-say/she-say, but he knew his friend was feeling himself way too much lately. Plus how could he close his ears when most of the information came from people who had no reason to lie.

"What you doing out here with these gorillas?", Cleofis replied looking directly at Gabe. "It's a little too late for you to be out here", he continued. "I wouldn't want cho' Momma to call them people if one of these niggaz smack you out here."

A couple hustlers giggled as Gabe eased in closer to see what they was betting for. "A nigga put they hands on me, I bet you couldn't pay him to put his hands on anybody else when I get through with his ass."

Cleofis bent down to scoop something Puncho was handing to him on the sly. "Gone get down chump they only shootin c-notes", said Cleofis as he stood back straight observing over the dice game like he was cutting.

"Naw I'm cool, I'm just watching", Gabe looked as Puncho threw seven and eleven like there was no tomorrow, talking plenty of shit with a girly like voice.

"What you want fo' an ounce", asked Cleofis as he bent back down to grab some more cash.

"Eight", Gabe said with the rising of his eye brows.

"Well let me holla at you real quick." Cleofis put his forearm on Gabe's shoulder and directed him to the side so they could speak in private. "Let me call this Mark and see if he still wants it."

Gabe stared at his friend as he use a cell phone with an uncoverable sneakiness drowning his face. "Come now, hurry up, the nigga got a bank roll big enough to choke a mule", Cleofis spoke into the phone with a low pitch, and then quickly ended the call. "Oh they straight, G' they already got it from somebody else"

"A'ight", said Gabe as the two walked back up on the dice game. Gabe watched the gambling for another brief minute before coming to the conclusion that the atmosphere was too weird. Something was up, he just couldn't put his finger on it and because he was climbing up more in the drug game he felt it was best to vacate the premises.

Gabe wasn't in his car good when deep voice demanded cash from the crap game. "Ya'll know what the fuck this is, lower that shit", they barked. "Click clack, click clack", was the sound of the automatic as they elevated bullets into the chambers. The two bandana masked gun men seemed like they dropped out of the sky judging how swift they were.

Gabe watched momentarily out his window as the robbers laid down everybody at the dice game. Shhit I'm glad I just left, he reflected, pulling off quickly. I knew something was about to happen.

The next day Kiara bought Gabe some strange gossip. "All I'm saying is Makeela say the faggot told her personally", shouted Kiara.

"That's bullshit", Gabe began for the second time. "Makeela just mad because he probably stopped fuckin' with her ass. And you should tell yo' dumb ass friend to stop spreading that shit fo' she get herself killed."

"Why would the faggot lie? Especially on somebody like him, where he could get himself hurt?"

"The same reason a lot of other hoes lie", replied Gabe refusing to believe the slander behind his friend's name. "That type of shit don't even sound right Kiara, just listen to yo'self. Even though he a rotten nigga, that's just some pure hating comin' from yo' girl mouth."

Gabe and Kiara were now staying together in an average apartment on the Westside funded by drug money. They were in love and rarely enjoyed each others company.

"It's not a big deal Gabriel", Kiara exclaimed with a slight giggle. "But cho' friend might be a doo-doo chaser", her giggles burst into a high pitch laugh.

"Ha ha ha", said Gabe. "You wouldn't want nobody spreading no lying ass rumor about you like that."

"Your right baby but this year two thousand, and more and more tuff guys are starting to come out the closet with that homosexual shit."

"I hear you, but people need to know facts befo they go yapin' about shit like that."

Gabe couldn't wait to catch Cleofis so he could find out who stuck him up last night. And when seeing an unfamiliar car parked outside Mrs. Jackson's house he knew the villain had to be inside. Cleofis greeted Gabe with half closed eye lids and a soft smile. "What's up little homie?"

"I'm big homie", Gabe responded, wondering why he was smiling after last night's robbery.

"Who the fuck stuck ya'll up last night?"

Stepping further into the living room Gabe could see a familiar face. It was Bootleg sitting at the living room table counting some cash. Glancing at the bandana and mag on the table sitting next to the cash, Gabe knew what happened before he Cleofis could respond.

"Come on 'gee' use yo' head, you think a nigga really gone stick me up", replied Cleofis. "You know them niggaz out there had it comin, but the only nigga cake I really wanted was Puncho's. Everybody else can have they cheese back"

"Hmph, you niggaz trip", said Gabe, greeting Bootleg with a nod. He remembered Bootleg from the county jail when he was Cleofis' cellmate. Bootleg had a restlessness about himself that made him conscious about him.

"Gee" Cleofis started excitedly, "We had some hoes last night boooy, woooo, weeee, these bitches was poppin' 'X', getting naked, fuckin' each other, the whole nine. I'm telling you, you need to try some ex home boy, you just don't know what you missing. A nigga still feel good."

Gabe gave Cleofis a look like he was bugging. "Man I ain't fuckin' with that shit, they say its worse then cocaine"

"Don't be believing that shit, I fuck with it and you know I ain't no hype."

"Not yet at least", Gabe spoke seriously.

"Well you know what chump?", Cleofis said grabbing a pile of cheese of the table. "You can take yo' square ass on somewhere, 'cause as you see I got the money, power and respect."

"And you like to eat pussy", Gabe said under his breath, going to the kitchen and opening the refrigerator.

Bootleg dropped the money out of his hand as he chuckled heavily at the remark. "Damn 'Moe'", he replied. "Every body know you eat pussy!"

"I see you cheerleading for the brick" Cleofis didn't sound too happy. "This brick the one eat pussy and nigga I heard how you be havin yo' face up Kiara's ass." Bootleg laughed as Cleofis continued. "I should've neva hooked you up with that fine ass bitch 'cause now you walking around with cho' head bigger than what it already is."

"Tisssssss", Gabe sighed as he walked past him headed for the front door. "They say you fucked some faggot but that couldn't be true 'cause you too gangsta fo' that." Gabe slammed the front door right behind his words.

Gabe was half way to his vehicle when Cleofis swung the front door open. "THAT'S WHY NIGGAZ wanna KILL yo' ASS NA", he shouted "Cause you always playin' too much, phony ass nigga!" Cleofis continued like a raging bull as Gabe pulled away. "Bootleg soon as you get a chance I want you to stick that nigga, I'm tired of that bricks mouth. If it wasn't fo' me, niggaz woulda stuck his ass up a long time ago."

"Oh trust me", said Bootleg. "If the nigga wouldn't have left five seconds sooner I woulda laid his ass down along with everybody else last night."

Gabe and Cleofis' slick comments to each other was starting to cross the line, for neither man felt the love they once had for each other was there anymore, but this was something that was none discussable though they could see it in each others eyes they rarely let it show in each others presence. Gabe wasn't naive to the fact that Cleofis could have him stuck up. But Gabe knew Cleofis couldn't do it himself because of the history between the two barred them from doing things to each other with the other ones knowledge. But that didn't mean Gabe didn't hear about Cleofis' jealous threats and though he heard it didn't stop him from coming around.

Natalie ended her phone call with her big sister just before pulling into Mrs. Jackson's drive way. She blew her horn until Cleofis came out.

"Damn I was coming", said Cleofis, coming out and strolling around to the driver side window.

"You know how you be taking yo' sweet ass time. Oh and here go your food."

Cleofis smiled at his son briefly that was strapped into a car seat in the back. Then shifted his smile to a frown. "Yo brotha Gabe gone make me wack his ass."

"What he do?" asked Natalie.

"What don't he do, on top of I think that nigga had something to do with Shawndra's murder…I'm telling you I'm getting tired of that cowards mouth", he took a sip from his drink then glanced around outside. "You gone be attending that boy's funeral."

"If you feel that way about him then tell him to stop coming over."

"I told him", Cleofis started lying, something Natalie was growing more and more aware of. "But you know the nigga wanna be me, when he need to be himself."

"Somebody told me you and some boy name Punchy or Puncho got robbed last night."

"What", replied Cleofis.

"Yeah, and they said Gabe had something to do with it."

"Number one ain't no nigga stuck me up, and number two you know Puncho's name 'cause they say you used to holler at the nigga."

Natalie raised her cheek bones as if she didn't know what he was talking about. "Don't give me that stupid ass look", he continued. "Just because I was locked up don't think I ain't have my ear to the streets."

"You musta didn't, 'cause if you did you would know that I wasn't hollering at anybody."

"Yeah right, you lying ass bitch, mufuckas seen ya'll together."

"Pleeeease, that boy came over Mandy's house a couple times when I was over their, he used to try and holla at me but I always let him know, wasn't shit happening." He sucked his teeth vividly, letting her know he didn't believe her. "Now I carried on conversation with him a couple times but once I found out y'all was into it I ended the conversations."

"Just listen to yo' self, you lying ass hoe, you just said you' carried conversation on until you heard we was into it with each other."

"You not fenna keep calling me out my name", Natalie was beginning to get upset. "I don't know who you letting send you off like that but if I was fuckin' with that nigga I wouldn't be fuckin' wit'chu."

With in a split second Cleofis had reached his hand into the car and started choking her. He was tired of her smart mouth, already in a bad mood and he was quite ready to leave her for a chick that was a few years older then her.

"I…can't…breath", she cried trying to remove his hands from around her neck. Cleofis' Wendy's meal was now food for the ants as it spilled on to the pavement of the driveway.

"Bitch I'll kill you…you hear me bitch if I ever find out you gave that pussy up while I was gone, on my daddy grave I'mma kill you."

Tears rolled down Natalie's now red dimpled imprinted cheeks. "So you gonna choke me in front of yo' son like this?" She managed to get out as he loosened the grip some.

Natalie felt a quick relief of breathing just before he released one hand to punch her with a closed fist while the other squeezed her neck extremely tight. "Let…me…go", she gagged for air kicking her legs as she reached for the button to roll up the window. She was able to maneuver out of his grip once the pain from the window rolled up on his arm started to kick in.

"BITCH LET ME GO!" Cleofis yelled with his arm stuck in the window trying to stop her from putting the car in reverse.

Natalie rolled down the window just enough for him to remove his arm then she quickly rolled it back up. With the car now in reverse she tried to swiftly pull off when Cleofis shattered the window with a vicious punch. "Yeah you killed her!", she shouted in fear. "You killed Shawndra Coleman", she had backed into the street and let her emotions flow for a few seconds while Cleofis stood angrily in the driveway.

"That's what'chu think bitch huh, that's what'chu think?" he looked for something to throw at the car.

"You killed Shanwdra Coleman", Natalie screamed louder wanting nosy neighbors to hear her.

"Stupid bitch", Cleofis ran out into the street knowing that she would pull off before he could harm her.

"I can't believe this bitch ass nigga punched me in the face like I was a fuckin' man", Natalie cried to her big sister over her cell phone. "Hold on a minute", she pulled to the side of a street. "Look at my damn baby, he got glass all on his face. That bitch don't even give a shit about his own son."

"That punk mufucka need to be dealt with, I'mma call Jooney and them", said her sister. "They'll take care of him."

"Don't call em. 'Cause I'm through with that maniac and I don't want him to have a reason to bother me no mo."

Natalie wanted a way out also, she had missed him when he was gone for five months, but frankly she was tired of his controlling ways, his lying the painful sodomizing and his lack of financial support for Cleofis Jr. He could have a pocket full of money and would only give Natalie a twenty here and there then a go brag about all the money he spend on his son.

"So what I told ya?", voiced Bones. "Naw ya pockets got the mumps, keep pushin' that diesel like that, you'll have the town like Bruno when he hit that lick for them five thangs. That nigga already had chips but with them five thangs of diesel that dude got rich as a motherfucka."

I knew that shit couldn't have been mixed, Cleofis said under his break. "You talking about back in '96 right, when me and cuz was doin' are thang."

"Yeah", Bones exclaimed, getting prepared to inject some heroin into a vein in his boney arm. "I swear to you CJ I helped the man count millions and he always had a bad bitch fo' me to fuck."

Cleofis was starting to get his feet wet in the heroin distribution, he knew very little about it. Customer to selling cocaine since a young teen, heroin was a stab in the dark for the gangster. But after hearing old timers boast about the financial gain it would give you, Cleofis figured he'd jump knee deep in the trade. Knowing that Bones was once Bruno's trusty chef, which was now strung out on the shit. Cleofis used him for a tester and an adviser. When he was beginning to stumble across some disturbing news.

"So exactly how much you think he made off them five thangs of diesel", Cleofis asked then mumbled under his breath, "That rotten ass nigga deserved everything he got, muthafucka probably made a fortune."

"Too much…too much", Bones voice dropped to a whisper as a leather belt fiend out of his left hand, and the H's sensation flooded his veins relaxing his body.

"So what's to it", asked Bootleg seated on a couch cross from Cleofis and Bones.

"Itsssssss cool young blood", said the half eye open in outer space Bones.

"I'm telling you 'Moe' we should keep our business right over here in the valley." Bootleg stood scratching his braids. "Fuck the Cartels and the Durrels they too fuckin' hot ova there."

Cleofis kinda ignored his new protégé as the thought of all the money Bruno made without him was starting to sink in. Drowned in a XXL gray Avirex sweater along with jet black pants with Avirex shoes he rose to his feet like a man working a nine to five. "Let's roll joe."

He could see it now. He'd be rich in no time especially the way his money was starting to climb. Bruno may have gotten over way more then him, but what's done was done. The two made motion for the door where they were welcomed by the bright beams of the sun as they strolled towards Bootleg's hooptie.

Puncho and Big C were posted up in the valley waiting on Cleofis and Bootleg to return to the hooptie they were spotted in. Big C was one of those gunslangers from Harvey a 6'3", 300 hundred pounded, well-built dark skinned man, with an itchy finger, short temper, and was a member of the conservative Vicelords.

Word had gotten back about Cleofis' roll in the robbery that was devised for Puncho. Puncho wanted to wait until nighttime but Big C wanted Cleofis brains on the pavement during the daylight followed by Puncho. The two tried to creep Cleofis and Bootleg from behind.

"A young blood!" shouted Bones from his screen door. "Ay you forgot chow phone." Turning to the direction of Bones' voice Cleofis immediately peeped the gun men. "Oh shit", he managed to blurt out as gunfire exploded in his direction. Taking cover behind a near by tree he reached for his knee knocker as Bootleg who they paid no attention to started blazing his mag like crazy.

"Who the fuck want it with moe?", shouted the daring Bootleg.

Cleofis unfolded from around the tree like a bat out of hell. "Whatch'all wanna do?" he let off four rounds grazing Puncho's stomach which lead them to retreating. "Run you cowards", he yelled.

Over thirty gun shots were fired in the Westside Valley Projects where little kids play on the swings and other accessories provided by the city. Police, task, and detectives swarmed the valley like bees to honey asking questions that they never received the correct answer to.

The valley was usually a quiet domain for low income residence. Though it was draped with addicts and dealers, the valley wasn't usually a shooting ground for static between rivals.

A couple weeks later Cleofis and Bootleg decided to walk through the north side of the small town. They wanted to catch anybody who associated with Puncho. Cleofis knew that niggaz slipped on Sundays and he was going to take full advantage of the opportunity. Not in the heart of the north side yet Cleofis' uncanny sense observed Big C, sitting in a short body Cadi arguing with some chick.

"Ay 'b' you see what I see?"

"Naw, what's up is it one of them niggaz?"

"Hell yeah", Cleofis replied after fully identifying the rival. "Take yo' heat out. Follow me, we gonna cut through them houses on the side."

This was the way Cleofis love to catch his victims, sitting in their cars like sitting ducks. Big C must have thought he was safe because he was pulled up in a back yard of a house. Jogging from between some closely built houses he crept the couple with such swiftness that Big C didn't even have time to react. "You pussy ass nigga what's up now", Cleofis barked with the barrel inches from Big C's face. "Niggaz you move I'll kill ya!"

"Please don't kill him Teflon", the chick clearly knew who the villain was, "Please Teflon , please Teflon."

Bootleg stood posted behind Cleofis waiting to put some slugs in Big C also. "Shoot that nigga 'Moe.'"

"Please don't, please don't kill me T", Big C's life flashed in front of his eyes as he seemed to be having a heart attack. "I'm through T, I'm through."

"You through", said Cleofis as he bit his bottom lip holding his firearm like a skill police officer.

"I mean I'm gone from it moe", Big C begged with tears in his eyes. "I'm gone from it."

"Please don't kill him Teflon", the chick screamed again. "He won't retaliate I promise."

Looking closely Cleofis noticed this was a face he'd seen before, it was Melissa, Jackpot's ex girlfriend, he emerged his murderous mean mug off his face. "You betta be gone from it."

"He is", said Melissa. "He won't bother you."

Cleofis had always wanted to sex Melissa but never got around to it. And looking into her fearful pretty eyes made him change the murder that was on his mind. He was letting pleasure get in the way of what he came to do. "Come on 'B'-- let's bounce."

"Damn 'moe' you letting 'em alive."

"Just come on nigga", it was because of Melissa he gave Big C a pass if only the terrified fella knew.

CHAPTER 17

Misery Loves Company - 2001

"I'm sorry for playin' you shady, but that knuckle head kept telling me to watch myself around you, telling me not to let you in if you came over."

"Yeah I figured it was something that clown said, 'cause you sure started treating me like a stranger."

"That's cuz that big nose punk had me thinking you killed Shawndra. His story just don't add up for one, and for two you never struck me as cold hearted."

"Well it's still some minds that insist I had some role in her death, but that's just how Kankakee is, that's why I realize I have no friends, before you even told me I already knew he tried to get people to convince the cops I did it…he the fuckin' reason so many women look at me strange."

"I can believe it, but what gets me is if he ain't have nuttin to do with her death why is he trying to put it off on people… I know Cleofis done shot a couple a niggaz but do you really think he killed Shawndra?"

"I don't know", Gabe shrugged his shoulders. "They was saying JW did that shit."

"Maybe that boy JW helped."

"Hardly doubt that, them two hated each other and Cleofis would've tried to slug JW on sight."

"Well if Cleofis did have anything to do with it, the police a find out sooner or later and if I was you I would stop associating myself with his snake ass, 'cause you know they say he had you stick up Puncho and them at the dice game."

"Yeah I know about that too, that's why I been watching Puncho's click like a hawk. A nigga that's street smart would know that I had nuttin to do with that robbery I was just stopping through", Gabe swallowed. "And I don't fuck with dude like that. We speak and shit but that's it."

"Come on now", Natalie spoke absurd. "You know you was a Capone like the rest of them dummies."

Seeing that she was just being silly he smirked slight. "Please that's yo' mans and them getting them ridiculous tattoos on each other."

"Well you know their Chief got his covered up, now from what I hear."

"I don't even think it's a Capone gang anymore. Jackpot locked up, JW dead, Berry locked up, and Cliff and Disco doing they on thang." Giving her twenty dollars that she came to get. He continued, "It's a shame Cleofis making all that change on the Westside but ain't givin' you a dime fo' my nephew who look just like his ass."

"Yeah I know that's why it's momma's baby, daddy's maybe. You only his uncle and you done damn near gave me more then Cleofis had since he been born." She slumped her body deeper into her brother's couch. "I ain't fucked with that horn face dead beat in a year", she spoke honestly. "I got niggaz that wanna holla but they scared 'cause mighty mouse is out here terrorizing."

Gabe laughed at his half sisters, names for Cleofis. "You shouldn't be even thinking about a man right now anyway", he knew she liked to gossip, so he tried to be careful about what he said around her. "You got a good job so just keep working, get cho' self on a budget and save. And forget a man 'cause that ain't gone do nuttin but knock you off yo' focus." He spoke as if he was the same age as the now 33 year old woman. "Let Cleofis trick his money off on as many tramps as he want too, cuz when he fall he gone be right back in yo' face." Natalie shook her head in agreement as the thought of him hearing Cleofis wanted to kill him unleashed his tongue. "I know yo' car is messed up and all you have is this regular Thunderbird, but shit a get better."

"I know but it's just hard fo' me to stand by and watch him take care of that old bitch Holly who done already told people she only want him for his money."

"So what!" Gabe was becoming agitated by her unhappiness. "You far from ugly, you only got two kids, stop letting what this dude do affect the way you live."

Natalie loved the way her and her little brother was back corresponding but she hated the truth, which he never would bite his tongue once she got the quiet fella talking.

"You heard that shit about him being a faggot", Natalie braced herself not wanting to look like a fool if Gabe hadn't heard it.

"Yeah I heard about that", Gabe replied, glancing at TV. "But I don't believe it, even though he done gave me every reason to hate him I ain't gone allow nobody to shit on his name 'cause I grew up with the nigga and that rumor don't fit his character."

"How you know", she said with tears in her eyes, She got emotional whenever speaking about the gangsta for so long, which drove her to saying things that she didn't believe herself. "Ain't no telling where that nasty nigga a stick his dick."

Gabe's eye brows rose as he cared not to speak about the man he'd grown to distrust.

Natalie left Gabe's place with her tears still building up in her eyes, she couldn't understand why Cleofis didn't want to help with their son that looked just like him. But far deep down inside she loved him more since they'd been apart, than when they were together though she wouldn't admit it to anyone including herself. And the thought of Holly, upset her more. She'd known Holly when they were in their early twenties. She felt 'cause Holly knew Cleofis was her baby's daddy, that she would consider him off limits. But Holly was enjoying herself with the young thug. She was thirty-six, with a twenty-one year olds body, mediocre on the looks, brown skin, slightly cocked eyes with reader type glasses and she had a walk that could tame a dragon. Plenty of hips with plenty of ass she had Cleofis paying every bill in her house, rent, car note and taking care of her two kids. Never holding a job for long she depended on lucrative drug dealers to take care of her and what one wouldn't do the other would.

Natalie just wanted to have a conversation with the woman who she felt was keeping food out of her son's mouth. Her two kids never went hungry but this was her excuse for wanting to speak with Holly. She psyched herself up to believe. What was really going on was that she was losing integrity, her composure and Cleofis memory was pulling her off her square. She even started to make up rumors about Holly to destroy the low valued reputation she already had.

Riding home from church with her daughter Dasia, Natalie's peaceful mind state immediately shifted when seeing Holly drive past her. Suddenly her whole attitude changed so she decided to make a u turn and follow her. She wanted some answers, hoping by friendly introduction she could get some in the mist of a lady like conversation.

Putting her pride along with her dignity to the side, she followed Holly all the way home, pulled up behind her and hopped out of the Thunderbird. Wearing a soft white open jacket with matching knee high skirt, poppy print bias shell and white high heels. She had her hair pressed straight down and bump under at the edges looking like she just jumped out of a magazine. Nails done, jewels on wrist, neck and ears. Holly didn't know whether to show attitude are ask for a autograph as she turned and saw Natalie approaching.

"Is it something you want bitch?" Holly let her mouth open wondering what Natalie could possibly want after trying to run her name down in the dirt.

"Why it's gotta be like that, I didn't come over here on no bullshit I just wanted to talk to you."

"About what tramp?"

"I just wanted to let you know that I have nuttin against you", she began in a bashful like manner. "I just would like Cleofis to take care of his son", she moved her hands harmlessly. "You know how it is."

"Naw, I don't know how it is 'cause he takes care of my two girls", Holly snapped her neck. "But I'mma tell you like this you dumb bitch", her finger started tapping Natalie's forehead as she began to get riled up. "Say some mo shit bout me and I'mma stomp that ass, hear me hoe."

Natalie took a couple steps back. "I'm not even tryin' to fight with you", thinking about her daughter in the car along with her white dazzling fit she tried to turn and walk away but Holly started throwing a tremendous amount of punches, landing a couple to her face.

Holly slid forward, and Natalie took over trying her best not to mess up her fit. "Momma momma", said Dasia as she rushed over to try and break up the fight. Natalie was taking care of her business and by Dasia interfering, it gave Holly a chance to maneuver out of the attack.

"Yall tryin' to jump our momma", was heard before Holly's teenage daughters started wailing on helpless little Dasia. Dasia couldn't even put up a fight against the two savage acting girls. They beat her bloody then moved on to helping their mom.

Pinning Natalie to some mud on the curb the three punched, kicked and spit all on her bald up body. Natalie was praying that they'd stop -- she didn't know how many more times her head could bang up against the concrete without causing brain damage.

Dasia watched from the ground as they stumped and spit on her mother for the last time before motioning towards the house. "And you can go get cho' sista, that fat bitch Mandy, and even tell Cleofis if you want to", Holly shouted. "This bitch got the nerve to come over my house!" were her last words, before the house door slammed behind her and her daughters.

Natalie and her daughter climbed into the Thunderbird and sped off. Embarrassed and humiliated tears fell down her dimples uncontrollably as she rushed her daughter to the hospital. "Do it hurt bad?", she asked referring to the gash in Dasia's head.

"Yessss ma, please take me to a hospital."

"I'm taking you, I'm taking you."

After returning from the hospital Natalie dropped Dasia off at home and started zooming to Mandy's. Very hysterical she phoned Mandy while weaving through traffic.

"Get yo', shit these bitches just jump me and Dasia."

"Whaaat, quit playin."

"No, I ain't playin' I'm on my way to get you right now."

"Who jumped ya'll?"

"Holly and her Amazon ass daughters, I just brought Dasia home from the hospital she had to get stitches and-

"Girl you ain't gotta explain", Mandy cut her off. "I'm getting my shit right now just pull up and honk."

Natalie was barely on Mandy's Street when she seen the multitude of jet black tinted out Crown Victoria's covering over half the block. It was the task force and they were raiding Mandy's crib. Natalie couldn't believe it as she drove past the scene slowly she could see Mandy walking out in hand cuffs followed by Fox. With the windows rolled up she couldn't quite here what Mandy was saying but she knew she was snapping.

Damn! I told her about selling out of her house like that. She rubbed her aching not on her forehead. They must have come in there soon as we hung up from each other.

Later that night, Cleofis was feeling good himself as he stood in front of Ben's recently open lounge for the young people. Holding a glass of Courvoisier he stationed himself in front of the entrance with the off duty police officers that ran the metal detector over your body.

The officers didn't like the way he stood there like he owned the place catching the attention of many lovely women and the recognition from hustlers. Sporting a majority yellow Ackademack outfit if you didn't know who he was he would still grab your attention with his gear. Thinking about the money green brand new

Lexus SC300 Coupe he was about to hop into in a minute, the freshly faded attention getter spoke to the arrivals with such jazziness.

The Lexus belonged to Mark Galante who had now turned his secretive powder habit into an expensive crack habit and started pondering his new Lexus out to Cleofis for an eight ball a day. Like other opportunities Cleofis fully took advantage of this one feeling that he would eventually swindle the lawyer out of the luxurious vehicle.

"Hey ladies", he spoke to Makeela and Melissa who was looking very jazzy. This was the first time he'd seen these two women together.

"Hey Teflon", said Melissa, with an 'I appreciate you for not shooting me' type wave. Makeela tried to ignore the villain.

"Ay Keela com` ear" shouted Cleofis surely missing bending the rump shaker over.

"What'chu want?", said Makeela fearing that he might have heard that she had started the silent rumor about him being a faggot but she turned and walked towards him wants seeing the off duty police officers.

"Plug me witcho' girl?"

"Who, Melissa?" asked Makeela as she swallowed the fear in her throat.

"Yeah and make show you tell her how good a nigga doin' in the streets."

"All, ok I'll tell her what'chu said", when she put her back towards him she rolled her eyes. *This nigga don't even care that me and him used to stay together,* she thought as she stepped into the lounge.

Melissa had been on his mind since that day he heard her pleading and crying for Big Cs life.

Bones was waiting patiently in the Lexus with a mag just in case Cleofis needed it. He had promised him some diesel if he sat quietly the whole time while he was in the lounge but now he was ready to shift into his grimy mode. Not in need for cash he did things because he felt he could get away with it, so the plot to rob Puncho, after peeping him circling the area, beat on his skull like a migraine.

"Yo", said Cleofis, tapping on the Coupe window making Bones jump out of his nod. "I'm fenna stick that nigga Puncho", he continued when Bones rolled down the window. "Hit the lock we gone follow this coward."

Already witnessing Puncho try to kill Cleofis, Bones couldn't help but ask. "Why you gonna rob 'em when he tried to kill yo?"

"'Cause the niggaz a coward", he started as he jumped into the passenger seat and told Bones to pull off. "I already caught that nigga Big C and made him shit on himself." The exaggeration seemed 100% percent true. "Now I'mma just rob Puncho in person instead of sending my goon -- fuck wackin' him, that shit'll bring too much heat from them people and they already know we into it."

As the two sat down, the street from what they hoped to be Puncho's destination. Cleofis' mind ran rapidly, "You think we shoulda kept followin' em."

"Naaaaa", said Bones. "He'll show up here befow it gets too late."

"You know Holly wooped Natalie right?", Cleofis replied feeling very pimpish about the ordeal as he watched the scene like a hawk.

"I heard, I heard they say Natalie was looking like a swan till they dirtied her up."

"Yeah, I felt sorry for her but she the one took her dumb ass over there. Man I miss her and my son, but Holly got that pus that a break up a happy home."

Bone's giggled very heavily, "You know Mandy got raided."

"You bull-shittin'."

"For real, Task came in that bitch, kicked the door down, caught that big bitch with like two ounces hard."

"Hmph, that bitch gone tell on somebody and it ain't gone be me…I told her ass to stop dumping out of her crib like that."

Meanwhile, Shanice was over a friend's house when she peeped Cleofis and somebody else she didn't know parked outside. She almost didn't know who he was but the street light that wasn't far away gave her just enough light into the Coupe to know it was Cleofis on the passenger side. First she got kinda leery 'cause she thought he might be trying to get on some stick up shit with her 'cause a lot of folks knew she had money. But once she realized the two was scoping out somebody else she wondered who could it be, then it hit her, Puncho's sister stays on the next block up.

She grabbed her cell phone quick and called Puncho, she had his cell number from the numerous times he tried to holla at her. She wanted Puncho to be full aware of the man she literally hated.

"Talk to me."

"Is this Puncho?"

"Depends on who wanna know."

"This Shanice, the one you break your neck to-

"Awwwwww, what's up wit'chu, I see you finally decided to call a nigga."

"Yeah, but it's nothing like what'chu think, I just wanted to pull yo' coat about some shit."

"Speak yo' mind."

"You a gangstafied ass nigga right", Shanice wanted him to feel like a top gun.

"Right."

"So tell me why Teflon and another dude sitting down the street from yo' sister's house looking like they waiting for you to show up."

"How you know?", asked Puncho.

"'Cause I'm over my girl house staring right at em, through the blinds."

"Nooo shit…well good looking out and what do I owe for this information."

"I might let you take me shoppin' up north if yo' bankroll big enough."

"Shhhhit you already know it is-

"Well I'mma let you go", she cut him off before he started spitting some game. "Cause I know a gangsta gotta go handle his business."

"Ain't that, that Deville pulling up", said Bones.

"Shou'll and the fuck is, hurry up pull up", demanded Cleofis. "Pull up in the middle of the street so I can hop out the same time he hops out." There was no scared nervous feeling, just a feeling if invisibleness. Puncho wouldn't expect me to pull up in a Lexus. He thought. And this stunt will show them niggaz just how bitch made they are.

Puncho didn't even turn to see who was approaching in the small vehicle he just start walking around the front of the Deville at a slow pace showing the approaching Lexus nothing but the back of his leather jacket.

Cleofis swung the Coupe door open, clutching a pretty big automatic. He skipped a little to try and catch up with the half way to the house door Puncho.

After already hearing a car door open the foot steps hitting the concrete swiftly was the last thing Puncho needed to here before he turned around and started blazing before he even leveled his gun.

The first shot hit Cleofis right up under his heart making him do a one eighty where he dropped his mag to the ground and began to run. The second and third flew past his head, so close that he could hear the whistle.

Puncho chased up behind him to get a better shot by this time Bones had sped off. The fourth shot inserted into the back of his right arm and the fifth tore through his right hand making him pick up his speed like a track star.

Puncho let off five more rounds of his ten shot clip, but came up empty on the results.

"Shhhhit", Cleofis shouted, jiggling his hand from the pain. The night wind seemed to blow through the hole in his hand and his right arm was becoming paralyzed.

Running through three blocks of back yards, luckily a resident let him in through the back door of their house or else Puncho's crew who was coming the neighborhood would of probably found him.

Big C with three more of Puncho's goons was chilling in the back ground itching for a piece of the action, but all an all they wanted Puncho to prove that his murder mouth was capable of results. So they strategized a plan and told Puncho they'd be in the cut which enhanced his small amount of courage.

Next day… Natalie swung by Gabe's and Kiara's apartment to drop the news on Gabe. Gabe hadn't let her in the door before she started, "You know yo' boy got shot last night."

"Mmm-Hmm I heard", Gabe spoke nonchalantly.

"They say he might not live", she replied not really knowing the status of the situation.

"Ssso", Gabe spoke with such unconcern as he took a bite out of some breakfast Kiara had prepared for him. "From what I hear he checked his self out of the hospital already."

"Well I don't know. So many people saying so many thangs", Natalie started gibbering at the mouth. "They saying the same people that shot Bruno back in 96 shot em."

"Maybe", Gabe replied not giving a shit. "Baby! Bring me some orange juice", he called to Kiara who was in the bed room.

"Probably was that bitch Holly who set him up", said Natalie. "Maybe he'll calm his ass down now and take care of his son", she spoke to Kiara as she brought Gabe some juice. She continued, "You know me and Holly got fightin' the other day. I didn't even wanna fight the bitch. I had just come from church with Dasia and all I was tryin' to do was talk."

"Yeah, I was starting ask you where that knot on yo' head came from", Gabe almost smirked but when he looked at her features a little more, he could see it wasn't a laughing matter. Her lip was busted and her left eye was puffy. "I hope she look worse then you."

"Them bitches jumped me", Natalie voice raised, desperate for sympathy, eager for her half brothers momentarily company. "Her and them big ugly ass daughters of hers, you should see what they did to yo' niece." She wanted him to act as a protector over a half sister and niece he'd just became to know a couple years ago that only came around when she wanted something or wanted somebody to listen to her problems.

Should've ever took yo' ass over there tryin' to talk, Gabe reflected before speaking. "Just be cool let a little time go by", he started the advice. "She'll think it's cool after she see you a couple times, then when she's comfortable, pick up something and knock the hell out of her. Trust me she want even know what hit her."

CHAPTER 18

SPRING TIME, 2002

Melissa's naked feet swished dryly across Mrs. Sterling's tiled floor, as she went to go fetch Cleofis some Jack Daniels out his grandmother's liquor cabinet. Melissa had finally responded to his invitation a couple of days earlier. When she seen the Kankakee Journal that showed James (Jackpot) Love being indicted by the grand jury for two counts of first degree murder. All this time she thought Cleofis was a snake and was responsible for Shawndra Coleman's death, but the newspaper held her long for ex boyfriend accountable, who was just about to be released for doing half of a six year bid.

In the same turquoise silk gown she used to wear for Jackpot with nothing on under, she returned up the wide carpeted steps that led to Cleofis' bedroom. He'd been staying at grandmother Sterling's house since he got shot, either there or Holly's house, but he felt safer at his grandmothers.

"I still can't believe it", she began, pouring him a glass and glancing at the two day old paper that showed Jackpots face on the front of it. "The whole time I'm thinking you did that to Shawndra and it was this nigga." She grabbed the news paper, climbed into the rocking chair, looked at Jackpots picture for the hundredth time, and took a swig from the Jack Daniels she poured for herself.

"I tried to tell everybody", the shirtless villain replied, shuffling some powdered coke around with a king of hearts playing card on an end table. "Teflon don't get down like that, Shawndra was my woman, she had my seed in her stomach, on my dead daddy I was gone make her my wife." He buried his face into the raw powder, snorting like a child with a bad cold and grunting like a pig with his nose.

"Boy you betta slow down befow you kill yo' self", said Melissa.

Cleofis shuddered, then stuck his finger in the powder, glided it through every inch of his gums, then laid back on the bed he was sitting on and started to flap his arms like a little kid making an angel in the snow.

"That's some dust buster you got there", Melissa referred to his nose. "How long yo' granny gone be gone?"

"Long enough for me to pipe you down", he stood quickly off the bed, dropped his pants and brandished his erect sprout. Pouring some powder on it he started stroking himself until his soldier felt raw, raw in a sense where he wouldn't have to be there mentally to perform a couple of hours without going limp.

Melissa and Jackpot use to toot powder furtively before he turned himself in on the six year bid back in 99. She stopped when he left, but since Cleofis was now treating his nose, she reincarnated the habit she once had for hers.

Cleofis resorted to snorting powder to relieve stress, murderous memories, paranoia, and the uncomfortable bullet that was still stuck up under his heart. Now twenty years old, gray hairs fluctuated through out the young man low cut and he constantly kept his emerging beard shaved. His weight was at an all time low, and his once progressing climb to the top in the heroine game was now almost at the bottom. If it wasn't for his knowledge of how some people still feared him he would most definitely be broke.

He used to rarely indulge in drinking hard liquor and smoking trees, and he never snorted, though he smoked a mac joint with Bruno as a teen.

Cleofis always liked to be on guard and focused as much as possible, but his conscious was becoming too much for him to bear, and Al Pacino in Scarface seem to keep everything under control while inhaling tremendous amounts of coke.

"I thought you'd never cum", Melissa gasped after coming up for air like she was being held under water. Her silk gown was drenched from his sweat. "I'm fenna go get in the shower."

"Mmm hmm", Cleofis muttered as he stretched his nude body across the bed exhausted. As Melissa went down stairs he closed his eyes and let his numb brain drift off into the day.

"Cleofis", Shawndra shouted as she stood with her back to him at the kitchen counter peeling potatoes. "I thought I asked you not to let your friends smoke that weed in here."

"What", Cleofis replied mesmerized by her presence.

"You heard me", she said. "And don't try and tell me they wasn't 'cause I can smell it even though its very light, I ain't playing Cleo-

Cleofis interrupted her mouthing by squeezing her so hard she gasped. "It's really you, I'm not dreaming", he lifted her off her feet as he squeezed her.

"Boy! What the hell wrong with you put me down."

Sitting her feet to the ground he spun her around only to be viciously frightened by the repulsive flesh revealing hole opened on the upper part of her forehead. Grabbing the left side of his chest he struggled for air, for his heart burned from horror.

"Why did you let them do this to me Cleofis", her eyes watered and the suffering in them was deep and painful like the love he had subconsciously accumulated for her since her death. "Why Cleofis, why Cleofis…"

"Why, is some hoochie down stairs in my bathroom taking a shower, Cleofis you hear me", Shawndra's voice suddenly sounded like Mrs. Sterling's. It was Mrs. Sterling breaking him out a detrimental sleep. "I done told you befo' about them skeezers", she waved her long thick finger in his direction. "She got to go", she pushed her glasses closer to her eyes.

"Damn! Granny quit motherfuckin' tripin", his right hand rubbed the hole under his heart and the other rubbed his chest. Every word that came out of Mrs. Sterling's mouth seemed like a closed fist punching him in the back of his skull.

"What the hell you dreaming about that got you looking like you having a heart attack, boy you too young to be grabbing yo' chest, maybe if you stop doing so much dirt in the street yo' little ass a be able to get some sleep."

Luckily Melissa had put a sheet over the lower part of his body. "Jus give me a minute", he spoke exhausted, as he thought for a second that he might be nude before realizing there was a sheet covering him up.

"Give me some money since you think this a hoe house", Mrs. Sterling turned his pants on the floor up side down and his little wad of cash dropped in her hand. "Awww and you been drinking my liquor too, huh motherfucka?" She peeled off three twenties and dropped the pants no quicker than she turned around. "And clean that shit off my end table", the words traveled with her down stairs.

Cleofis said very little as he sat at the edge of the bed with his head in his crossed arms, resting on his lap. He was still trying to pull himself together mentally and physically.

Cliff and Disco were now both selling weight independently. The two had distanced themselves from Cleofis -- they had become their own men and realized they didn't need him to prosper largely in the drug trade. And being that they never were the grimy type they were never really cut out for the Capone crew that was now departed. By this time neither trusted Cleofis as far as they could throw him.

Berry was free again, but steered clear away from Cleofis for the statement he had forced him to make on Jackpot still bothered him. And the threat he made about bringing Berry down with him all led him to believe Cleofis was a rat, but that was something he wouldn't disclose to many.

Berry was starting to click with Gabe, somebody he thought he'd never click too tight with. But after being around Gabe awhile he could see that he was a real nigga and far sharper in certain avenues, which Cleofis wasn't.

Gabe was now a leading name as one of the city's biggest drug dealers. He could most definitely sell you a slab or two. Twenty two years old he'd grown into an extremely handsome 6 foot tall young man who always kept his facial hair lined, crisp and cut.

100% self made he'd created more envy and jealousy then he ever had for himself. But he still wasn't *'stenjie'*, plenty of dealers ate off his plate to the point where they wasn't hungry.

Kiara still was the leading lady in his life and for her love loyalty and respect he bought her a brand new Buick Century in cash before purchasing himself a jet black Navigator. Gabe never liked that much attention, so rims was a no-no along with sounds, it was already bad enough that he had an expensive truck with no job. Disciplined and smart there were very few people who could purchase coke from him personally, they would have to go through his right hand and in a way that was becoming Berry.

Jackpot was extremely angry when thinking his freedom was around the corner then to be halted by first degree murder charges. Plus Melissa wasn't accepting his calls or responding to messages sent through other people. If only he knew she was sleeping with the person she always told him to stay away from.

Since the shooting Cleofis had toned down that Teflon the untouchable image. He told detectives who shot him, and they picked up Puncho in a heart beat. Puncho was now out on a 25,000 bond. He was basking in high street credibility and was letting it rip through the streets that Cleofis told on him about the shooting. This dude ain't no gangsta, real gangstas retaliate instead of telling who shot em. Though he was enjoyed being praised for the one to tame the beast, he would dodge an area if it was said Cleofis was there. As bad as Cleofis wanted revenge he knew the smart thing to do was to wait like he'd been doing. The reality of him being a rat still could not set in street characters minds. And the villain kept a different side of the story for curious minds.

Floating through the tough North Side Cartel streets in his Navigator, Gabe rarely stopped when block huggers called his name, but on this in particular day it was a voice he'd known since a young teen. "Homeboy!" It was Cleofis standing with a group of thirsty young wolves. So Gabe hit the block and swung back around to see what he wanted. It had been quite some time since the two spoke face to face.

"Want me to hop in wit'chu", said Cleofis as he stepped in front of the crowd and walked up to the driver side window.

"Naw I'll get out", Gabe replied with fearlessness in his tone, he wanted every nigga that was staring to know that he wasn't scared to jump out the truck and correspond just because he was selling bricks.

"I been sending messages fo' you to get at me, what, you don't wanna fuck with me no mo?"

"No, it ain't that", Gabe exclaimed as he glanced under his truck at the antifreeze that was dripping. "I just feel niggaz not following by the rules that was taught when we was younger." He expressed more when they strolled up the block, "Motherfakaz saying you told the detectives Puncho popped you and the way I came up I was taught not to tell who shot-

"That nigga a fuckin' lie", Cleofis roared cutting him off. "They picked him up fo' that shit 'cause a witness seen him shoot me. What the hell I look like telling on that coward ass nigga", the lie was powerful. "Man you need to get cho' facts straight before you question me about some shit like that." The two turned around at the end of the block. "But anyway I got these young cats out here that look up to me, so they all put they chips together and give it to 'em", he passed a wad of cash to Gabe very slick like and continued. "Count that when you get to the crib and bring something back presentable fo' these cats."

"I'll see what I can do", Gabe put the cash in his Burberry jeans pocket, looked over at the starving young wolves that he reflected was plotting on him along with Cleofis and got into his truck.

"Don't be all day", yelled Cleofis before Gabe pulled off in the lustful Lincoln Navigator.

"I thought you said you wasn't fuckin' with dude", Berry was disappointed in the man he felt was on top of his game.

"I ain't fuckin' with dude like that, but the dude just gave me fifty-eight hundred of them little niggaz chips in the Cartels, so as long as he giving me the change first-

"Yeah I feel you, but the nigga done already slipped up and told some hoes that he gone get in good wit'chu until he finds the stash. Then the nigga say he gone burn you. So of course the nigga gone try and gain yo' trust back by trusting you with his and shawty an them money on the block."

"I know, I ain't stupid", Gabe said

"An, another thing, it's a chance the snake nigga might tell on you, remember that Bo Pete shit, that nigga was gone trick on me about that. And they say the nigga done tricked on a few cats but mufuckaz be scared to speak on the shit 'cause they think dude a kill em."

"Dude tells me, witnesses seen Puncho pop him, but I looked at the nigga like yeah right."

Gabe had stopped by Berry's to holler at him about Cleofis' brought business, he knew before hearing criticism from Berry that he should turn the business down but if the snake was going to be bringing him lump sums of cash it was worth the risk. And considering he felt two steps ahead of Cleofis why not build to his empire by collecting about six gees every couple days when the buyer waits for you to return with the goods. When the nigga tries to get close I'll just push him away, Gabe reflected.

"Bay!" shouted the enthusiastic mouth, followed by Bootleg and Bones as he walked in Holly's front door. "Everybody startna see how JW and Jackpot wanted me dead so bad that they killed Shawndra. Jackpot surprised me though, I ain't even know he was in on the shit." The three walked to the basement, "So much for friends" followed behind his body.

"I told you anyway!", Holly shouted loud enough for him to hear as she sat on the couch upstairs puffing on a Newport. "What's done in the dark will come to the light, now all them hypocrites owe you an apology."

The three plopped down on the ran down furniture that was in the basement, put Shyne's debut album in the CD player and let the

Bad Boy Anthem play out the speakers. Cleofis laid a small bag of snow on a small chair then proceeded to open it.

"They say old girl Mandy dumping again", said Bootleg, practically rubbing his hands together ready to toot the powder.

Cleofis had damn near everybody that was around him inhaling the white. "That bitch outta have a badge, how many niggaz she done set up."

The fact of the matter was Mandy hadn't told or set anybody up. In case Cleofis said the lie, so much so that the whole town started to believe it, which was something she hated him for.

Cleofis tongue never stopped with slander on peoples names, and even though he was being proven to be dishonest by some who kept it real, a lot of wannabes still listened to the lies that they would turn to rumors unaware that they were false. So many still wanted to follow him even if it was down a self destructing path.

"Ay 'T' how long you think it a take you to get the nigga", Bone's scratched his scar flooded face waiting on a response.

Cleofis played with the red flaps on his nostril, he couldn't feel his nose and soon couldn't feel his face. "Soon…very soon….man this powder got me not able to feel my face.

"I knowww", said Bootleg. "I wonder where Gabe get this from."

"Now this how the shit used to be in the eighties", replied Bones. "Damn near pure without the cut, shhhoot that youngsta just don't know what he got."

"Ow he know what he got that's why the lame clocking them dollars, soon as I get 'em to trust me, it's ova, I'mma be about five bricks richer."

"You thank the nigga copping that much work", asked Bootleg.

"On everything I love I know a nigga that's buying a brick and getting fronted a brick from the nigga so I estimate five at the least."

Bootlegs hunger mode kicked in. "Why don't we just kidnap the lame and make him tell us where it's at."

"Yeah I thought of that as plan B, if all else fails, but when you kidnap a nigga you gotta catch him at the right time and the right place so a motherfucka can't say they seen you snatch 'em up." Cleofis flinched repeatedly from the high as he spoke fast.

Melissa finally decided to drive to the state prison to see Jackpot. He wrote so many letters swearing his innocence and begging for her visits that he eventually hit on a soft spot she still had for him. The state had not yet transferred Jackpot to the Kankakee county jail because it was still a couple weeks left in his sentence. After the state got their time out of him, they would send him back to Kankakee County to await trail for the murder of Shawndra Coleman and her unborn seed.

The four hour drive was tiresome and to think she would have to drive back was more. But Melissa walked into the visiting room with a smile even after the forty-five minute wait. She died her hair blonde which didn't look right on her and wore a red jogging outfit that Jackpot had purchased for her not long after they met.

When seeing Jackpot stroll from behind a door where they thoroughly search the convict before entering, she narrowed her smile to a straight face vividly showing him she wasn't moved by his presence. The navy blue one piece state wear fit sorta big on the in desperate need for a hair cut, shave, and depressed looking Jackpot.

"How you doing James", Melissa spoke as he took a seat at an assigned table for the both of them. "Sorry I ain't been down to see you lately, I got a new job and it takes up most of my time, so I don't be home when you call and I really don't be having the time to write."

Jackpot could tell immediately that she was back snorting powder by the look on her face she probably tooted some right before she came in, he said to himself while shaking his head in disappointment, with the left corner of his mouth pulled back. "Look Melissa", his elbows set on the cold steel table. "I didn't do this shit", he nodded for her to move in closer, putting her stoned unfoolable covered with make up look to the side. "Cleofis and JW did this shit, I was just their."

"What do you mean", stupidity swam in the pit of her stomach as he reached over and gently grabbed her right hand.

"Dude you fuckin' with is foul", said Jackpot as her face got stuck with a how did you know look.

"That stool pigeon ass nigga the reason I'm in here." As he took a stressful deep breath she asked, "How is he the reason you in here? And how did him and JW kill Shawndra, when I thought the two was at war with each other? You don't gotta lie to me James."

At that moment he gripped her hand a little, for everything he was about to tell her was the truth.

"Remember when I told you that nigga JW called my cell making threats and shit." Melissa shook her head yes as he solidified his courage to tell her. "Well when I met with him I called Teflon so they could squash the bee, at first neither one wanted to holla at each other but I stepped from around JW and explained to 'T' how it would be good to squash the beef and just make cuz work it off or something. But Teflon had other plans in mind." Like what Melissa's facial expression expressed. "At the time Shawndra had stolen five gees that was ours, and she kept telling people she was gone tell on 'T' about that townhouse murder, so 'T' fixed it to where if JW wacked Shawndra his debt from the eighth he took would square them even. And JW wanted to be a killer so bad… they both sat around, planned everything out for a couple days… so once everything was mapped out, Teflon dropped me and JW off a couple of blocks from her apartment. We wanted to get dropped off closer cause it was raining that night. But we didn't argue we just ran till we reached her crib. I knocked on the door 'cause we knew she wouldn't have opened it up for JW."

All the talking from the other inmates getting visits seemed to seize as Melissa pictured every word that was coming out of his mouth inside her mind. "I told her 'T' was stranded and that we needed her to take us to go get him, she came because…..she trusted me. When we got on Brifman Road JW told her to pull over with the gun waved in her face. She called out to me as I was sitting in her back seat but I just froze, it was like somebody had cut out my tongue. She begged for me to save her and I wanted to but I couldn't", Jackpot squeezed her hand tighter and his remorseful watery eyes went on. "JW shot her…Teflon was waiting in a get away right up ahead of us, and he got out walked up and shot her a second time as me and JW headed to the car. I could barely walk my legs was so weak…it was blood everywhere!"

Melissa snatched her hand back it was like she could hear Shawndra's screams when Jackpot was holding it. "Why, why couldn't ya'll do something else, you didn't have to kill her?"

"I know, but I let that rotten ass nigga trick me. Shawndra wouldn't have never told on him she just wanted his attention and that money she took was basically hers 'cause the nigga owed her it from the five thousand dollar loan she took out for him."

"How could he do that to the woman who was carrying his seed, how could he", Melissa asked with deep compassion for the slain woman.

"I don't know", Jackpot rubbed his forehead saying. "All I know is there is not a night that goes by when I don't hear her screams, it's like she hunts me, then I wake up after the loud gun shot."

"Well why isn't the police charging him too?"

"Because the nigga covered his tracks, he was wearing gloves, me and JW wasn't, so not only had my hands touched the gun earlier that day but we both gave him are bloody clothes. 'T' said he was gone burn 'em but he never did. I guess the detectives questioned his snitch ass and he got scared, but he still played it smart he made a statement on JW first that's, why JW was trying to skip town when he had that car accident. Then the snake nigga had somebody or himself place the gun he shot Shawndra with under my moms central air conditioner in the back yard. And he placed my clothes in a bag at a hypes house and told the hype to make a statement saying I put them there. He had Berry make a statement saying he heard me and JW plotting to kill Shawndra to make him feel it 'cause we couldn't get close to him. I'm telling you, its so many niggaz on my four twelve you'd think it was a concert…this snitch even had the nerve to say me and JW was running the Capone crew and he got that low down dirty ass Mark Galante helping him. Only mine and JW finger prints was in the car, they got all they needed to lock me up and throw away the key. This nigga got the whole shit in his favor, scared phony witnesses and the whole city thinking him and JW was still at war. I ain't pull the fuckin' trigger, I swear."

"But you went and got her", Melissa said as she stood up and turned around begging to leave.

"Baby I'm sorry", he grabbed her arm firmly. "I love you and I need you."

"Take your hands of me", she shouted.

"So you just gone leave me like this", Jackpot replied embarrassed by her hostility. "The nigga you fuckin' the one killed her."

By this time correctional officers were rushing to intervene. "Don't you ever call me, don't you ever write me", Melissa screamed as Jackpot said to the officers, "This bitch freaking out."

Don't send me no mo messages, and I hope they give your ass the electric chair along with Cleofis."

An officer grabbed her arm to escort her to the exit at a quicker pace then she was going. Jackpot returned to the strip search room as if the whole scene was nothing to him.

Melissa slapped the dashboard of the car at her stupidity wondering how she fell for Cleofis' lies. Cleofis put her under the impression that the townhouse massacre was nothing more then a group of people who was responsible for it but then tried to put the accusation off on him. And he really had her fooled with the Shawndra Coleman slaying. She'd told herself that she could never be involved with a man who killed a woman but to her naïveté's she was involved with one of the men who murdered Shawndra Coleman and one who helped.

CHAPTER 19

Unbelievable and Unexpected

Cleofis and Bootleg was rotating around on feet when they spotted Natalie's Thunderbird at the hair store. Noticing his sons car seat in the back with a male sitting on the passenger side he wondered who Natalie had sitting in the thunderbird he brought for her with his son in the back seat. Walking up on the car he told Bootleg to wait off to the side. A large man was fettling with the radio when Cleofis barked, "Who the fuck is you and what the fuck you doing in my car with my son."

The dude looked up with astonished eyes that in a split second turned to a mean mug so brutal that it could kill an elephant in its tracks. It was Chopper, Travis' huge 6'3" wide shouldered football playing looking brother, who Cleofis was almost a 100 percent sure wrote that death threat to him in the county and probably was one of the assassins waiting in the grass when he touched down from the Gillmen incarceration. Chopper didn't even have a neck from the looks of him and his dark brown skin along with the rest of his handsome ingredients was all a woman needed to feel proud and protected.

"Chopper nigga, and who is you 'cause this car belongs to the lady that's in the stow."

"Well.....", Cleofis was scrambling for words, never seen Chopper up close, the mean mug with his size, intimidated the frown shown at first into a cautious expression. "Is she in the store?"

"I guess", Chopper replied with a nigga you knew that look. Just then Natalie stepped out carrying some bags filled with hair products. "What do you want?", she shouted ignorant like when seeing Cleofis.

"Nothing I was just stopping to see my son."

"Well you see don't you, 'cause I have to go", she said getting into the car quickly.

"Damn you ain't gotta try and leave so quick." Cleofis felt like a chump as he refused to give eye contact to Chopper who was giving him a vengeful stare.

"You don't never try an see yo' son no other time", she pulled off quicker when observing Bootleg walking up to possibly help Cleofis get on some bullshit. But what she didn't know was that her baby daddy wasn't prepared for the sight of Chopper and the shot gun wounds, drugs, betrayal and tarnished reputation made him question his killer's instinct. It was like a feeling of being dethroned he didn't have the heart to mumble a word of gangsta shit to the big brother of Travis, who was riding smoothly with his son and baby's mother.

"Who was that nigga?", ask Bootleg

"Her brother from Chicago", Cleofis lied not wanting to think of his enemy in between his baby mother's legs. And how could he explain a nigga chilling in a car bought for Natalie by him, and just letting them pull off.

"Fuck that hoe 'Moe', let's hit the Cartels?"

"Watch yo' mouth 'cause I don't speak on yo' baby momma so don't speak on mine." Cleofis spat, turning from the direction Natalie drove off in.

More into their stroll, the two weren't far from Blue Fairy Park so they decided to see who was all out there. Disco and Cliff was playing B ball against Puncho and Big C for a nice healthy pot. Amongst a gun slinging crew that started whispering when seeing Cleofis approach, Puncho made sure they followed him to this ruthless park were so many people had been murdered. Aware of Cleofis' powder habit Puncho felt the villain would become dangerous sooner or later especially with the hush rumors of him being a snitch.

"Make sure that burner ain't on safety", whispered Cleofis who had no burner. Bootleg was like his bottom boy, doing whatever even if it meant wacking a nigga. Cleofis wanted no trouble just like the previous encounter, but now wanted to hang at the park with the odds against him if something did happen.

"Moe we need to motion from over here, I bet you all these chumps got heat."

"So, all them niggaz cowards, them fools ain't gone get on shit unless I do."

"Teflon", called Disco from the basketball court, "Com'eer."

Cleofis signaled for the jubby dealer to come to him instead. Who the fuck this fat fuck think I am he betta come to me?"

"What's up T", Disco spoke, walking up. "Them niggaz over there ain't on shit." He was referring to Puncho's crew on the opposite side of the court. "But Puncho wanna holla at you."

"Well tell 'em to come holla." Cleofis crossed his arms in a defiant sorta way, making himself look more swollen in his wife beater. "Keep an eye on them niggaz", he shrugged his elbow into Bootleg's arm as Disco went to go relay the response. Phony ass nigga used to be real now he fuckin' with them phony ass niggaz who shot me. I shoulda spit in the niggaz face.

"Yo T", Puncho's moose like voice uttered, with a wave of his hand directing Cleofis to walk with him to the parking lot. "I ain't on shit, I just wanna holler at you."

Cleofis said nothing as he stepped off with Puncho to the parking lot. Bootleg was Jumpy and slightly nervous not knowing what was about to happen. As the two rivals put the distance between the two behind them Cleofis started, "What the fuck you want, if its about that court shit you gone have to pay me twenty five grand if you don't wanna do no time", he constantly tried to catch eye contact with Puncho, like Chopper was with him. But Puncho's eyes fluctuated from the trees to Cleofis waist randomly.

Taking all the courage inside of him Puncho said, "I thought you was playin' it the street way."

Cleofis' guts twisted with a year of anxiety and a rush of recklessness swept over his frame. "Motherfucka! If I don't get paid you can kiss these streets goodbye." Seeming to grab a hold of his wanting to kill him feeling, he further explained. "I'm playin' chess, that's why I made the statement. You up, I'm down and right now -- you in check, and if I don't get what I want you'll be in mate." He turned his back on Puncho with such disrespectful body language. This was because he knew Puncho still feared him by the scariness of his voice and the tremble of his small fat frame.

Years ago it would have been a murder with rivals stationed on the Blue Fairy grounds, but common sense was wise, everybody knew it wasn't the time and no longer the place for such dumb moves with police patrolling the area non stop.

Cleofis called Natalie's cell and house phone for day's harassing her about the individual she had in her car. "How you gone have some nigga in the car I bought for you and my son. And the nigga my enemy at that, you gone make me wack you and his ass. I'm telling you that motherfucka a hurt my son to get back at me, there's a lot of shit you just don't know."

But Natalie always hung up in his face, though she wanted him, she loved the fact that he was jealous and that it was eating him up to know she was moving on. Knowing the situation could get dangerous at any time she actually liked the attention and knew that Chopper wasn't afraid of Cleofis or his threats. Secretly Chopper was master minding a plan to murder Cleofis while daily laying pipe to Natalie who was blind to the life long enemy of her baby's daddy. It had been six long years since Travis' murder and it still affected Chopper like it was yesterday. To murder Cleofis, washed over his body like a title wave, but the knowledge of incarceration kept his mind at work on a smart way to get him and to get away with it.

Gabe, Cleofis, Holly and Kiara were all off to the Harris Casino Boat in Joliet. Cleofis' business with the Cartel youngster was now bringing ten gees every couple of days to Gabe. And the two childhood friends was conversing daily, Gabe having the phat pockets decided to invite Cleofis and Holly up to the casino to have some fun. With the Navigator driven by Kiara, Cleofis sat in the back seat with Holly, envy fluttered his mind, jealousy circled in his eyes. Lusting over Kaira was in his heart, and crossing Gabe was on his soul. Ever since they'd broken ties with each other, Cleofis wanted to see Gabe fall more then ever, and he psyched himself out to believe Gabe was against him. When it really was his paranoid conscious which led him to betray Gabe and many of his friends with subconsciously thinking they were betraying him.

"So Kiara", Cleofis replied from the back seat. "When you and this nigga getting married?"

Kiara giggled as she wipped the SUV around some vehicles to jump off on an exit. "I don't know you would have to ask him, he the one feel it's too soon."

"Boy it's been about 4 years now you better marry this girl."

"Maybe one day but fo' nah I'll chill."

"Bay, why you getting in they business", said Holly.

"Its cool", said Gabe, "that's why his nose is big 'cause he so nosy."

"Aight chump we ain't gone talk about you", Cleofis tapped the back of Gabe's shoulder. "Kiara, I hope you getting this nigga fo' every penny, 'cause trust me he got it...I never thought I'll see the little nigga on top of his game so tight."

Gabe took in the compliments as new angles to get him to drop his guards.

"All I need is him, forget the money, car, clothes and shit. I love him for better or worse."

"Well ain't that sweet", spoke Holly.

Cleofis bit his bottom lip and snarled from jealousy, Gabe having a fine stick by your side woman just teed him completely off in silence.

"Dang it's packed, we might not be able to find a parking spot", Kiara circled the three story parking lot looking for a spot.

"Right there baby", said Gabe. "Right where them old people pulling out."

All four were dressed to impress, Holly kinda felt odd 'cause of her age but she barely let it bother her, sometimes she felt like a counselor to Cleofis and his friends.

The two hustlers started off at the crap table where they lost a little bread, then wound up going to the high rollers room and started to gain. With Kiara hovering over his shoulder, Gabe split two aces on the black jack table and doubled down on both. "Good job baby you won", clapped Kiara when watching the dealer turn over two tens on top of his aces. She made her man feel good while Holly was asking hers for money every time he won some. Black jack paid off well, winning Gabe 4,800 and Cleofis 2,300 before they both decided to quit, rent some hotel rooms next to each other where Cleofis fucked his women and Gabe made love to his. While screwing Holly, Cleofis fantasized about Kiara, if only I could fuck that fine bitch he visualized Kiara's face along with her slight moans traveling through the walls, it turned him on so bad that sleep wasn't an option for Holly.

That night, early in the morning the two met up in the hallway to discuss business as the women slept like infants.

"On the real gee, I bet'chu this dude I know in St. Louis a get you a betta price on them slabs you getting."

This nigga just trying to count my pockets…I know damn well he can't get me a better deal then what I'm getting…how the fuck he gone no I'm copping slabs anyway. "I'm cool, I'm cool. The connect I'm fuckin' with lookin out fo' me, so why jump on another boat", replied Gabe.

"All I'm sayin", Cleofis study tried to convince Gabe. "Is why pay what'chu payin' when you can pay less."

I never told you how much I'm paying. "If I need yo' connect I'll let you know. So I see them little niggaz dumping good on the Cartels."

"Ow yeahhhh, but they really wanna get they hands off in the diesel and dude in St. Louis got that too. If you gone keep them little niggaz bizness you gotta supply them with everything they want." Cleofis searched Gabe's face for signs of possibility.

"I'm straight with what I'm doing now", Gabe was becoming tired of hearing about dude in St. Louis and Cleofis could see it so he stopped pushing the issue for now.

When they got back to Kankakee they dropped the ladies off and bent some blocks. Riding past the scene where Cleofis got shot at, he focused in on Shanice who was pulling off in Puncho's Deville. "I wonder is she fuckin' with dude?"

"Who?"

"Puncho, I wonder if that bitch Shanice fuckin' with him?"

"Aw yeah, I coulda been told you that and from what I hear the bitch got a whole new wardrobe, thanks to that nigga."

"I ain't even think that bitch a fuck with a nigga from here, let alone the coward who shot me."

"Well you know how shit is when a nigga it. The bitch flirted with me a couple times but that's as far as it went 'cause I wouldn't never creep on Kiara."

"Get the fuck outta here", Cleofis laughed. "I know Kiara fine an' all, but Shanice a bad mufaka and I know if she offered you a sample you'd take it."

"I ain't you bruh', I got control plus it's all one nut anyway, so I might is well stay with my chick."

"I can dig it. I keep forgetting you got an old soul like me. But check this though, I fucked the shit out of Disco's baby momma last week, got head and everything. Hoe talking about she been wanting a nigga since grade school."

"You gone get that bitch severely beat", Gabe cruised through Wendy's drive through and placed an order.

"He know how that hoe is, so I don't see why he won't leave her", chuckled Cleofis. "You know a mufucka gonna try and say I'm tooting powder", Cleofis shockingly switched to another subject that Gabe had heard, but never brought up. "What they gonna be sayin about me next", putting it in the air Cleofis figured Gabe heard so it was necessary for him to comment on the true accusation by swearing they were false. "Let me find out who the fuck said that shit and I'mma put that nigga to sleep", he barked "What the fuck I look like turning into a hype."

The more Cleofis went on about the rumors and denied them the more Gabe was beginning to believe they must be true. Cleofis' mistake, whether in his right state of mind, or not was always taking silence for illiterate, lame, or weakness. So Gabe not saying anything, always made Cleofis thinks he was soaking up all of the lies as truth. But Gabe clearly knew how to separate the little percentage of truth from the majority of lies.

Natalie's house phone rang as Chopper walked out of her apartment door. "Hey little bro", she peeped the caller ID. "Act like you can't call me since you ballin' now."

"You know I be busy, I just dropped yo' baby daddy off."

"I thought you didn't mess with him like that."

"I don't, it was just business, but I believe the nigga fuckin' with that shit."

"You just now hearing that", she spoke like she'd known since it first began. "People been saying that, and alot of other shit about him wanting to rob and kill you."

"Yeah I know about that, that's why I'm keeping him close."

"I even know this girl that said that James Love guy girlfriend said Cleofis put the second hole in Shawndra Coleman, and that JW person put the first."

"Don't surprise me one bit."

"She also said Cleofis turned states on Jackpot that's why they charging him."

"That don't surprise me either."

"What I want to know", Natalie laughed hilariously into the phone. "Is he a homo or not. I been itching to ask my friend George have he heard anything but I'd be embarrassed."

"I don't know about that one, I can't picture CJ going that route."

"But I'mma ask George when I go get my hair done today if he ever heard anything."

"Let me know what he say?"

"You know I will. Why don't you and Kiara come over later on so you can see your niece and nephew?"

"Aight."

"Make sure you be here and be careful 'cause Cleofis gonna try and pull it sooner or later."

"I know, I know. One!"

George had just finished up with Natalie's hair, he spun her around in the chair and handed her a mirror. Damn I'm fine, but the hair due make a bitch look flawless. She was feeling herself, especially since the new man in her life seemed to put on an excellent performance in bed. And gave her all the attention she wanted. "I left my money in the car", she did on purpose. "Follow me and I'll give it to you." Not wanting to ask him in front of everybody in the shop, when she handed him the money embarrassment made her smile first. "Have you ever heard anything about Cleofis…", she blurted with a stuck smile to prepare herself for the worst. George was just about to turn and go back in shop.

"Like what unparticular." Usually to ask him something wouldn't ever be this hard, but this was about the man she loved and she just had to know.

"Well you know, doing the type of stuff you do."

George gave her a strange look before it dawned on him. "Trust me girl you don't wanna know."

"Yes I do", her face fluctuated to a serious look. "Please just tell me the truth do you know of one of your male friends that's done been with him."

"Natalie", George said with an un-proud but arrogant look, "I've been with him."

"Stop playin", Natalie started laughing to cover the knife in the heart she'd just felt. "George I know you gotta be lying, when this happen?"

"I'm not going to tell you girl cuz you gonna get mad."

"Believe me, I won't get mad it ain't like I want his nasty ass."

"It was a day you was at the grocery store with Mandy, I stopped by your crib for you and he opened the door. He told me you was gone and asked me did I have the equipment to cut his hair in my car. I went to the car, came back in and cut his hair. I was about to leave when he said hold on a minute. He went to the bathroom took a quick shower and came out with the towel wrapped around his waist…..

"Why you stop?", said Natalie hurtfully eager to hear more. "Finish telling me."

George's hand touched his cheek. "I feel so bad 'cause I know he was your man at the time and I couldn't resist that nice body of his."

"I won't get mad I promise just finish telling me."

"He asked me to put some lotion on his back so I did, then he asked me to suck his dick so I did."

"Stop playing", Natalie said again but with less laughter.

"I think that was all he wanted till he seen how talented I was, then he wanted some booty and I put it on 'em like he was my man." Natalie's face was stuck in shock as she pictured the unbelievable scene. "And girl I see what they say 'cause he ain't packing shit, only time I could feel it real good was when he spread my-

"George! I don't need to hear anymore details, I get the point", she spoke through clenched teeth trying very hard to cover up her anger.

"I'm sorry girl, but I just couldn't help myself."

"Mmm-Hmm, where you'll get busy at?"

"On the couch in the living room by the big screen."

Natalie let George get back in the shop and flew home where she cried in private. The fact that Cleofis messed with a man, bothered her womanhood. Wasn't she pleasing him a lot when they was together. Didn't she suck him how he wanted to be sucked, didn't she fuck him how he wanted to be fucked, didn't she cook for him, clean for him and sometimes dream for him?

I shoulda known from how he used to like to fuck me in my ass all the time, and my stupid ass used to let him. Right under my damn roof he was fucking a man, George at that. Was I too much for him…God how could this be, how could the man that I still loved so much be a bisexual, how? How could he do this to me and my son?

Gabe had just kicked his feet up in his lazy boy, and Kiara was changing into her night clothes. They had just returned from Natalie's place where they were suffocated with the news she found out about Cleofis.

Natalie never stopped gossiping about the uncovering of her baby daddy's sexuality, and the two stuck around till they couldn't take anymore.

Now at home Gabe had some uncovering news of his own, as Kiara walked from the bedroom in her blue berry Victoria Secrets see through lingerie, she was a little confused about the large gorgeous diamond ring sitting on the love seat with a card. But she immediately fixed the look into a tearful smile when seeing the joyful grin on Gabe's face.

"I know you didn't", she picked up the five carat ring along with the card that read. I loved you when I first met you. I love you now and I want to love you forever, will you merry me? Gabe spun up out the chair to meet her warm hugs and love full kisses.

"Yes baby oooooh I love you so much", her Chinese eyes was no match for the tears that ran out of them. All she wanted to do was make love to her fiancé.

Raising-up his shirt, she started kissing his navel, and worked her way up to his chest as she slowly removed his shirt.

"Birrrrrang Birrrrrang…Birrrrrang Birrrrrang!"

Gabe didn't want to answer his cell phone, but Kiara insisted as she kissed his chest.

"Yyyeah."

"A nigga in room fifteen looking for something sweet for his stay", it was Cleofis, meaning him and the little Cartel hustlers had 15k and to come get it. And bring back something sweet upon return.

"I'm a little tied up right nah, let me hit you back."

"Take yo' face out that pussy for a minute." Kiara darted her back as if she tasted something nasty. "We need you nah, the block is dumping."

"Tell that fool to call back with his disrespectful ass", said Kiara.

"Man 'C' I'm a little busy."

"M-O-B nigga plus you know how these little niggaz pockets be burning."

"Go on out Gabe", said Kiara not wanting to hold him back from his business, "But hurry back."

"I'll be through there in a minute", Gabe said to Cleofis.

Chopper was getting ready to call it a night and go to Natalie's house, when he seen Cleofis jumping into the passenger side of a black Navigator truck. Bitch ass motherfucka killed my brother. He couldn't take it anymore six years was to long.

Zooming over to his mother's house he retrieved her 357 out the hallway closet, his mother was in a deep sleep as he jumped back into his grey Mercury and searched the city for the Navigator. With intoxication mixed with marijuana, he believed he held in his hand the problem solver that would rid him and his mother of the revenge they carried in their hearts.

Gabe clutched his hammer in the pocket of his jacket, and stirred the truck wheel with the other. It was pretty late to be doing a fifteen thousand dollar hand off but this was Gabe, when others was scared to make moves late at night he would seize the opportunity for huge profit.

"There you go", Cleofis sat a brown paper bag on the arm rest just after getting into the high seated SUV. With a grim look on his face that the dark couldn't even hide. "That's fifteen stacks, and you can take yo' hand off yo' pistol nigga, I ain't gone rob you."

"Hmph", Gabe smirked, "I ain't worried."

Cleofis adjusted his seat back and slouched down in it as if he was trying to hide from somebody. Gabe, barely able to see Cleofis' face now used his ears and instinct for the possibility of a struggle, 'cause he'd made up in his mind that Cleofis might pull his mag out but it would be swiftly knocked out his hand or fought over. Why the fuck did I come out to see this grimy nigga late at night like this…It was no turning back now, whatever was going to happen was going to happen.

"Look nigga why don't you give us a slab fo' that fifteen, and let me get the rest to you as soon as I make it."

"I already told you befo'", Gabe tried his best to stay on a main street. "A motherfucka can't owe me shit."

"All that fuckin' bread we been bringing you", viciously rolled off his tongue. "The way we been dumping you should be frontin us a brick."

"Is you slow or just can't hear straight?"

"You know what you gotta jazzy fuckin' mouth, a real jazzy fuckin' mouth", hissed Cleofis. Bullshit was most definitely in the air, and tension was boiling in the seconds of silence. Both strapped up, it was too dark outside for lip boxing somebody could get killed.

"I'll drop you off and bring you something back sweet for the fifteen, or you can take yo' chips else where."

"Why you always gotts bullshit", Cleofis said aggressively. "I'm tryin' to expand and yo' bitch ass won't give me a hand."

Gabe could see that Cleofis wasn't going to exit his truck until he struck a deal or used his gun to kill. "Be cool", Gabe spoke calmly to the hostile acting villain. "I'll bring you back a brick, but I won't the rest of my chips in two days."

Because of the aggression level in the air Gabe knew where it was headed, so he smartly ended the disagreement by telling Cleofis what he wanted to hear. With intentions on giving him his fifteen grand in the morning with some made up excuse Gabe was about to end their business together. He could clearly see that Cleofis' hunger would never be able to be quenched, and to avoid a dangerous situation from occurring, disguising his true plan was necessary

Gabe wasn't scared one bit and never really let Cleofis intimidate him, but it was time to cut him loose. Very disciplined Gabe knew when it was time to pull out.

"Be right back", said Gabe, dropping Cleofis off around the Cartels. Making a right turn on Birch Street he glanced at the brown paper bag full of money. As much as he wanted the lump sum of cash he knew the best thing to do was take it back in the morning with an excuse he hadn't made up yet. 'Cause it was no way he was about to let him owe anything. Halfway to his crib Kiara called his cell phone.

"Where you at?"

"I'm almost home."

"You don't gotta go back out do you, 'cause I know how it is when you dealing with dude."

"Naw I'm straight, I'm cutting his ass off anyway, shit getting to risky and ain't no telling with that faggot ass nigga has up his sleeve."

"I tried to tell you he was a homo, but I guess it took yo' sista to tell you for you to believe it."

"I wouldn't have believed her if George wouldn't have told her to her face. I don't wanna even think about the shit, especially how close me and the niggas used to be. Its still hard for me to picture him being a faggot."

"Yeah I know and I'm glad you decided to leave his rotten ass alone 'cause he ain't nothing but trouble." Kiara could see the headlights of the Navigator as she looked out their bedroom window that gave you a nice long view of the up coming traffic on the street. Her knees deepened into their full sized bed that she gazed out the window on top of. Excited like a kid in Walt Disney World, she couldn't wait for her new announced fiancé to return into the apartment.

She called a couple friends and family to let them know the great news. Bliss covered her beautiful face as she sprinted to the window in the front room that gave a view of the property parking lot Gabe was pulling into. Kiara was on cloud nine, haven't felt so much joy since the couple first met. She watched anxiously as Gabe parked the SUV and turned off the lights. Just then a grey Mercury pulled into the parking lot very slowly. Kiara could tell Gabe had to be counting some money or looking for something because his head was down and dangling. The Mercury pulled slowly into the empty parking space on the passenger side of the black SUV and the next thing that was heard was loud silence breaking gunfire that could wake up a hibernating bear. All six shots mentally hit Kiara's body as four of them in reality tore through Gabe's body leaving him slumped over on the trucks horn which serenaded the neighborhood.

The gray Mercury then reversed, backed out and peeled out the parking lot into very little traffic. Kiara was devastated she had no strength in her legs that released her body on to the floor after trying to walk to the entrance door. She tried to scream but the horrifying sight took her voice away and she quivered as a drop of her never seeing Gabe alive again swept down her spine.

God…no…please not Gabriel…please don't let him be dead, Lord…I need him.

Please I need him…please let him be alive God… he's my husband and I need him.

CHAPTER 20

Wrong One

Natalie was returning from Gabe's funeral in her Thunderbird driven by Mandy. Dasia and Cleofis Junior were in the back seat quiet as church mice. Mandy wanted to say something to her friend but she just didn't know what to say. Natalie was crying internally she just couldn't figure out why Chopper would kill Gabe then his own life. It made no since to her but it made a lot of since to Cleofis.

Cleofis had thought he'd seen that gray Mercury pass by when jumping into the truck with Gabe. And it didn't take a genius to figure out what happen after that. Chopper, thinking Cleofis was still in the Navigator pulled up on the passenger side and just started shooting without properly identifying who was in the SUV. Then when he found out the next day that it was Gabriel Smith he killed, and that there was nobody else in the truck. He went to visit his brothaz grave sight for the last time and put the same 357 used to kill Gabe to his temple, said his prayers and blew a third of his skull off onto the cemetery grass.

Cleofis showed up to the funeral with his brother Lonzale, they both had their tee shirts air brush with Gabe's face along with other friends family and associates of the deceased. Kiara screamed more than Gabe's mother. Berry shed a tear and mean-mugged Cleofis the whole time as if he was responsible. Pastor Evens said a few scriptures from the Bible. And Natalie cried over her brothers' casket making Dasia and Cleofis Jr. feel her emotions, so much that they cried too.

A lot of ballers were happy to see Gabe go, for Gabe was slangin' so much weight it was starting to drive some of their loyalist to the table where everybody ate good except the untrustworthy.

Authorities seized the fifteen grand and the truck. So Cleofis and the Cartel youngsters were now bottom of the barrel broke. And Cleofis constantly called and harassed Kiara about if Gabe had anything that could be compensated for the loss of fifteen grand. Kiara would repeatedly go off, swearing Gabe never kept anything in her possession, but the truth was he most certainly did. She knew where all Gabe's money and drugs were. Stuffing both into two suit cases, she hopped into her Century and left for New York to live permanently and to see about modeling, Gabe always advised her to get into.

"I think Chopper thought yo' brotha was Teflon", squirmed out of Mandy lips. Knowing Natalie wasn't in a good mood Mandy took a deep breath and prepared herself for her response.

"Why would you say that", Natalie asked in a very saddened tone.

"'Cause Chopper is Travis' big brother", Mandy went on when she looked as if she didn't know who Travis was. "Remember them three dudes that got murdered in that townhouse back in 96 that they say yo' baby daddy killed."

"Yeah."

"One of 'em was Travis, and Travis is Chopper's little brother. They say Chopper and his mother never let that go."

"Why are you just now telling me this?"

"'Cause I thought you knew girl, I thought you was just trying to make Teflon mad, by sleeping with his enemy."

"I knew that Cleofis was implicated in them townhouse murders from when I worked at the county, but I didn't know Chopper was one the victims brothaz, else I wouldn't have ever dealt with the man. Cleofis was tryin' to tell me not to mess with dude, but I thought he was just jealous."

"Naw, he was telling you that for a reason, but forget his faggot ass anyway. He the reason why I can't cop from down here, 'cause he told everybody I was the police."

Dasia rolled her eyes and turned her nose up in the back seat. She liked Cleofis and wanted her mother to get back with him, and Mandy's big mouth was not helping one bit. She didn't care that they said he was a murderer, in a weird way it made feel proud that the man that used to call her his daughter was like the bad guys on the TV screen.

"You need to stop selling that shit anyway, 'cause you the last person I want to see locked up."

"That might be too late, my lawyer say the states offer is six years. So I might as well dump till it's time to go, at least I would be able to stack me some change."

"Well you know how the state is. You can get a better deal than six years, trust me. When I was working at the county I done seen the state come from 30 to 6 in some cases."

Natalie had quit her job at the Kankakee County Jail about a month ago. She missed the juicy gossip from her trusted circle of co-workers, and the attention from hundreds of inmate men. But working that tiresome second job just wasn't worth it. Now that she only worked at her first fantastic paying job, she has time to sleep and more time with her two children.

Mandy was glad that her friend was conversating – it was helping to break the silent sadness that was in the air.

"I hope so 'cause I don't wanna be away from my kids for six years you'd probably be coming to my funeral 'cause I don't think I could live six years with out them"

"I bet'chu I could", said Natalie with surprising humility. "Them kids of yours so bad they oughta be called children of the damned."

Dasia laughed quick, high pitched and sorta obnoxious agreeing fully with her mother.

"What you laughing about Dasia?", said Mandy.

"Yeah what'chu laughing about", replied her mother. Dasia said nothing as her cheeks drew red and her body flooded with embarrassment, she just stared at her pink Nike shoes.

"I done told you about listening in on grown folks conversation haven't I?"

"Yes mom."

"Ok then, well I don't wanna have to tell you again." Natalie shifted her conversation back to Mandy. "Anyway girl aunt De-De probably gone be gone soon, the nursing home say that cancer is taking its told on her."

"That's the one you used to keep huh?"

"Yeah, my favorite auntie and I was her favorite niece"

Bootleg was entering Mrs. Sterling house with out anybody inviting him in. "You must be tryin' to get ya self shot motherfucka, don't ever walk in this house unannounced", Mrs. Sterling momentarily went off. "CJ you better tell yo' little friend, broke down brick layer or whatever hell his name is, don't be just walking up in here 'cause I, I'll kill 'em."

"Sorry about that Mrs. Sterling", Bootleg spoke respectfully, standing on the doormat. Cleofis glanced up at Bootleg from the sofa giving him an, is you out your mind look.

"Granny you shoulda just shot his ass 'cause that nigga know better", smiled Cleofis as Bootleg pulled up a chair from the dinning room.

"I see you representing your boy to the fullest", Bootleg was referring to the air brush shirt if Gabe.

"The nigga was my little homey back in the day, it's sad that I ain't have a chance to wack 'em myself, and snatch up them bricks he was holding."

"I told you, we shoulda got that lame a long time ago, but you chose to wait. Nah look at you, fifteen thousand lost, back to being broke again." Bootleg spoke humbly agitated with a dash of aggression. "And with that bitch Kiara, what did I say… let's snatch her up and make that bitch tell us where its at, but noooooooo, you said you got this and now the bitch done skipped town with the bricks and the chips. You losing yo' touch moe, for real you losing yo' touch." He pointed his finger in a scolding manner.

"Shut-the-fuck-up, what's done is done", Cleofis glided off the couch, got the house phone and plopped back down on the couch. He was trying to debate on calling Natalie or not, when the phone rang. "Who dis?"

"Is CJ there?"

"Yeah this me who is this?"

"This Kim, your first love."

"Girl please I was young and dumb then. And how the hell you get my Grandma number."

"It hasn't changed since we was teenagers, and I saw it in my old phone book so I decided to call."

"So what the fuck you want?"

"Nuttin' much, but you know that bitch Melissa out here running her mouth about that Shawndra Coleman shit, she saying that you popped ole girl the second time and that you ratting on Jackpot."

"You believe that shit?"

"That's not important I was just letting you know about that foul bitch you fuckin' wit."

"I don't fuck with her no mo', so whatever that hoe say don't bother me one bit."

"Mmm-Hmm.....somebody was saying you was fucking around with that faggot George."

Cleofis picked the phone up and threw it through the dinning room, where it landed in the kitchen snatching the cord out the wall when it reached its limit.

"I'm tired of this shit", he shouted, standing quickly. "That's all the fuck everybody do is gossip."

"Boy what the fuck wrong with you?", yelled Mrs. Sterling "You going crazy or something?"

"Yeah granny they making me go crazy", he paced the old fashion rug with his temper rising. "Every time I turn around granny they either saying I did something or somebody did something to me."

"Well just leave -- go where they can't talk about you no mo'."

The recklessness moved with him like a shadow. He missed Natalie. He missed Shawndra Coleman who he kept a picture of on the dresser at his bedroom of Mrs. Sterling's. In his mind he didn't believe he killed Shawndra, so why was everybody accusing him. He also psyched himself out to believe he wasn't bisexual, that he wasn't a powder head and that him and Shawndra would have been married if she was still alive.

Deep down inside he missed Gabe, a friend that never followed his lead. A feeling of hopelessness, not able to trust, and never knowing if the state or the Feds would pick him up for something from the past, all was leaning on his conscious. He'd done so much dirt that his paranoia was starting to turn him into a borderline psycho.

CHAPTER 21

Seems Like A Change

Ben's Tavern wasn't crowded at all but it was a nice wager going on the pool table. All the young folks stopped trying to sneak into the tavern since Ben's lounge was open on the other side of town, they mostly all went there to hang out now. But on this quickly fallen evening, Disco and Cliff was shooting pool for a hundred a game at the tavern against some out-of-towners watched by a handful of old folks.

Cleofis got word of it through an old heroine addict he used to sex, so he and Bootleg went and got dressed for the occasion. All black from head to toe with their eyes covered by dark colored baseball caps, the two wossed into Ben's with guns drawn demanding the four gamblers to pay handsomely.

"Damn 'Moe' we suppose to be brothaz", started the calmly spoke Disco. Cleofis spat in his eyes making him blink then greeted his fat pudgy face with the butt of the gun.

"If we was brothaz I wouldn't have to take this cheddar", he reached into Disco's tight husky Encye pants pulling out a roll of twenties. "I could just ask fo' it, but you niggaz see me in the hood everyday and turn your head like I ain't the one who put you cowards on."

"C, mon nah Cleofis", shouted old Ben. "Don't bring that street shit in my place of bizness."

"Shut the fuck up", Bootleg waived his barrel in Ben's direction. "You betta be glad it's just these niggaz that's getting stuck."

"Chill out", Cleofis replied to Bootleg. "Ben's a cool old man, don't disrespect him."

"I tried to help you out", cried Cliff terrified after seeing the butt hit Disco in the face. "But you was always tripin 'Moe', you know I don't get down like that, on Black Stone all you had to do was ask." Cliff held his hands visible hoping his old friend would give him a break.

"Fuck that", Cleofis fired a loud shot into the ceiling discouraging any thoughts of anybody trying to call the police or trying to make a fast retreat. "I gave you cowards life", he punched Cliff in his hooked like nose. Not as sturdy as Disco, Cliff tumbled to the ground. "And in return you bitch made niggaz continuously fucked with the nigga that shot me."

Disco could see that his old friend was becoming a little emotional on top of the anger that came in with him, and this made him fear for his life.

"Ya'll marks come off that dust too", barked Bootleg at the two out-of-towners. "Wrong place at the wrong time", he said, collecting their cash.

"Cleofis", yelled anger rising Ben. "You got what you came for nah get the fuck outta hear."

"A'ight", Cleofis spoke respectfully. "But the next time I have to come take money from these two bitches I'mma take they life too."

Ben shook his head as if he understood, pointing in the direction of the exit.

The police was called after the two left but none of the four men wanted to press charges so it was pointless.

Cleofis and Bootleg made off with thirty three hundred and twenty three dollars all together. And Holly was slightly happy when he came in her house with rent money that she was three days late on. She was getting ready to put him out until he produced what she needed.

Cleofis would rob every month if he had to make sure Holly's household was straight, or he would credit coke out until the first of the month and demanded double sometimes triple for his wait. Holly heard about his powder habit and she knew that's what him and his friends had to be doing in her basement, which was why their noses was always red along with their eyes. But as long as he took care of home she would act blind to his activities.

"Look what I got fo' my son bay!" Cleofis stood in front of Holly with a little kid's seven hundred dollar chinchilla coat. "My little side kick gonna love daddy when he see this coat."

Holly leaned forward in her kitchen chair. "Look nice", she rubbed her hand through the little mink, leaned back into her chair and blew out a ring of smoke from her Newport. Clearly making the coat absorb the smoke, and clearly looking uninterested in the face. "Pretty soon you gone be ova there tryin' to take care of that bitch, and you know she wants you, that's why she always riding that raggedy Thunderbird past my house."

"Ain't nobody thinking about her I'm just tryin' to do mo for my son."

"Well I wouldn't want to take out of no kid's mouth, so you should just pack your shit and go stay with her." Holly gave him a mean look, mixed with why you didn't buy my kids a chin-chilla.

"See that's the reason why we can't get no where 'cause you always think I want her...damn! Can a man just buy his son something nice? And I'm tired of you telling me I can pack my shit, whenever you get in one of your moods. I only stay here 'cause you want me too, actually I like staying at my grandmas, but if I want to stay here permanently I be damned if I gotta pack my shit when I been the only adult in this bitch paying bills."

"It ain't like they won't get paid without you", she nodded her head to the right sharply and flicked the ashes of her New Port into a pop can. Spreading her thick legs open that caused her already low cut shorts to pull back where if you was looking in between her legs you could actually see her panty-less ungroomed bush, she pointed directly at it like it was where a pitcher threw a strike. "Cause this right here will see to it that all bills be paid in advance if I wanted it to."

"You a hoe just like the rest of em", Cleofis stuffed the Chin Chilla back into the bag. "And I wish you woulda been talking that shit befow I went and stuck them niggaz up fo' yo' ass."

Holly knew he wouldn't get violent with her while her daughters were in the house, so she showed her ass a little more. "What you stick 'em up fo' a measly thirty three hundred, nigga you washed up and everybody knows it. You walk around here like you some threat. Well niggaz don't see you as a threat no mo, niggaz see you as a clown." Cleofis just stood and looked at her for a minute, then went into her room to grab his hammer. "Where ya going", asked Holly in a ranking tone as he tucked his hammer into his waist and proceeded for the door. "I'm not through talking to ya ass!"

"Fuck you, you cock eyed bitch, you lucky I don't kill you." Cleofis stormed out the house. "Hoe you must got me confused with one of yo' kids or something."

"Naw but you got a little dick like one", Holly tried shouting out before he slammed her front door.

Headed to Natalie's House on foot he made all the short cuts as possible to lessen his chances of having an encounter with the police. At the same time he reminisced about Natalie.

If only she would be how I want her to be…me and her could possibly make a family…but she runs her mouth too much, too nosy, not trustworthy in all the areas I need her to be the most trust worthy…I know I used to creep a lot on her but I'm a man and men do things like that…I wonder if she found out about me and George, what the fuck is wrong with me why can't I control my dick.

Natalie was at home trying to potty train little Cleofis. "I'm not playin' with chow ass", she yelled at his little joking face. "If you don't pee in that pot you ain't getting no ice cream."

Natalie poured herself a glass of Kool-Aid, turned on Ashanti's 'Foolish' song on her stereo and returned to the kitchen where her son was sitting on his pot.

It's gonna be hard raising a boy without his farther, he's far different then Dasia was at his age…and damn he looks just like his daddy…it's a shame how that sorry big nose bisexual still here in the form of his son. It look like horn nose carried him himself and I just pushed him out……man I sure miss how that nigga used to suck on this pussy and though his dick was little he still knew how to work it… Hmmmmmmm Natalie blew through her nose, standing in the kitchen door way. Am I wrong for missing him after all the shit he put me through? Lord knows I would take him back if he would just do right but that a probably never happen 'cause the thought of him fucking a man on my couch just discusses me…how could he do that, how could he become a drug addict, how could he be so stupid as to think Holly doesn't want him for nothing more then a cash machine……what happened to the young ambitious man that I met with charm and intellect.

Cleofis could hear the Biggie Smalls beat laced with Ashanti's beautiful voice as he stepped to the door. "See every time I get the strength to leave you, you always tell me that you need me, and I'm weak 'cause I believe you, and I'm mad because I love you. So I stop and think that maybe, you would learn to appreciate me, but it all remains the same you ain't never gonna change."

Cleofis knocked on her door before the music switched to another cut.

"Who is it?", Natalie asked assertively.

"Teflon", said Cleofis with shamefulness in his voice.

"Can I help you with something", she said with a pissed off look, soon as she opened her door.

"I got a coat for my little man."

"Hmph", Natalie sucked her teeth. Dead beat ass nigga only brought him a coat. "Come in, you can give it to him yo'self he's in the kitchen on the pot."

She couldn't help but smell his Burberry cologne that she breathed in deeply as he passed and went into the kitchen.

"Hey look what daddy got fo' ya", he took the expensive coat out of the bag with the seven hundred dollar tag still on it.

Little Cleofis stood off his pot where he'd just surprisingly peed in with a done something wrong look on his face.

"What's wrong?", asked his father as he moved in closer to observe. "You pee pee in your pot, use a big boy!" He started clapping cheerfully for his son and Natalie joined in with him feeling very proud that her son was sharing this learning experience with both his parents.

Thirty minutes flew pass and Cleofis now played on the beige carpet living room floor with his little mini me. He could already see that his son was demanding, independent and a leader like himself. "So what's on your agenda today?", asked the playing with his son farther.

"Why", Natalie replied with an offensive look.

"I wasn't trying to be in your business, I just want to know if ya'll wasn't going no where could I take him to the park."

"I don't think that would be a good idea."

"Ok then, it's cool", he said as he playfully fought with his son enjoying every moment. "I'll just stop by and give you some money for him from time to time", he then pulled out five twenties and handed them to her. She immovably accepted the cash.

Was he changing?, she thought. *Or was this a way for him to try to get back in good with her.* We'll see, he acting like he about to start doing his part or something...maybe he just want some ass... maybe he don't love me no more and just want to be apart of his sons life...that's unlikely he's up to something.

The shocking visit had Natalie secretly excited for some reason, maybe he was growing up.

By the end of the year Cleofis was turning out to be a supportive father, giving Natalie cash every couple of weeks and in return she let him spend all the time he wanted with Cleofis Jackson Jr. They were conversing twice a week and hints were dropped about starting another relationship. But both had too much pride to just come out and tell the other what they wanted.

During this platonic period of time Natalie found a friend in Cleofis that she never thought she would meet she truly felt he was growing up and she started to build a brick wall around the images of him fucking George.

Cleofis was beginning to understand the struggles and worries of an independent black woman in America. And how many have low self-esteem which leads them down the wrong path, and there's no one there to tell them how truly beautiful they are instead hustlers, pimps and murders trick them mentally. Some control them physically sweeping them through the dirty inner streets where they become unclean and lower their value, lower then their self esteem. Only through the Lord Jesus Christ can these women be un-blind-folded, cleansed, and reborn.

Aunt De-De died and left Natalie a hundred thousand dollars, far more then she had gave her sisters and brothers which was very little. Natalie was always De-De's apple of her eyes and with no children she considered her a daughter. Natalie would always tend to her auntie's needs when other family members shyed away from her. No one knew how large De-De's estate was until she died then everybody wish they'd treated her good as Natalie did. Now Natalie was riding in style and searching for a house to buy.

CHAPTER 22

February 2003

Cleofis rested his back up against the hard bark of a tree off in the cut with a nice view of the passing vehicles on a Cartel block. Though darkness covered the majority of the tree shielding him from any visibility, the youngsters hugging the side walk knew he was there, but they were the only ones. It wasn't a very dark night, considering the way the clouds fully covered the moon, but it was a cold one. One that had him blowing through the sides of a closed fist to heat up his hands. The light brown insulated Co heart coat along with overalls and some tan Timberland boots made him look like he was going to a construction sight at night. But this was hustling gear to the block huggers, dumping packs through the night. The weather was at a fluctuating period, a period black folks called flu weather. One day it was warm and the next it was freezing cold.

Just as snow flakes started to fall from the sky decorating the top of the soil, a first class SUV had turned onto the block. Cleofis could tell it was an expensive wip by the neon lights that seemed to catch every youngster's attention on the block. Who is that in that truck... must be a sell, spoke the youngsters. The truck drove slowly as if it was a hype looking for some rock. Cleofis pushed himself off the tree with his upper body to get a good look at what he made up in his mind to possibly be the FEDS or the police. But as the alpine white BMW slowly approached he could see that it was a woman looking from right to left. Squinting his eyes, he was sort of surprised to see who it was. *Natalie? What the hell she doin' over here at this time of night*, he smirked. *She got that BMW I told her she should get.*

"Ay!" He shouted waving his hand like he was landing a plane, "over here!"

Natalie was just about to pick up speed when she heard his voice, "Cleofis", she yelled, rolling down the window with flacks landing on her face. "Right here", he came from the left rear of the truck, "Girl you can't be riding slow like that through here, these niggas a think you a hype. "How else was I supposed to find you", she said with tremendous amount of interest in her voice. "Hop in for a minute, I'll bring you back."

He instantly noticed the spice in her body language from looking at her through the window. Not having to ask him twice he shot into the passenger seat quicker than a bullet. He could smell her Chanel perfume as he relaxed into the gray leather, inhaling the spanking new aroma of a new wip.

Natalie was most definitely dressed to impress, in the chilliness of February, wearing a purple soft leather knee high skirt with purple stockings, a black long sleeve shirt covered by an open purple soft leather jacket, black leather Fendi shoes and a sophisticated hair do that didn't hide the diamonds in her ears. Rested on her chest was a gold chain link with a picture of her aunt Dee Dee.

"So you went and got the X5 like I suggested huh."

"Yeah", she replied like a person who would say yes to anything with a face done in elegant make up.

"This here is niiiice, I know it hit you fo' a nice piece of change", Cleofis felt like he could go to sleep in the luxurious comfortable heated seats.

"Yeah too much, but it's nice and I like it."

"Where my son at home, with Dasia?"

"Yep… they both knocked out on the couch sleep at the new place."

"So, you bought a house too!"

"Yep, and I would like for you to stay over tonight, 'cause I be feeling a little uncomfortable in that big house."

Cleofis had heard she inherited some money form a relative but he never asked how much it was, besides it wasn't his business, but with a 2002 BMW X5 truck and a purchase of a house he wondered just how much did she inherit. He'd been a good father and her asking him to stay the night encouraged him to make a move on her, "tah tah tah, don't touch the kitchen if you ain't licking", she said to him as he reached over into her seat for a feel.

"You know I'll suck the shit out this pussy so quit playin."

At that note she lifted off the seat and pulled her skirt up with on hand while controlling the wheel with the other. Spreading her pretty caramel legs a little, Cleofis could see she was panty-less, and revealing her sheer neatly triangle cut silky patch.

"Mmm, mmm, mmm", he softly spoke, "I can't believe you girl, you sooo nasty."

"Only for you", she giggled and reclined her seat so he could play with it intensely as she drove to her new house.

Natalie bought a house on the not to bad part of the north side, cream colored on the outside it was a two story house, with three bedrooms up stairs along with a bathroom and a stair way that led to a full sized attic. The down stairs held a big cream carpeted living room attached to a polished wood floor dining room, medium sized kitchen connected to a second bedroom, a big full tiled basement. Sizable two car garage and an average beautiful green grass backyard.

So far she'd put thirty thousand done on her house, paid thirty thousand for her BMW truck, bought her and her kids some clothes, and was contemplating on buying Dasia a four thousand dollar car. She paid off her student loan and bought a little more furniture.

Cleofis was familiar with the sizable house but just didn't know exactly which one it was 'til they arrived. Stepping through the door they walked through the short hall way, glanced at Dasia and little man crashed on the couch snoring and headed up stairs to Natalie's room.

They were tongue kissing before they even got through her bedroom door. Natalie could taste the Newport he smoked hours ago, on his moist mouth and Cleofis watched her honey brown eyes shut in a dance to what he thought was the bed but turned out to be her black wooden dresser.

"Sit me on the dresser" she spoke with silk in her voice, setting her on the dresser he watched with silent compassion for a moment, "strip", she demanded with seductive authority. Cleofis did as he was told and Natalie pushed everything off the dresser. "I want it with my clothes on", Cleofis was fully nude when she laid across the shiny dresser top, pulled her skirt to her waist line and flung her legs open again. Her plump pink pussy lips opened automatically revealing strings that bridged from lip to lip surrounded by a clear coating, and displaying a long dark lusting tunnel.

"Hand me the remote to the radio off the bed", she asked gently before he got into action. Pressing play on her CD player that held Alicia Keys in the changer she put Fallen on repeat and cut it up fairly loud. It had been almost three years since she last gave herself to him, and the song Fallen seemed to fit the mood just right. As he kneeled down to submerge his face in the open wet womb, he surprised her by lifting her up in the air with her legs resting on his shoulders.

For a second she thought he was gone eat while holding her up in the air, but she kinda figured she was too heavy, that's why she wasn't surprised when he fell butt first in the bed, then laid his back on top of the plush silk cover, setting her directly on his face. As she rode his face like a slow intense lap dance, he curled his arms around her thick thighs trying to push his tongue as far into her tunnel as possible. Even as his tongue wiggled between her legs he made plans on how to convince her to put him back on his feet. He fought off the desire just to give himself up to the love making completely. He used all his mental power to control the love irrupting inside of him. How can I fall in love with her again, after she fucked my enemy…? Just like Kim… But damn I'm bugging, she didn't know… Should I give my self to her?

In an instinct everything inside of Natalie seemed to want to come out. Her knees trembled as she slid her arms behind her back and laid her palms on his tightened stomach. The feeling of his tongue licking from her tunnel to her clit, sent shock waves through her body, causing her to unconsciously moan his name, allowing herself to be involuntary possessed.

Her flesh seemed to crawl with unbearable sensations and as Alicia Keys hit a high note at the end of the song Natalie hit a high note of her own, acting as if she was transforming into something, screaming until every bit of sensation built up inside of her released out of her body, liquid covered the bottom half of Cleofis face dripping to a puddle being soaked into the cover.

"Damn you taste good", he said pushing her onto his chest, licking his top lip. Still in sort of a trance, Natalie felt drained not knowing if her body could regain strength, but Cleofis quickly diminished that when he laid her on her back and started bouncing up and down like a six four.

"Slow down", she moaned as her body started reconstructing, "Make love to me?"

Natalie wrapped her arms around his neck moving their bodies closer to each other as she rolled her tongue in his ear, he slowed down the tempo.

Cleofis avoided long eye contact with her love stricken eyes, and the wet slapping sound from penetrating back and fourth inside of her sent him into a faze of wanting to undress her but she refused for the idea of him not getting the whole package would enhance is desire to satisfy her even more. And she knew this

Turning her over on her stomach, the soft purple leather skirt covered half of her bottom, that glistened from light sweat and Cleofis dove back into her rapidly, swirling around in her face like a Farris wheel. Natalie enjoyed every bit of it and often demanded he stop so she could put in her mouth what was feeling so damn good.

In the middle of the night Natalie was awakened by his tossing and turning along with understandable sleep talk. She kinda worried for a minute for the scene bought her back to when she had her old house prayed for after the encounter with what she felt was super natural. But this was different Cleofis was having a nightmare about something.

"I changed my mind.... But it was too late.... I had no choice..... You was gone tell on me, I had to do it.... I'm sorry Shawndra." His breathing was hard, and he was speaking clear as if he was awake. "I promise you I wanted to stop him... But it was too late... I had to make sure you were dead:.. Shawndra listen to me, please just listen to me... See you always running yo' mouth... You gone make me wack yo' ass again." Cleofis shifted his head in the opposite direction on Natalie's and continued, "I squashed that shit with JW 'cause he my cousin... I know you don t want him over here... I'm sorry, I'm sorry please... I'm sorry. Natalie's inside felt funny for it wasn't just something somebody told her she now knew for a fact that Cleofis murdered Shawndra Coleman with help of followers.

Any woman with any sense would have left him alone when he gave her herpes, and fucked a faggot on her couch, but now that she heard out of his own unconscious mouth that he had committed the infamous slaying, instead of dismantling all ties she sympathized for the lost soul. Feeling like she could heal him of all things she wrapped him up in her arms and whispered in his ear, "Everything is going to be okay", she rubbed his head and back, putting him back into a more peaceful sleep after pulling him up on her comfortable cleavage. She prayed for his soul before returning back to rest herself. It seemed like soon as she closed her eyes they were opened to the smell of smoke coming through a vent in her room. "Oh shit the house on fire, not even checking to see if Cleofis was on the side of her, she raced down stairs butt naked and all. By the time she hit the bottom step the smoke alarm was going off. She could see the smoke was coming from the kitchen along with movement of dishes.

"I know yo' momma probably up by nah, with all that noise." She could hear Cleofis say. Reaching the kitchen she could see him cracking a window, and Dasia waving a towel under the detector. "What's going on down here", she suddenly caught both of their attentions, "I'm making you and Dasia some breakfast bay."

"Some breakfast", she drew her head back, "Boy you don't know how to cook."

"Look Ma", said Daisa directing attention to the warm breakfast laid out on the kitchen table.

"Well lookie here", Natalie smiled thankfully though the smoke bothered her eyes, "If this is the breakfast then what are you burning", she grabbed a coat out of the hallway closet to cover the front of her naked ness.

"I spilled some stuff in the oven that's all, ain't no big deal. Gone and throw some clothes on so we can eat breakfast as a family before Dasia goes to School."

"Okay", she said simply and went to fetch a long tee shirt.

"I'm glad you are back", replied Dasia as they took a seat at the table waiting for Natalie to return.

"I'm glad I am too, and I'm sorry for not being here when I was supposed to."

"It's okay", then Dasia then dropped her head with a whisper, "You think you can talk mom into buying me this Corsica, 'cause when she takes a long time to make up her mind it usually means no."

"I'll see what I can do", Cleofis poured orange juice into the three cups he set up for them.

"Just give me a couple of days."

"Give me a couple of days with what", Natalie said jokingly walking back into the kitchen wearing a long Winnie the Pooh pajama shirt.

"A couple of days 'til I ask you to marry me", he grinned letting her know it was none of her business in a gentle way.

The three of them filled their bellies up and Daisa rushed off to school, happy that her little brothers' daddy was back home. That meant her mother would stop being so miserable and finally put her intensions else where, 'cause Dasia was fifteen and felt grown as her mother. In one year she grew taller than her mother just as thick as her mother and her 36c was catching up to her mother's 34D. With smooth ebony skin and long black hair like Natalie's she would be approached by grown men on the regular, but her lust rested in the hands of a boy a year older than her. Cleofis could tell by the way she carried herself that she was sexually active but wouldn't dare mention it to Natalie, who still felt her daughter was a virgin.

"I think Dasia has a crush on you", Natalie rubbed her full belly and sighed, "she used to tell me she think you sexy and I asked her what sexy was, she gone say she don't know how to explain it. But from the day we stop talking she asked about you like you used to be her man or something."

"It's normal for young girls to have crushes on grown men, as long as they don't act on it."

"I wish she would call her self flirting with you, I'll snatch out all that good hair she inherited through me."

Natalie could feel the cool morning air blowing on the bottom half of her legs, "Ohh, air blowing through that window", she rose to go shut it. "Its not smoky in here anymore, and what were you dreaming about last night?"

"I don't recall me dreaming about anything, why was I talking in my sleep or something?"

"No", she lied convincingly, "You were just tossing and turning… all I hop is that you don't bring anything into my house like you did at the first one."

"What is you talking about", one side of his face frowned.

"I remember when I had to have your mother and Pastor Evans come by and bless the first one. Too much weird shit was going on and it was because of the things that were on you."

Cleofis blew through his nose as if he didn't want to hear any of it, "What you tryin' to say?"

"……Don't be dropping no evil off in this house, is all I ask", she began picking up the dishes off the table and carrying them to the sink.

"How you know something came in here on me, maybe it came in from –."

"Let's not make this a big issue okay", she cut him off speaking nice but stern."

"Cleofis left it alone for the print of the booty through the long shirt was starting to turn him on while watching her put away the dishes, especially the way the middle back of the shirt seemed to sink in above her rump, "Ready fo' round two", he asked so proudly. She didn't think he would leave the conversation alone so swiftly. "If you ready I'm ready", she was happily obliged wanting a nice hard screw before she went to work.

Cleofis and Natalie grew closer through the weeks of satisfying sex, love making, intimacy, parent hood, and companionship. He'd talked her into buying Daisa the Corsica but she could only drive it with an adult in the car. Natalie was slowly but showily letting him see her BMW, while she worked and when she did he would always be there to pick her up from work on time.

Everything was going like she envisioned Cleofis had moved his stuff from his grandmoms and Holly's then moved it in with her. He would watch their son while she was at work she wouldn't have to worry about Dasia having company while she was gone though Cleofis would let her have company as long as they wasn't fowdy. Cleofis liked to hold friendly conversation with her fully developed female friends that adored him and was drawn to him by the things Dasia bragged he did in the streets.

Besides his constant begging to be put back on his feet, Natalie couldn't ask for a better man. He was very respectful and she stopped socializing with friends and family for she was caught up in the rapture. And nobody could tell her nothing she felt the love of her and their son was the cure to all his problems. Cleofis was starting to feel financially embarrassed again still pitching twenty dollar bags from the Cartel blocks. He was growing strongly impatient -- He felt his value was for to much to be taking risk for such petty amounts of dollars. Since the first night he stepped foot in her house he slowed down on snorting powder and drinking heavily. No doubt Cleofis felt he was ready to ball till he fell again.

James (Jackpot) Love was now at Kankakee County Jail awaiting trail on the Shawndra Coleman slaying. Word spread rapidly through the facility about the statement Cleofis made on him and Jackpot showed as many inmates as possible so they could all see proof of the rat. His pretrial was starting and his lawyers were going over the evidence of the case. Prosecutors knew one of their star witnesses would be Cleofis (Teflon) Jackson and they hoped to find out everything that happened.

Det. Diamond kept visiting Jackpot trying to persuade him to testify about what really happened in exchange for a low double digit sentence. But Jackpot consistently proclaimed his innocence saying someone is trying to frame me.

Puncho was dismissed of all charges once Cleofis took the stand retorting. "I don't remember it was dark. I don't remember…I said, I don't remember." Puncho gambled on the odds of him stating he shot him 'cause he wasn't going to pay him shit. Puncho knew Cleofis wouldn't want to ruin his already tarnished reputation a gangsterfied ass nigga. So his chance of leaving the court house was high, and Shanice was right there to celebrate the innocent verdict with her man.

Cleofis was just arriving from visiting his mother with little Cleofis. Usually he would come through the side door, but because he lost his side door key he came through the front one.

The front door didn't make much noise at all because of the furnace that was humming you wouldn't know someone was coming in the house. Little junior was curled up in his strong arms sound asleep as he footed to the living room to lay him down on the couch. Natalie was at work still and Dasia wouldn't be home for another thirty minutes. So the villain made his way down to the basement for a self played game of pool on the pool table Natalie bought a couple days ago, only to be stunned by an unusual sight. Dasia was riding some boy on the basement couch in the far left corner. Not aware that Cleofis could see her she pounced up and down like she was on top of a big rubber ball. Glancing at a picture frame, she immediately could see the reflection of Cleofis standing on the stairs watching her. At first she began to stop but when peeping he wasn't saying nothing she rode the teenage boy harder and arched her back more.

Cleofis just watched for a minute while she moaned louder and acted as if she didn't have a back bone, jerking her body back and forth. Looking at her ass half way covered by her shirt, roll back and forth made it quite clear that she had been having sex for awhile. Cleofis started too interrupt, but changed his mind went upstairs and relaxed.

That little girl got a grown women ass, man that mutherfucka big. big black shiny booty I bet you that little nigga don't know what to do with all that, Cleofis thought, but I'mma let her have her fun but this a be the last time in this house. She knows better than to fucking up in here, what if her momma would of came home early and caught her.

Dasia let her company out the side door and headed up the second story to take a shower. She could hear Cleofis walking down to the first story before she ran the water.

Cleofis was bagging up some twenty sacks of coke on the living room table when Daisa came down stairs with a towel wrapped around her chest down to her thighs

"Seen my shoes Teflon?"

Turning to his left he could see that she was standing there holding the back of the towel with one hand and stroking her hands through her wet hair with the other looking like a young beautiful version of her mother.

"Noll, but you can't be just fucking niggaz in the house like that, what if yo' momma woulda came home early?"

"What's the matter", she spoke sexy. "You see something you like, and you jealous 'cause somebody else getting it."

"Little girl I don't-

"Don't little girl me, I saw you looking with chow sexy ass."

"I wasn't lookin at shit and if I catch you fuckin' again I'mma tell yo' momma. 'Cause you sure got her fooled into thinking you a virgin."

"I thought you was a real nigga, real niggaz don't snitch."

"I ain't no snitch, I just don't wanna see you become a hoe like a lot of these tramps in the streets, plus I got a lot love fo' you that's the reason why."

Dasia went to look for her so called shoes behind a couch and bent over purposely in front of Cleofis' view. "So you got love fo' me like I'm one of yo' bitches." He clearly saw her hairy womb sticking out as the back of the towel raised up around her butt cheeks. "Or like a step daughter?"

"Like a step daughter", he growled. "Now take yo' ass upstairs and put on some clothes."

She walked past him throwing her hips hard, and then dropped her towel purposely just before reaching the stairs. "Woops", she shouted childishly.

Cleofis was becoming pissed at the sight of her nude body. "Didn't I say go put on some clothes", he picked up his light brown Timberline and threw it at her.

"Ok, ok", she quickly put the towel over her body and ran upstairs.

"And bring yo' ass straight down stairs after you get dressed", he yelled loud enough for her to hear him downstairs.

Coming back downstairs with an appropriate garment, Cleofis demanded she take a seat across from him. Feeling like an O.G. in the game he went through the disadvantages of being labeled as a hoe. How important it was for her to stay low on the number of men she messed with. He knew she was going to have sex regardless so he explained how important it is to keep one partner. And how if she didn't do this, men wouldn't respect her even after years went by. Cleofis let her know that though she was an attractive young lady he would always look at her like a daughter.

Dasia sat there listening to his hour long speech nodding her head to his suggestions and solutions. It seemed as if she was taking heed to everything that was being said and he enjoyed listening to his own wise tongue speak.

It was about the middle of April when Natalie came strolling up her walk way yapping seriously on her cell phone. "Like I told you befo' he only here so that him and my son can spend time. I'm not fucking him", she lied.

"This is Mandy you talking to, I been known you since 78 when I beat you up in the hallway at school. And only time a man drives your car or should I say thirty thousand dollar BMW truck is when he's piping you down."

"I swear-

"Oh quit it and I don't care, what you say that faggot been staying there for at least a month or better. I'm telling you, you need to leave that dope fiend, faggot, disease having motherfucka alone."

"Disease having", Natalie played as if she was stupid.

"Don't act like you ain't heard about that shit he got, all the hoeing he do the faggot probably got that package." Mandy felt good the more she roasted the person that ruined her street credibility.

"For the last time I'm not fucking him", Natalie insisted, sticking her key into her side door.

"And since he's been around he's been a completely changed man." Coming into her apartment she instantly smelled the aroma from her favorite candle raspberry. She had had a long day at work and to come to a clean good smelling house was a relief. It was the last day of the week and all she wanted to do was rest, knowing that the house was clean it was easy to do that 'cause Cleofis took care of it from top to bottom.

"I'll call you back", Natalie closed the side door behind her went through the hallway, and discovered him slouched on the couch in the living room watching. Hoodlum.

"Who was you talking to bay?"

"Mandy", said Natalie as her eyes scowered the cleanest. "So you musta really been in a good mood to clean up the whole house today."

"Anything fo' you", he motioned for her to come sit between his legs for a massage.

"Little man with my momma and Dasia somewhere around here."

"When will he be---"

A loud knock from the side door interrupted her. "Ill get it", Dasia shouted from the basement answering the door with some tight cut off shorts just shy of some daisy dukes.

"You here for Teflon huh?"

"Yeah", Bootleg's eyes dropped to her thighs.

"Well come on in I'll get 'em fo' you."

"Who is it", shouted Natalie enjoying her shoulder massage.

"Its Bootleg", she said, walking into the living room.

"If you don't put on some bigger short", Natalie started as Cleofis climbed over her to see his company at the door." I will get up from here and beat you into the floor."

Dasia stumped upstairs mumbling. "Keep stumping", she shouted. "And I'mma stump you with cho' fast ass."

"Damn", said Bootleg. "You betta keep that little heifer away from me 'cause man ……"

"You touch her and I'll kill you", Cleofis let him know that he was serious not giving him a chance to comment on it anymore.

"You bugging 'Moe', you bugging…have you been asking her for some doe 'cause I'm tired of this petty shit."

"She won't budge", Cleofis gave him a nigga you talking too loud look. "I don't think she got any left."

"Well it's time to get grimy nigga", Bootleg smacked his hands louder than to crash symbols. "Lets mag up and go stick a vic."

"Be cool", Cleofis announced. "It's only a matter of time befow something comes up."

"Fuck that let's rob till we come up on enough to cop some weight."

"Just be cool", he tapped on his shoulders. "Let me think some shit out and I'll get back up wit'chu."

"Easy for you to say", Bootleg felt Cleofis was getting to comfortable with Natalie. He felt Cleofis was deserting him because Natalie was seeing to it that Cleofis had everything he needed. Bootleg was basically homeless sleeping from crack house to crack house, the only thing he knew how to do was rob and slang coke. This was the way he survived.

"Every since you've moved in this place you been on some soft shit and them little packs you giving me to dump, I could wip my ass with."

Natalie could hear bits of the conversation through the movie noise. She didn't like Bootleg -- he gave her an impression of an untamed animal though Cleofis could quickly tame him. She rouse to her feet to eaves dropped some more.

"I told you, you can sleep down in the basement till we come up with something 'cause I'm tired of taking penitentiary chances for the petty shit too, and these bitch ass niggaz gone squeal once a mutherfucka start makin it unsafe for 'em to come out, and I don't know about you but I can't get knocked no mo 'cause them people ain't gone play with my ass. I'm the most sought nigga to catch in Kankakee all a snitch gotta due is breathe my name", he slit his own throat with his index finger demonstrating what the system a due if having a solid case.

"Cleofis", yelled Natalie from the other end of the hall. "You gonna finish my massage or what?"

"Yeah bay."

"Look at you 'Moe'", Bootleg was disappointed. "Who wearing the panties her or you?"

"I'm wearing the panties", Natalie stepped in full view. "And I would like for yo' disrespectful ass to leave my house."

"You betta holla at chow girl 'Moe'."

"You heard her nigga. You already know how yo' mouth is."

Natalie was proud that Cleofis bagged her up, she thought he might of felt she was tripping.

"Obviously you done forgot who yo' homies is…nigga I was there when this chick was sleeping with the enemy."

"ENOUGH", came along with a heavy muff that sent Bootlegs head flying to the corner of the wall making a loud thump. "I told ju about cho' mouth, bitch nigga."

"It's like that huh? -- It's like that?", spoke the embarrassed friend.

"Mufucka it's like that, if you ain't got no respect for her you ain't got no respect for me", he opened the door and literally pushed him out.

"What going on?", asked Dasia who just flew down the stairs.

"Nothing nosy…Cleofis took care of it", Natalie plopped back down on the carpet in front of the couch ready to continue with her massage. Just as Cleofis started stretching back over her to proceed another knock came from the door.

"I know dis nigga ain't still by my door", Cleofis raised the right cushion of the couch up and retrieved a 38 snug. "Watch out", he replied to Dasia on her way to answer. "Imma get the do', go back upstairs", suspecting trouble he flung the door open pointing his revolver directly in the face of his mother. "Damn Momma, I'm sorry I thought you was-

"Boy get that thang out my face", she cut in. "What's wrong with you", Mrs. Jackson stepped in with her grandson clinging to her hand. "I see you ain't gone never change."

"I just had to throw Bootleg out", he stuck the strap in his back pocket. "And I thought you was him tryin' to bring some drama."

"Mommy, mommy", little Cleofis flew passed his daddy and into his mothers arms. "Grandma took me to the Lincoln Park Zoo."

"Oh she did?" Natalie picked him up squeezed him. "Was he acting bad", she asked.

"He was fine", Mrs. Jackson smiled. "Though he wouldn't stop staring at the rhinos."

"One of them probably reminded him of his daddy", Natalie laughed at her own joke harder then Mrs. Jackson.

"Ha ha ha", expressed Cleofis. "I bet'chu it was a gorilla there that looked exactly like you."

Mrs. Jackson laughed harder at her son's joke showing her undeniable loyalty to him. "I'm so happy to see you two still together. I always said you'll make a cute couple and y'all most definitely made a beautiful son." Natalie and Cleofis smiled confidently. "So I can expect to see you two in church Sunday riiiight?"

"We'll be there", Natalie answered for her baby daddy's undecided face.

"Good", said the soft spoken and humble Christian. "Ill be expecting you both", she cleared before exiting.

"So what's to it lil moe", Cleofis built the pyramid with his little sons hands. "Nuttin 'Moe'", said the 3 year old.

"Don't be teaching my son that shit", yelled Natalie. "He already bad enough", the little boy hit the left side of his chest with a bald fist mimicking his farther. "All is well", he mumbled aware of his mother's disappointment hoping she didn't hear him.

"I'm well on your- Natalie began when the door erupted with a serious loud knock. "What is this everybody knocked on my door when I get off work day."

"I'll get it, I'll get it", Cleofis answered with a frowned face, but shifted to a worried one when staring in the eyes of a sheriff police officer accompanied by Det. Diamond.

"Cleofis Jackson", asked the sheriff. It wasn't any use of lying because Diamond could spot him from a mile away and most definitely up close.

"What's up?"

"I have a subpoena to serve you and I would like for you to sign right here", the sheriff pointed to a black line on a white sheet of paper.

"Fo' what, what am I getting softened fo'?"

"You're a witness in the Shawndra Coleman murder", Diamond answered for the sheriff with a lotto hit smile.

CHAPTER 23

How could he give so much pleasure, but then 'cause so much pain?

Cleofis hadn't expected a visit from the Sheriffs for at least another month in a half because the trial wasn't until June, but the department thought they would play it smart by finding him early so they wouldn't have to search for him when it was time to testify.

He was becoming stressed like hell with knowing he was going to have to testify against Jackpot, that he was sure would assemble a lot of people to observe the testimony.

Natalie temporarily stopped his deterioration when she entrusted him with her last twenty thousand dollars. Telling him, "Now you can get on your feet but you gotta promise me you going to pay me all my money back…cause that's the last of it if you mess that up we a be broke."

Cleofis quickly snatched Bootleg back up for muscle, snatched Bones 'cause he knew all the hypes and started grinding like it was no tomorrow. Setting up shop in a crack house directly across the street from Holly and another spot in the Durrels sectioned off from Puncho and his crew.

Stepping into the crib to weigh out a half a ounce for a customer he wondered was his baby Momma home yet because it was about that time. "Anybody home", he shouted as he slid a metal tray from under the living room couch containing chunks of hard cocaine on the top.

"I'm here", yelled Dasia from the bathroom connected to the kitchen. "Tell ma I went to the YMCA to go swimming if she not pulling up, when I pull off."

"I think you betta tell her that yo' self." The cocaine was so hard he had to wrap his shirt around it and break it with his teeth. "Cause she ain't fenna be fussing with me. But I tell you what, if you go get yo' lil brotha from the daycare I'll talk her into letting you stay a couple hours pass curfew."

"Bet", she said from the bathroom through the kitchen and into the living room where he was weighing the coke out. "Like my swim suit", she stood proudly like Mrs. America. At the instant attention of Cleofis she spun around in a circle showing off her lustful pink swim suit that look like it was ready to pop from holding so much tits and ass. With a trunk like a horse, and a chest like a celebrity implant, Her chocolate beautiful radiant skin tone on top of her black hair made her closely resemble Ki Toy of Outkast, "I Like the Way You Move", video.

"It's straight", it was hard for him to take his eyes off her and she knew it. But he had to remain the adult in this situation. "Don't you think you should put that on when you get there?"

"Yeah but I just wanted to know that it was tight."

"Oh it's definitely tight", Cleofis meant in the leaving less to the imagination way. "Gone and go get cho' brotha, your mother should be hear about time you come back."

Hearing Dasia leave out the side door he quickly shot upstairs to stash some cash in the attic. This was the only place in the house, Natalie rarely went to. And Cleofis couldn't stand her keeping tabs on the fedi that was being made. So to put it there would be to leave her in the blind about the status she requested every week. She always demanded to know how he was doing, and deep inside this irked the shit out of him. Never the less it was her money and his plan was to make himself twenty grand before giving back twenty grand.

His thumb fingered through the big faces in his hand as he opened the attic door and crept up a small amount of stairs. With only one small window it was slightly dark even with the sun gleaming through. The thin wooded floor seemed to want to fall in at his every step. He was stashing the bills in a full size deserted mattress he'd sliced a spacey hole in. making sure the cram was stuffed by the rest of it loot he proceeded to exit when he accidentally knocked over a shoe box full of pictures. Starting to leave the spilled mess he decided to quickly pick them up. As he did so a picture of him and Natalie when he came home in 98 captured his attention.

Man my bay looking fly… seems like yesterday……I never thought she would be the one.

Bunched in the back of the picture was a few others, sliding the picture of them two to the shoe box, the next picture brought his jealousy back to life. "Fucking nasty bitch!" It was a picture of Chopper strolled out across her canopy bed butt ass naked with his fist on waist like a superhero. What fumed him the most was the size of his cock and it wasn't even erect the brother was most definitely hung like a horse.

His teeth clenched and his jaw bone's flickered from building anger. His eyebrows damn near touched his eye lashes from insecurity. If only his Johnson was bigger. Gazing at the picture he shook his head thinking about how Chopper musta been killing her with that package.

No wonder why that pussy so big, niggaz put pipe to her the size of that. Cleofis knew he wasn't the biggest man down there but what little confidence he possessed from making Natalie climax was out the window. How can I compete with something like this?

He stuck the picture deeply into his Sean John jeans, looked through the rest of the scattered pictures, left them as is and headed out the attic. He knew Natalie had bigger in the bed room, but he always felt nobody could compete with the way he worked her and certainly not the way he sucked her pussy.

He probably was making the bitch cum fourteen times. And the way Natalie explained it was like Chopper meant nothing to her. Bitch ass nigga meant everything that's why she took a picture of the nigga. The discovery was really putting a cramping in Cleofis ego.

He could hear her coming through the side door as he pondered down the stairs onto the first floor.

"Where's little Cleofis?", asked Natalie. "It's been time to pick him up from the day care."

"Chopper went to go get him", Cleofis stood with a straight face as she toed pass him through the kitchen to the bedroom.

"What", she pulled her work pants down and sat on the toilet thinking she misunderstood him.

"You heard what I said, Chopper motherfucka!"

"Why must you start with that mess, I already told you it wasn't even like that with me and dude."

"Fuck if it wasn't, you hoe", Cleofis moved closer to the cracked bathroom door

"See", Natalie patted her pus and pulled her pants up. "We can't get no where 'til you completely let the past go, I don't bring up that Shawndra shit or that Holly shit."

"Beat it with the shenanigans we talking about yo' hoe ass, seems to me like you and Chopper was fuckin' on the regular."

"Like I told you befo'", she stood in the mirror trying to swipe a piece of hair out an eye with tissue. "Yeah I fucked em, not that many times but I fucked him", she knew better then to tell the complete truth, because it would hurt him.

He bit his lip hard trying to show her she better get terrified because he was pissed. She toed past him again not paying him any attention as she opened the refrigerator to some left over ribs.

"You must think I'm a God damn fool Natalie, do it look like I got fool written across my face?" His closed fist slammed repeatedly into an open hand, he become more angry as she rolled her honey brown eyes and got the munching on some cold ribs. "Dude was piping yo' ass down and I bet you he didn't even have to wait for the pussy. 'Cause you know how you do -- you was fuckin' me when I was in the county."

Natalie made a loud popping noise with every finger she sucked the barbeque sauce of off. Sitting on her bar stool she figured as long as she stayed silent things would eventually die down until he flung Choppers Polaroid picture up out of his pocket.

"I bet'chu that's exactly what you did with his dick, bitch!" He laid the picture on her lap.

"Oooooh so you've been through my things", she replied after a giggle. A sharp moment of silence occurred. And she could feel him staring through the side of her head so she nervously smirked.

"BITCH!" Cleofis came from down under with a spit flying smack. The smack was the push he needed. "Huh, shit ain't funny now is it huh?"

Natalie had to brace herself to swallow a piece of rib that he knocked down her throat. Before she could react, Cleofis wrapped his arm around her neck like a python squeezing harder at every breath she took. "What! Bitch, you gone try an fight me?" Bringing her body down to the floor he laid her on her back and released her. "I wish you would get up", he stood with her head between his feet drawing back his fist threatening to punch her.

"I can't believe you just did that to me", she cried hysterically, holding her neck breathing rapidly. Laying on the hard cold floor all the love she felt for him was temporarily replaced with hate. As her ears picked up the sound of Dasia coming through the side door she sprung up on her feet like an athlete. "Ill kill you", she dropped her head rushing him throwing wild punches. Dasia ran to her mothers rescue followed by little Cleofis.

"Get your hands off my momma", she broke in between the two. "Stop momma stop", yelled Dasia. Little Cleofis started to yell at the top of his lungs at the unusual sight.

"Hold chow momma Dasia 'cause if she hit me again."

"Just leave", Dasia tried her best to hold her mother back. "Cause I'm not fenna continue to hold her back."

"If you don't let me go girl, I swear I'mma beat yo' ass", flipped Natalie. "You don't know what he just did to me!"

"Yall still can't be fighting in front of my brother", Dasia reminded.

Natalie broke from her daughters grip and chased Cleofis who just sprang out the door. "You not leaving in my truck you faggot mufucka." About time she reached the outside he was closing the door of the SUV. "Cleofis! You leave in my truck I'mma call the police!" By this time he was peeling rubber.

"Call them people on me and you'll never see yo' twenty stacks"

Wanting to call the police she thought about the twenty grand and quickly changed her mind. She would have to get her money back before anything.

Cleofis hung out at Holly's the majority of the day, pulling the BMW in the back of her yard to hide it from Natalie. Holly was very much annoyed by his presence but looked at it as a financial gain 'cause she was well aware that he was back on his feet.

For hours he tried convincing her to give him some pussy, but she refused hoping he would make a financial commitment, she would care less that he was over there in Natalie's truck or that that's where he'd been for the last two months. The gold digger wanted her car paid off completely and wasn't giving up no ass till he agreed.

"Let's talk about it some more in the truck?"

"Ok!" Holly laughed inside knowing he just didn't want to agree to her terms in front of her teenage girls. "I'll be right back in", she told her girls as she opened the backdoor and lit a Newport in the fresh night air.

"Must you tell them nosy girls yo' every move?" Cleofis unalarmed the truck with a key device.

"Them my daughters and I'll tell them whatever I want to", she snapped entering the vehicle.

"Keep running that mouth of yours and I'mma close it permanently", he spoke serious but with humor.

"Nice truck…you and your wife probably feel like the shit!"

"She ain't my wife and I don't even fuck with her like that no mo."

"As of….."

"Stop with chow shit and give a nigga some of that thang."

"Like I told you before", she smacked her coochie through her sweat pants. "Missy needs her car paid off, and a guarantee that you gone take care of me and my girls."

Giving her his word they climbed to the back seat. While he pushed the seats forwards for more space, she purposely put her cigarette out on the seat burning a hole in the leather. This was her little way of saying she'd been in Natalie truck and what was she going to do about it. Consciously knowing she was going to tell a friend about her spiteful act she laughed inside trying to picture how Natalie would respond to the news.

Cleofis slid her sweat pants down, popped his soldier out his zipper and started ramming her from the back. Rocking the truck back and forth, Holly allowed her mental to make the activity better than what it was, so that she could cum multiple times and drip on the seat and floor purposely. With her chin pinned to the window she blew her breath on it making fog like a child playing. Hopping to leave every possible scent her body could produce in the SUV, catching a charlie-horse drove her to arch her back more knowing this would make the villain explode inside of her.

Natalie was cleaning her basement when she could hear Cleofis come through the side door accompanied by someone. "Bay", he called from the first story, "Where's the cordless phone?" She didn't respond when she moved the basement couch to sweep and discovered a semen-filled rubber. It made her shut her eyes for a minute. *I can't believe this shit.* She picked-up the nut-filled condom with some rubber gloves and marched upstairs to confront 'Mr. Man'.

"So I see you just so careless now that you leave evidence in the basement", she dangled the rubber in his face.

"That ain't mine", he presented a crazy look

"Well just who the fuck is it then, 'cause Dasia ain't fucking!"

Cleofis gave her a think again look. "Like I said the shit ain't mine so quit questioning me about it."

"No motherfucka just a couple weeks ago you was beating my ass over a fuckin' Polaroid picture that was taken when I wasn't even dealing with you."

"Whatever, whatever", he waved her off and continued to look for the cordless. "Wait a minute", lifting a couch pillow up he replied.

"Did you and one of them nasty hype bitches of yours leave that fuckin' shit in the basement?"

"Yeah my back moe", exclaimed Bones catching on quickly to the lie.

"I outta make yo' ass clean the whole basement for that wild ass shit. That mean that shit been down there for 3 days", clearly angrily scowled the hype.

"You mean to tell me you let him", Natalie pointed with hostility in her voice. "A dirty ass hype fuck another dirty ass hype in my basement where Dasia and her friends study at."

"Excuse me Mrs., but ain't nuttin dirty about old Bones."

"You can leave my fuckin' house if you don't like it."

"Calm down bay", Cleofis moved close to her. "Do you want me to make 'em clean the whole basement?"

"Nope", she turned, went and through the condom away and returned to the basement. Natalie could barely finish cleaning the basement she was so angry. She knew better than to believe that it was Bones in her basement but it was no sense in arguing since the hype took the rap. It was no way Cleofis was going to confess to anything unless he was caught red handed.

Since the smacking and chocking, Natalie allowed him to completely do what he wanted to do. She submitted the little power she possessed, convinced that this was to keep him around. He disrespected her to her face more than ever before, he fronted her off more then ever before, and barely took over her house making it a revolving door for hidden criminals such as himself. He made her give him sex at the snap of his fingers, fucking more bitches in her truck, switching from her and Holly's bed every other day, and his aggression level in her house was rising.

Natalie only received five of the twenty thousand she gave him back and waited silently and patiently for the rest. She received plenty of word about his activities, but always turned the other cheek. All dogs' run when you let them off the leash, as long as they returned and took care of home it was ok, was her new theory.

But Cleofis was becoming more and more stressed the closer the trail approached. Back to tooting powder everyday, he was snorting more then ever before. Loosing himself in the bottle, he was consuming liquor more then ever before. Whatever to rid his conscious of Shawndra Coleman and the tricks Jackpot's lawyer would try to pull, if he got on the stand. He moved around at an extremely fast past as the raw seemed to eat at the back of his skull.

Natalie strutted past Cleofis in complete regretful disgust with her nose turned up. Nasty mufucka got a outbreak thats why he ain't bring his ass to the bedroom last night...God I wish I never met that nasty little dick mufucka.

Cleofis lay in a slight sleep on the couch as Natalie passed, going upstairs to the room. He'd just finished mentally counting his funds before drifting. Sleeping with both hands in his colorful boxers was a dead give away to Natalie. She knew he must be having one hell of a herpes outbreak by the way he fidgeted around in his sleep, rubbing his private and making a painfully twisted face.

Picking up the ringing cordless she almost didn't answer when seeing it was Mandy on the ID. She just wasn't in the mood for gossip. She took the day off -- made sure the kids were at school and daycare, and just wanted some peace and quiet.

"What?" Natalie whispered as if she was resting.

"Daaaamn, nigga got you whispering in your on house hu?"

"Girl what do you want?"

"I was just calling 'cause I seen both vehicles at home, and I know homo drives the BMW and you always have the Corsica."

"Well a bitch took off today", she put sound to her voice. "Hoping to have some peace."

"Well I guess you shouldn't be talking to me then."

"Why, you got something to tell me?"

"Nuttin' major, but them feds want yo' baby daddy real bad. They came at me offering me a deal to set him up."

"When was this?"

"Yesterday girl, they knocked on my door and everything. Talking about I'll have a squeaky clean record if I set him up."

"What'chu say?"

"Hell naw, I'mma 'G' what I look like snitching even if that homo told everybody I was. I politely told 'em to get the fuck out.

But if I was you id tell that faggot to stop all that traffic through your house."

"It don't be a lot of traffic through here", Natalie said in denial and naively.

"Whaaaateva, I sure wish I was Holly."

"Why?"

"'Cause she gets her bills, rent and car paid by another niggaz women."

"Who said that?"

"Come on girl, I know you helped that nigga out and his ass ova there helping Holly ass. Taking care another bitch with cho inns, and they say the bitch be all in ya truck and shit."

"It ain't my inns if he is spending something on that bitch 'cause I got my shit back", she felt stupid the more she lied and made excuses. "And I hardly doubt if that bitch done been in my shit!"

"Quit fooling yourself girl, that bitch been bragging about how she been putting out cigarettes in ya shit."

"She must've been in somebody else truck 'cause I cleaned mine the other day and I ain't see shit. That bitch just mad 'cause he don't want her ass, yeah he probably still fucking her but this is where home is!" Natalie took a hard swallow because she was just asking Cleofis a couple days ago about the holes, and he claimed they were from blunt ashes. She wanted to take her truck but felt powerless even when she got angry with him. Knowing Holly was being accompanied in her truck upset her but she figured confronting him was useless. She just couldn't find the courage to shake the devil.

"Open yo' eyes and quit being brain washed by your feelings? If you don't when that fool fall he gone take you with him. I been hustling since 89, trust me on this one?" Natalie was trying to reply but Mandy continued. "And they say the nigga been talking about wacking you."

"I hear you girl, but I got this don't trip", she was tired of the gossip

"Alright, but if you need to beat that bitch down call me, and if you need to cut that homo speed dial me!"

"You know I will", she replied kinda amp-ed. "Ill check ya later." Natalie hung up wondering how much of the gossip to believe. Mandy wasn't always right, but the thought of him plotting on her life was serious. Why would he? She asked herself, but then again, why did he kill the people he did, the info was mind boggling and interrupted her mood to rest.

What if he does want me dead.....that can't be true 'cause why would he be stupid enough to tell someone...I'm just gone stop picking up the phone when that barring of bad news call.

When the alpine white BMW truck pulled up across the street from Holly's, the hypes released the blinds and scrambled to the door. "Teflon, Teflon, ay Teflon", they barely gave his feet a chance to touch the pavement. "What's the business", said Cleofis with a three day dirty all white Gucci summer outfit on.

"Bootleg ain't been by all day and yo' girl across the street wouldn't give us a number to reach you", a missing two front teeth hype replied. "It's been so many people coming through with big faces and you know we itching fo' a fix!"

"Be cool I gotta little somethin' on me, let's step in the house." Cleofis stuck his hands in his dirty shorts to retrieve a pack, still feeling very uncomfortable down there. Stepping into the desperately in need for a cleaning house, usually the stinjie would make him front someone off about keeping it clean, but it seemed to not bother him as he poured a cup of Kool-Aid out of a jug, known for smokers to drink out of.

"Bootleg left here yesterday with some pretty little thang, ain't been back since", said a tiny dwarf like lady.

"He betta hope she worth it 'cause I'm fucking him up on sight", he gave everybody in the house a dub sack.

"Thanks T... my maaan... you a life saver... nigga got the Bombay", was some of the appreciating terms that spat.

When night fell Cleofis was back at the spot to see if Bootleg made it back yet. Reentering, he noticed everybody in the house was sleep or relaxed. He toed to a small round table in the kitchen, copped him a squat, and pulled out a sandwich bag of white. Dumping it on a plate he dropped his face in it snorting and licking in a circle. Lost in the plate he didn't notice Bootleg come out a back room with that beautiful little thang on his side.

"Scarface, Scarface slow down", humored his buddy.

"What?" Cleofis lifted his head up with the bottom half of his face covered in sparking china white and his eyes the color of blood. "Angie…what the fuck you doing here", he tried to quickly wipe his face as if he was busted. "She wit'chu 'B'."

"What'chu think", said Bootleg with a smirk. "She gets high."

"Don't be putting my business out there like that", Angie snapped.

"Well you do" Bootleg walked over to Cleofis pimpishly. "She told me she new you 'Moe', just befow I stuck 12 inches in her."

"Get the fuck outta here." Cleofis smacked his own leg. This was unbelievable to him, and if he wasn't tuned up on powder he would have quickly realized how skinny and undernourished she looked. She'd cut her baby doll hair short, her skin tone looked like the color of a dead body, and her teeth looked rotten. But she still maintained some beauty, not nearly as much as she thought, but enough to feel sad for the lost soul. "So now you taking back shots for the rock huh?"

"Not like how your friend is putting it", Angie slightly pouted. "But I……."

"Quit being in fuckin' denial", Bootleg cut in. "The way you was hitting that missile, woooo, weeeee, it was like you was beaming up to Scottie."

Cleofis laughed at the comment heavily as he stood and wosed up on Angie. "Why you fuckin' with this loser, when you could be fuckin' with a winner?"

"Get yo' hating ass outta here 'Moe', you see she already with a champ."

"Let her choose", a grin struck his face.

Angie said nothing for a few seconds. Bootleg glanced over at her undecided-able face and could see submission in her look. "We got history", was her excuse when she glided next to Cleofis.

"Alright bitch, but you just fuck up the best thing that ever happened to you." Bootleg turned and headed for the door.

"Slow your roll 'B'…you need to be posted at the spot you know a nigga missed a ton of cheddar earlier."

"Fronting ass nigga", Bootleg mumbled before turning around and spinning to the back room he emerged from. "Alright big shot whatever you say."

Angie clung to Cleofis like a shadow over the approaching days. He drove around with her as if she was a star, barely making it home to Natalie some nights. So caught up in the zone he still hadn't realized how bad she really looked. Bootleg felt his buddy was loosing it, because hustlers knew the chick was a hype. But you couldn't tell Cleofis shit once his mind was set, it was set.

Angie got hooked on cocaine by her basketball star boyfriend in Green Bay who she always would do anything for. He messed up his scholarship and his feeling like a failure led him to the habit which he dragged Angie into. He eventually landed himself back in trouble with the law, leaving Angie to fear for her next high alone. Stealing from her parents a few times was enough for them to turn their backs on her. Now she was back in Kankakee playing for self in an underworld that groomed some of the grimiest.

"Just take a hit, if you don't like it then…" Angie spoke, patting some cocaine on the tip of a pipe with her index finger.

"What the fuck, you tryin' to turn me into a hype?"

"Naw boy, you only a hype when you get strung out, but I'm a big girl, I know how to handle my shit, you don't see me out there stealing and shit do you?"

"You got a point…I used to always wonder what was so fantastic about this shit for mufuckaz to be acting the way they do." Cleofis was tempted to try coke in a rock form. How bad could it be if Angie fucking with the shit…besides a nigga strong minded this shit can't get me hooked I'm a soldier?

They both sat on the edge of a bed in one of the Durrel projects. They just finished having sex and the two sharp pulls from the pipe she was trying to convince Cleofis to try made her eyes buck.

"Damn is it really better than sex like they say."

"You'll never know…… until you try", she stretched across the bed with out a care in the world, this was what she lived for now, them little moments of cloud nine.

"No way could it be betta than the dick I just gave you", he looked at her for a response and got nothing but giggles. Cleofis looked gazingly at the pipe in her hand that she slowly let go of. "Fuck it, you only live once." He picked it up and put it between his lips.

Sergeant Fox and Det. Diamond sat down the street from Holly's in a tinted out Chevy Impala. Drugs certainly wasn't Diamond's field, but he'd become so obsessed with putting Cleofis behind bars one way or another.

Fox didn't like the company of Diamond, but they shared the same hunger for the target. Fox was trying to see who he could turn into an informant. Peeking through some night vision binoculars it had to be somebody running in and out of there he could turn. Usually he would go squad up for a raid, but he knew if he struck and missed, it would make the villain relocate.

"How much money you think he making a day?", asked Diamond from the passenger side.

"That brown monkey probably pulling down three thou a night in bags, which a probably escalate to six thou in a couple weeks."

"He gotta be bringing in more than that by the looks of that BMW truck he got."

"That truck belongs to that black bitch that used to be a correctional officer -- word is some relative passed and left her a 100-grand."

"Uhh haa……it's a shame how women like her have so much going for their self until they get involved with dirt bags like him. I bet you he doesn't think twice about the lives he's took."

"The coon hasn't responded to Puncho's landing gun shots", Fox puffed from a Camel and blew some up in his nose. "Cleofis is a little bitch, nobody really respects him anymore -- sure he's getting money, but with his habit that I hear he has, he'll slip up soon enough for us to nab his black ass before the Feds do."

"Seems like they've been having a hard time", replied Diamond.

"Only 'cause he's up and down so much, it's just like with us, every time we get close the monkey he goes broke. I never saw a nigger as stupid as this filth, now his cousin Bruno back in the early nineties."

"I remember him. That was that guy some Chicagoans killed -- barely could identify him from the chunks missing out his face."

"He was smarter than just about any of these dope pushing niggers I ever seen, that fucker ran the city, when he had dope everybody had dope. And it was difficult to locate the nigger 'cause they say he had houses from here to California, so we could never keep him under a microscope."

Diamond was not a prejudice law man like Fox and though he hated the drug pushers he didn't hate the color of their skin or the way they looked.

Bootleg was in the company of his younger brother Sirus who just got out the joint for manslaughter. Sirus was taller and for much thinner but had always been a go getter that bagged down from no one. With corn rolls like his big brother, the Darth Vader wasn't the least attractive.

The two sat in the apartment of a hood rat Sirus paroled to, chopping it up.

"Niggaz in the joint say you out here fuckin' with that rat ass Teflon", Sirus began cutting straight to the chase. "And they say he got you tooting powder."

"Nigga please, yeah I did a line here and there, but I'm my own man. And I'm only fuckin' with dude so I can get on."

"Well you ain't gotta worry no mo, 'cause I got connected and it's gone be lavish for the both of us-"

Sirus speech was cut of by a loud chuckle. "Yo little ass acting like you fenna get it."

"I am", Sirus broadcasted. "And if you start bringing that nigga Teflon around I'mma knock his shit back 'cause I don't like that chump.....quit letting that snitch treat you."

"Ain't no nigga treating me", Bootleg started smacking his fist into an open hand. "On Blackstone I started to body that nigga, call himself testing me...he eventually got the picture."

"If you fuck with em", Sirus spoke like he was the big bro. "Imma stop fuckin' with you."

Bootleg was internally embarrassed, wanting to press up on his lil brother but left it alone for his love for him chained his actions.

Plus when Sirus fought he fought 'til one of you was seriously hurt or dead.

Natalie slept deeply on her right side, resting her head on her right arm. Positive that Cleofis was lying next to her, she subconsciously rolled to her left, expanded her arm to feel his body, but was fully awaken by the cool feeling of the empty spot on his bed side.

Her eye lids shot open, were was he, it had to be early night morning. She thought. Lifting up and touching the cold floor with bare feet, she could still hear Dasia's radio playing that she usually left on through the night. "107.5 WGCI", a disc jockey's voice sprang from the radio box as she stepped from her door way. The bathroom to her left would be her first destination before calling Cleofis' cell phone, but she could hear whispers right before another song played. This little heifer think she slick, probably some boy in there, if it is I'm gonna beat her ass.

Natalie tip toed up to the cracked door anxiously ready to burst into the room and beat Dasia down in front of her company.

Listening and peeking through the opening she could clearly see her daughter stretched out across the bed. With her legs cocked open, somebody was down in between them doing some garden work, but whom? She couldn't quite see for the opening only allowed her so much sight. Nasty lying little bitch she was fully ready to crash the sessions, but for some reason didn't. She stood there and watched for a few seconds at her daughters wide open moaning mouth from the satisfaction. Little hoes moaning like she been doing this for awhile...I can't believe I bragged about her being a virgin.

Leveling her eye to the peek hole to see exactly who this teenage boy could be, who had his face shoved in Dasia's center, Natalie suddenly became sick to her stomach. Cleofis…an over whelming feeling of wanting to vomit swept over her, she flicked her eyes several times wishing with all her might that this was a dream. Her face became red and tears blurred her vision, she wiped them only to be swept away by more. She glanced back through the crack to make sure her daughter was really allowing Cleofis to orally penetrate her. But she was, and was enjoying every minute of it.

Murder lit up in her mind like a winning slot machine. How could he…..how could she…do this to me…God, how could they hurt me like this. She cried silently through her trembling breathing, constantly wiping her face she was stuck not knowing how to react or what to say. As a mother she was ashamed to have her as a daughter. As Cleofis' baby mother she was ashamed to have him as the farther of her child. She most definitely wouldn't be able to look at either the same ever again.

Where was her courage, she asked herself. Where was her courage to bust down the door and go insane? What she was seeing she would never believe if someone told her. The two glances lasted seconds but her heart would be shattered for what seemed like a eternity as she walked back to her room and got under the covers sobbing barely being unheard through her daughters radio. Her face flushed through her eyes, nose and mouth. She cried like a wounded animal with a sound she couldn't imagine herself producing.

Cleofis wondered into their bedroom thirty minutes later, took off his clothes and got into bed. Natalie immediately was flooded with the stink of some heavy liquor. She had her back to him trying to keep her cries silent. "Nat you up", he lashed over and tapped her back. Getting no response he expanded his body over to look at her face. "Nat you up", he asked again with sweat dripping from his head. She tried her best to put on the best imitation of deep sleep as possible, slightly frowning from the stink of her daughters pussy on his breath. Everything inside her wanted to go crazy, she felt she was caging a beast but why, what was stopping her from picking up the phone calling the police and then acting a fool knowing they were on they way.

She played sleep for some time before she realized she just couldn't sleep next to the monster. Rising to her feet, It took Cleofis no time till he was snoring and she rushed to dress not wanting him to wake him. Packing week's worth of clothing, she slipped out the side door and disappeared into the night.

CHAPTER 24

You're The Reward

Natalie returned home permanently after staying at Mandy's for a couple weeks she would stop home frequently when no one was there to check, mail, calls, get more clothes, and things of the sort. Mandy baby-sat little Cleofis while Natalie was at work. Dasia would call when Natalie was gone but she would always keep it short asking her daughter what she wanted. Deep down inside Dasia knew in some way her mother found out about her and Cleofis, why else would she stay away from her own home so long.

Cleofis would call snapping but Natalie would hang up on him until he came correct, he wanted to know why she and his son hadn't been home, but deep down inside he knew also, though he played the jealous roll as if she was staying with some dude.

The whole two weeks she was gone, Cleofis and Dasia fucked like jack rabbits in just about every area of the house. He just couldn't get enough of the pretty young thang, and she just couldn't get enough of his rough image. He snorted plenty powder in front of the teen and took her around his activities in her Corsica because Natalie didn't leave the BMW for either of them. In a way he enjoyed having Dasia at his call, giving him pleasure like her mother when they first met, and loved teaching her to give head like a porn star. For a youngster Dasia started to love it up the ass, he'd taught her just like others where he made them adjust to the thumb first. But he seriously missed Natalie and his son and he was becoming extremely pissed when she returned.

With her body laid across the sofa she rested the back of her head on the arm rest, gazing up at the ceiling in deep thought. She asked Mandy to watch little man until she got settled. What the hell should I do, she thought, closing her eyes trying to vision the future, maybe he thought she was me…God…he's my sons father and she's my daughter…what do I do? She instantly jerked her head to the side bringing herself to the vengeful other personality she created over the weeks. Fuck his bitch ass…I'm gonna get his ass back for this shit…..he done crossed the wrong one.

She started to drift into her thoughts unaware that she was coming into a slight sleep. In some strange way she could feel someone standing over her, it was a weird feeling that washed over her body sending her eyes to open quickly. It was Cleofis standing over her clutching a large automatic with a murderous look in his eyes, silently.

"What the fuck?", she fearfully jerked and maneuvered the back of her body to the back of the couch. "What you jumpin fa, you scared", he looked her up and down in a distasteful manner. "I ain't gone kill you, but if you leave like that again I will, that's my word", he snarled at her frantic posture which fed his intimidation. "Ok, ok", she was going to beg for her life before he demanded she never do it again.

"Where my son at?" Cleofis tucked the mag in his string tide sweat pants waist and stood shirtless waiting on a reply.

"He's at Mandy's", she was catching her breath.

"I don't know what concocted you to leave, leaving me here to raise that bad ass daughter of yours, but it betta not happen again, understand?" He put up a mean mug making it seem like she was in the wrong.

"Whatever, whatever just leave me be", she glanced at his size noticing for the first time how he was becoming thinner, his jaw structure was sinking, it was like he was shriveling up and had that look like if you was to touch him you would catch a disease and die. He was gradually getting thinner before she left, but she paid it no attention then.

She layed back in her formal position when he tossed five stacks on her upper body. "That's five stacks, I'mma give you yo' ten soon", she stuffed it between her left thigh and back pillow of the sofa.

"Where them truck keys at I gotta make a run?"

"You not driving my truck."

"Later with that shit, give me the fuckin' keys so I can go pick up some cheddar", he lied, he missed the luxury SUV and wanted to go stunting perhaps holler at some hoes, that's why he threw her the five grand trying to let her know he'd been hustling but she was well aware of what his aim was and she wasn't having it.

"I told you no", she gave him a keep fucking with me look and I'm gone clown.

"You always tripin", he walked off and went upstairs not wanting her to bring something up he didn't want to hear.

Would he kill me she thought was what Mandy said true, did he want her dead. Obviously not then but soon maybe or maybe he just wanted to scare her into seeing everything his way. Never the less the mentally distressed woman had to come up with something quick.

Today was the day he was supposed to testify in the James (Jackpot) Love trial, a day that had him on the edge. He was contemplating on skipping town until the trial was over.

Why the fuck do they need me to testify…..fuckin' D-A gotta trick up his sleeve…I know they gone try and pull some bullshit. The warm water from the shower hit his face while these thoughts rambled.

Berry Hilton probably wouldn't recall his statement unless threatened about the Bo Pete murder gun again.

Disco and Cliff sure wasn't going to recall there statements after being stuck up by him and bootleg.

And most of the addicts he paid to make statements were nowhere to be found. But still the job of exposing Jackpot as an accomplice was done well.

A sense of fear rattled Cleofis' fear of getting on the stand against another man. In just an hour this would have to be done.

Not wanting to get out the shower though the water was becoming cold he enjoyed it. For the hot June afternoon was very humid outside. He wished he could just stay in the shower as if it was a time capsule and come out in the future when things passed over.

When Natalie realized that this was the date Cleofis had to come into court and get on the stand she called Mandy. Listening to the water running upstairs she knew he couldn't hear her as she told Mandy about arranging for little man to go someplace else so that they could go be nosy at the trial.

Natalie had made it a mental note to be there to see the snitch who portrayed himself as the realest nigga, to get on the stand to testify against Jackpot. And so far Jackpot wasn't saying shit. Knowing he had to do this, partially to ease some of her emotional pain. She knew this would be a tremendous blow to what was left of his street cred.

She hurried out the house into the sun blazing day while he was still in the shower upstairs.

Arriving to the Kankakee court house she caught the elevator to the top floor where they tried the felon cases. Soon as the elevator opened for her to get off she could see Mrs. Coleman, Shanice, Melissa and a crowd of spectators outside the designated court room. She didn't know Mrs. Coleman, Shanice, or Melissa personally but she knew who they were and they knew who she was, Cleofis' baby momma. She could see Mrs. Coleman and Shanice mumbling as she took a seat on a hard mahogany bench a couple yards away from the crowd waiting on Mandy.

I know they over there talking about me she said to herself but they ain't gotta make it so obvious. Everybody seem to be waiting on the accused to show, knowing he would come out the same elevator

Natalie just emerged out of, they seemed to be riled up preparing to either spit or show support.

Natalie glanced over at Mrs. Coleman and gently made eye contact with her heart broken eyes. Natalie wanted to say something like sorry for the loss of your daughter, but Shanice whispered something in her ear to break the eye contact. Whatever Shanice whispered, Natalie was sure had something to do with Mrs. Coleman strolling around the crowd and walking towards her.

"Isn't your name Natalie", she asked kindly, standing over her.

"Yes it is, who wants to know", Natalie looked up at her with slight animosity thinking the lady was about to act nasty 'cause Cleofis was her baby daddy.

"Hello", she stuck her hand out for a shake. "I'm Mrs. Coleman, Shawndra Coleman's mother, nice to meet you."

"Nice to meet you too", Natalie glanced over at the clock high in the ceiling.

"So how are you and your family doing, I heard you and Cleofis have a little boy together."

"Yeah we do and the family's just fine, how bout yours?"

"Oh, were surviving that's about all we can do after the loss of Shawndra."

All of a sudden Natalie felt uncomfortable, was this women going to say something rude to her

"So how are you and Cleofis getting alone, if you don't mind me asking?"

"Were fine, it's not like were together he's just there for his child", Natalie started fidgeting through her purse looking for nothing.

"Well from a mother to a mother how would you feel if somebody killed your daughter?"

How did she even know I had a daughter.....alright about now I wouldn't care what happened to her nasty little ass...yes I would, I'm just very very upset with her.

"I would feel terrible", said Natalie rocking her legs from the discomfort. "But I wouldn't blame those who had nothing to do with it."

"Meaning who Cleofis Jackson", Mrs. Coleman darted her head to the side. "He is to blame for this, I don't care how many people they take to trail, I know he killed my baby and left a motherless granddaughter."

"If he did, than he will be punished", Natalie couldn't understand why she was not admitting what she knew for fact was true. "I know he's not a angel-

"Damn right", Mrs. Coleman cut in, "Not even human if you ask me. What about all them other people he killed like that little white boy Toby, don't that mean anything to you."

"Yes it does and I'm so sorry for your loss, but he still is my sons farther."

"I'm sorry", she touched Natalie's lap. "Your right that is your sons father no matter what, and I'm sorry if I offended you 'cause your not the one I'm upset with."

At that moment Mandy stepped out the elevator. "Ay girl", she shouted. Mrs. Coleman rose to her feet said take care at that point and toed back to where Shanice was leaning against the railing. "Teflon's down stairs girl", Mandy walked past and sat where Mrs. Coleman just rose from. "I got to see this shit", she rubbed her hands together then asked. "What did Shawndra's mother want with you?"

"Nothing important, just asking me how I'm doing and stuff."

"Did she say anything about Teflon or Jackpot?"

"Naw not really, but its something I want to tell you about him and, but you gotta promise you won't say nothing."

"I promise."

"And after I tell you it's a big big favor I want you to do."

"Anything for you."

Cleofis emerged from the stairs and in an instance started to receive a lot of stares. He dropped his head not willing to look at the dirty looks as he strolled into the District Attorneys office. "Could you tell the D-A I'm here", he said to an unattractive mixed secretary with braces. "Hold on one second", she picked up a phone, informed the prosecutor of Cleofis' presence and said. "Just take a seat outside the court room -- he'll speak with you when he comes out."

This made Cleofis frown, why couldn't he pop a seat in the office. Fuck-a just want me to sit out here and deal with the madness. Cleofis took a seat in the far left corner as far away from the crowd as possible. I should leave this bitch and make them search for me. Listening more and more to the loud enough for him to hear threats made him feel extremely uncomfortable and nervously scared.

For the first time Natalie could see the lost little boy in him as she stared at him across the room. To her it looked like he was a misguided young boy who was swallowed by the mouth of the beast. Staring to have sympathy for his pleading for help nervous eyes she was snapped back to the vengeful personality when Mandy spoke.

"That's some fucked up shit, nasty rotten nigga gone put his mouth on Daisa... you know they probably fucked." Mandy gave Cleofis a distasteful evil stare. "All this time I'm thinking he hit you or somethin' and this dog ass nigga done fooled with your daughter. Girl you ain't gotta ask me twice for you, I'll do anything."

Cleofis could see the two eyeing him with evil intentions and made a mental note to watch the two, but whatever they were conjuring up was the least of his problems. He was busy watching his surrounding though it was county officers around he wasn't putting it past somebody to try an take a swing at him. If looks could kill, the look Mrs. Coleman and family was giving him would knock his soul right out his body.

The opening of the elevator doors seemed to send a room temperature breeze through the crowd when they opened. Surrounded by four armed county officers Jackpot stepped from out the elevator with confidence in an orange one piece, chains around wrist, waist, and ankles jumpsuit. Briefly glancing around, he could see his supporters and opposition. Cleofis didn't look him in the eyes. Melissa gave him a crazy look, his supporters was saying silent prayers while waving and the opposition made an earful of threatening remarks.

"Back up out the way", yelled the officers ordering them to clear the double doors to the courtroom. They all backed up and let them enter, then piled into the court room behind them taking up a lot of space on the hard mahogany row seats. Everybody except for Cleofis entered, he was still waiting to speak with the D-A

The D-A walked out of his office wrapping up a conversation with Jackpot's tall Italian lawyer. "Just give me a minute", said the D-A as he departed from the lawyer and came over to speak with Cleofis. The lawyer went inside the courtroom and advised the judge that the D-A would be in shortly. "How you doing Mr. Jackson" Point Dexter took a seat beside him holding a black brief case.

"Living", Cleofis shifted his elbows so they'd rest on his lap. "Do ya'll need me to testify today?"

"Nap, nap Mr. Jackson we thought we did, but it all have to be in August after we go over some recent statements."

"What recent statements?"

"Oh, that's confidential for now but I advise you not to stray too far away." The geek stood, allowing his beige slacks that were flooding to almost meet the top of his dress socks. "We most definitely need your testimony", stroking his hand through his funny colored tie he walked off whistling his small pink lips.

"Well-well-well, if it ain't missing in action", Cleofis sat at the kitchen table of his crack spot across the street from Holly's house. "What did you get abducted by aliens or something, you sure got the right name, Bootleg. 'Cause you most definitely not the real thing."

"Nigga", Bootleg began with a dark pitch. "I been out in the street making moves unlike you, trick master."

"Look at who you with", Cleofis guzzled the last of the Wild Irish Rose that was in his hand and cut his dull brown eyes from the liquor in the direction of Angie. "I know this bitch right here getting somethin' out cha, you always disappearing with her."

"You disappear with her more then any one of us", Bootleg responded, "Besides she's tired of getting her pussy ate."

"Say word" said Sirus, who came in behind his big brother chuckling at the rapid come back.

"I see both of you niggaz some clowns, ya'll should join the fuckin' circus." Cleofis was sloppy drunk and in a fronting mood, not aware of the blood running from his nose."

"Look at his dope fiend ass", Sirus tapped his big brother. "That raw habit got his nose bleeding."

"You bitch ass niggaz", he kept wiping the blood while it ran as if it was nothing to him. "Need to stop being the bitches that you are and go make me some chips."

"Dog you must be referring to someone else 'cause I'm nobody's bitch", Sirus didn't take the word lightly for the joint he was in bread man of respect. On top of that he wasn't one of his workers and he didn't fuck with him like that.

"That nigga just drunk", Bootleg made excuses for the disrespect.

"Naw dog, drunk or sober don't let this coward disrespect you like that."

"The last tough toney who called me a coward is in hell, is that where you wanna be?" the liquor gave him a feeling of invisibility as his eyes flickered in confidence under the dim kitchen light.

"I don't care how many lames you bodied nigga you fuck with me-

"Noc that bullshit off", Bootleg intervened again. "Respect each others gangsta."

"Well you betta holler at yo' tough little brotha fo' I touch 'em up."

"Snitch ass nigga who the fuck you think I am", Sirus stepped in front of the seated villain, in a challenging way towering over him with a ready for whatever look. In a snap of a finger Cleofis drew the hammer from is waist and sat it on his lap. "What'chu think I won't 'deaden' you 'cause you 'b' little brotha?"

"All so you wanna take it there", Sirus smiled sinister like. "You pulling yo' heat on me?"

"Naw bitch", Cleofis stood quick with the hammer to his side and cocked it. "If I raise this boy yo' ass gonna be pushin up daises."

"That's my brotha 'Moe'" said Bootleg stepping directly in Cleofis face filling the space between the two barking dogs.

"Fuck if it is", replied Cleofis. "I'll bury this nigga right nah, gimme my other sword", he reached at Bootlegs waist when he began to block it off but seen that careless look in his dull eyes. "Move the fuck out the way", Cleofis now clutched to hammers at his side breathing steam from his blood stained nostrils.

"I ain't fenna let you pop my lil bro", Bootleg wouldn't budge scared of his friends actions.

"Come on let's leave", Angie stepped to the side of Cleofis. "Mommas gone take you home, you've had a little too much to drink" for some unexplainable reason he listen to her and let her pull him to the door while Bootleg remained in front of Sirus like a shield.

"See you around dead man", Cleofis growled as Angie shut the door behind them.

Sirus was far pumped about the situation he didn't even want to fuck with Cleofis but his brother advised that it would be wise to make a few chips before they did they own thing. Hoping to milk the now $5,000 a night spot off bags out of a couple a thousand before they shook it. Sirus uncontrollably had another plan. Wasn't no man no matter his reputation going to pull a gun on him and don't use it.

Angie didn't know where to take the drunk powdered up fella she'd used one of the hype cars from the spot and was told to return straight back afterwards. "Where do you want me to take you baby, 'cause I gotta get this car back?" She reached over to rub his leg hoping to calm the raging soul.

"I shoulda murk that bitch nigga, mufacka gone call me a snitch, shit I'm a o-g in this shit hear, I was wacking niggaz back in the nineties, these new millennium niggaz think they gangsta." He held both mags on his lap as he blew more steam off not paying any attention to what Angie was saying. "Imma start back wackin' niggaz, on Blackstone, who the fuck they think they dealing with?"

"I know Boo, but I have to get this car back tonight so can you please tell me where you going."

"What happened to us", Cleofis again ignored her request and started on an emotional note. "Look at what the fuck we've become Angie, I used to wanna marry you now you're just like me, a fuckin' fiend." his voice got softer by the second. "Just look at me, I'm surprised I even lived this long….. Fucking D-A got a trick up their sleeves, they think I killed that girl." Tears started slowly dripping. "I loved the shit out of her and I love Natalie."

All the emotional drama was blowing her recent high, Bootleg and Sirus gave her for busing down. But she knew better to offend him because the red wine had him under some sort of trance it was like all his pain was coming out due to the bottle.

"Toby, Muddy..... And what the fuck I kill Muddy for......", he buried his face in his palms and cried deep and heavy, and loud. "Ill probably never make it to heaven... don't know good woman want me... everybody hates me", Seeped through sobs.

What was Angie to do with this emotional gangsta, she wanted to lay him on her lap and pat him but the whole scene made her agitated. All she wanted to do was get back to the spot and hump for some more rock.

Just then his cell phone rang snapping him out of the emotional state. "Who's this?" his words slurred.

"Mandy, what'chu doing?"

"Chilling, what made you call me, I thought you hated me from what I was told."

"No, I don't hate you, I was just a little salty but it's all good. I was just sitting here in the bed tonight thinking about your big tasty dick in my mouth and how I would love to drink you up."

Cleofis didn't hear anything but the last sentence that sounded like a blast to him. His senses were twirping, sensing danger but the two hammers would protect him he though. "Hold that thought I'll be through there." It wasn't nothing like a good head doctor and he knew from experience Mandy was one of the best. "Keep the back door open."

"Alright; but hurry my mouth is watering."

If it was a set up fuck it, thought Cleofis I'mma go out blasting. The state of mind he was in wouldn't allow him to give two shits about danger.

Angie pulled up a couple houses before Mandy's, watched him as he swung the car door open, slung his legs around and sat there with his back to her trying to conceal his weapons. At that point, she saw some cash hanging half way out his back pocket. Fear halted her from trying to pick pocket, but the unawareness he carried gave her the courage to try. "It'll be alright", she tapped the lower part of his back just an inch from the cash. "Gone in'nerr and sleep that monkey off ya back." Within a blink of an eye she gently grabbed it and under, threw it to the back seat when he turned showing half of his face.

"Watch me", he uncontrollably spit saliva. "Watch me as I walk around to the back."

"Ok", Angie nodded, trembling from fear he might have noticed the theft and from the anticipation of another hit. She watched him as he staggered and stumbled his way out of her view.

"Shhhhhhhhh", Mandy whispered with her index finger over her own mouth as she led the loud talking villain to her bedroom. "The kids is asleep", she held his hand so he wouldn't fall, instantly recognizing he was intoxicated made her lure him quicker not wanting to wake the kids.

The Richard Wild Irish Rose made Mandy's fat sloppy frame look very appealing in a thick way to the nearly out of it fella. "Bada Bing", he spoke as she closed her bedroom door behind them and he brandished the two hammers from his waist sides. "CLINK, CLINK" was the sound as he tapped both of the barrels together and fell into a couch chair by her bed. Both weapons rested at the edge of the arm rest clutched tightly in his hands as he stared at her in a silent lustful but madman state.

His penis held a bulge in his Gucci jeans like he'd been taking Viagra. Mandy was sorta scared but quickly shook it off figuring he was just being cautious. Hoping down on all fours she crawled over in between his legs, unzipped his zipper, popped it out and started slowly making him disappear in her mouth. The two guns that were inches from her head didn't bother her as she brandished more saliva while pulling more frequent.

"That's what I'm talking about, suck that dick.....you supposed to be Natalie's friend but you can't keep my dick out yo' mouth, hu bitch, can you."

Mandy looked up at him, with her jumbo shaped eyes, and running wild hair piece. "Just relax big man I know you probably had a stressful day earlier with all that court shit." She downed it and came back up. "We was just there to see what was going on", she downed him again and before she came up he replied. "You, Natalie and the rest of them gossiping bitches is nosy... shhit watch the teeth?" He tightened his grip on his mags, assuming she scaved him on purpose. "You keep taking her in when she runs off and I'mma put you on my list."

"Boy you crazy", she darted back and started jacking him off making precum ooz, then took to it like it was a Carmel on a Sunday. "I bet you like that you big bad ass motherfucka."

"Damn right", he loosened up his grip on the weapons and started to relax more. "This Teflon the untouchable I ain't never been down for a murder", he was feeling himself just as much as he was feeling the outstanding blow job.

Mandy deep throated him again slowly soon as his had hit the back of her throat she could feel a tingle from the warm gushing nut. "Get all of it" he whimpered as his toes curled in his white air force ones. Like a person being shocked to avoid the flat line his body lifted then dropped like it was lifeless after releasing.

"Where you going?", he mumbled though with very little energy, his arms dangling, barely griping the two mags.

"Somebody knocking at the door, I'll be right back."

"Just don't answer it", he was barely able to keep his head from leaning into a slight sleep.

Mandy couldn't make what he said as she left the bed room door cracked and headed to her back door to see who was knocking.

Cleofis was dozing off but his paranoia took a hold of his drowsiness when hearing foot steps approaching the room door his automatics rose to the direction of the door like Denzel off 'Training Day'.

"It's just me", Mandy replied in a deep breath. "Please don't point them thangs at me?"

Cleofis brought the two Rottweillers down to his lap slowly. "Who was at the do'?"

"That was one of my customers -- she just came and got the last of my yack."

"Girl I told you befo' the last time you got raided to quit making moves where you lay yo' head at. You ain't gone learn 'til them people come kick this bitch in again."

"I don't go no where else to hustle, and a bitch gotta do what she gotta do to pay bills", she pulled a wad of cash out her bra and started counting. This made Cleofis set his heaters to the side and check is back pocket. "A mufucka done got me", he checked is fronts then started feeling through out his jeans. Lifting up the chair pillow his hands sunk into the cracks wishing it wasn't true. "If that bitch got me, I'mma kill 'er", referring to Angie.

"You think I could get three an a half fo' these two stacks", Mandy asked politely not wanting to rattle him no more than what he already was.

"Let me use your phone", she gave it to him still waiting on a response. "Hold on Mandy let me make this call, 'cause somebody fenna get hurt.....hello, this 'T' come get me, I'm on the Southside on the corner of Eleventh and Main." Mandy could hear some women responding kinda teed off, before Cleofis spoke again. "I ain't got time to hear that shit right now weigh up ninety eight and bring ya ass, 'cause I got some heads to go bus."

Holly pulled up on the corner of Eleventh and Main, gave Cleofis the three and a half ounces and waited as he jogged back to Mandy's to make the transaction.

"What's going on 'bay' who you mad at", asked Holly as he returned seeming like he appeared out the darkness pulling the handle of her car door.

"I don't know who the fuck got me, but I gotta couple ideas", he closed the car door, motioned for her to pull off then started counting the damp from breast sweat money Mandy gave him. "Damn this bitch could have least let this shit sit out to dry or something."

"Don't be having me bring shit to them bitches you be fuckin", Holly snapped. "Cause I know you Cleofis-

"Quit cho' fuckin' yapin", he cut in with viciousness. "I wouldn't fuck that big bitch if she was the last bitch on Earth."

"Oh.....I thought you said she was the police."

"Naaaaaaa I just made it up 'cause she was always being too nosy."

The next morning Cleofis sat in sort of a daze at Holly's kitchen table with his back to her steel chair, he rubbed his forehead continuously from hangover and his stomach was in his back.

Holly was fixing some sunny side up eggs to go with the waffles that just had jumped out the toaster. He never had to ask Holly to prepare breakfast when he stayed over, she knew the way to a man's heart was through his stomach as well as his dick. So when she would cook breakfast she always made sure it was the bomb like what she felt was between her legs.

"Here you go bay", Holly sat his plate in front of him then proceeded to go fetch some orange juice. The sudden look on his face concerned her. The look on Cleofis' face was like he was in another world or something. Slob drooled from the side of his mouth and snot ran from his nose. "Cleofis you ok", she asked but he gave no response it was like he was in la-la land, completely gone from this Earth.

Holly could look into his distressed, coked up, paranoid eyes and tell he couldn't even see her standing in front of him. "See", she began loud and ignorant. "Yo ass out there getting high off yo' own supply", as she poured his glass of orange juice in front of him she could see he was mumbling something. She tried reading his lips for a second before spinning back to the refrigerator to put the orange juice up.

Walking past him to go entertain herself in front of the living room tube, it dawned on her. SHAWNDRA! "So you miss yo' girl huh?" Holly lit a short of a cigarette, kicked her right foot up on her end table and crossed over it with her left one. "I hope you covered yo' tracks good Mister, 'cause Mrs. Coleman not letting that rest till they have you too."

Just as quick as he drifted was just as quick as he clicked back in. "Damn bay you sure fix this fast", he spoke as if she never said anything, like he was unaware of the sudden pause.

"Boy you a walking time bomb", Holly shook her head giggling while blowing the smoke out her nostrils.

"Where the fuck did that come from?" One side of his face twisted. "See that's the reason why we can't ever have a good time 'cause of your mouth, always thinking the worst of me."

"Noll you got it backwards you must think the worse of yourself, why you over there day dreaming about Shawndra with your face runnin' like a fiend."

"Fuck you Holly, I'm more of a man then any of them clowns you used to fuck wit."

"Hmph", she started with a nigga I know you ain't claiming such a title look. "You more of a man then LL Cool J as long as you pay these bills."

"You know what", he scooted his chair back. "I'mma go an' leave fo' I beat the soul outta you", he spit his mouth full of food out his mouth. "Nasty ass food, taste like yo' nasty ass pussy."

"Mus' ain't that nasty, tiny little man", Holly replied as he headed for the front door. "Your tongue bigger then yo' dick…run over there to yo' baby mommas house and tell her my daughter needs new Jordan's."

"Whatever hoe, at least her pussy don't stank", he slammed the door before letting her respond.

"I was searchin fo' yo' ass all last night", Sirus spoke with uncontrollable anger. "Pussy motherfucka upped burner on me last night."

"Who?" asked Puncho, rolling a white owl full of purple haze on Shanice's front two steps outside her house.

"Rat ass Cleofis, I'm telling you I'mma blow his shit back on sight."

Puncho grinned a boss type grin, then brushed cigar tobacco off his Louie V shorts. "If I let you have the forty you betta make sure you lay 'em down permanently." Sirus agreed to the terms he already concocted himself as Puncho yelled for Shanice through the screen door. "Yo brotha ain't fuckin' with dude no mo or somethin'?" Puncho asked firing up the tip of the blunt.

"Fuck Bootleg this coward be letting dude treat his ass."

"Boy if you wasn't my dog from way back I'd think you was the enemy", Puncho replied as he grabbed a forty cal. out of Shanice's hand through the screen she opened behind him. "Make show you lay 'em down", the 40 cal passed from one hand to another.

"Who you about to go to prison for?", Shaince asked sarcastically.

"Mind yo' business woman, but if you must know he fenna go lay down Teflon", said Puncho.

"For real", she replied vengefully surprised with malice in her eyes. "In that case you should give him the chopper baby, that way he won't miss."

"That won't be needed", said Sirus. "This'll do the job just fine", he concealed the weapon under the front of his shirt tucked into a belt.

"Wanna hit this green?"

"Naw I'm good, thanks fo' lookin out thow…Cleofis a be on the front page by the morning that's my word."

Bump! Bump! Bump! Bump! Bump! Bump!

"Go away Cleofis", shouted Holly. "Go where the pussies don't stank." Holly was stretched out on her sofa watching next Friday, not wanting to be bothered with Cleofis after their harsh argument. "Get, away from my door", she yelled after hearing a second knock. She smiled to herself excitedly knowing she locked the top lock so there was no way he could get in.

BUMP! BUMP1 BUMP! BUMP!, the knocks got louder. She flung off her couch in full pursuit to curse his ass out. "Go to your baby momma's house", she screamed, slinging the front door curtain to the side.

"It's the FBI open the door maam", one bullet proof vest agent's shouted.

Holly was totally caught off guard, if only she would have kept her mouth shut they wouldn't have known somebody was home. "Yes", she opened the door with a visible attitude but only enough for herself to be seen.

"FBI maam", one out of the three agents flashed a badge. "Were looking for Cleofis Jackson and our sources tell us it's a big possibility he's here so if we could just search the house-

"Not without a search warrant", she crossed her arms defensively.

"Now look Mrs.", said a familiar face walking up from shutting her fence. "We can do this the easy way or the hard way." It was Det. Diamond gladly assisting the FBI, she knew him just from his dedication to solving some of Kankakee's vicious murders.

"If you want to know where he is, just ask, don't start making threats."

"Well where is he?", asked Diamond.

"Not here", a smirk struck her face. "Around this time of the day he's usually at Natalie's, you'll should know that by now."

"Well we've been there already", said a white balled clean cut husky agent.

"Well like I said he's not here, but if you'll watch his baby mommas spot then he'll show up 'cause he probably want be back here today."

"Well thank you", Diamond replied. "I hope your telling the truth."

Cleofis leaned up against Natalie's two car garage, finishing off the last of some snow out a sandwich bag. After licking every corner of the bag he brushed the bottom half of his face off and strolled quickly up Natalie's walk way. He knew her and Dasia was home from their two vehicles parked outside. "Where yo' momma at, up stairs", he asked walking pass the living room where Dasia was sitting on the love seat.

"Yep", she said never looking his way. Knowing better to not pay him any attention when her mother was there.

"Why you not at work?", asked Cleofis, stepping through the bedroom door.

Natalie quickly gave him none of your business look then returned to watching Waiting to Exhale on her DVD. Lying in the bed on her stomach and sitting up on her forearms she clapped with excitement. "That's right burn his shit girl, burn it", she was enjoying the 'Angela Bassett burning her husband's stuff' scene.

Cleofis sucked his teeth pulled out one of his two hammers and laid it on her dresser. "Why you watching this shit, when you done seen it fifty million times?" Cleofis expressed, taking a seat at the top of the bed, tapping her on the ass.

"Don't touch me", she turned back at him with an evil look on her face.

"Damn, my bad. I guess I ain't the right nigga", he rose and headed for the bedroom door.

"Naw, you just got the wrong Knowles" she made sure she stated clear enough before he walked back down to the first story.

Sirus had just cut through a field and was beginning to cross an alley approaching the back of Natalie's garage. He barely got any sleep the night before thinking about murdering Cleofis so much kept him awake.

Patting the 40 through his shirt he reenacted last nights scene over and over in his head. Then he reenacted what he was going to do to Cleofis. Slowing up directly behind Natalie's garage he came to a halt, leaned his back up against the wood and lit up a square to calm his recklessness. I should just knock on the door, ask for him and blow his shit off right there.

Cleofis' mind was flicking like a child playing with a view master and he was moving around quickly throughout the house looking for some sandwich bags. "Have you seen my sandwich bags?"

"No, not lately", Dasia looked at him for the first time since he'd been there. "But, can you give me some money so I can put some gas in my car 'cause I'm tired of sitting in this house."

"Girl you better get out and walk on this nice summer day."

"Please, it'd be a cold day in hell befow Dasia Knowles walks when she got a car."

"You must don't wanna get out that bad", he flicked an opening through the blinds covering the window of the front door unconsciously. "SHHHIT", he yelled watching two unmarked cars pull up with feds hoping out. "Natalie!" he shouted upstairs. "The Feds here." Cleofis tossed his other hammer to Dasia, told her to put it in her purse and zoomed out the side door.

Sirus could hear some one running towards his direction. He flung the cigarette bud, reached for the 40 and peeked from around the garage. It was Cleofis running towards his direction not even looking in front of him. Sirus wielded the automatic so swift, stepped from around the garage quick and leveled it. When Cleofis saw who was standing in his path it didn't make any sense at first, then it came to him, that's when he knew it was all over. "Thought you was gone pull a pistol on me and get away with it", said Sirus with the look of death in his eyes. "FLACOW! FLACOW!"

The two shots seemed like they ended Cleofis' life as he halted with a victimized look in his eyes. Seeing Sirus' body drop in front of him made him a little confused. "Put your hands up Cleofis", ordered Diamond who instantly appeared. Fully focused on Cleofis, Diamond waited until the Feds cuffed him before checking the pulse of Sirus who he'd just shot twice. "The ambulance is on its way", said Diamond as he kicked Sirus' gun further away from his hand. "Try not to move."

About time the ambulance arrived everybody and they momma was outside. They all watched from a watching distance as they threw Sirus' body on a stretcher and into the ambulance.

Det. Diamond walked over to the unmarked car with Cleofis in the back seat. The Feds rolled down the back window so he could speak. "Luckily I came to your rescue or else that young man back there would of put you in a coffin."

"Betta that than what these feds probably pick me up for", Cleofis tried to sound as tough as possible.

"Anyway what's the charge?"

"Drug trafficking."

"Drug trafficking" his eyebrows rose. "Get the fuck outta here."

"I'm not playing", replied Diamond. "Take a look at your son", Diamond directed Cleofis' attention to Mrs. Jackson exciting her vehicle with little man in her arms. "The next time your free, he'll be your age", he smirked very proud that Cleofis would be long gone off the streets.

"I'll give you anybody you want", said Cleofis feeling like his heart was ripped out his chest when seeing his mother and son. "You know anybody uh fuck with me, I'm telling you I could get ya'll so many people they'll give you a reward when I get through."

Diamond laughed and shook his head. "Don't you get it, you're the reward", he then gave the agent a high five that was in the front seat and turned his back on the hopeless face gangsta.

CHAPTER 25

Revenge Is A Dish Best Served Cold

Natalie gawked over how beautiful she looked, gazing into a hand mirror at Fresh Fades and Hair Do's. George had just finished her hair and she sat proudly in a customer chair feeling like all eyes were on her in the shop. "What I owe you George?"

"Nuttin girl, you know better then to ask me that."

"Well I was just checking 'cause I know it's been awhile since we spoke."

"Aw girl its still love", he gave her a fast hug. "How you been holding up?"

"I'm just fine, getting alone very well without that maniac in my life", she was on her feet and grabbing for her purse that her ringing cell phone was in. "Call me later", she said to George as she headed for the shops entrance. "Who the fuck is this calling me private?"

"It's me, I had somebody call you on three way."

"What do you want?"

"What do you mean what do I want?", it had been a week since the Feds picked him up in the back of her house and ever since then he'd been calling the house phone but she never accepted. "Why haven't you been accepting my calls?"

"I don't understand what purpose you would have to call my house why don't you call Holly?"

"Look 'bay' I don't got time fo' the shit I'm down here hurting, I need some cheddar and I need you to tell these people I need to see a doctor."

"Poor baby maybe if Dasia would of picked up the phone it would have been possible."

"Don't make me reach through this phone and choke the shit outta you!"

"Wow! I'm so scared, I'm trembling right now. What do you want you child-molesting faggot, snitch ass dope fiend?"

"Why you calling me all them names?"

"Cause that's what you are and I advise if you don't want who ever on the phone to hear your business then shut the hell up."

"Well if you feeling these things I suppose I can't change your mind, but your girl foul then a muthafucka."

"Who?"

"Mandy, the bitch set me up with the Feds, what I need you to do is go over there and talk to her."

"Cleofis", Natalie spoke with unconcern-ness in her tone. "I told her to set your rotten ass up, and she did it as a favor for me after I seen you and Dasia enjoying yourselves. I hope you didn't think I would let you get away with that did you?" Natalie waited for a response but got none so she continued. "All that rotten shit finally done caught up with your rotten ass, and I was the one who saw to it."

"You one evil bitch", he managed to utter.

"No, I just made sure justice was served. You did sell her three and a half ounces, Cleofis Jackson or is it Teflon? You'll find yo'self a nice girlfriend in there, nice life Bitch!"

Natalie ended the call as she hopped into the passenger-side of her BMW truck driven by Mandy. She felt cleansed, brand new and ready for another chapter in her life. "That was Cleofis girl!"

"For real, what he say?"

"Mandy set me up", Natalie impersonated his recent heard voice. "I said no kidding I'm the one who came up with the idea, and gave the ok. If only you could have heard the silence on the phone girl, the faggot probably in his cell crying his heart out", she started laughing uncontrollably for the certainty of revenge electrified her like a new experience. This got to be the next best thing to an orgasm she reflected.

"So where we off to?", asked Mandy.

"Home, so I can get dressed and go find me a man."

THE GAME IS CHESSNOT CHECKERS!

MASTERMIND

A ROBERT RICKS URBAN TALE

MASTERMIND

By Robert Ricks

SNEAK PREVIEW!

CHAPTER 1

The Promise

AKA

Mr. Kittles pulled into the freshly paved parking lot of the Saints and Sinners Baptist Church, turned off the air, rolled down the windows, and sat for a moment, savoring the smell of the new black top. He loved the strong pungent aroma and how it glistened when the sun hit it. Sort of like him, he thought as he grabbed the briefcase from the back seat and pulled his 5′11 frame from the red Lexus.

His new black Timbs made a crackling sound as he trudged his way to the church door and punched in the last four digits of his social. He took the stairs two at a time until he reached the third floor, then punched 1987 into the second pad.

That was a date that not even old timers disease would allow him to forget.

By the time the green light flashed, the lock clicked, and he entered, the transformation was complete. He was no longer Mr. Kittles, nor little Clarence Kittles, A+ student. He was no longer a barber, a boyfriend, nor a brother, but the equivalent of all the above marinated in pain: He was Clear.

He walked through the door and made his way around the oblong redwood table, greeting his captains one by one. He sat, opened his briefcase, pulled out four manila envelopes and passed them to his right.

The soft white light illuminated his Tootsie Roll colored skin, as he scanned faces looking for signs of confusion. Although he knew nothing about stocks, bonds and Dow Jones reports, what he did know was that nine ounces of cocaine, thirty thousand dollars in cash, and twelve years had made him very wealthy. Oh, he thought, let's not forget about the well-educated white broad and the street-wise fat kid. Clear followed the Henry Ford philosophy. He didn't need to know everything he just needed to surround himself with people who did.

Black, South-Side captain, pushed the papers forward a bit, and sunk into his chair.

Marwon, East-Side captain, stuck up a finger indicating he needed another minute and continued reading.

Daemon, West-Side captain, looked at Clear, smiled and said comically, "We some rich motherfuckers. We white folks rich."

Big Mack, the fat kid, North-Side captain, second in command, sat expressionless, saying nothing… Doing nothing.

"Any questions?," Clear asked. Silence confirmed comprehension.

"Okay, gentlemen, if you would pass all that incriminating shit forward, I'll retain a copy which you are free to examine at any time." Then with a slight smirk, he asked, "What in the hell is white folks rich, Daemon?"

Daemon looked up from the paper and smiled, which made him look much younger than his twenty-six years. He was the newest member of the organization, but he had served faithfully for nearly eight years. He was only eighteen when Clear and Mr. Roebuck magically turned manslaughter into self-defense, and twenty-five to life into five years probation.

"Well let me tell you," Daemon responded. "See, 'cause I'm an authority on white folks. I study their greedy asses. I believe they wipe their butts from side to side to preserve toilet paper, but that's an ongoing study. Now there's three kinds a rich; white folks rich, black folks rich, and nigga rich: white folks rich is when you got so much damn money you got to build little tax shelters to hide the shit. Black folks rich is when you got a house next to the white folks with the money. And nigga rich is when the bill collectors ain't on your ass, you got a stash under your mattress, two blunts on the dresser, and a half a bag of party wings deep frying in Crisco."

"Nigga, you crazy," Black said between chuckles.

"Excuse me? I'm eccentric. Poor folks go crazy," Daemon elaborated.

As the balance of the envelopes came forward, Clear sat staring at his Rolex, waiting for the second hand to make its way around for the second time. Calming himself as he looked across the table at Mack, he attempted to crawl into his head, looking for the screw that was loose or the bulb that was blown, because Mack was his man, and he would rather repair him than junk him.

"What's up wit' you, Mack?", he asked, trying to establish boundaries where once no boundaries existed.

"What you mean, what's up with me?", Mack responded.

"You okay?"

"Yeah. I'm straight", Mack said, tilting his head a little and adjusting his fitted baseball cap.

"Then why are you selling dope out of the hotel, man?"

Mack looked around the room and exhaled loudly as if the question aggravated him.

"Because I'm their man. Thousands float in and out of that hotel, and I decided it looked better in our pockets."

"You decided! You fucking decided..."

Clear paused, leaned back, once again composing himself, and nodded his head.

"So you doing your own thang now. Kinda liberating yourself from the mundane activities of this organization," he said.

Duplicating Clear's actions, Mack leaned his chair back.

"Naw, it ain't like that. I figure I can make some decisions to keep shit moving, too."

"But you can't," Clear said, leaning forward, throwing diplomacy to the wind.

"Why fuckin' can't I?"

Clear stood up, placed his hands on the table and pressed forward. "This organization didn't change when you went to the penitentiary for that bullshit, Mack. We're like the Borg and once you're assimilated, the collective needs to know everything you think! In fact, everything you think you thought. Therefore, from this point forward, you can disregard any thoughts you might have concerning day-to-day operations. I disseminate information around this bitch. I am the collective."

The heat from Clear's words obviously burned Mack's ego. Clear could see the fire in his eyes as nouns, verbs, and adverbs danced in his head, authorizing a response that could possibly get him killed.

This nigga didn't know nothing about hustling. He was one of them burger flippin', French fry shakin' motherfuckers. I should have just jacked his ass way back then. That's what Mack probably thought. And he was probably on the verge of giving voice to his thoughts when Clear noticed Marwon's and Daemon's hands simultaneously sliding underneath the table. Mack had obviously noticed too.

"You. . .you right, man," Mack said. "I…I just feel a little pressured Clear, feeling like I'm not holding my weight. I been home damn near six months man and every time I look up, y'all lacin' my pockets and shit."

Clear sat back down, licking his lips to conceal the smile forming on his face. He knew Mack well, thirteen years well, and he was fully aware that he was being served some heart warming, melodramatic, bullshit. So he called him to the carpet.

"Don't give me that shit, Mack. You doing exactly what you wanna' do. The same shit you were doing before you went to jail, parlaying and chasing ass. But you're fucking with the illusion, and when the illusion is gone, we're nothing but common street thugs throwing bricks at the penitentiary."

Mack bobbed his head up and down, as if he was in perfect agreement with what Clear was saying. Clear glanced over at Marwon, Daemon, and Black, whose eyes were veering neither left nor right, and defying the principles of blinking.

Clear got up, walked around the table and placed his hands on Daemon and Marwon's' shoulders.

"I'm not about to do a day in jail behind your bullshit, Mack. And if you never sell another bag of dope, or make another financial contribution, your presence will always be felt in this organization. But remember… this shit is until death do us part… and please don't make me do us part."

Clear proceeded around the table, collected the envelopes, and embraced his Captains once more. But the warmth that once confirmed him and Mack's camaraderie was now gone. And in that instant, Clear knew, and he walked out attempting to embrace the inevitable.

Preview

He didn't stop to talk to Pastor Williams, he walked straight out of the church, hopped in his car, got on the expressway and headed for the highway.

The windows went up, the air came on and the seats in the 1998 Lexus coupe went back. Pac blasted through the Boeing speakers, cruise control initiated and the speedometer read minus 120 miles per hour, the odometer was going backwards. Backwards into endless streams of yesterdays, back to a time where memories were buried deep inside of harsh realities that weren't really real.

The night he crawled into the dumpster behind McDonalds looking for food to feed his little brother and sister wasn't real.

The standing in the lines at the Open Door Mission, silently praying that they didn't run out of stale bread and almost spoiled hot dogs wasn't real.

The garbage bag of day old donuts resting against the wall at the House of Mercy wasn't real. And the sparkle that appeared in Dayja's eyes when the kind lady gave her two donuts just for being four and a half, wasn't real.

The diaper rash that was still discernable even after Dayja entered Miss Nash's first grade class wasn't real.

The head lice and ringworm that left bald spots in Brandon's head weren't real.

The degenerates and derelicts and prostitutes who were way past their prime weren't real, they only appeared real when they burrowed themselves in the living room. Smoking, drinking, and geekin' as if their house was a clubhouse for society's rejects.

His little brother's blood splattered all over the family-size boxes of Tylenol and Advil wasn't real. But... it all seemed real then.

The only thing that was real was The Promise. . . Oh, and of course, the psychological disfiguration that comes from living a nightmare.

CHAPTER 2

A Clear Sunday

"You here because your Mama on welfare and you can't afford a hair cut?". Toby said to Wakim.

"I can afford to kick your ass. The only reason you talking smack is because I'm in this chair," Wakim responded.

Clear shouted from the back room. "Wakim! What I told you about cursin' in my shop?"

"I'm sorry, Mr. Clear, but Toby said I was on welfare."

Clear walked out from the back and onto the barber floor.

"Why you here, Toby?", he asked walking over to his station to retrieve his car keys from the drawer.

Toby cocked his head to the side and announced without any apprehension, "Because my Mama said if you crazy enough to cut hair for free then she smart enough to send me down here."

"Is that so?", Clear said.

Black laughed as he continued to cut Wakim's head.

Clear dropped the keys back into the drawer then turned and patted his chair. "C'mon, Toby," he said.

"You not my barber, Black my barber."

"I'm gonna be your barber today," Clear responded.

Toby got up and climbed into his chair. Clear took the edgers, shaved one side of Toby's Afro off then handed him the mirror.

"You like that?", Clear asked. " I call it the crazy man cut." He tried hard not to laugh.

"Mr. Clear, you not gon' leave my hair like this, are you? My Mama gonna spaz-out on you."

"Tell your Mama the crazy man did it, and if she got eight dollars, he smart enough to fix it."

"Come on, Mr. Clear, it's Sunday. I'm gonna have to go to school like this tomorrow."

Clear handed him one of the many baseball caps that hung on the coat rack in the corner. Toby looked up at him, climbed out the chair, walked to the door then shouted "Fuck you," and ran out.

Clear and Black laughed but Wakim wasn't amused at all.

He turned to Clear and said, "I'll catch him and beat his ass if you want me to, Mr. Clear."

"That's okay, Wakim. Life is gonna beat his ass."

He hung his barber jacket on the coat rack, retrieved his keys, shaped up Wakim and headed home.

Clear hated cutting hair on Sundays. The getting up and getting there was one of the problems. But once he was there and all the little boys said, "Good morning Mr. Clear," and all of their tired, over-taxed Mamas looked at him as if he were the best thing since peanut butter and reduced daycare, that made the mornings worthwhile. Sure some of their parents had the eight dollars to pay for their kids' haircuts, but most of them didn't. And for Clear those were the ones that really mattered.

Clear pulled into the driveway, turned off the car and sat for moment. He moved his head from side to side trying to work out the kinks in his neck as he turned to retrieve the flowers from the back seat. He often bought Porsha flowers, just as a small token of his appreciation. She cooked, cleaned, washed, smiled, laughed, scratched his head, massaged his shoulders, and spent his money. Ain't no cheat in a fair trade, he thought, smiling as he stuck the key in the door.

"Hey, Boo," Porsha said while she ran down the stairs.

"Hey, Baby," Clear responded.

"Are those for me?." she asked.

"Oh, shit," Clear responded and stuck the flowers behind his back. "Naw, they for our new neighbor, a housewarming gift."

"Oh," Porsha said cheerfully. She walked up to him with her lips puckered and arms extended. She pressed her lips to his and put her arm around his waist. Then she snatched the flowers from behind his back.

"Bitch won't get these, you're not tracking hair on her carpet," she said, and turned and went in search of a vase.

"What's for dinner?", Clear asked, following her into the kitchen.

"I don't know, go and ask the bleached blonde next door."

"You know her number?", he asked, teasing.

"Keep it up, Clear, and you'll be wearing these flowers and this vase."

Clear laughed and put his arms around her waist as she leaned over the sink to fill the vase.

"How was your day, baby?", he asked as he pulled her to him and kissed the nape of her neck.

"It was good, until the cable went off and I was stuck with four channels. Football, football, golf, and an infomercial about zits or wrinkles, some kind of face stuff."

"Did you call the cable people?", Clear asked as he walked over to the stove and lifted the top on the stewed pork chops.

"Time Warner's people don't work on Sundays. Nobody works on Sundays except you, and all the little Clear wannabes at the barbershop", Porsha smiled, then took Clear's hand and led him into the dining room.

"Why you dissin' my boys, Porsha?", Clear asked, pulling out a chair from the table.

"I'm not dissin' em," she said with a smirk. "If I was a man I would follow your crooked ass too."

Porsha went into the kitchen and pulled two plates from the cabinet. She piled the mushroom and onion gravy on top of the Uncle Ben's rice, and laid two stewed pork chops neatly beside the diced green beans that she had seasoned with beef bouillon, just the way her man liked them. She placed two medium sized slices of Jiffy corn bread in a saucer, because Clear didn't like his corn bread soggy. One small scoop of rice, one pork chop and a thin slice of corn bread was all she had, because her figure was bangin' and she intended to keep it that way.

Porsha stood at the refrigerator all of two minutes, tortured by the choice between pink lemonade and diet Pepsi. Pink lemonade won and she retrieved another glass from the cabinet and filled it with her weakness.

She sat across the table from Clear, silently praying over their food.

Clear didn't start eating until she was finished, but he didn't indulge in the prayer ritual.

"Some lady called. I wrote her name on the pad by the phone. She said she turned in the plane ticket and was taking the bus, and she told me to tell you that if God intended for her to fly, he would've made her an angel."

"If God intended for her to travel he would have gave her some damn money," Clear responded.

"Some things are more important than money, Clear," Porsha said, setting him up.

"Like what, Porsha?"

"Love, family, eternal life."

Clear looked at her and shook his head. "You definitely need to get out more. Love is a feeling. You can't eat it, sleep in it, nor drive it. And if I'm broke, show me you love me by giving me some money. And eternal life? The jury's still out on that shit. If I'm gonna pay ten percent of my gross earnings for my whole life to secure a place when I'm dead, I need to see that shit in writing."

"It is in writing, read your Bible," Porsha responded.

"Which Bible? From which religion, or which translation from which religion?", Clear asked, sounding a bit more abrasive than he probably had intended.

"We're awful hostile today," Porsha responded.

"I'm not hostile, Porsha, I'm real. Religion in the black community has become an excuse to sit around and wait for something to happen. Instead of getting off your ass and making something happen. You ride through the ghetto and the only thing you see black-owned is the Churches. Not the houses we live in, the businesses we slave at, not even the cars we drive. You would think, that if we can take ten percent of our salary and invest it in the hereafter, that we probably could take another ten percent and invest it in the right fucking now."

"I'm not even going there with you, Clear," Porsha said as she got up and walked into the kitchen to get the hot sauce.

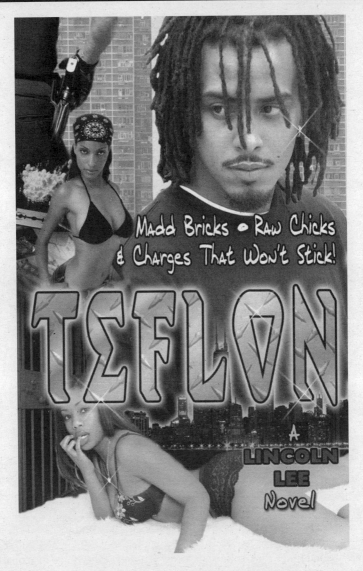

"TEFLON" DESCRIPTION

Cleofis Jackson a.k.a. **"Teflon the Untouchable"** is a young hood-rich hustler that the FED's have not been able to make murder-charges stick.

Having been trained by one of the best, **Bruno** (his cousin), the #1 Kingpin in Chicago destined for the 'Hood Hall Of Fame', Teflon desires to achieve everything Bruno has! Blood is normally thicker than water. But when Teflon finds out that his main-girl and first-love (Kim) is about to become Bruno's baby-mama, it's about to be on!

Teflon is ruthless and murder is his calling-card -- but it doesn't detour a steady stream of raw ghetto-girls all dying to become his ride-or-die chick.

Natalie is a thick 5'3", gap-toothed, big-booty part-time correctional officer that has a thing for thugs and does many favors for Teflon. **Holly** is a grimey gangsta-chick that's all about the dollar, but doesn't like competition for Teflon's attention and ain't never scared to hand-out a beat-down. **Shawndra**, 10-years older than Teflon, works for Bruno as a 'mule', while simultaneously getting dangerously close to Teflon when she begins visiting him during a short-stint in jail. **Kim**, though a chicken-head, is the only women that Teflon has a weakness for, having known her since they were 15-years old.

When Teflon forms his own crew, 'The Capone Gang', and sets out to control the street, his crew's loyalty and honor gets tested. Everyone knows that if you fail Teflon's test, you'll never see tomorrow's daylight.

Gabe is Teflon's protégé and one of his boyz from the block that he's now puttin'-up on game, just as Bruno had done for him. Everything between them is all good, that is, until Gabe starts making his own moves, calling his own shots and begins gaining power.

When Teflon makes the cardinal mistake of starting to use some of his own product – he begins to become paranoid -- about everyone and everything!

Adding gas to an already red-hot fire, a long-kept secret of Teflon's is found-out! Teflon is then threatened, which is the last thing that anyone should do!

Feeling like his hand is forced, Teflon resorts to planning a set-up and murders. But his new drug-habit is scratching and denting the hell-out of his normally sound and rock-solid judgment – putting everything in jeopardy, including his freedom and his life! – Proving it's possible for anything to be penetrated – even Teflon!

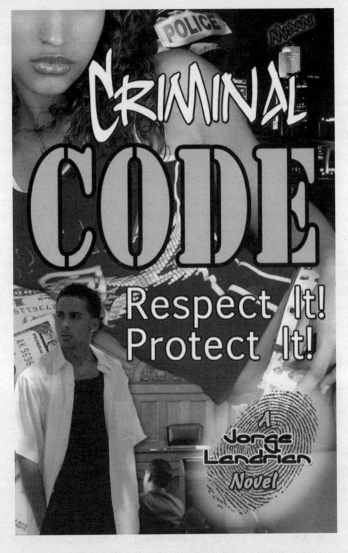

"CRIMINAL CODE" DESCRIPTION

Jorge Gomez, a Miami-bred black-Cuban hustler believes in living by the 'Code' and dying by the 'Code'. After serving a 5-year bid on drug-possession charges, refusing the Fed's offers for him to become a snitch, Gomez gains an early release due to the recommendations of a corrupted Correctional Officer that he'd done favors for while in jail.

Though Gomez' is true to his code of loyalty to his friends and family, he returns to find that Doris, his wife and baby-mama to his two kids hasn't been faithful to the code.

After his release, Gomez decides to relocate, setting his sights on virgin drug territory. He meets **Mark Goodman**, a drug dealer himself, who helps Gomez get back into the only game he's ever known. But when the script gets flipped and it's Goodman needing Gomez, a double-cross creates a deadly situation between the two.

Donna Schultz a.k.a **'Iceburg'** is a real down-a** chick that falls for Gomez, but her wealthy father (Bruce) wants her to have nothing to do with a hood-gangsta.

Bruce Schultz (Donna's dad), a Cadillac dealership owner who long-ago turned his own dirty-money into a respectable business is dead-set on making sure that his daughter will not be put in jeopardy by Gomez' lifestyle and is willing to do anything to ensure it --- even murder! Having many connections, he enlists the help of Federal Agents and Local Police to try take out Gomez – permanently!

Kiki, a life-long friend of Gomez from Miami, is nicknamed **'The Friendly Ghost'** because of his ability to get into cars, houses and pockets undetected. A true believer of the code, Kiki's always down for whatever – whenever.

Sexy **Sandra Perez** is a law-school student and in debt to one of Gomez' boyz (Jimmy). She's forced to work as a phone-sex operator for Jimmy as a way to repay her debt of school tuition. Gomez has a soft-spot in his heart for Sandra and buys her freedom from Jimmy. Later, when a botched-hit attempt on Gomez' life fails, Sandra lives up to the code, as she's now an Assistant District Attorney with crucial information on witness identity that she supplies to Gomez.

Gomez has vowed to never see the inside of a jail again! When he learns of a former drug-associate who's considering becoming an snitch for the Feds, putting in danger everything he's achieved, it's time to live by the code, die by the code or kill by the code!

"MASTERMIND" DESCRIPTION

Clarence Kittles a.k.a. **'Clear'** is the mastermind behind his New York crime-crew, The Black Mob. But, he's more than just street-smart. Clear knows exactly how to organize and keep his biz on the down-low, disguising his true identity through a legitimate business, a barbershop.

Growing up in poverty, he vows never to go back to that life again. Anyone trying to hook-up with him better understand one thing -- Clear is a stickler for rules! Understanding that most hustlers get caught by not following them, he has no patience for rule-breakers and quickly turns into the most ruthless man when dealing-out punishment. On the flipside, most people in the community have come to know Clear as the *'Ghetto Robinhood'*, an up-standing businessman who gives away free haircuts to kids of women on welfare and donates money to churches.

Magic Jr. is a smart-youngster who basically grew-up without a father just like Clear. When they meet, Clear can't help but think about how much Magic Jr. reminds him of his deceased brother, Brandon. He begins to treat Magic Jr. like a younger brother, even hooking him up with his sister (Dayja) while schooling him on the game.

Dayja is Clear's little hot-mama sister that he's trying to wrestle free from the grips of the Child Protective Services system that he'd originally had her placed into because of her wild ho-like behavior. She's also the main reason that he works so hard at the game, so that he can provide her with anything that she wants.

Magic Sr., was a drug-addict during Magic Jr.'s early childhood. It wasn't until Magic Jr.'s teen-years that he even knew the man that he was named after. Having endured the bad-side of the game, Magic Sr. cleans himself up and decides to now profit from the very same game that had him strung-out by becoming a dealer. When he chooses to set-up his operation on drug-turf that belongs to Clear, that action could lead to a deadly conflict.

Big Mac is the co-founder of The Black Mob and Clear's boy from way back. But, just because he was there at the beginning doesn't mean that he's immune from the rules that he helped to create – Clear ain't having it!

Porsha is Clear's ride-or-die chick that is like a mother to Dayja. She is no stranger to thugs and the drug-game. She says that she's down for whatever and will do anything for Clear, but has never been tested.

Candy is a booty-shakin' stripper turned conniving strip-club owner. Despite her name, there ain't nothin' sweet about her, as her only goal is to take care of #1 – herself! And she's so grimey, that she'll do it in anyway possible.

As Clear becomes frustrated by some of his crew's lack of discipline that can threaten his freedom, he begins to systematically reduce the size of The Black Mob, one-by-one. He knows that even though he's got cops on his payroll -- that may not be enough to overcome careless mistakes.

At times, Clear feels like he's the only one who truly understands that 'The Game' is chess, not checkers!

"LEGIT BALLER" DESCRIPTION

Jay Bernard has been dedicated to his craft as a baler. That is, until his deeds land him a 14-year bid in the Federal Pen on drug-charges.

Kim, Jay's supposed 'Bonnie' to his 'Clyde' wastes no time in cutting ties after his sentencing by moving her game to the new Baller-Kint (Paris).

During Jay's incarceration, sexy Summer Foster, proves to be a better friend than anyone who'd benefited from Jay's life-style. Though from the same hood, Summer has managed to rise-up, earning a college degree and currently an M.B.A. student at Harvard.

After his early-release, Jay finds it hard to avoid the only life he knows, even with the love and encouragement from an old-friend (Summer) for him to go 'Legit' – Old habits, just seem to die hard!

The complete opposite of Jay's gangsta, Summer views him as much more than just hard-rock – but a true diamond-gem! However, Jay's past and the streets keep calling him.

Paris views himself as a street-rival of Jay's even before his stint in prison, and now feels threatened that Jay may want to re-claim everything back – his drug territory and his woman (Kim)!

When the inevitable confrontation arises between Jay and Paris, the next move could be the last!

"Gritty Urban Realism At Its Best! ... Legit Baller Is The Truth!"
Lynne D. Johnson, VIBE MAGAZINE

"HUSTLERS" DESCRIPTION

Popcorn & Bay-Bay have been boyz for what seems like forever. Since they were 'shorties' growing up in Richmond-VA, as the crowned Street-Prince-boys to their OG-fathers who carried notorious reputations in VA's streets as true hustlers, nothing separated the two of them -- until both of their fathers fell victim to the hood.

After the deaths of their fathers, Bay-Bay's mother decides to relocate to Miami, Florida – temporarily ending their contact.

Several years later, Popcorn & Bay-Bay are all grown-up and reunite with plans of taking 'The Game' to the highest level – fulfilling their destiny as Street-Royalty.

Peaches, a hood-sophisticated dime-piece and Popcorn's wifey, is thoroughly satisfied with the kinky-work he's puttin'-down in the bedroom, but suspects that Popcorn is cheating on her with his life-long female friend (Yolanda) who he seems to always be around.

When Popcorn suddenly starts disappearing at night and begins flashing more cash than his 'lawn-business' could possibly provide, Peaches doesn't feel like she even knows who he really is.

As Popcorn seeks to gain revenge for his brother's murder, he wants to know if he can totally put his trust in Peaches? Is she just a dime? Or is she truly his 'to-the-grave' Ride-Or-Die chick?

Out for her own personal-revenge to satisfy her suspicions of Popcorn's indiscretions, Peaches makes a decision that will come back to haunt both of them.....maybe forever!

Money, Betrayal and the constant Struggle-for-Power are just the normal territory for Real Hustlers!

"This Joint Is So Hot!....Ghetto-Fab!.... ...Game Has To Be Recognized!"
- Terry Shropshire, Rolling Out Magazine

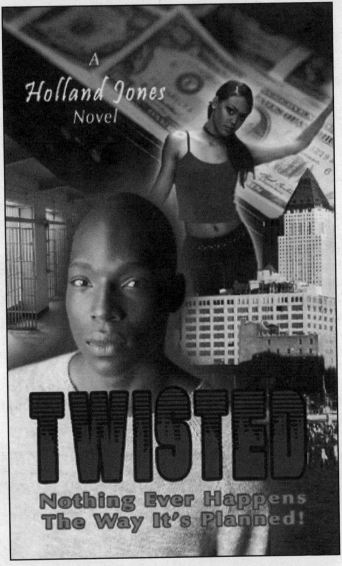

"TWISTED" DESCRIPTION

Nadine, a sultry, ghetto-fine conniving gold-digger, will do whatever it takes to make sure that she is financially set for life -- even at the cost of breaking-up a family.

When Wayne, Nadine's man since high-school, is sentenced to two years in prison for a crime he did not commit, he's betrayed by the two people he trusted the most—his woman (Nadine) and his cousin (Bobo).

Asia, a curvaceous diva and designer-clothing boutique owner with a wilder-side sexual-preference becomes an unlikely confidant to her best-friend Nadine's man (Wayne) during his incarceration.

Meanwhile Bobo, one of VA's most notorious and most successful Street-Entreprenuers, manages to hustle his way into staring down a possible life sentence.

Now that the roles are reversed, it's Bobo who's now facing some serious prision time, as Nadine tries to do whatever it takes to keep her hands on the secret stash of cash hidden in a suitcase that Bobo left behind.

Money, greed and sex always have as a way of gettin' things ***Twisted!***

"Daaaaayummmmmm! Holland Jones brings it! A hood-licious story that combines deceit, murder, freaky sex and mysterious-twists! You gotta get this one!"

-- Winston Chapman, Best-Selling Author of ***Caught Up!*** and ***Wild Thangz***

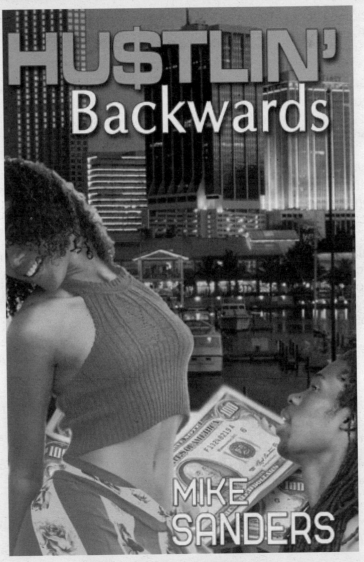

"Hustlin' Backwards" DESCRIPTION

Capone and his life-long road dawgz, June and Vonzell are out for just one thing.... To get rich!....By any means necessary!

As these three partners in crime rise up the ranks from Project-Kids to Street-Dons, their sworn code of "Death Before Dishonor" gets tested by the Feds.

Though Capone's simple pursuit of forward progression as a Hustler gains him an enviable lifestyle of Fame, Fortune and all the women his libido can handle – It also comes with a price.

No matter the location – Miami, Charlotte, Connecticut or Puerto Rico – There's simply no rest for the wicked!

WARNING: HUSTLIN' BACKWARDS is not the typical street-novel. A Unique Plot, Complex Characters mixed with a Mega-dose of Sensuality makes this story enjoyable by all sorts of readers! A true Hustler himself, Mike Sanders knows the game, inside and out!

"Fast-Paced and Action-Packed! Hustlin' Backwards HAS IT ALL -- Sex, Money, Manipulation and Murder! Mike Sanders is one of the most talented and prolific urban authors of this era!"

"NASTY" DESCRIPTION

Life-long friends, Nate & Moe, are certified players! Both have used their jobs in the entertainment industry to their advantage with the women they meet.

Moe is a well-known radio DJ in New York, while Nate is doing his damage with a pen as a magazine writer in Baltimore.

When Nate loses his job in B-more and moves back to New York to freelance for one of the hottest urban magazines, a controversial article he writes about star music artists that are using drugs could lead to his permanent down-fall.

Moe warns Nate about releasing the article, but Nate's regaining of success has him feelin' himself too much – Now he's making big-cash and begins feeling like he's untouchable! Playing women may only get him slapped, but playing with the industry's hottest hardcore rappers that have millions to lose from the article could get Nate 'slumped'!

Kaneecha (Moe's girl), is a sexy-diva clothing model and nympho without a conscience. Kaneecha's always gotta have it, whenever, where-ever! But a horny-night decision may come back to haunt her.

Tierra is a blunt-smoking, hood drama queen from Queens, NY. Though she's known Nate for a long time, it wasn't until he resurfaced in New York years later that she recognized that she wants a piece of that! Later, she views Nate as the answer for her baby-daddy drama.

Janettea (Nate's 'main-girl') is an independent sophisticated-dime that's doing her own thing with interior designing, but can also cop an attitude with a quickness! And, she ain't above giving a beat-down to a hoochie she thinks is sexin' Nate.

All the dirt Nate's doing begins to catch-up with him. Having twice narrowly escaped the hardcore rapper's crew of henchmen seeking revenge against him – he might not be so lucky the next time! Doing the ultimate dirt to his boy Moe, has serious consequences of its own! And, his player-ways gets him played!

It's just the price you pay for being NASTY!

"DRAMA!" DESCRIPTION

Destiny Smith, a young sexy diva, is intent on living the wild-life – a path that puts her on a collision course with nothing good! Spoiled by her boyfriends and protective brother (Chicago), she feels like the world owes her and she'll settle for nothing less.

Sexin' a ball-player, fightin' hoochies, back-stabbin', lyin' and cheatin' are all fair game in the ordinary day of Destiny.

When Destiny's wild behavior catches-up with her and lands her in serious trouble with the law, it's up to her brother (Chicago) to again rescue her. Having no choice, Chicago accepts a favor from a rogue cop -- a favor that he'll soon regret taking – one that will cost much more than they're willing to pay!

Though Chicago takes it upon himself to look-out for his full-grown sister, especially after the broad-daylight murder of their mother – he's also struggling with his own personal-demons. On-and-off relationships with hoodish girlfriends, money problems, court battles, consistent drama-situations in Destiny's life and the rogue cop's increasing strong-arming of him – all of these things are beginning to wear him down to a breaking point.

Chicago tries his best to hold it together – keep from going gangsta, and solving problems in his normal way...with a gun! – But when the tables are turned on him and he smells a set-up that threatens his life, he's forced to take matters into his own hands!

And, when an unexpected event reveals the identity of his mother's killer, placing him face-to-face with them, it's definitely gonna be ON!....There's NO WAY and NOBODY that can stop the *DRAMA*!

"DYME HIT LIST" DESCRIPTION

Rio Romero Clark, is an Oakland-bred brotha determined to remain a Playa-For-Life!

Taught by the best of Macks (his Uncle Lee, Father and Grandfather), Rio feels no woman can resist him. And he knows that his game is definitely tight, considering that he's as a third-generation Playa.

It is Rio's United-Nations-like appreciation for all types and races of women, from the Ghetto-Fab to the Professional, that leads him to the biggest challenge of his Mack-hood, Carmen Massey.

Carmen, a luscious southern-Dyme, at first sight, appears to be just another target on Rio's ***Dyme Hit List!*** Possessing a body that's bangin' enough to make most brothas beg, mixed with southern-charm that can cause even the best playa to hesitate, Carmen's got Rio in jeopardy of getting his Playa-Card revoked.

Burdened with the weight of potentially not living-up to the family Mack-legacy, Rio must choose between continuing to love his lifestyle or loving Carmen.

Unexpectedly tragedy strikes in Rio's life and a dark secret in Carmen's past ignites a fire that threatens to burn-up their relationship, permanently.

"***Dyme Hit List*** is On-Fire with Sensuality! This story is pleasingly-filled with lotsa lip-folding scenes! Curtis Alcutt is a bright new star in fiction!"

-- Winston Chapman, Best-Selling Author of *"Wild Thangz"* and *"Caught Up!"*

"SHAKEDOWN" DESCRIPTION

Paris Hightower, is a sexy young thang who falls in love with the man of her dreams, Tyree Dickerson, the son of very wealthy Real Estate tycoons. But there's a problem.... Tyree's mother (Mrs. Dickerson) thinks that her son is too good for Paris and is dead-set on destroying the relationship at all costs.

After Mrs. Dickerson reveals a long-kept secret to Paris about her mother (Ebony Hightower), a woman that abandoned Paris and her brother more than fifteen years ago when she was forced to flee and hide from police amidst Attempted-Murder charges for shooting Paris' father --- Paris is left in an impossible situation.

Even though the police have long given-up on the search for Ebony Hightower (Paris' mother), the bitter Mrs. Dickerson threatens to find her and turn her in to authorities as blackmail for Paris to end the relationship with her son.

Paris knows that Mrs. Dickerson means business – she has the time, interest and money to hunt down her mother. Left with the choices of pursuing her own happiness or protecting the freedom of her mother, a woman she barely knows, Paris is confused as to the right thing to do.

As the situation escalates to fireworks of private investigators, deception, financial sabotage and kidnapping, even Paris' life becomes in danger.

Just when Paris feels that all hope is lost, she's shocked when she receives unexpected help from an unlikely source.

"Be careful who you mess with, 'cause Payback is a ......! *Shakedown* combines high-drama and mega-suspense with the heart-felt struggle of the price some are willing to pay for love!" -- Winston Chapman, Best-Selling Author of *"Wild Thangz"* and *"Caught Up!"*

"BUSTED" DESCRIPTION

Arianna, Nicole and Janelle each have met a charming man online at LoveMeBlack.com, a popular internet-dating website.

Arianna Singleton, a sassy reporter who moves to Philly to further her career as a journalist, finds herself lonely in the big 'City of Brotherly Love' as she seeks a brotha-to-love online. After several comical dates with duds, she thinks she's finally met a stud.

Nicole Harris, a sanctified Public Relations Executive residing in Maryland puts her salvation on-hold when she begins living with a man that she's met on-line. Stumbling across her new beau's e-mails, she realizes that his Internet pursuits didn't end just because they now share the same zip code.

Janelle Carter, a Virginia Hair Salon Owner spends her nights cruising the Web taking on personas of her sexy, confident clients. A business arrangement that she makes on-line brings her face-to-face with a man she thinks is her destiny.

The lives of Arianna, Nicole and Janelle collide in a drama, as they discover that they've all been dating the same man....Chauncey, a brother that makes a habit out of loving and leaving women that he's met thru LoveMeBlack.com.

The three of them plot to exact their revenge on the unsuspecting Chauncey, as an unforgettable way of letting him know that he's been ***BUSTED***!

"Rhonda Swan 'brings it' in this comical story that's a warning to wanna-be players as to what can happen if they ever get ***Busted***!"

-- Winston Chapman, Best-Selling Author of *"Wild Thangz"* and *"Caught Up!"*

"Slick"
DESCRIPTION

Dana & Sylvia have been girlfriends for what seems like forever. They've never been afraid to share everything about their lives and definitely keep each other's secrets ... including hiding Dana's On-The-DL affair from her husband, Jonathan.

Though Sylvia is uncomfortable with her participation in the cover-up and despises the man Dana's creepin' with, she remains a loyal friend. That is, until she finds herself attracted to the very man her friend is deceiving.

As the lines of friendship and matrimonial territory erodes, all hell is about to break loose! Choices have to be made with serious repercussions at stake.

If loving you is wrong, I don't wanna be right!

"SLICK!!! .... Ain't That The Truth! Brenda Hampton's Tale Sizzles With Sensuality, Deception, Greed and So Much Drama – My Gurrll!"

- MYSTERIOUS LUVA, BEST-SELLING AUTHOR OF *SEX A BALLER*

"Wild Thangz" DESCRIPTION

Jazmyn, Trina and Brea are definitely a trio of Drama-Magnets - the sista-girlz version of Charlie's Angels. Young & fine with bangin' bodies, the three of them feel like they can do no wrong – not even with each other.

No matter the location: Jamaica, Miami, NYC or the A-T-L, lust, greed and trouble is never far from these wanna-be divas.

Jazymn has secret dreams that if she pursues will cause her to have mega family problems. Though the most logical of the group, she can get her attitude on with the best of them when pushed.

Trina wasn't always the diva. Book-smarts used to be her calling-card. But, under the tutoring of her personal hoochie-professor, Brea, she's just now beginning to understand the power that she has in her traffic-stopping Badunkadunk.

Brea has the face of a princess, but is straight ghetto-fab -- without the slightest shame. As the wildest of the bunch, her personal credos of living life to the fullest and to use *'what her mama gave her'* to get ahead, is constantly creating drama for Jazymn and Trina.

When past skeleton-choices in Brea's closet places all three of them in an impossible life-and-death situation, they must take an action that has the most serious of consequences, in order to survive!

The very foundation of their friendship-bond gets tested, as each of them have the opportunity to sell-out the other! The question is, Will They?

Wild Parties, Wild Situations & Wild Nights are always present for these Wild Thangz!

Best-Selling Author of "*Caught Up!*", Winston Chapman weaves yet another suspenseful, sexy-drama tale that's a Must-Read!

"Wild Thangz is HOT! Winston Chapman shonuff brings the HEAT!"

-- Mysterious Luva, Essence Magazine Best-Selling Author of *"Sex A Baller"*

"STILL CRAZY" DESCRIPTION

Kevin Allen, a rich, handsome author and self-reformed 'Mack', is now suffering from writer's block.

Desperately in need of a great story in order to renegotiate with his publisher to maintain his extravagant life-style, Kevin decides to go back to his hometown of Chicago for inspiration. While in Chi-town, he gets reacquainted with an ex-love (Yolanda) that he'd last seen during their stormy relationship that violently came to an end.

Unexpectedly, Yolanda appears at a book-event where Kevin is the star-attraction, looking every bit as stunningly beautiful as the picture he's had frozen in his head for years. She still has the looks of music video model and almost makes him forget as to the reason he'd ever broken off their relationship.

It's no secret, Yolanda had always been the jealous type. And, Kevin's explanation to his boyz, defending his decision for kicking a woman that fine to the curb was, "She's Crazy!".

The combination of Kevin's vulnerable state in his career, along with the tantalizing opportunity to hit *that* again, causes Kevin to contemplate renewing his expired Players-Card, one last time. What harm could one night of passion create?

Clouding his judgment even more is that Kevin feels like hooking-up with Yolanda might just be the rekindling needed to ignite the fire for his creativity in his writing career. But, there are just two problems. Kevin is married! ....And, Yolanda is *Still Crazy!*

"Darrin Lowery deliciously serves up.....Scandal & Sexy-Drama like no other! *STILL CRAZY* has all the goods readers are looking for!" -- *Brenda Hampton, Author of "Slick"*

"Sex A Baller"
DESCRIPTION

Mysterious Luva has sexed them all! Ball players, CEO's, Music Stars -- You name the baller, she's had them. And more importantly, she's made them all pay......

Sex A Baller is a poignant mix of a sexy tale of how Mysterious Luva has become one of the World's Best Baller Catchers and an Instructional Guide for the wanna-be Baller Catcher!

No details or secrets are spared, as she delivers her personal story along with the winning tips & secrets for daring women interested in catching a baller!

PLUS, A SPECIAL BONUS SECTION INCLUDED!

Baller Catching 101

- Top-20 Baller SEX POSITIONS (Photos!)
- Where To FIND A Baller
- Which Ballers Have The BIGGEST Penis
- SEDUCING A Baller
- Making A Baller Fall In Love
- Getting MONEY From A Baller
- What Kind Of SEX A Baller Likes
- The EASIEST Type of Baller To Catch
- Turning A Baller Out In Bed
- GAMES To Play On A Baller
- Getting Your Rent Paid & A Free Car
- Learn All The SECRETS!

BY THE END OF THIS BOOK, YOU'LL HAVE YOUR CERTIFIED BALLER-CATCHER'S DEGREE!

"CAUGHT UP!" DESCRIPTION

When Raven Klein, a bi-racial woman from Iowa moves to Atlanta in hopes of finding a life she's secretly dreamed about, she finds more than she ever imagined.

Quickly lured and lost in a world of sex, money, power-struggles, betrayal & deceit, Raven doesn't know who she can really trust!

A chance meeting at a bus terminal leads to her delving into the seedy world of strip-clubs, big-ballers and shot-callers.

Now, Raven's shuffling through more men than a Vegas blackjack dealer does a deck of cards. And sex has even become mundane -- little more than a tool to get what she wants.

After a famous acquaintance winds-up dead -- On which shoulder will Raven lean? A wrong choice could cost her life!

There's a reason they call it HOTATLANTA!

"HYPED"
DESCRIPTION

Maurice LaSalle is a player – of women and the saxophone. A gifted musician, he's the driving force behind MoJazz, a neo-soul group on the verge of their big break. Along with his partner in rhyme and crime, Jamal Grover, Maurice has more women than he can count. Though guided by his mentor Simon, Maurice knows Right but constantly does Wrong.

Then Ebony Stanford enters Maurice's world and he begins to play a new tune. Ebony, still reeling from a nasty divorce, has just about given up on men, but when Maurice hits the right notes (everywhere) she can't help but fall for his charms.

While Maurice and Ebony get closer, Jamal is busy putting so many notches on his headboard post after each female conquest, that the post looks more like a tooth-pick. When a stalker threatens his life, Maurices warns him to slow his roll, but Jamal's hyped behavior prevails over good sense.

Just as Maurice is contemplating turning in his player card for good, stupidity overrules his judgment and throws his harmonious relationship with Ebony into a tale-spin. When it appears that things couldn't get any worse, tragedy strikes and his life is changed forever!

A Powerfully-Written Sexy-Tale, *HYPED* is a unique blend of Mystery, Suspense, Intrigue and Glowing-Sensuality.

"Buckle Up! HYPED Will Test All Of Your Senses and Emotions! LUKE Is A Force To Be Reckoned With For Years To Come!" -- WINSTON CHAPMAN, ESSENCE MAGAZINE BEST-SELLING AUTHOR OF "CAUGHT UP!" AND "WILD THANGZ"

"CRUNK" DESCRIPTION

Imagine a Thug-World divided by the Mason-Dixon Line........

After the brutal murder of four NYC ganstas in Charlotte, the climate is set for an all-out Thug Civil War – North pitted against South!

Rah-Rah, leader of NYC's underworld and KoKo, head of one of the Durty South's most ferocious Crunk-crews are on a collision course to destruction. While Rah-Rah tries to rally his northern Thugdom (Philly, NJ & NY), KoKo attempts to saddle-up heads of the southern Hoodville (Atlanta, South Carolina & Charlotte).

Kendra and Janeen, a southern sister-duo of self-proclaimed baddest b*****'s, conduct a make-shift Thug Academy to prepare KoKo's VA-bred cousin (Shine) to infiltrate NYC's underground, as a secret weapon to the impending battle.

The US Government, well-aware of the upcoming war, takes a backseat role, not totally against the idea that a war of this magnitude might actual do what the Government has been unable to do with thousands of life sentences -- Rid society completely of the dangerous element associated with the Underground-World.

Suspensfully-Sexy, Erotically-Ghetto and Mysteriously-Raw. CRUNK will leave you saying, Hmmmm?

"Get Ready For A Wild & Sexy Ride! Twists & Turns Are Abundant! An Instant Urban Classic Thriller! Tariq, Rudd & Jones Are Definitely Some BAD BOYZ! Errr'body Gettin' CRUNK!"

BLACK PEARL BOOKS INC.

ORDER FORM

Black Pearl Books Inc.
3653-F Flakes Mill Road- PMB 306
Atlanta, Georgia 30034
www.BlackPearlBooks.com

YES, We Ship Directly To Prisons & Correctional Facilities
INSTITUTIONAL CHECKS & MONEY ORDERS ONLY!

TITLE	Price	Quantity	TOTAL
"Caught Up!" by Winston Chapman	$ 14. 95		
"Sex A Baller" by Mysterious Luva	$ 12. 95		
"Wild Thangz" by Winston Chapman	$ 14. 95		
"Crunk" by Bad Boyz	$ 14. 95		
"Hustlin Backwards" by Mike Sanders	$ 14. 95		
"Still Crazy" by Darrin Lowery	$ 14. 95		
"Twisted" by Holland Jones	$ 14. 95		
"Slick" by Brenda Hampton	$ 14. 95		
"Hyped" by Luke	$ 14. 95		
"Dyme Hit List" by Curtis Alcutt	$ 14. 95		
"Busted" by Rhonda Swan	$ 14. 95		
"Shakedown" by Nubian James	$ 14. 95		
"Hustlers" by Ronald Quincy	$ 14. 95		
"Legit Baller" by Jerry Blackshear	$ 14. 95		
"Street Games" by Eric Myrieckes	$ 14. 95		
"Nasty" by Rahsaan Ali	$ 14. 95		
"Drama!" by Tia Hines	$ 14. 95		
"Criminal Code" by Jorge Landrian	$ 14. 95		
"Freak Unleashed" by Cindy Cox	$ 14. 95		
"Mastermind" by Robert Ricks	$ 14. 95		
"Teflon" by Lincoln Lee	$ 14. 95		

Sub-Total	$
SHIPPING: ___ # books x $ 3. 50 ea. (Via US Priority Mail)	$
GRAND TOTAL	$

SHIP TO:
Name: ______________________________
Address: ____________________________
Apt or Box #: __________
City: ______________ **State:** _____ **Zip:** _____
Phone: _________ **E-mail:** _______________